EDITED BY
STEPHEN JONES

VISITANTS

Stories of
FALLEN ANGELS & HEAVENLY HOSTS

Ulysses Press

For full copyright information see pages vii–viii.

Published in the United States by
Ulysses Press
P.O. Box 3440
Berkeley, CA 94703
www.ulyssespress.com

ISBN 978-1-56975-838-0
Library of Congress Control Number 2010925867

Printed in the United States by Bang Printing

10 9 8 7 6 5 4 3 2 1

Acquisitions Editor: Keith Riegert
Managing Editor: Claire Chun
Editorial and production: Lily Chou, Lauren Harrison, Judith Metzener
Front cover design: Yasmin Amer
Cover photos:© Grafissimo/istockphoto.com (wing), © rotofrank/
    istockphoto.com (clouds), musinus2/istockphoto.com (man)
Interior illustrations: © Larz Photography/shutterstock.com (angel),
    © Potapov Alexander/shutterstock.com (feather)

Distributed by Publishers Group West

For
PETE & NICKY
Whom I am blessed to call friends.

CONTENTS

Acknowledgments

Special thanks to Keith Riegert and the staff of Ulysses Press, Dorothy Lumley, Milt Thomas, Elizabeth Harding and all the contributors, who have been angels to work with . . .

INTRODUCTION
An Angelology, of Sorts

CELESTIAL MESSENGERS or instruments of divine retribution? Heavenly guardians or Hellish demi-gods? Angels can mean many things to many people . . .

The term "angel" is a combination of the Old English word *engel* and the Old French word *angele*. Both are derived from the Latin word *angelus*, and entered the English language in very early times, denoting a supernatural being of kindly qualities. In the Bible it translates as Hebrew and Greek words meaning "messengers" (or the *Malachim*), and first appears in the Old Testament in the phrase "angel of the Lord"—the title given to the divine messenger who told Hagar that she would give birth to Ishmael.

More recently, "angel" has been used to describe various notions of spiritual creatures found in many other religious traditions, ranging from the Qur'an to Kabbalah to New Age mysticism.

By the late fourth century a hierarchy was established among the angels, with many taking on specific names and roles. Amongst the highest ranks of archangels is Metatron, who is often depicted as a scribe. Michael is God's warrior, while Gabriel serves as a messenger or force of justice. Raphael is God's healer, Uriel leads us to destiny, and Seraphims are the "burning ones" who protect the gates to the Garden of Eden.

In Jewish and Christian mythology, angels are God's courtiers or intermediates, helpers of men. They are often described as beautiful, winged creatures of light. Sometimes they are described in theological texts or depicted in art as androgynous or even female. But there are also other kinds of angels—harbingers of doom or dispensers of swift and powerful justice. And then there are the Fallen Angels, such as Lucifer and, of course, Malach HaMavet, the Angel of Death.

A poll conducted in 2007 discovered that sixty-eight percent of Americans believed that angels and demons were "active" in the world. A survey the following year by Baylor University's Institute for Studies in Religion found that fifty-five percent of Americans—including one in five who said they were not religious—were convinced that they had been protected by a guardian angel during their life. Perhaps even more remarkably, according to four separate polls conducted last year, a far larger percentage of Americans believed in the existence of angels than those who believed in global warming.

A 2008 survey of Canadians recorded that a mighty sixty-seven percent believed that angels really existed while, in the UK, a 2002 study found that people said to have had experience of angels either described the "classic" image of a human figure with wings, a remarkably beautiful and radiant figure, or a shining countenance of pure light. These sightings were often accompanied by visions, a pleasant fragrance or the feeling of being pushed or lifted out of danger.

This new anthology reflects many interpretations of these remarkable creatures, with original and occasional reprint stories by some of the world's leading fantasy, horror and science fiction authors:

Neil Gaiman's "Murder Mysteries" is a celestial murder mystery with the Act of Creation at its heart. Jane Yolen and Ian R. MacLeod present us slightly skewered Biblical stories about angels, and Arthur Machen's "The Bowmen" gave rise to perhaps the most famous angel mythology of modern times.

The protagonists of the stories by Sarah Pinborough, Lisa Tuttle and Brian Stableford find themselves having unexpected encounters with angelic creatures of sorts, while it is guardian angels that come to the aid of humans in the tales by Graham Masterton, Michael Marshall Smith and Peter Crowther.

Michael Bishop's contribution is a one-act play that, in part, addresses the question of angelic sex. In Steve Rasnic Tem's tale, an artist only paints what he can see, and Jay Lake gives us five very different vignettes about angels.

The "angels" depicted in the stories by Chelsea Quinn Yarbro, Hugh B. Cave and Richard Christian Matheson are not necessarily of the supernatural variety, while the entities encountered in the work of Robert Shearman and Ramsey Campbell most definitely are—and in the most terrifying way.

Those angels found in the contributions from Yvonne Navarro, Mark Samuels and Conrad Williams are also of the decidedly darker variety as well.

A computer programmer converses online with angel avatars, with disastrous consequences, in Robert Silverberg's "Basileus," and as the End of Days fast approaches, a group of beautiful strangers herald the coming Apocalypse in Christopher Fowler's poignant tale.

Through these twenty-seven very different stories, the authors explore our acceptance or fear of angels, at a time when many people are questioning their own beliefs and the need to perhaps once again trust in some kind of divine intervention or spiritual guidance.

Of course, this being a genre anthology, I can't actually guarantee that it will all necessarily end in a good way . . .

Stephen Jones
London, England
July 2010

MURDER MYSTERIES
Neil Gaiman

NEIL GAIMAN recently became the first person ever to win the Newbery Medal and the Carnegie Medal for the same children's novel, *The Graveyard Book*, which spent more than fifty-two consecutive weeks on the *New York Times* best-seller list. The book has also won the Hugo Award, the Booktrust Award and many others.

The ever-busy author also has out a book of poems, *Blueberry Girl*, illustrated by Charles Vess; *Crazy Hair*, a new picture book with regular collaborator Dave McKean; the graphic novel compilation *Batman: Whatever Happened to the Caped Crusader?* (with art by Andy Kubert); and *Stories*, an anthology of all-new tales co-edited with Al Sarrantonio.

During the past few years, Gaiman co-scripted (with Roger Avary) Robert Zemeckis' motion-capture fantasy film *Beowulf*, while Matthew Vaughn's *Stardust* and Henry Selick's *Coraline* were both based on his novels. He wrote and directed *Statuesque*, a short film starring Bill Nighy and Gaiman's fiancée, singer/songwriter Amanda Palmer, and he has also just written an episode of *Doctor Who* for the BBC.

He is very happy.

"'Murder Mysteries' was the hardest story I've ever written," admits Gaiman. "I'd never done a classical detective story, the kind that plays fair with the audience, before, and it took draft after draft until I got it right.

"Some years later I turned it into a radio play. Then P. Craig Russell took my story and the radio script and turned it into a graphic novel. And I got a phone call recently to tell me that it might be turning into a movie.

"So I'd like to thank Peter Atkins, all those years ago, for reading eleven different drafts of this, until I got it right."

The Fourth Angel says:

> Of this order I am made one,
> From Mankind to guard this place
> That through their Guilt they have foregone,
> For they have forfeited His Grace;
> Therefore all this must they shun
> Or else my Sword they shall embrace
> And myself will be their Foe
> To flame them in the Face.

—Chester Mystery Cycle:
The Creation, and Adam and Eve, 1461

THIS IS TRUE.

Ten years ago, give or take a year, I found myself on an enforced stopover in Los Angeles, a long way from home. It was December, and the California weather was warm and pleasant. England, however, was in the grip of fogs and snowstorms, and no planes were landing there. Each day I'd phone the airport, and each day I'd be told to wait another day.

This had gone on for almost a week.

I was barely out of my teens. Looking around today at the parts of my life left over from those days, I feel uncomfortable, as if I've received a gift, unasked, from another person: a house, a wife, children, a vocation. Nothing to do with me, I could say, innocently. If it's true that every seven years each cell in your body dies and is replaced, then I have truly inherited my life from a dead man; and the misdeeds of those times have been forgiven, and are buried with his bones.

I was in Los Angeles. Yes.

On the sixth day I received a message from an old sort-of-girlfriend from Seattle: she was in LA, too, and she had heard I was around on the friends-of-friends network. Would I come over?

I left a message on her machine. Sure.

That evening: a small, blonde woman approached me, as I came out of the place I was staying. It was already dark.

She stared at me, as if she were trying to match me to a description, and then, hesitantly, she said my name.

"That's me. Are you Tink's friend?"

"Yeah. Car's out back. C'mon: she's really looking forward to seeing you."

The woman's car was one of the huge old boat-like jobs you only ever seem to see in California. It smelled of cracked and flaking leather upholstery. We drove out from wherever we were to wherever we were going.

Los Angeles was at that time a complete mystery to me; and I cannot say I understand it much better now. I understand London, and New York, and Paris: you can walk around them, get a sense of what's where in just a morning of wandering. Maybe catch the subway. But Los Angeles is about cars. Back then I didn't drive at all; even today I will not drive in America. Memories of LA for me are linked by rides in other people's cars, with no sense there of the shape of the city, of the relationships between the people and the place. The regularity of the roads, the repetition of structure and form, mean that when I try to remember it as an entity all I have is the boundless profusion of tiny lights I saw one night on my first trip to the city, from the hill of Griffith Park. It was one of the most beautiful things I had ever seen, from that distance.

"See that building?" said my blonde driver, Tink's friend. It was a red-brick art deco house, charming and quite ugly.

"Yes."

"Built in the 1930s," she said, with respect and pride.

I said something polite, trying to comprehend a city inside which fifty years could be considered a long time.

"Tink's real excited. When she heard you were in town. She was so excited."

"I'm looking forward to seeing her again."

Tink's real name was Tinkerbell Richmond. No lie.

She was staying with friends in a small apartment clump, somewhere an hour's drive from downtown LA.

What you need to know about Tink: she was ten years older than me, in her early thirties; she had glossy black hair and red, puzzled lips, and very white skin, like Snow White in the fairy stories; the first time I met her I thought she was the most beautiful woman in the world.

Tink had been married for a while at some point in her life, and had a five-year-old daughter called Susan. I had never met Susan— when Tink had been in England, Susan had been staying on in Seattle, with her father.

People named Tinkerbell name their daughters Susan.

Memory is the great deceiver. Perhaps there are some individuals whose memories act like tape recordings, daily records of their lives complete in every detail, but I am not one of them. My memory is a patchwork of occurrences, of discontinuous events roughly sewn together: the parts I remember, I remember precisely, whilst other sections seem to have vanished completely.

I do not remember arriving at Tink's house, nor where her flatmate went.

What I remember next is sitting in Tink's lounge, with the lights low; the two of us next to each other, on the sofa.

We made small talk. It had been perhaps a year since we had seen one another. But a twenty-one-year-old boy has little to say to a thirty-two-year-old woman, and soon, having nothing in common, I pulled her to me.

She snuggled close with a kind of sigh, and presented her lips to be kissed. In the half-light her lips were black. We kissed for a little, and I stroked her breasts through her blouse, on the couch; and then she said:

"We can't fuck. I'm on my period."

"Fine."

"I can give you a blow job, if you'd like."

I nodded assent, and she unzipped my jeans, and lowered her head to my lap.

After I had come, she got up and ran into the kitchen. I heard her spitting into the sink, and the sound of running water: I remember wondering why she did it, if she hated the taste that much.

Then she returned and we sat next to each other on the couch.

"Susan's upstairs, asleep," said Tink. "She's all I live for. Would you like to see her?"

"I don't mind."

We went upstairs. Tink led me into a darkened bedroom. There were child-scrawl pictures all over the walls—wax-crayoned drawings of winged fairies and little palaces—and a small, fair-haired girl was asleep in the bed.

"She's very beautiful," said Tink, and kissed me. Her lips were still slightly sticky. "She takes after her father."

We went downstairs. We had nothing else to say, nothing else to do. Tink turned on the main light. For the first time I noticed tiny crows' feet at the corners of her eyes, incongruous on her perfect, Barbie-doll face.

"I love you," she said.

"Thank you."

"Would you like a ride back?"

"If you don't mind leaving Susan alone . . . ?"

She shrugged, and I pulled her to me for the last time.

At night, Los Angeles is all lights. And shadows.

A blank, here, in my mind. I simply don't remember what happened next. She must have driven me back to the place where I was staying—

how else would I have gotten there? I do not even remember kissing her goodbye. Perhaps I simply waited on the sidewalk and watched her drive away.

Perhaps.

I do know, however, that once I reached the place I was staying I just stood there, unable to go inside, to wash and then to sleep, unwilling to do anything else.

I was not hungry. I did not want alcohol. I did not want to read, or talk. I was scared of walking too far, in case I became lost, bedeviled by the repeating motifs of Los Angeles, spun around and sucked in so I could never find my way home again. Central Los Angeles sometimes seems to me to be nothing more than a pattern, like a set of repeating blocks: a gas station, a few homes, a mini-mall (donuts, photo developers, laundromats, fast-foods), and repeat until hypnotized; and the tiny changes in the mini-malls and the houses only serve to reinforce the structure.

I thought of Tink's lips. Then I fumbled in a pocket of my jacket, and pulled out a packet of cigarettes.

I lit one, inhaled, blew blue smoke into the warm night air.

There was a stunted palm tree growing outside the place I was staying, and I resolved to walk for a way, keeping the tree in sight, to smoke my cigarette, perhaps even to think; but I felt too drained to think. I felt very sexless, and very alone.

A block or so down the road there was a bench, and when I reached it I sat down. I threw the stub of the cigarette onto the pavement, hard, and watched it shower orange sparks.

Someone said, "I'll buy a cigarette off you, pal. Here."

A hand, in front of my face, holding a quarter. I looked up.

He did not look old, although I would not have been prepared to say how old he was. Late thirties, perhaps. Mid-forties. He wore a long, shabby coat, colorless under the yellow street lamps, and his eyes were dark.

"Here. A quarter. That's a good price."

I shook my head, pulled out the packet of Marlboros, offered him one. "Keep your money. It's free. Have it."

He took the cigarette. I passed him a book of matches (it advertised a telephone sex line; I remember that), and he lit the cigarette. He offered me the matches back, and I shook my head. "Keep them. I always wind up accumulating books of matches in America."

"Uh huh." He sat next to me, and smoked his cigarette. When he had smoked it halfway down, he tapped the lighted end off on the concrete, stubbed out the glow, and placed the butt of the cigarette behind his ear.

"I don't smoke much," he said. "Seems a pity to waste it, though."

A car careened down the road, veering from one side to the other. There were four young men in the car: the two in the front were both pulling at the wheel, and laughing. The windows were wound down, and I could hear their laughter, and the two in the back seat (*"Gaary, you asshole! What the fuck are you onnn mannnn?"*) and the pulsing beat of a rock song. Not a song I recognized. The car looped around a corner, out of sight.

Soon the sounds were gone, too.

"I owe you," said the man on the bench.

"Sorry?"

"I owe you something. For the cigarette. And the matches. You wouldn't take the money. I owe you."

I shrugged, embarrassed. "Really, it's just a cigarette. I figure, if I give people cigarettes, then if ever I'm out, maybe people will give me cigarettes." I laughed, to show I didn't really mean it, although I did. "Don't worry about it."

"Mm. You want to hear a story? True story? Stories always used to be good payment. These days . . . ," he shrugged, ". . . not so much."

I sat back on the bench, and the night was warm, and I looked at my watch: it was almost one in the morning. In England a freezing new day would already have begun: a work-day would be starting for those who could beat the snow and get into work; another handful of old people, and those without homes, would have died, in the night, from the cold.

"Sure," I said to the man. "Sure. Tell me a story."

He coughed, grinned white teeth—a flash in the darkness—and he began.

"First thing I remember was the Word. And the Word was God. Sometimes, when I get *really* down, I remember the sound of the Word in my head, shaping me, forming me, giving me life.

"The Word gave me a body, gave me eyes. And I opened my eyes, and I saw the light of the Silver City.

"I was in a room—a silver room—and there wasn't anything in it except me. In front of me was a window, that went from floor to ceiling, open to the sky, and through the window I could see the spires of the City, and at the edge of the City, the Dark.

"I don't know how long I waited there. I wasn't impatient or anything, though. I remember that. It was like I was waiting until I was called; and I knew that some time I would be called. And if I had to wait until the end of everything, and never be called, why, that was fine, too. But I'd be called, I was certain of that. And then I'd know my name, and my function.

"Through the window I could see silver spires, and in many of the other spires were windows; and in the windows I could see others like me. That was how I knew what I looked like.

"You wouldn't think it of me, seeing me now, but I was beautiful. I've come down in the world a way since then.

"I was taller then, and I had wings.

"They were huge and powerful wings, with feathers the color of mother-of-pearl. They came out from just between my shoulder blades. They were so good. My wings.

"Sometimes I'd see others like me, the ones who'd left their rooms, who were already fulfilling their duties. I'd watch them soar through the sky from spire to spire, performing errands I could barely imagine.

"The sky above the City was a wonderful thing. It was always light, although lit by no sun—lit, perhaps by the City itself: but the quality of light was forever changing. Now pewter-colored light, then brass, then a gentle gold, or a soft and quiet amethyst . . ."

The man stopped talking. He looked at me, his head on one side. There was a glitter in his eyes that scared me. "You know what amethyst is? A kind of purple stone?"

I nodded.

My crotch felt uncomfortable.

It occurred to me then that the man might not be mad; I found this far more disquieting than the alternative.

The man began talking once more. "I don't know how long it was that I waited, in my room. But time didn't mean anything. Not back then. We had all the time in the world.

"The next thing that happened to me was when the angel Lucifer came to my cell. He was taller than me, and his wings were imposing, his plumage perfect. He had skin the color of sea-mist, and curly silver hair, and these wonderful grey eyes . . .

"I say he, but you should understand that none of us had any sex, to speak of." He gestured towards his lap. "Smooth and empty. Nothing there. You know.

"Lucifer shone. I mean it—he glowed from inside. All angels do. They're lit up from within, and in my cell the angel Lucifer burned like a lightning storm.

"He looked at me. And he named me.

"'You are Raguel,' he said. 'The vengeance of the Lord.'

"I bowed my head, because I knew it was true. That was my name. That was my function.

"'There has been a . . . a wrong thing,' he said. 'The first of its kind. You are needed.'

"He turned and pushed himself into space, and I followed him, flew behind him across the Silver City, to the outskirts, where the City stops and the Darkness begins; and it was there, under a vast silver spire, that we descended to the street, and I saw the dead angel.

"The body lay, crumpled and broken, on the silver sidewalk. Its wings were crushed underneath it and a few loose feathers had already blown into the silver gutter.

"The body was almost dark. Now and again a light would flash inside it, an occasional flicker of cold fire in the chest, or in the eyes, or in the sexless groin, as the last of the glow of life left it forever.

"Blood pooled in rubies on its chest and stained its white wing-feathers crimson. It was very beautiful, even in death.

"It would have broken your heart.

"Lucifer spoke to me, then. 'You must find who was responsible for this, and how; and take the Vengeance of the Name on whomever caused this thing to happen.'

"He really didn't have to say anything. I knew that already. The hunt, and the retribution: it was what I was created for, in the Beginning; it was what I *was*.

"'I have work to attend to,' said the angel Lucifer.

"He flapped his wings, once, hard, and rose upwards; the gust of wind sent the dead angel's loose feathers blowing across the street.

"I leaned down to examine the body. All luminescence had by now left it. It was a dark thing; a parody of an angel. It had a perfect, sexless face, framed by silver hair. One of the eyelids was open, revealing a placid grey eye; the other was closed. There were no nipples on the chest and only smoothness between the legs.

"I lifted the body up.

"The back of the angel was a mess. The wings were broken and twisted; the back of the head stove in; there was a floppiness to the corpse that made me think its spine had been broken as well. The back of the angel was all blood.

"The only blood on its front was in the chest area. I probed it with my forefinger, and it entered the body without difficulty.

"*He fell*, I thought. *And he was dead before he fell.*

"And I looked up at the windows that ranked the street. I stared across the Silver City. *You did this*, I thought. *I will find you, whoever you are. And I will take the Lord's vengeance upon you.*"

The man took the cigarette stub from behind his ear, lit it with a match. Briefly I smelled the ashtray smell of a dead cigarette, acrid and harsh; then he pulled down to the unburnt tobacco, exhaled blue smoke into the night air.

"The angel who had first discovered the body was called Phanuel.

"I spoke to him in the Hall of Being. That was the spire beside which the dead angel lay. In the Hall hung the . . . the blueprints, maybe, for what was going to be . . . all this." He gestured with the hand that held the stubby cigarette, pointing to the night sky and the parked cars and the world. "You know. The universe."

"Phanuel was the senior designer; working under him were a multitude of angels laboring on the details of The Creation. I watched him from the floor of the Hall. He hung in the air below the Plan, and angels flew down to him, waiting politely in turn as they asked him questions, checked things with him, invited comment on their work. Eventually he left them, and descended to the floor.

"'You are Raguel,' he said. His voice was high, and fussy. 'What need have you of me?'

"'You found the body?'

"'Poor Carasel? Indeed I did. I was leaving the Hall—there are a number of concepts we are currently constructing, and I wished to ponder one of them, *Regret*, by name. I was planning to get a little distance from the City—to fly above it, I mean, not to go into the Dark outside, I wouldn't do that, although there has been a some loose talk amongst . . . but, yes. I was going to rise, and contemplate.

"'I left the Hall, and . . . ,' he broke off. He was small, for an angel. His light was muted, but his eyes were vivid and bright. I mean really bright. 'Poor Carasel. How could he *do* that to himself? How?'

"'You think his destruction was self-inflicted?'

"He seemed puzzled—surprised that there could be any other explanation. 'But of course. Carasel was working under me, developing a number of concepts that shall be intrinsic to the Universe, when its Name shall be spoken. His group did a remarkable job on some of the real basics—*Dimension* was one, and *Sleep* another. There were others.

"'Wonderful work. Some of his suggestions regarding the use of individual viewpoints to define dimensions were truly ingenious.

"'Anyway. He had begun work on a new project. It's one of the really major ones—the ones that I would usually handle, or possibly even Zephkiel,' he glanced upward. 'But Carasel had done such sterling work. And his last project was *so* remarkable. Something apparently quite trivial, that he and Saraquael elevated into . . .' he shrugged. 'But that is unimportant. It was *this* project that forced him into non-being. But none of us could ever have foreseen . . .'

"'What was his current project?'

"Phanuel stared at me. 'I'm not sure I ought to tell you. All the new concepts are considered sensitive, until we get them into the final form in which they will be Spoken.'

"I felt myself transforming. I am not sure how I can explain it to you, but suddenly I wasn't me—I was something larger. I was transfigured: I was my function.

"Phanuel was unable to meet my gaze.

"'I am Raguel, who is the Vengeance of the Lord,' I told him. 'I serve the Name directly. It is my mission to discover the nature of this deed, and to take the Name's vengeance on those responsible. My questions are to be answered.'

"The little angel trembled, and he spoke fast.

"'Carasel and his partner were researching *Death*. Cessation of life. An end to physical, animated existence. They were putting it all together. But Carasel always went too far into his work—we had a terrible time with him when he was designing *Agitation*. That was when he was working on Emotions . . .'

"'You think Carasel died to—to research the phenomenon?'

"'Or because it intrigued him. Or because he followed his research just too far. Yes.' Phanuel flexed his fingers, stared at me with those brightly shining eyes. 'I trust that you will repeat none of this to any unauthorized persons, Raguel.'

"'What did you do when you found the body?'

"'I came out of the Hall, as I said, and there was Carasel on the sidewalk, staring up. I asked him what he was doing and he did not reply. Then I noticed the inner fluid, and that Carasel seemed unable, rather than unwilling, to talk to me.

"'I was scared. I did not know what to do.

"'The angel Lucifer came up behind me. He asked me if there was some kind of problem. I told him. I showed him the body. And then . . . then his Aspect came upon him, and he communed with The Name. He burned so bright.

"'Then he said he had to fetch the one whose function embraced events like this, and he left—to seek you, I imagine.

"'As Carasel's death was now being dealt with, and his fate was no real concern of mine, I returned to work, having gained a new—and I suspect, quite valuable—perspective on the mechanics of *Regret*.

"'I am considering taking *Death* away from the Carasel and Saraquael partnership. I may reassign it to Zephkiel, my senior partner, if he is willing to take it on. He excels on contemplative projects.'

"By now there was a line of angels waiting to talk to Phanuel. I felt I had almost all I was going to get from him.

"'Who did Carasel work with? Who would have been the last to see him alive?'

"'You could talk to Saraquael, I suppose—he was his partner, after all. Now, if you'll excuse me . . .'

"He returned to his swarm of aides: advising, correcting, suggesting, forbidding."

The man paused.

The street was quiet, now; I remember the low whisper of his voice, the buzz of a cricket somewhere. A small animal—a cat perhaps, or something more exotic, a raccoon, or even a jackal—darted from shadow to shadow among the parked cars on the opposite side of the street.

"Saraquael was in the highest of the mezzanine galleries that ringed the Hall of Being. As I said, the Universe was in the middle of the Hall, and it glinted and sparkled and shone. Went up quite a way, too . . ."

"The Universe you mention, it was, what, a diagram?" I asked, interrupting for the first time.

"Not really. Kind of. Sorta. It was a blueprint: but it was full-sized, and it hung in the Hall, and all these angels went around and fiddled with it all the time. Doing stuff with *Gravity*, and *Music* and *Klar* and whatever. It wasn't really the universe, not yet. It would be, when it was finished, and it was time for it to be properly Named."

"But . . ." I grasped for words to express my confusion.

The man interrupted me.

"Don't worry about it. Think of it as a model, if that makes it easier for you. Or a map. Or a—what's the word? *Prototype*. Yeah. A Model-T Ford universe." He grinned. "You got to understand, a lot of the stuff I'm telling you, I'm translating already; putting it in a form you can understand. Otherwise I couldn't tell the story at all. You want to hear it?"

"Yes." I didn't care if it was true or not; it was a story I needed to hear all the way through to the end.

"Good. So shut up and listen.

"So I met Saraquael, in the topmost gallery. There was no one else about—just him, and some papers, and some small, glowing models.

"'I've come about Carasel,' I told him.

"He looked at me. 'Carasel isn't here at this time,' he said. 'I expect him to return shortly.'

"I shook my head.

"'Carasel won't be coming back. He's stopped existing as a spiritual entity,' I said.

"His light paled, and his eyes opened very wide. 'He's dead?'

"'That's what I said. Do you have any ideas about how it happened?'

"'I . . . this is so sudden. I mean, he'd been talking about . . . but I had no idea that he would . . .'

"'Take it slowly.'

"Saraquael nodded.

"He stood up and walked to the window. There was no view of the Silver City from his window—just a reflected glow from the City and the sky behind us, hanging in the air, and beyond that, the Dark. The wind from the Dark gently caressed Saraquael's hair as he spoke. I stared at his back.

"'Carasel is . . . no, was. That's right, isn't it? *Was*. He was always so involved. And so creative. But it was never enough for him. He always wanted to understand everything—to experience what he was working on. He was never content to just create it—to understand it intellectually. He wanted *all* of it.

"'That wasn't a problem before, when we were working on properties of matter. But when we began to design some of the Named Emotions . . . he got too involved with his work.

"'And our latest project was *Death*. It's one of the hard ones—one of the big ones, too, I suspect. Possibly it may even become the attribute that's going to define the Creation for the Created: if not for *Death*, they'd be content to simply exist, but with *Death*, well, their lives will have meaning—a boundary beyond which the living cannot cross . . .'

"'So you think he killed himself?'

"'I know he did,' said Saraquael. I walked to the window, and looked out. Far below, a *long* way, I could see a tiny white dot. That was Carasel's body. I'd have to arrange for someone to take care of it. I wondered what we would do with it; but there would be someone who would know, whose function was the removal of unwanted things. It was not my function. I knew that.

"'How?'

"He shrugged. 'I know. Recently he'd begun asking questions—questions about Death. How we could know whether or not it was right to make this thing, to set the rules, if we were not going to experience it ourselves. He kept talking about it.'

"'Didn't you wonder about this?'

"Saraquael turned, for the first time, to look at me. 'No. That *is* our function—to discuss, to improvise, to aid the Creation and the Created. We sort it out now, so that when it all Begins, it'll run like clockwork. Right now we're working on Death. So obviously that's what we look at. The physical aspect; the emotional aspect; the philosophical aspect . . .

"'And the *patterns*. Carasel had the notion that what we do here in the Hall of Being creates patterns. That there are structures and shapes appropriate to beings and events that, once begun, must continue until they reach their end. For us, perhaps, as well as for them. Conceivably he felt this was one of his patterns.'

"'Did you know Carasel well?'

"'As well as any of us know each other. We saw each other here; we worked side by side. At certain times I would retire to my cell, across the city. Sometimes he would do the same.'

"'Tell me about Phanuel.'

"His mouth crooked into a smile. 'He's officious. Doesn't do much—farms everything out, and takes all the credit.' He lowered his voice, although there was no other soul in the gallery. 'To hear him talk, you'd think that *Love* was all his own work. But to his credit he does make sure the work gets done. Zephkiel's the real thinker of the two senior designers, but he doesn't come here. He stays back in his cell in the City, and contemplates; resolves problems from a distance. If you need to speak to Zephkiel, you go to Phanuel, and Phanuel relays your questions to Zephkiel . . .'

"I cut him short. 'How about Lucifer? Tell me about him.'

"'Lucifer? The Captain of the Host? He doesn't work here . . . He has visited the Hall a couple of times, though—inspecting the Creation. They say he reports directly to the Name. I have never spoken to him.'

"'Did he know Carasel?'

"'I doubt it. As I said, he has only been here twice. I have seen him on other occasions, though. Through here.' He flicked a wingtip, indicating the world outside the window. 'In flight.'

"'Where to?'

"Saraquael seemed to be about to say something, then he changed his mind. 'I don't know.'

"I looked out of the window, at the Darkness outside the Silver City.

"'I may want to talk with you some more, later,' I told Saraquael.

"'Very good.' I turned to go.

"'Sir? Do you know if they will be assigning me another partner? For *Death*?'

"'No,' I told him. 'I'm afraid I don't.'

"In the center of the Silver City was a park—a place of recreation and rest. I found the angel Lucifer there, beside a river. He was just standing, watching the water flow.

"'Lucifer?'

"He inclined his head. 'Raguel. Are you making progress?'

"'I don't know. Maybe. I need to ask you a few questions. Do you mind?'

"'Not at all.'

"'How did you come upon the body?'

"'I didn't. Not exactly. I saw Phanuel, standing in the street. He looked distressed. I enquired whether there was something wrong, and he showed me the dead angel. And I fetched you.'

"'I see.'

"He leaned down, let one hand enter the cold water of the river. The water splashed and rilled around it. 'Is that all?'

"'Not quite. What were you doing in that part of the City?'

"'I don't see what business that is of yours.'

"'It is my business, Lucifer. What were you doing there?'

"'I was . . . walking. I do that sometimes. Just walk, and think. And try to understand.' He shrugged.

"'You walk on the edge of the City?'

"A beat, then, 'Yes.'

"'That's all I want to know. For now.'

"'Who else have you talked to?'

"'Carasel's boss, and his partner. They both feel that he killed himself—ended his own life.'

"'Who else are you going to talk to?'

"I looked up. The spires of the City of the Angels towered above us. 'Maybe everyone.'

"'All of them?'

"'If I need to. It's my function. I cannot rest until I understand what happened, and until the vengeance of the Name has been taken on whoever was responsible. But I'll tell you something I *do* know.'

"'What would that be?' Drops of water fell like diamonds from the angel Lucifer's perfect fingers.

"'Carasel did not kill himself.'

"'How do you know that?'

"'I am Vengeance. If Carasel had died by his own hand,' I explained to the Captain of the Heavenly Host, 'there would have been no call for me. Would there?'

"He did not reply.

"I flew upwards, into the light of the eternal morning.

"You got another cigarette on you?"

I fumbled out the red and white packet, handed him a cigarette.

"Obliged.

"Zephkiel's cell was larger than mine.

"It wasn't a place for waiting. It was a place to live, and work, and *be*. It was lined with books, and scrolls, and papers, and there were images and representations on the walls: pictures. I'd never seen a picture before.

"In the center of the room was a large chair, and Zephkiel sat there, his eyes closed, his head back.

"As I approached him he opened his eyes.

"They burned no brighter than the eyes of any of the other angels I had seen, but somehow, they seemed to have seen more. It was something about the way he looked. I'm not sure I can explain it. And he had no wings.

"'Welcome, Raguel,' he said. He sounded tired.

"'You are Zephkiel?' I don't know why I asked him that. I mean, I knew who people were. It's part of my function, I guess. Recognition. I know who *you* are.

"'Indeed. You are staring, Raguel. I have no wings, it is true, but then, my function does not call for me to leave this cell. I remain here, and I ponder. Phanuel reports back to me, brings me the new things, for my opinion. He brings me the problems, and I think about them, and occasionally I make myself useful by making some small suggestions. That is my function. As yours is vengeance.'

"'Yes.'

"'You are here about the death of the angel Carasel?'

"'Yes.'

"'I did not kill him.'

"When he said it, I knew it was true.

"'Do you know who did?'

"'That is *your* function, is it not? To discover who killed the poor thing, and to take the Vengeance of the Name upon him.'

"'Yes.'

"He nodded.

"'What do you want to know?'

"I paused, reflecting on what I had heard that day. 'Do you know what Lucifer was doing in that part of the City, before the body was found?'

"The old angel stared at me. 'I can hazard a guess.'

"'Yes?'

"'He was walking in the Dark.'

"I nodded. I had a shape in my mind, now. Something I could almost grasp. I asked the last question:

"'What can you tell me about *Love*?'

"And he told me. And I thought I had it all.

"I returned to the place where Carasel's body had been. The remains had been removed, the blood had been cleaned away, the stray feathers collected and disposed of. There was nothing on the silver sidewalk to indicate it had ever been there. But I knew where it had been.

"I ascended on my wings, flew upward until I neared the top of the spire of the Hall of Being. There was a window there, and I entered.

"Saraquael was working there, putting a wingless mannequin into a small box. On one side of the box was a representation of a small brown creature, with eight legs. On the other was a representation of a white blossom.

"'Saraquael?'

"'Hm? Oh, it's you. Hello. Look at this: if you were to die, and to be, let us say, put into the earth in a box, which would you want laid on top of you—a spider, here, or a lily, here?'

"'The lily, I suppose.'

"'Yes, that's what I think, too. But *why*? I wish . . . ,' he raised a hand to his chin, stared down at the two models, put first one on top of the box then the other, experimentally. 'There's so much to do, Raguel. So much to get right. And we only get one chance at it, you know. There'll just be one universe—we can't keep trying until we get it right. I wish I understood why all this was so important to Him . . .'

"'Do you know where Zephkiel's cell is?' I asked him.

"'Yes. I mean, I've never been there. But I know where it is.'

"'Good. Go there. He'll be expecting you. I will meet you there.'

"He shook his head. 'I have work to do. I can't just . . .'

"I felt my function come upon me. I looked down at him, and I said, 'You will be there. Go now.'

"He said nothing. He backed away from me, toward the window, staring at me; then he turned, and flapped his wings, and I was alone.

"I walked to the central well of the Hall, and let myself fall, tumbling down through the model of the universe: it glittered around me, unfamiliar colors and shapes seething and writhing without meaning.

"As I approached the bottom, I beat my wings, slowing my descent, and stepped lightly onto the silver floor. Phanuel stood between two angels, who were both trying to claim his attention.

"'I don't care how aesthetically pleasing it would be,' he was explaining to one of them. 'We simply cannot put it in the center. Background radiation would prevent any possible life-forms from even getting a foothold; and anyway, it's too unstable.'

"He turned to the other. 'Okay, let's see it. Hmm. So *that's Green*, is it? It's not exactly how I'd imagined it, but. Mm. Leave it with me. I'll get back to you.' He took a paper from the angel, folded it over decisively.

"He turned to me. His manner was brusque, and dismissive. 'Yes?'

"'I need to talk to you.'

"'Mm? Well, make it quick. I have much to do. If this is about Carasel's death, I have told you all I know.'

"'It is about Carasel's death. But I will not speak to you now. Not here. Go to Zephkiel's cell: he is expecting you. I will meet you there.'

"He seemed about to say something, but he only nodded, walked toward the door.

"I turned to go, when something occurred to me. I stopped the angel who had the *Green*. 'Tell me something.'

"'If I can, sir.'

"'That thing.' I pointed to the Universe. 'What's it going to be *for*?'

"'For? Why, it is the Universe.'

"'I know what it's called. But what purpose will it serve?'

"He frowned. 'It is part of the plan. The Name wishes it; He requires *such and such*, to *these* dimensions, and having *such and such* properties and ingredients. It is our function to bring it into existence, according to His wishes. I am sure *He* knows its function, but He has not revealed it to me.' His tone was one of gentle rebuke.

"I nodded, and left that place.

"High above the City a phalanx of angels wheeled and circled and dove. Each held a flaming sword which trailed a streak of burning brightness behind it, dazzling the eye. They moved in unison through the salmon-pink sky. They were very beautiful. It was—you know on summer evenings, when you get whole flocks of birds performing their dances in the sky? Weaving and circling and clustering and breaking apart again, so just as you think you understand the pattern, you realize you don't, and you never will? It was like that, only better.

"Above me was the sky. Below me, the shining City. My home. And outside the City, the Dark.

"Lucifer hovered a little below the Host, watching their maneuvers.

"'Lucifer?'

"'Yes, Raguel? Have you discovered your malefactor?'

"'I think so. Will you accompany me to Zephkiel's cell? There are others waiting for us there, and I will explain everything.'

"He paused. Then, 'Certainly.'

"He raised his perfect face to the angels, now performing a slow revolution in the sky, each moving through the air keeping perfect pace with the next, none of them ever touching. 'Azazel!'

"An angel broke from the circle; the others adjusted almost imperceptibly to his disappearance, filling the space, so you could no longer see where he had been.

"'I have to leave. You are in command, Azazel. Keep them drilling. They still have much to perfect.'

"'Yes, sir.'

"Azazel hovered where Lucifer had been, staring up at the flock of angels, and Lucifer and I descended toward the city.

"'He's my second-in-command,' said Lucifer. 'Bright. Enthusiastic. Azazel would follow you anywhere.'

"'What are you training them for?'

"'War.'

"'With whom?'

"'How do you mean?'

"'Who are they going to fight? Who else *is* there?'

"He looked at me; his eyes were clear, and honest. 'I do not know. But He has Named us to be His army. So we will be perfect. For Him. The Name is infallible and all-just, and all-wise, Raguel. It cannot be otherwise, no matter what—' He broke off, and looked away.

"'You were going to say?'

"'It is of no importance.'

"'Ah.'

"We did not talk for the rest of the descent to Zephkiel's cell."

I looked at my watch: it was almost three. A chill breeze had begun to blow down the LA street, and I shivered. The man noticed, and he paused in his story. "You okay?" he asked.

"I'm fine. Please carry on. I'm fascinated."

He nodded.

"They were waiting for us in Zephkiel's cell: Phanuel, Saraquael and Zephkiel. Zephkiel was sitting in his chair. Lucifer took up a position beside the window.

"I walked to the center of the room, and I began.

"'I thank you all for coming here. You know who I am; you know my function. I am the Vengeance of the Name: the arm of the Lord. I am Raguel.

"'The angel Carasel is dead. It was given to me to find out why he died, who killed him. This I have done. Now, the angel Carasel was a designer in the Hall of Being. He was very good, or so I am told . . .

"'Lucifer. *Tell me* what you were doing, before you came upon Phanuel, and the body.'

"'I have told you already. I was walking.'

"'Where were you walking?'

"'I do not see what business that is of yours.'

"'*Tell me.*'

"He paused. He was taller than any of us; tall, and proud. 'Very well. I was walking in the Dark. I have been walking in the Darkness for some time now. It helps me to gain a perspective on the City—being outside it. I see how fair it is, how perfect. There is nothing more enchanting than our home. Nothing more complete. Nowhere else that anyone would want to be'

"'And what do you do in the Dark, Lucifer?'

"He stared at me. 'I walk. And . . . There are voices, in the Dark.

I listen to the voices. They promise me things, ask me questions, whisper and plead. And I ignore them. I steel myself and I gaze at the City. It is the only way I have of testing myself—putting myself to any kind of trial. I am the Captain of the Host; I am the first among the Angels, and I must prove myself.'

"I nodded. 'Why did you not tell me this before.'

"He looked down. 'Because I am the only angel who walks in the Dark. Because I do not want others to walk in the Dark: I am strong enough to challenge the voices, to test myself. Others are not so strong. Others might stumble, or fall.'

"'Thank you, Lucifer. That is all, for now.' I turned to the next angel. 'Phanuel. How long have you been taking credit for Carasel's work?'

"His mouth opened, but no sound came out.

"'Well?'

"'I . . . I would not take credit for another's work.'

"'But you did take credit for *Love*?'

"He blinked. 'Yes. I did.'

"'Would you care to explain to us all what *Love* is?' I asked.

"He glanced around uncomfortably. 'It's a feeling of deep affection and attraction for another being, often combined with passion or desire—a need to be with another.' He spoke dryly, didactically, as if he were reciting a mathematical formula. 'The feeling that we have for the Name, for our Creator—that is *Love* . . . amongst other things. *Love* will be an impulse which will inspire and ruin in equal measure . . . We are,' he paused, then began once more, 'we are very proud of it.'

"He was mouthing the words. He no longer seemed to hold any hope that we would believe them.

"'Who did the majority of the work on *Love*? No, don't answer. Let me ask the others first. Zephkiel? When Phanuel passed the details on *Love* to you for approval, who did he tell you was responsible for it?'

"The wingless angel smiled gently. 'He told me it was his project.'

"'Thank you, sir. Now, Saraquael: whose was *Love*?'

"'Mine. Mine and Carasel's. Perhaps more his than mine, but we worked on it together.'

"'You knew that Phanuel was claiming the credit for it?'

"'. . . Yes.'

"'And you permitted this?'

"'He—he promised us that he would give us a good project of our own to follow. He promised that if we said nothing we would be given more big projects—and he was true to his word. He gave us *Death*.'

"I turned back to Phanuel. 'Well?'

"'It is true that I claimed that *Love* was mine.'

"'But it was Carasel's. And Saraquael's.'

"'Yes.'

"'Their last project—before *Death*?'

"'Yes.'

"'That is all.'

"I walked over to the window, looked out at the silver spires, looked at the dark. And I began to speak.

"'Carasel was a remarkable designer. If he had one failing, it was that he threw himself too deeply into his work.' I turned back to them. The angel Saraquael was shivering, and lights were flickering beneath his skin. 'Saraquael? Who did Carasel love? Who was his lover?'

"He stared at the floor. Then he stared up, proudly, aggressively. And he smiled.

"'I was.'

"'Do you want to tell me about it?'

"'No.' A shrug. 'But I suppose I must. Very well, then.

"'We worked together. And when we began to work on *Love* . . . we became lovers. It was his idea. We would go back to his cell, whenever we could snatch the time. There we touched each other, held each other, whispered endearments and protestations of eternal devotion. His welfare mattered more to me than my own. I existed for him. When I was alone I would repeat his name to myself, and think of nothing but him.

"'When I was with him . . .' he paused. He looked down. '. . . nothing else mattered.'

"I walked to where Saraquael stood; lifted his chin with my hand, stared into his grey eyes. 'Then why did you kill him?'

"'Because he would no longer love me. When we started to work on *Death* he—he lost interest. He was no longer mine. He belonged to *Death*. And if I could not have him, then his new lover was welcome to him. I could not bear his presence—I could not endure to have him near me and to know that he felt nothing for me. That was what hurt the most. I thought . . . I hoped . . . that if he was gone then I would no longer care for him—that the pain would stop.

"'So I killed him; I stabbed him, and I threw his body from our window in the Hall of Being. But the pain has *not* stopped.' It was almost a wail.

"Saraquael reached up, removed my hand from his chin. 'Now what?'

"I felt my aspect begin to come upon me; felt my function possess me. I was no longer an individual—I was the Vengeance of the Lord.

"I moved close to Saraquael, and embraced him. I pressed my lips to his, forced my tongue into his mouth. We kissed. He closed his eyes.

"I felt it well up within me then: a burning, a brightness. From the corner of my eyes, I could see Lucifer and Phanuel averting their faces from my light; I could feel Zephkiel's stare. And my light became brighter and brighter, until it erupted—from my eyes, from my chest, from my fingers, from my lips: a white, searing fire.

"The white flames consumed Saraquael slowly, and he clung to me as he burned.

"Soon there was nothing left of him. Nothing at all.

"I felt the flame leave me. I returned to myself once more.

"Phanuel was sobbing. Lucifer was pale. Zephkiel sat in his chair, quietly watching me.

"I turned to Phanuel and Lucifer. 'You have seen the Vengeance of the Lord,' I told them. 'Let it act as a warning to you both.'

"Phanuel nodded. 'It has. Oh it has. I, I will be on my way, sir. I will return to my appointed post. If that is all right with you?'

"'Go.'

"He stumbled to the window, and plunged into the light, his wings beating furiously.

"Lucifer walked over to the place on the silver floor where Saraquael had once stood. He knelt, stared desperately at the floor as if he were trying to find some remnant of the angel I had destroyed: a fragment of ash, or bone, or charred feather; but there was nothing to find. Then he looked up at me.

"'That was not right,' he said. 'That was not just.' He was crying; wet tears ran down his face. Perhaps Saraquael was the first to love, but Lucifer was the first to shed tears. I will never forget that.

"I stared at him, impassively. 'It was justice. He killed another. He was killed in his turn. You called me to my function, and I performed it.'

"'But . . . he *loved*. He should have been forgiven. He should have been helped. He should not have been destroyed like that. That was *wrong*.'

"'It was His will.'

"Lucifer stood. 'Then perhaps His will is unjust. Perhaps the voices in the darkness speak truly after all. How *can* this be right?'

"'It is right. It is His will. I merely performed my function.'

"He wiped away the tears, with the back of his hand. 'No,' he said, flatly. He shook his head, slowly, from side to side. Then he said, 'I must think on this. I will go now.'

"He walked to the window, stepped into the sky, and he was gone.

"Zephkiel and I were alone in his cell. I went over to his chair. He nodded at me. 'You have performed your function well, Raguel. Shouldn't you return to your cell, to wait until you are next needed?'"

The man on the bench turned towards me: his eyes sought mine. Until now it had seemed—for most of his narrative—that he was scarcely aware of me; he had stared ahead of himself, whispered his tale in little better than a monotone. Now it felt as if he had discovered me, and that he spoke to me alone, rather than to the air, or the City of Los Angeles. And he said:

"I knew that he was right. But I *couldn't* have left then—not even if I had wanted to. My aspect had not entirely left me; my function was not completely fulfilled. And then it fell into place; I saw the whole picture. And like Lucifer, I knelt. I touched my forehead to the silver floor. 'No, Lord,' I said. 'Not yet.'

"Zephkiel rose from his chair. 'Get up. It is not fitting for one angel to act in this way to another. It is not right. Get up!'

"I shook my head. 'Father, You are no angel,' I whispered.

"Zephkiel said nothing. For a moment my heart misgave within me. I was afraid. 'Father, I was charged to discover who was responsible for Carasel's death. And I do know.'

"'You have taken your vengeance, Raguel.'

"'*Your* vengeance, Lord.'

"And then He sighed, and sat down once more. 'Ah, little Raguel. The problem with creating things is that they perform so much better than one had ever planned. Shall I ask how you recognized me?'

"'I . . . I am not certain, Lord. You have no wings. You wait at the center of the city, supervising the Creation directly. When I destroyed Saraquael, You did not look away. You know too many things. You . . . ,' I paused, and thought. 'No, I do not know how I know. As You say, You have created me well. But I only understood who You were and the meaning of the drama we had enacted here for You, when I saw Lucifer leave.'

"'What did you understand, child?'

"'Who killed Carasel. Or at least, who was pulling the strings. For example, who arranged for Carasel and Saraquael to work together on *Love*, knowing Carasel's tendency to involve himself too deeply in his work?'

"He was speaking to me gently, almost teasingly, as an adult would pretend to make conversation with a tiny child. 'Why should anyone have "pulled the strings," Raguel?'

"'Because nothing occurs without reason; and all the reasons are Yours. You set Saraquael up: yes, he killed Carasel. But he killed Carasel so that I could destroy *him*.'

"'And were you wrong to destroy him?'

"I looked into His old, old eyes. 'It was my function. But I do not think it was just. I think perhaps it was needed that I destroy Saraquael, in order to demonstrate to Lucifer the Injustice of the Lord.'

"He smiled, then. 'And whatever reason would I have for doing that?'

"'I . . . I do not know. I do not understand—no more than I understand why You created the Dark, or the voices in the darkness. But You did. You caused all this to occur.'

"He nodded. 'Yes. I did. Lucifer must brood on the unfairness of Saraquael's destruction. And that—amongst other things—will precipitate him into certain actions. Poor sweet Lucifer. His way will be the hardest of all my children; for there is a part he must play in the drama that is to come, and it is a grand role.'

"I remained kneeling in front of the Creator of All Things.

"'What will you do now, Raguel?' He asked me.

"'I must return to my cell. My function is now fulfilled. I have taken vengeance, and I have revealed the perpetrator. That is enough. But—Lord?'

"'Yes, child.'

"'I feel dirty. I feel tarnished. I feel befouled. Perhaps it is true that all that happens is in accordance with Your will, and thus it is good. But sometimes You leave blood on Your instruments.'

"He nodded, as if He agreed with me. 'If you wish, Raguel, you may forget all this. All that has happened this day.' And then He said, 'However, you will not be able to speak of this to any other angels, whether you choose to remember it or not.'

"'I will remember it.'

"'It is your choice. But sometimes you will find it is easier by far not to remember. Forgetfulness can sometimes bring freedom, of a sort. Now, if you do not mind,' He reached down, took a file from a stack on the floor, opened it, 'there is work I should be getting on with.'

"I stood up and walked to the window. I hoped He would call me back, explain every detail of His plan to me, somehow make it all better. But He said nothing, and I left His Presence without ever looking back."

The man was silent, then. And he remained silent—I couldn't even hear him breathing—for so long that I began to get nervous, thinking that perhaps he had fallen asleep, or died.

Then he stood up.

"There you go, pal. That's your story. Do you think it was worth a couple of cigarettes and a book of matches?" He asked the question as if it was important to him, without irony.

"Yes," I told him. "Yes. It was. But what happened next? How did you . . . I mean, if . . ." I trailed off.

It was dark on the street, now, at the edge of daybreak. One by one the streetlights had begun to flicker out, and he was silhouetted against the glow of the dawn sky. He thrust his hands into his pockets. "What happened? I left home, and I lost my way, and these days home's a long way back. Sometimes you do things you regret, but there's nothing you can do about them. Times change. Doors close behind you. You move on. You know?

"Eventually I wound up here. They used to say no one's ever originally from LA. True as Hell in my case."

And then, before I could understand what he was doing, he leaned down and kissed me, gently, on the cheek. His stubble was rough and prickly, but his breath was surprisingly sweet. He whispered into my ear: "I never fell. I don't care what they say. I'm still doing my job, as I see it."

My cheek burned where his lips had touched it.

He straightened up. "But I still want to go home."

The man walked away down the darkened street, and I sat on the bench and watched him go. I felt like he had taken something from me, although I could no longer remember what. And I felt like something had been left in its place—absolution, perhaps, or innocence, although of what, or from what, I could no longer say.

An image from somewhere: a scribbled drawing, of two angels in flight above a perfect city; and over the image a child's perfect handprint, which stains the white paper blood-red. It came into my head unbidden, and I no longer know what it meant.

I stood up.

It was too dark to see the face of my watch, but I knew I would get no sleep that day. I walked back to the place I was staying, to the house by the stunted palm tree, to wash myself, and to wait. I thought about angels, and about Tink; and I wondered whether love and death went hand in hand.

The next day the planes to England were flying again.

I felt strange—lack of sleep had forced me into that miserable state in which everything seems flat and of equal importance; when nothing matters, and in which reality seems scraped thin and threadbare. The taxi journey to the airport was a nightmare. I was hot, and tired, and testy. I wore a T-shirt in the LA heat; my coat was packed at the bottom of my luggage, where it had been for the entire stay.

The aeroplane was crowded, but I didn't care.

The stewardess walked down the aisle with a rack of newspapers; the *Herald Tribune*, *USA Today* and the *LA Times*. I took a copy of the *Times*, but the words left my head as my eyes scanned over them. Nothing that I read remained with me. No, I lie: somewhere in the back of the paper was a report of a triple murder: two women, and a small child. No names were given, and I do not know why the report should have registered as it did.

Soon I fell asleep. I dreamed about fucking Tink, while blood ran sluggishly from her closed eyes and lips. The blood was cold and viscous and clammy, and I awoke chilled by the plane's air conditioning, with an unpleasant taste in my mouth. My tongue and lips were dry. I looked out of the scratched oval window, stared down at the clouds, and it occurred to me then (not for the first time) that the clouds were in actuality another land, where everyone knew just what they were looking for and how to get back where they started from.

Staring down at the clouds is one of the things I have always liked best about flying. That, and the proximity one feels to one's death.

I wrapped myself in the thin aircraft blanket, and slept some more, but if further dreams came then they made no impression upon me.

A blizzard blew up shortly after the plane landed in England, knocking out the airport's power supply. I was alone in an airport elevator at the time, and it went dark and jammed between floors. A dim emergency light flickered on. I pressed the crimson alarm button until the batteries ran down and it ceased to sound; then I shivered in my LA T-shirt, in the corner of my little silver room. I watched my breath steam in the air, and I hugged myself for warmth.

There wasn't anything in there except me; but even so, I felt safe, and secure. Soon someone would come and force open the doors. Eventually somebody would let me out; and I knew that I would soon be home.

THE HOUSES OF THE FAVORED

Jay Lake

JAY LAKE lives in Portland, Oregon, where he works on numerous writing and editing projects. His most recent books include the novel *Pinion* from Tor Books; the novellas *The Specific Gravity of Grief* from Fairwood Press and *The Baby Killers* from PS Publishing; and a new collection, *The Sky That Wraps*, from Subterranean Press.

His short fiction appears regularly in literary and genre markets worldwide. He is a winner of the John W. Campbell Award for Best New Writer, and a multiple nominee for the Hugo and World Fantasy awards.

"I first wrote this set of stories as part of a proposed project with Bruce Holland Rogers," explains the author. "Bruce set me to his concept of a symmetrina, which is to say, writing to a very precise word count. It's an interesting kind of limitation, which binds the writer to the form in a way that we don't usually experience.

"I found the experience very focusing—not to mention the fun of finding five different ways to talk about angels gone bad. Just because they're good doesn't mean they're nice."

I SMELL LAMB'S BLOOD. Walking the dusty streets sword in hand, I hear only silence. High, silver clouds sweep moon's brightness like the linen wrapping a lover's face. These clouds are mine, the silence my shroud. There are tasks no one should be forced to, not even by the loving hand of He Is Who He Is.

One of my brothers stands in a grove of olives and pomegranates, waving a flaming sword, occasionally killing snakes. A symbolic post, with little business to execute.

Others were sent to despoil virgins and lay waste to cities. Symbolism *and* execution, but at the end, they went home with their hands clean and clear consciences. Sinners live for punishment, after all.

But here is a city of a million beating hearts crowded together on the banks of their Father River, now sleeping. In my presence, the dogs are silent, the vultures huddled uneasily on temple roofs. Even the louche crocodiles doze among their muddy reeds.

Who He Is has charged me with vengeance. Not Eden's dangerous hungers, nor Sodom's hot sins. Here it is only for me to still the hearts of ten thousand sleeping sons. Most of them innocent of any sin worse than craving the breast or a sweet, or perhaps a pretty girl.

My feet bring me to the stony regard of a jackal-headed god. "You, friend," I whisper, "are at least honest in your falsehood. I wear Heaven's gleaming mantle as I set about my murders."

A thin spray of dust trails from the jackal's muzzle as his smile cracks open a little wider.

Fang, I tell myself, I am the tooth of God. He Is Who He Is, and it is I who will render flesh.

Honest acknowledgement is needed of the suffering that will arise with the morning sun. Suffering simply to make a point. Though the pain reaches my heart, I tear all my feathers loose to lay them at the jackal's feet, each great pinion radiant with holy power. The blood from my back I smear upon my face and hands, coat my sword with, echo of the lamb's blood on the houses of the favored. Many and legion, I step into the darkest shadows to wound the hearts of ten thousand mothers.

AN INFESTATION OF ANGELS
Jane Yolen

JANE YOLEN has been called "the Hans Christian Andersen of America" (*Newsweek*) and "a modern equivalent of Aesop" (*New York Times*).

A prolific author, editor and poet of fantasy, science fiction, folklore and children's books, she is a winner of the prestigious Caldecott Medal, two Nebula Awards for short fiction and the World Fantasy Grand Master Award.

Her most recent releases include her 300th book—however, she is not exactly certain which one it is! These include the novel *Except the Queen* (written with Midori Snyder) and a fantasy graphic novel, *Foiled*. She is currently working on a redacted young-adult fairy tale novel, *Snow in Summer* (which she describes as "an Appalachian Snow White").

"I wrote (and originally published) 'An Infestation of Angels' a number of years ago while thinking about biblical stories of angels," recalls Yolen. "God only knows why. And She hasn't thought fit to tell me.

"I think a bird might have dropped something on my car that morning. Certainly I have had other instances when small irritations have encysted in the brain and turned into a bitter pearl."

THE ANGELS CAME AGAIN TODAY, filthy things, dropping golden-hard wing feathers and turds as big and brown as camel dung. This time one of them took Isak, clamping him from behind with massive talons. We could hear him screaming long after the covey was out of sight. His blood stained the doorpost where they took him. We left it there, part warning, part desperate memorial, with the dropped feathers nailed above. In a time of plagues, this infestation of angels was the worst.

We did not want to stay in the land of the Gipts, but slaves must do as their masters command. And though we were not slaves in the traditional sense, only hirelings, we had signed contracts and the Gipts are great believers in contracts. It was a saying of theirs that "One who goes back on his signed word is no better than a thief." What they do to thieves is considered grotesque even in this godforsaken desert-land.

So we were trapped here, under skies that rained frogs, amid sparse fields that bred locusts, beneath a sun that raised rashes and blisters on our sensitive skins. It was a year of unnature. Yet if any one of us complained, the leader of the Gipts, the faró, waved the contract high over his head, causing his followers to break into that high ulullation they mis-call laughter.

We stayed.

Minutes after Isak was taken, his daughter Miriamne came to my house with the Rod of Leaders. I carved my own sign below Isak's and then spoke the solemn oath in our ancient tongue to Miriamne and the nine others who came to witness the passing of the stick. My sign was a snake, for my clan is Serpent. It had been exactly twelve rotations since the last member of Serpent had led the People here, but if the plague of angels lasted much longer, there would be no one else of my tribe to carry on in this place. We were not a warrior clan and I was the last. We had always been a small clan, and poor, ground under the heels of the more prosperous tribes.

When the oath was done and properly attested to—we are a people of parchment and ink—we sat down at the table together to break bread.

"We cannot stay longer," began Josu. His big, bearded face was so crisscrossed with scars it looked like a map, and the southern hemisphere was moving angrily. "We must ask the faró to let us out of our contract."

"In all the years of our dealings with the Gipts," I pointed out, "there has never been a broken contract. My father and yours, Josu, would turn in their graves knowing we even consider such a thing." My father, comfortably dead these fifteen years back in the Homeland, would not have bothered turning, no matter what the cause. But Josu's father, like all those of Scorpion, had been the anxious type, always looking for extra trouble. It took little imagination to picture him rotating in the earth like a lamb on a holiday spit.

Miriamne wept silently in the corner, but her brothers pounded the table with fists as broad as hammers.

"He *must* let us go!" Ur shouted.

"Or at least," his younger, larger brother added sensibly, "he must let us put off the work on his temple until the angels migrate north. It is almost summer."

Miriamne was weeping aloud now, though whether for Isak's sudden bloody death or at the thought of his killers in the lush high valleys of the north was difficult to say.

"It will do us no good to ask the faró to let us go," I said. "For if we do, he will use us as the Gipts always use thieves, and that is not a happy prospect." By *us*, of course, I meant me, for the faró's wrath would be visited upon the asker which, as leader, would be me. "But . . ." I paused, pauses being the coin of Serpent's wisdom.

They looked expectant.

". . . if we could persuade the faró that this plague was meant for the Gipts and not us . . ." I left that thought in front of them. The

Serpent clan is known for its deviousness and wit, and deviousness and wit were what was needed now, in this time of troubles.

Miriamne stopped weeping. She walked around the table and stood behind me, putting her hands on my shoulders.

"I stand behind Masha," she said.

"And I." It was Ur, who always followed his sister's lead.

And so, one by one by one, the rest of the minon agreed. What the ten agreed to, the rest of the People in the land of the Gipts would do without question. In this loyalty lay our strength.

I went at once to the great palace of the faró, for if I waited much longer he would not understand the urgency of my mission. The Gipts are a fat race with little memory, which is why they have others build them large reminders. The deserts around are littered with their monuments— stone and bone and mortar tokens cemented with the People's blood. Ordinarily we do not complain of this. After all, we are the only ones who can satisfactorily plan and construct these mammoth memories. The Gipts are incapable on their own. Instead they squat upon their vast store of treasures, doling out golden tokens for work. It is a strange understanding we have, but no stranger than some of nature's other associations. Does not the sharp-beaked plover feed upon the crocodile's back? Does not the tiny remora cling to the shark?

But this year the conditions in the Gipt kingdom had been intolerable. While we often lose a few of the People to the heat, to the badly-prepared Giptanese food, or to the ever-surprising visit of the Gipt pox, there had never before been such a year: plague after plague after plague. There were dark murmurs everywhere that our God had somehow been angered. And the last, this hideous infestation.

Normally angels stay within their mountain fasts, feasting on wild goats and occasional nestlings. They are rarely seen, except from afar on their spiraling mating flights when the males circle the heavens, caroling and displaying their stiffened pinions and erections to their females who watch from the heights. (There are, of course, stories of Gipt women who, inflamed by the sight of that strange, winged masculinity, run off into the wilds and are never seen again. Women of the People would never do such a thing.)

However this year there had been a severe drought and the mountain foliage was sparse. Many goats died of starvation. The angels, hungry for red meat, had found our veins carried the same sweet nectar. Working out on the monuments, walking along the streets unprotected, we were easier prey than the homed goats. And the Gipts allow us to carry no weapons. It is in the contract.

Fifty-seven had fallen to the angel claws, ten of them of my own precious clan. It was too many. We *had* to convince the faró that this plague was his problem and not ours. It would take all of the deviousness and wit of a true Serpent. I thought quickly as I walked down the great wide street, the Street of Memories, towards the palace of the faró.

Because the Gipts think a woman's face and ankle can cause unnecessary desire, both had to be suitably draped. I wore the traditional black robe and pants that covered my legs, and the black silk mask that hid all but my eyes. However, a builder needs to be able to move easily, and it was hot in this land, so my stomach and arms were bare. Those parts of the body were considered undistinguished by the Gipts. It occurred to me as I walked that my stomach and arms were thereby flashing unmistakable signals to any angels on the prowl. My grip on the Rod of Leadership tightened. I shifted to carry it between both hands. I would not go meekly, as Isak had, clamped from behind. I twirled and looked around, then glanced up and scanned the skies.

There was nothing there but the clear, untrammeled blue of the Gipt summer canopy. Not even a bird wrote in lazy script across that slate.

And so I got to the palace without incident. The streets had been as bare as the sky. Normally the streets would be a-squall with the People and other hirelings of the Gipts. *They* only traveled in donkey-drawn chairs and at night, when their overweight, ill-proportioned bodies can stand the heat. And since the angels are a diurnal race, bedding down in their aeries at night, Gipts and angels rarely meet.

I knocked at the palace door. The guards, mercenaries hired from across the great water, their black faces mapped with ritual scars, opened the doors from within. I nodded slightly. In the ranks of the Gipts, the People were higher than they. However it says in our holy books that all shall be equal, so I nodded.

They did not return my greetings. Their own religion counted mercenaries as dead men until they came back home. The dead do not worry about the niceties of conversation.

"Masha-la, Masha-la," came a twittering cry.

I looked up and saw the faró's twenty sons bearing down on me, their foreshortened legs churning along the hall. Still too young to have gained the enormous weight that marked their elders, the boys climbed upon me like little monkeys. I was a great favorite at court, using my Serpent's wit to construct wonder tales for their entertainment.

"Masha-la, tell us a story."

I held out the Rod and they fell back, astonished to see it in my hand. It put an end to our casual story sessions. "I must see your father, the great faró," I said.

They raced back down the hall, chittering and smacking their lips as the smell of the food in the dining commons drew them in. I followed, knowing that the adult Gipts would be there as well, partaking of one of their day-long feasts.

Two more black mercenaries opened the doors for me. Of a different tribe, these were tall and thin, the scarifications on their arms like jeweled bracelets of black beads. I nodded to them in passing. Their faces reflected nothing back.

The hall was full of feeding Gipts, served by their slimmer women. On the next to highest tier, there was a line of couches on which lay seven massive men, the faró's advisors. And on the high platform, overseeing them all, the mass of flesh that was the faró himself, one fat hand reaching towards a bowl of peeled grapes.

"Greetings, oh high and mighty faró," I said, my voice rising above the sounds in the hall.

The faró smiled blandly and waved a lethargic hand. The rings on his fingers bit deeply into the engorged flesh. It is a joke amongst the People that one can tell the age of a Gipt as one does a tree, by counting the rings. Once put on, the rings become embedded by the encroaching fat. The many gems on the faró's hand winked at me. He was very old.

"Masha-la," he spoke languidly, "it grieves me to see you with the Rod of your people."

"It grieves me even more, mighty faró, to greet you with my news. But it is something which you must know." I projected my voice so that even the women in the kitchens could hear.

"Say on," said the faró.

"These death-bearing angels are not so much a plague upon the People but are rather using us as an appetizer for Giptanese flesh," I said. "Soon they will tire of our poor, ribey meat and gorge themselves on yours. Unless . . ." I paused.

"Unless what, *Leader of the People*?" asked the faró.

I was in trouble. Still, I had to go on. There was no turning back, and this the faró knew. "Unless my people take a small vacation across the great sea, returning when the angels are gone. We will bring more of the People and the monument will be done on time."

The faró's greedy eyes glittered. "For no more than the promised amount?"

"It is for your own good," I whined. The faró expects petitioners to whine. It is in the contract under "Deportment Rules."

"I do not believe you, Masha-la," said the faró. "But you tell a good story. Come back tomorrow."

That saved my own skin, but it did not help the rest. "These angels *will be* after the sons of the faró," I said. It was a guess. Only the sons and occasional and unnecessary still women went out in the daylight. I am not sure why I said it. "And once they have tasted Gipt flesh . . ." I paused.

There was a sudden and very real silence in the room. It was clear I had overstepped myself. It was clearer when the faró sat up. Slowly that mammoth body raised with the help of two of the black guards. When he was seated upright, he put on his helm of office, with the decorated flaps that draped against his ears. He held out his hand and the guard on the right pushed the Great Gipt Crook into his pudgy palm.

"You and your People will not go to the sea this year before time," intoned the faró. "But tomorrow *you* will come to the kitchen and serve up your hand for my soup."

He banged the crook's wide bottom on the floor three times. The guard took the crook from his hand. Then exhausted by the sentence he had passed on my hand—I hoped they would take the left, not the right—he lay down again and started to eat.

I walked out, through doors opened by the shadow men, whose faces I forgot as soon as I saw them, out into the early eve, made blood red by the setting sun.

I could hear the patter of the faró's sons after me, but such was my agitation that I did not turn to warn them back. Instead I walked down the street composing a psalm to the cunning of my right hand, just in case.

The chittering of the boys behind me increased and, just as I came to the door of Isak's house, I turned and felt the weight of wind from above. I looked up and saw an angel swooping down on me, wings fast to its side in a perilous stoop like a hawk upon its prey. I fell back against the doorpost, reaching my right hand up in supplication. My fingers scraped against the nailed-up feathers. Instinctively I grabbed them and held them clenched in my fist. My left hand was down behind me scrabbling in the dirt. It mashed something on the ground. And then the angel was on me and my left hand joined the right pushing up against the awful thing.

Angel claws were inches from my neck when something stopped the creature's rush. Its wings whipped out and slowed its descent, and its great golden-haired head moved from side to side.

It was then that I noticed its eyes. They were as blue as the Gipt sky—and as empty. The angel lifted its beautiful blank face upward and sniffed the air, pausing curiously several times at my outstretched hands. Then, pumping its mighty wings twice, it lifted away from me, banked sharply to the right, and took off in the direction of the palace where the faró's sons scattered before it like twigs in the wind.

Two times the angel dropped down and came up with a child in its claw. I leaped to my feet, smeared the top of my stick with the dung and feathers and chased after the beast, but I was too late. It was gone, a screaming boy in each talon, heading towards its aerie where it would share its catch.

What could I tell the faró that he would not already know from the hysterical children ahead of me? I walked back to my own house, carrying my stick above my head. It would protect me as no totem had before. I knew now what only dead men had known, the learning which they had gathered as the claws carried them above the earth! *Angels are blind and hunt by smell.* If we but smeared our sticks with their dung and feathers and carried this above our heads, we would be safe; we would be, in their "eyes," angels.

I washed my hands carefully, called the minon to me, and told them of my plan. We would go this night, as a people, to the faró. We would tell him that his people were cursed by our God now. The angels would come for them, but not for us. He would have to let us go.

It was the children's story that convinced him, as mine could not. Luck had it that the two boys taken were his eldest. Or perhaps not luck. As they were older, they were fatter—and slower. The angel came upon them first.

Their flesh must have been sweet. In the morning we could hear the hover of angel wings outside, like a vast buzzing. Some of the People wanted to sneak away by night.

"No," I commanded, holding up the Rod of Leadership, somewhat darkened by the angel dung smeared over the top. "If we sneak away like thieves in the night, we will never work for the Gipts again. We must go tomorrow morning, in the light of day, through the cloud of angels. That way the faró and his people will know our power and the power of our God."

"But," said Josu, "how can we be sure your plan will work? It is a devious one at best. I am not sure even I believe you."

"Watch!" I said and I opened the door, holding the Rod over my head. I hoped that what I believed to be so was so, but my heart felt like a marble in the mouth.

The door slammed behind me and I knew faces pressed against the curtains of each window.

And then I was alone in the courtyard, armed with but a stick and a prayer.

The moment I walked outside, the hover of angels became agitated. They spiraled up and, like a line of enormous insects, winged towards me. As they approached, I prayed and put the stick above my head.

The angels formed a great circle high over my head and one by one they dipped down, sniffed around the top of the Rod, then flew back to place. When they were satisfied, they wheeled off, flying in a phalanx, towards the farthest hills.

At that, the doors of the houses opened, and the People emerged. Josu was first, his own stick, sticky with angel dung, in hand.

"Now, quick," I said, "before the faró can see what we are doing, grab up what dung and feathers you find from that circle and smear it quickly on the doorposts of the houses. Later, when we are sure no one is watching, we can scrape it onto totems to carry with us to the sea."

And so it was done. The very next morning, with much blowing of horns and beating of drums, we left for the sea. But none of the faró's people or his mercenaries came to see us off, though they followed us later.

But that is another story altogether, and not a pretty tale at all.

SECOND JOURNEY OF THE MAGUS

Ian R. MacLeod

IAN R. MacLEOD's debut novel, *The Great Wheel* (1997), won the Locus Award for Best First Novel. Since then he has followed it with *The Light Ages*, *The House of Storms*, *The Summer Isles* (which won the Sidewise Award for Alternate History in both its novel and novella forms), the Arthur C. Clarke Award–winning *Song of Time* and *Wake Up and Dream*, forthcoming from PS Publishing.

MacLeod has twice won the World Fantasy Award, for novella and novelette, and his short fiction is collected in the Arkham House volume *Voyages by Starlight,* as well as *Breathmoss and Other Exhalations*, *Past Magic* and *Journeys*.

"I'd long been thinking of writing something based on what I suppose you might call this story's theological premise," reveals the author. "For a long while, I played around with using John the Baptist and Salome as the main protagonists, but I couldn't get it to work. Then, when Melchior came along, and, with a touch of T.S. Eliot's famous poem about the magi, everything snapped into shape.

"There's something horrible about angels, even when they're described as being at their most holy and brilliant, as a quick perusal of the Book of Revelation will show."

HE TRAVELED THE SAME WAY, but there was heat this time instead of the dark of winter, and nothing of the lands which he had passed through more than thirty years before was the same. Gone were the quiet houses, the patchwork fields, the lowland shepherds offering to share their skins of wine. Instead, there were goats unmilked, bodies bloating in ditches, fruit left to rot on the branch. And people were fleeing, armies were marching. Fear and dust hazed the roads.

He followed hidden tracks. He camped quietly and alone. He lit no fire, ate raisins and dry bread. He spoke no prayers. Although an old man, weak and unarmed, he felt resignation rather than fear. His camel was of far greater value than he was, and he knew he could never to return to Persia. At least, alive. The Emperor, if he ever knew of his journey, would regard it as treason, and the Zoroastrian priests would scourge his body for honoring a false god.

He came at last to the Euphrates. There were palms and green hills rising from the marshes, but the villages all around were empty. He sat down by the broad blue river as his camel drank long and loud, and quietly mourned for his two old friends. Melchior, who had first read of that coming birth in the scriptures of a primitive tribe. Gaspar, who had found the right quadrant in the stars to pilot their way. And, he, Balthasar, who had accompanied them because he had ceased to believe in anything, and wished to see the emptiness of all the world and the entire heavens proven with his own eyes. That, he supposed, was why he had chosen to bring an unguent for embalming corpses as his gift for this king he never expected to find.

A boat was moored, nudging anxiously into the current as if feared to be left alone in this greenly desolate place. It was evening by the time Balthasar had refound his resolve and persuaded his half-hobbled camel to board the vessel with murmured spells, then made small obeisance to the gods of the river, and poled into the inky currents beyond the reeds. The sky in the west darkened as sprites of wind played around him, but, even as the moon rose and stars strung the heavens, even as he re-moored the boat on the far side and set off across a land which soon withered to desert, the western horizon ahead remained aflame.

He knew enough about war to understand the dark eddies and stillnesses which he had already witnessed on his journey, but it seemed to him that the battleground he encountered as the dawn sun rose at his back and brightness glared ahead was the stillest, darkest place on earth. All Persians should be grateful, he supposed, that this resurgent Hebrew kingdom had turned its wrath against the Empire of Rome. A strategist would even say that war between powerful neighbors can only bring good to your own lands—he had heard that very thing said in the bars of Kuchan—but that presupposed some balance in the powers which fought each other. There was no balance here. There was only death.

Blackened skulls. Blackened chariots. Heaps of bone, terribly disordered. The way the Roman swords and shields were melted as if put to the furnace. The way the helmets were caved in as if crushed between giant fists. Worst still, somehow, was the sheer *value* of what had been left here, ignored, discarded, when every battlefield Balthasar had ever witnessed or heard of in song was a place ripe for looting. This great Roman army, with its engines and horses, with the linked plate metal walls of irresistibly fearless men and raining arrows, had been obliterated as if by some fiery hurricane. And then everything simply left. It was hard to find a way across this devastation. He had to blindfold his camel and sooth the moaning creature with quite visions of oases to keep it calm. He wished that he could blindfold himself, but, strangely, there was nothing here to offend his mouth and nose. There were no flies even as his feet sunk through puddled offal as he climbed mountains of bones. The only smell was a faint one of some odd kind of perfume, such as the waft you might catch from beyond the curtains of the temple of some unknowable god.

The noon sun was hot, but the blaze in the west had grown brighter still. He remembered that star, the one which Gaspar had been so certain would somehow detach itself from the heavens to lead them. Had it now reignited and settled here on earth? Was *that* what lay ahead? He swathed his face against the burning light and drifting ash. It seemed to him now that he'd always been destined to re-take this journey at the end of his life. If nothing else, it was due as penance.

The three men who had taken this journey before had thought themselves wise, and were acknowledged in their own lands as priests, kings, magi. Then, unmistakably even to Balthasar's dubious gaze, a single star had hovered before them, and did not move as the rest of the heavens revolved. It went beyond all reason. It destroyed everything he understood, but the people they asked as they passed through this primitive outpost of the Roman Empire could speak of nothing in their ragged tongue but vague myths of an ancient king called David, and of a great uprising to come. They did not understand the stars, or the ancient scripts. They only understood the gold which the three magi laid upon their palms.

Finally, though, they reached the city called Jerusalem. It was the administrative capital of this little province, and truly, from its fallen walls and the pomp with which the priests of the local god bore themselves, it did seem to be the remnant of a somewhere which had once been far greater. The local tetrarch was called Herod, and even to the cultured eyes of the three magi, his palace was suitably grand. It was constructed on a sheer stone platform with high walls looking out across the city, and surrounded by groves of fine trees, bronze fountains, glittering canals. Thus, the three magi thought, as they were led through mosaic-studded halls, does the Rome honor and sustain those who submit to its power.

They were put at their ease. They were given fine quarters, soft clean beds and hot baths. Silken girls brought them sherbet. Dancing girls danced barefoot. Here, at last, they felt that they were being treated as the great emissaries that they truly were. Herod, bloated on his throne, struck Balthasar as little man made large. But he could converse in the Greek, and the three magi could think of no reason why they should not ask for his advice as to the furtherance of their quest. And that advice was given—generously, and without pause. Astrologers were summoned. Holy books were unfurled, and the bearded priests of this region who clustered around them agreed that, yes, such was the prophecy of which these ancient scriptures spoke— of a new king, of the lineage of a king called David who had once made this city great in the times of long ago. The three magi were sent on their way from Jerusalem with fresh camels, full bellies and happy hearts. Herod, they agreed, as they rode toward the star which now seemed even brighter in the firmament, might be a slippery oaf, but at least he was a hospitable one.

The roads were clogged. It was the calling, apparently, of a census, despite it being the worst time of the year. Not an auspicious moment, either, Balthasar couldn't help thinking, for a woman to travel if she was heavy with child. He discussed again with Melchior as they pushed with the crowds and the sleeting rain past the camps of centurions and lines of crucified criminals. Remind me again—is this child supposed to be a man, or a god? But the answer he got from his friend remained meaningless. For how can the answer be both yes, and yes? How can something be both? Difficulties, then, with finding somewhere to reside, for all the documents of passage Herod had so kindly given them, and Gaspar's navigation was no longer so sure. For all that this star glowed out at them like a jewel set the firmaments both day and night, no one could offer guidance on their quest, and none bar a few wandering shepherds seemed to notice that the star was even there.

Then they came at last to a small town by the name of Bethlehem, and it was already night, and it was clear that whatever this strange light in the heavens signaled had happened here. They enquired at the inns. They spoke once again to the so-called local wise men, although this time, more warily. They made no mention of gods or kings. At the start of this journey, Balthasar had imagined himself—although he had never believed it would truly happen—being led to some glowing presence which would rip down the puny veils of this world. But he realized now that whatever it was that they sought would be painfully humble, and all three magi had began to fear for the fate of the family involved.

It was a stable, at the back of the cheapest and most overcrowded of all the inns. They would have been sent away entirely had not Melchior known to ask as the door was being slammed in their faces about a family from a town called Nazareth. So they had reached the place toward which the star and the prophecies had long been leading them, on the darkest and most hopeless of nights, and in coldest time of the year. There was mud, of course, and there was the ordure. There was little shelter. Precious little warmth, as well, apart from that which came from the fartings and breathings of the animals. The woman was still exhausted from birth, and she had laid the baby amid the straw in a feeding trough, and the man seemed . . . not, it struck Balthasar, the way any proud husband should. He was dumbstruck, and in awe.

They should, by rights, have simply turned and left. Offered their apologies for the disturbance, perhaps, and maybe a little money to help see this impoverished family toward their next meal. Balthasar thought at first that that was all Melchior planned to do when he stepped forward with a small bag of gold. But then he had fallen to his knees on this filthy floor before the child in that crude cot. And Gaspar, bearing a bowl of incense, did the same. These were the gifts, Balthasar now remembered, that his two friends had always talked of bearing. Now, he felt he had no choice but to prostrate himself as well, and offer the gift which he had never imagined he would be called to present. Gold, for a king, and frankincense, for a man of God—yes, those gifts were understandable, if the prophecies were remotely true. But myrrh symbolized death, if it symbolized anything at all. Then the baby had stirred and, for a moment, Balthasar had felt he was part of *something*. And that something had lingered in his mind and his dreams through all the years since.

He had spoken about that moment with Melchior as he lay on his deathbed back in Persia. Yes, his old friend agreed in dry whisper, perhaps a god really had chosen to manifest itself in that strange way, and in that strange place. Perhaps he had even moved the heavens so that they could make that long journey bearing those particular gifts. But Melchior was fading rapidly by then, falling into pain and stinking incontinence which the castings of spells and prayers could no longer assuage. As his friend spasmed in rank gasps, Balthasar couldn't bring himself to frame the other question which had robbed him of so many nights of sleep. For if that baby really was the manifestation of an all-powerful god, why had that god chosen to make them the instruments of the terror which happened next?

The three magi had left the stable at morning under a sky doused with rain, and they knew without speaking that they must return quietly and secretly to Persia, and should spread no further word. But, through their vain discussions in Herod's opulent palace, it was already too late. Rumors of a boy king was the last thing this restless province needed, and the remedy which Herod enacted was swift and efficient in the Roman way. Word came like a sour wind after the three supposedly wise men that every male child recently born in Bethlehem had been slaughtered, and they returned to their palaces in Persia half-convinced that they had seen the manifestation of a great god, but certain that that god was dead.

So it had remained in all the years since, through Balthasar's increasing decrepitude, and the loss of his wives, and deaths of his oldest friends. But then had come rumor from that same territory in the west of a man said to have been born in the very place and manner which they had witnessed, who was now performing great miracles, and proclaimed himself King of the race the Romans called the Jews. It had been four years, as Balthasar calculated, since this man had emerged as if from the same prophesies which Melchior had once shown him on those ancient scrolls. And it seemed to Balthasar now that this last journey had always been predestined, and that the only thing which he had been waiting for was the imminence of his own death.

He was entering a green land now. It was fertile and busy. The creeks bubbled with water so pure and sweet that he feared both he and his camel would never stop drinking. The roadside bloomed with flowers more abundant than those tended in his own palace grounds. Fat lambs baaed. The air grew finer and clearer with every breath. All the dust and pain and disappointment of his journey was soon cleansed away.

The first angel Balthasar witnessed was standing at a crossroads, and he took it at first to be a tall golden statute until he realized that it wasn't standing at all. The creature hovered two or three spans in the air above the fine-set paving on four conjoined wings flashing with many glittering eyes, and it had four faces pointing in each of the roadway's four directions, which were the faces of a man, a lion, an ox and an eagle. Its feet were also those of an ox. Somehow Balthasar knew that this creature belonged to the first angelic order known as Cherubim. There was a singing in his ears as he gazed up at the thing, which was too beautiful to be horrible. He didn't know whether to bow down in tears, or laugh out loud for joy.

"Old man, you have come as a pilgrim." It was merely a statement, sung by a roaring choir. "You may pass."

This land of Israel truly was a paradise. He had never seen villages so well tended, or lands so fecund. Trees bowed down with fruit even though it was too early in the season. Lambs leapt everywhere. The cattle were amiable and fat. He felt, amongst many other feelings, ridiculously hungry, but withheld from plucking from the boughs of the fig trees until he saw the many other travelers and pilgrims feasting on whatever took their fancy, and farmers freely offering their produce—plump olives, fine pomegranates, warm breads, cool wines, glistening haunches of meat—to all.

He knew that night was coming from the darkening of the eastern sky behind him, but the west glowed far too bright for any visible sunset to occur. A happy kind of tiredness swept over him. Here, he would merrily have cast himself down in these hedgerows, which would surely be soft as a feather bed. But a farmer came running to him from out of the sleek blue twilight, and insisted on the hospitality of his home. It was a square building, freshly whitened, freshly roofed. Olive lamps glittered, and the floor inside was dry and newly swept. He had never encountered somewhere so simple, yet so beautifully kept. The man himself was beautiful as well, and yet more beautiful were his wife and children, who sang as they prepared their meal, and listened gravely to Balthasar's tale of his journey and the terrible things he had witnessed, yet laughed when he had finished, and hugged him, and broke into prayer.

All he was seeing, they assured him, were the sad remnants of a world which would soon be extinguished as the Kingdom of their Savior spread. Their eldest son was fighting in the armies of Jesus the Christos, which they knew would be victorious, and they did not fear for his death. Even in a house as joyous as this, that last statement struck Balthasar as odd, but he kept his council as they sat down to eat on beautifully woven rugs, and the meal was the best he had ever tasted. Then, there was more song, and more prayer. When the man of the house finally beckoned Balthasar, he imagined it to show him the place where he would bed. Through a small doorway, and beyond a curtain there was, indeed, a raised cot, but a figure already occupied it; that of an elderly woman who lay smiling with hands clasped and eyes wide open as if gripped in eager prayer.

"Go on, my friend," Balthasar was urged. "This is my grandmother. You must touch her."

Balthasar did. Her skin was cold and waxy. Her eyes, for all their shine, were unblinking. She was plainly dead.

"Now, you must tell me how long you think she's been thus."

Troubled, but using his not inconsiderable knowledge of physic,

Balthasar muttered something about three to four hours, perhaps less, to judge by the absence of odor, or the onset of rigor in the limbs.

The man clapped his hands and laughed. "Almost two years! Yet look at her. She is happy, she is perfect. All she awaits is the Lord's touch to bring about her final return in the eternal kingdom which will soon be established. *That* is why we Christians merrily do battle against all who oppose us, for we know that we will never have to fear death . . ."

That night, Balthasar laid uneasily in the softness of the rugs the family had prepared for him, and was slow to find sleep. This clear air, the happy lowing of the cattle, the endless brightness in the west . . . And now the family were singing again, as if out of their dreams, and joined with their voices came the softer croak of older woman, calling with emptied lungs for her resurrection from undecayed death. In the morning Balthasar felt refreshed for all his restlessness, and the beast the family led from their stables was barely recognizable as the surly creature which had borne him all the way from Persia. The camel's pelt was sleek as feathers. Its eyes were wise and brown and compassionate in the way of no beast of burden Balthasar had ever known. He almost expected the creature to speak to him, or join with this family when they broke into song as they waved him on his way.

Thus, laden with sweetmeats and baked breads, astride a smooth, uncomplaining mount on a newly softened saddle, Balthasar completed the last leg of his strange second journey to Jerusalem. The brightness before him had now grown so intense that he would have feared for his sight, had that light come from the sun. But he could see clearly and without pain—see far more clearly than he had ever seen, even in the happiest memories of his youth.

The encampment of a vast army lay outside the great city's gleaming jasper walls. Angels of other kinds to the creature he had first witnessed—some were six-winged and flickered like lampflames and were known as the Seraphim; others known as the Principalities wore crowns and bore scepters; stranger still were those called the

Ophanim, which were shaped like spinning wheels set with thousands of eyes—supervised the mustering and training with the voices of lions. The soldiers themselves, Balthasar saw as he rode down among them, were like no soldiers he had ever seen. There were bowed and elderly men. There were limping cripples. There were scampering children. There were women heavy with child. Yet even the seemingly lowliest and most helpless possessed a flaming sword which could cut as cleanly through rock as it did though air, and a breastplate seemingly composed of the same glowing substance which haloed the city itself. Seeing all these happy, savage faces, hearing their raucous song and laughter as they went about their everyday work, Balthasar knew that these Christian armies wouldn't cease advancing once they had driven their old overlords back to Rome. They would turn east, and Syria would fall. So would Egypt, and what was left of Babylon. Persia would come next, and Bactrai and India beyond. They would not cease until they had conquered the furthest edges of the world.

He entered the city through one of its twelve great, angel-guarded gates. The paving here was composed of some oddly slippery, brassy metal. Dismounting from his camel, Balthasar stooped to stroke its surface just as many other new arrivals were doing. Like all the rest, he cried out, for the streets of this new Jerusalem truly were paved with gold. The light was intense, and there were temples everywhere, as you might find market stalls, whorehouses or watchman's booths in any other town. He doubted if it rained here, but the golden guttering ran red with steaming gouts of blood. The fat lambs, cattle and fowls seemed not to fear death as they were led by cheering, chanting crowds toward altars of amethyst, turquoise and gold. Balthasar, who had drooped his camel's rein in awed surprise, looked back in sudden panic. But it was too late. The crowds were already bearing the happily moaning creature away.

Most of the people here in Jerusalem wore fine but anonymous white raiments, some splattered with blood, but Balthasar recognized the faces and languages of Rome, Greece and Egypt amid the local Aramaic. Yet even when the strange pilgrims of darker and paler races he encountered spoke to him, he discovered that he understood every word.

The story which he heard from all of them was essentially the same. Of how two figures had appeared atop the main tower of what had then been the largest temple in this city on the morning of the Sabbath four years earlier. Of how one of the figures had been dressed in glowing raiments, and the other in flames of dark. And how the glowing figure had cast himself as if to certain death before the gathering crowds, only for the sky to rent from horizon to horizon as many varieties of angels flew down to bear him up. Even the most conservative of the local priests could not deny the supernatural authority of what they had witnessed. When the same figure had arrived the following day at the closed and guarded city on a white horse in blazing raiments and demanded entry, Pilate the Roman prefect, who was subsequently crucified for his treachery, ordered that the gates be flung open before they were broken down.

Everything had changed in the four years since. Jerusalem was now easily the most powerful city in the eastern Mediterranean, and Jesus the Christ or Christos was the most powerful man. If, that was, he could conceivably be regarded as a man at all. Balthasar heard much debate on this subject amid the happy babble as work toward celebrating his glory went on. Man, or god, but surely not both? It was, he realized, the same question he had asked Melchior many times on that earlier journey. He'd never received what he felt was a satisfactory answer then, and the concept still puzzled him now.

The city walls were still being reconstructed in places from more huge blocks of jaspar which angels of some more muscular kind bore roped to glowing clouds. For all the imposing depth and breadth of the finished portions, Balthasar could not imagine that this city would ever be required to defend itself. Many of the buildings, for all their spectacular size and ornamentation, were also works in progress, raised from the support of what looked like ridiculously frail scaffoldings, or perhaps merely faith alone, as new gildings and bejewelings were encrusted over surfaces already bright with gems. The Great Temple, which rose from the site of the far lesser building from which Christ had thrown himself down, was the vastest and most impressive building of all. Great blocks of crystal so sheer you could almost walk into them formed turrets which seemed mostly composed of fire and air.

Controlled and supervised by angels, crowds flooded the wide marble steps beneath arches of sardine and jasper. Most of those who came to worship were whole and healthy, but some, Balthasar noticed, bore terrible injuries, or were leprous. Others, perhaps impatient for the promised resurrection, bore the dead with them on crude stretchers, variously rotted or well-preserved. As was the case throughout the entire city, there were none of the expected smells. Instead, that fragrance which he had first encountered at the site of that battlefield was much stronger still. It was part spiced wine and part the smoke of incense, and part something which your reeling mind told you wasn't any kind of scent at all. The interior of the temple was, of course, extraordinary, but by now Balthasar was drunk and dizzy on wonders. Like the rest of the crowd, all he yearned for was to witness the presence of Jesus himself.

There he was, beyond all the sacred gates and hallways, enthroned at very furthest of the vast final court of the Holy of Holies, which Balthasar had no doubt was the largest interior space in the entire known world. Angels swooped amid the ceilings, and huge, strange beasts, part-lion and part-bird, guarded a stairway of rainbows, but the eye was drawn to the small-seeming man seated at the pinnacle on a coral, emerald and lapis throne.

In one way, Jesus the Christos seemed frail and small, dwarfed by these spectacular surroundings. You noticed that he wore his hair longer than might seem entirely manly, and that his raiments were no whiter than those worn by many in the crowd. Noticed, as well, his plain leather sandals and how, for all that he was past thirty, he still possessed a young man's thin beard. But at the same time, you knew without thinking he was the source of all the radiance and power which flooded from this city. At first he sat simply gazing down with a kind of sorrowful compassion at the wild cries, prostrations and offerings. Then he stood up from his throne and walked down the steps into the masses, and absolute silence fell.

A sense of eternity moved amongst them, and everyone in that great space felt humbled, and judged. It really did seem that some of the dead were resurrected with the touch of a hand, a few quiet words, and that the leprous regained their limbs, but equally a few of those who had imagined they had come here in good spirits collapsed as if dead. Then, without the Christos having come close to Balthasar, a clamor of trumpets sounded, and his presence vanished, and the audience was at an end.

Balthasar had come all this way, lived all these years, in search, he now realized, of just one undeniable glimpse of the absolute. Just to know that there was something more than the everyday magic—the dirt and demons—of this world. Some blessed certainty. That was all he'd ever wanted. Or so he'd believed. And now, the presence of a supreme being had been demonstrated to him and ten thousand other witnesses in this city of crystal and gold. So why, he wondered as he left the Great Temple with the rest of the milling crowds, did he feel so let down?

There was no way of telling in Jerusalem whether it was day or night. What stars he could see were probably the auras of angels, or glittered amid the impossible architecture which rose all around. But he noticed that a patch of deeper dark had settled at a corner of the Great Temple's wide outer steps. People were making a wide berth around it, and as curiosity somehow drew him closer he caught a jarringly unpleasant smell. Swarms of flies lifted and encompassed the shape of what he now saw was a man. Here, he thought, was someone so hopelessly sin-ridden as to be beyond even Jesus' help.

Balthasar felt in his pockets and pouch for what scraps and food and money he had left and tossed them in the poor creature's direction.

Not that he imagined that such material things would be of much use in this city, but what else could he do? He was turning and pondering if he was likely to find a place to sleep when a preternaturally long arm extended to grab the edge of his robe.

He allowed himself to be pulled back. The man had large brown eyes. He might once have been beautiful, if you ignored the flies and the sores and the rank and terrible smell which emanated from him. He licked his scabbed lips and looked up at Balthasar.

"You know who I am?" he asked in a voice which was a faint whisper, yet echoed in Balthasar's mind.

Just as in the temple, Balthasar knew and understood. "You are the Christos, the Christ—the same Christ, and yet a different one—as the Christ I have just witnessed perform many wonders in this temple."

"There is only one Christ," the man muttered, glancing around at the crowds which were already gathering around them, then up at the various angels which had started to circle overhead. "I am always here."

"Of course, my Lord, you are all-powerful," the theologian in Balthasar answered. "You can thus be in many places at once. And in many forms."

"I can be everywhere, and everything," Jesus agreed with a slow smile, bearing what teeth he possessed within his blackened mouth. "What I cannot be is nowhere. Or nothing at all."

Balthasar nodded. The crowd around them was still growing. "Do you remember me, my Lord? I and two of my friends, we once journeyed . . ." He trailed off. Of course Jesus knew.

"You brought that deathly unguent as your gift. Perhaps instead of asking me why you did so, Balthasar, as you were thinking of doing, you should ask yourself."

"My Lord . . . I still do not know."

"Why should you?" Jesus shifted his crouch on the temple steps, hooking his thin arms around his even thinner legs as the flies danced around him in a humming cloud. "Any more than you should know why you chose to return. After all, you are only a man."

Balthasar was conscious of the murmurs of the watching crowd—
He is Here. It is as they say. Sometimes He comes in pitiable disguise—
and the knowledge that Jesus already understood far more about his
thoughts than he was capable of expressing. "I returned, my Lord,
simply because I am a man. And because you are a god."

"*The* God."

"Yes." Balthasar bowed. His voice trembled. "The God."

"So . . . Why do you doubt?"

"I do not—"

"Do not try to lie to me!" Suddenly, Jesus the Christ's voice was
like the rumble of rocks. The sky briefly darkened. The circling angels
moaned. "You doubt, Balthasar of Persia. Do not ask me why, but you
doubt. You look at Me in awe but you cannot see what I am, for if you
did, if all was revealed, your mind would be destroyed . . . Yet, even
then, I wonder if you would believe in that instant of knowing? Or
even after a million eternities lived amid glories which would make
this city seem squalid as the stables in which I was born. Would you
believe then?"

"I am sorry, Lord. I simply do not know." Balthasar blinked. His
eyes stung. Terrible though it was, he knew that everything Jesus had
said was true. Without this accursed doubt which even now would
not leave him, he could not be Balthasar at all.

"I came to this world to bring eternal peace and salvation," Jesus
was saying. "Not just for the Jews, but for all humanity. I was born
as you witnessed. My parents fled Herod's wrath, and I was raised
almost as any human child, waiting for the time of my ministry arrive.
And when that time came . . ." He brushed the re-gathering flies from
around his eyes. "When it came, I sought knowledge and solace in the
wilderness for forty days, just as any penitent would . . .

"I fasted. I prayed. I knew I could bring down the walls of this
world, rip the stars from the heavens—indeed, just as you have
imagined, Balthasar, in your wilder dreams. Or I could have entered
this city as pitiably as you see me now, or as some holy buffoon riding

on an ass. I could have done all these things and many others. If, that was, I wished to discover how little compassion the men and women who populate this earth possess. Or perhaps . . . I could . . ." The flies were buzzing thicker. The stench seemed to have grown. A different emotion, which might almost have been interpreted as fear, played across the crawling blackness of Jesus' face. "I could, perhaps, have gathered a small band of followers, performed small deeds, and declared myself in ways which the priests would have found easy to challenge. I could have allowed them to bring about my death. All of these things I could have done so that men such as you, Balthasar, might ultimately choose to be redeemed. I could have died in an agony of unheeded screams, Balthasar . . ." Jesus smiled a sad, bitter smile. "If that was how your gift to me was intended . . ."

"But you cannot die, my Lord."

"No . . ." Jesus picked at a fly from his lips and squashed it between ruined nails. "But I can feel pain. I could have passed through this world as lightly as the wind passes over a field of barley. And human life would have continued almost as you know it now—and worse. Armies would march. People would suffer and starve and doubt my existence whilst others fought over the meaning of my words. Cities of stone and glass even more extraordinary than this one you see around you would rise and fall. Clever men like you, Balthasar, would learn how to fly just as you see these angels flying. Yes, yes, it's true, although I know it sounds extraordinary. Men would learn how to pass even beyond the walls of this Earth, and how to poison the air, and kill the living waters of the oceans. And all for what, Balthasar? What would be accomplished, other than many more lifetimes of pointless striving?"

"I do not know, my Lord."

"Indeed." Jesus shook his head. Then he laughed. It was a terrible, empty sound, and the flies stirred from him in a howling cloud. "Neither did I, Balthasar. Neither did I. And I was hungry in that wilderness, and I was afraid. There were snakes and there were scorpions . . .

And there were other things . . ." Jesus shuddered. "Far worse. It was in those last days of my torment when it seemed that the very rocks taunted me to transform them into bread, that I finally understood the choice I had to make. I saw all the kingdoms of this Earth spread below me, and I knew that I could take dominion of them. All I had to do was to show myself, cast myself from a high point of a temple so that all the angels in the heavens might rescue me. After all . . ." Jesus shrugged. "I had to make my decision. And this . . ." He looked around along the marble steps at the awestruck crowd, then around at the incredible spires and domes, then up at the heavenly skies. ". . . is the world I have made."

Even as Jesus the Christ spoke these last words, Balthasar and the crowd around him could see that he was fading. With him departed the droning flies, and the pestilential stink was replaced by the heady, sacred scents of the temple. He would be somewhere else, or had been in many other places already. Appearing as a glowing vision on some hillside, or leading with a tongue of swords at the front of one of his many armies. All that was left of the Christ now was what Balthasar had once feared he might be—just a trick of the light, a baseless hope turned from nothing more than shadow, and a last few droning flies.

Balthasar pushed his way down the steps and out of the crowd. He walked the golden streets of Jerusalem alone. He'd been thinking before of sleep, but now he knew that he would never find sleep, or any other kind of rest, within this city. It was all too much. It was too glorious. And he was still just a man. Perhaps he would just crumble to dust when all the rest of the believing, undoubting multitudes were resurrected. Sacrilegious though the thought was, it felt welcoming. He passed through one of the city's twelve great gates almost without realizing, and found his way through the encamped battalions as they joined with choirs of angels in celebration of their inevitable victory. Looking back at the city as the land finally darkened and rose, he wondered once again why an all-powerful God should feel the need to protect it with such large and elaborate defenses. Still questions,

Balthasar . . . Pointless doubts and questions . . . Walking on and away from the blazing light, he realized that what he needed was solitude, silence, clarity.

He was almost sure that it was night now, for his tired eyes caught something resembling the glint of stars in a blessedly black firmament. The ground was rough and dry and dusty. He began to stumble. He grew dizzy. He fell, and lost track of time until light came over him, and he winced and cried out and covered his face in awe, only to discover that it was merely the harsh blaze of the sun. This place truly was a wasteland, and in its way it was terrible. But it was beautiful as well, in the deathless heat-shimmer of its emptiness.

Balthasar walked on through places of stones and dry bones. Then, as evening came, he sought shelter from the sudden cold in a decayed hole at the edge of the mountains. Others had been in this cave before him. There was a sour stench, and there were carvings on the rocks. Squatting on the dark hard ground inside after willing a few sticks to make a fire, Balthasar traced these marks with his fingers. A babble of symbols in different alphabets honoring different gods, all of which he now knew almost for certain to be misguided. Still, he found these leavings of other seekers after truth oddly comforting.

Some of the most recent markings, he noticed, were written by one hand, and in Aramaic. Studying these scratches more closely in the firelight, he saw that they mimicked the words of the old prophecies which Melchior had once shown him, and he looked around at this squalid place in which he had sought shelter with a different gaze. Somehow, and for all that he had witnessed, it seemed beyond incredible that this decayed hole was the very place in which Jesus Christ had sought shelter in his time in the wilderness. Yet how could he doubt it, after all that he had heard and seen? The writing was loose and ill-composed—you could sense the writer's anguish—and terminated in a crude series of crosses.

The fire died. Balthasar sat alone in the dark, waiting for the return of the sun, and perhaps for an end to his own torment. He remembered again that first journey he had taken to this land with his two friends, and the subsequent slaughter of the innocents. Jesus had survived to fulfil the prophecies scrawled on these walls, yes. But what of all the others? Was *that* what his gift of myrrh had foretold, the pointless death of hundreds of children? And why—the question came back to him, although left unasked in Jesus' presence—had an all-powerful God permitted such a thing to happen? Why had pain and suffering been allowed into this world at all?

In the darkness, Balthasar shook his head. *Always the same with you*, he heard the Gaspar's voice saying. *You have too many doubts, too many questions.* Yet everything he had seen in New Jerusalem had left him unsatisfied.

A slow dawn was coming, rising from the east in gaunt, hot shadow. A cur dog howled. The wind hissed. Looking out across this landscape, Balthasar thought of Jesus squatting in this same cave, and wondered about his last days of torment, and about how he must have felt, and what he had seen. Then, as the heat rose and the sky whitened, Balthasar took a stick of charcoal from the remnants of his fire and began to make his own marks across the rough stone. It had been a long time since he had engaged in the practice of serious magic, but the shapes to make the necessary spell of summoning came to him with astonishing ease.

THE BOWMEN

Arthur Machen

ARTHUR MACHEN (1863–1947) was born Arthur Llewellyn Jones
in Wales. He worked as a clerk, teacher, actor and journalist
while writing stories of horror and fantasy rooted in the myths
of his homeland. H.P. Lovecraft named Machen as one of the
four "modern masters" of supernatural horror fiction (alongside
Algernon Blackwood, Lord Dunsany and M.R. James).

Probably best known for his classic 1894 novella "The Great
God Pan" (which Stephen King described as "Maybe the best
[horror story] in the English language") and the short story "The
White People," his novels include *The Innermost Light*, *The Shining
Pyramid*, *The Three Imposters* and *The Hill of Dreams*. His best
short stories are collected in *Tales of Horror and the Supernatural*.

The first major conflict between British and German forces during
the First World War occurred near the French village of Mons in
August 1914. The encounter ended with a bloody and humiliating
retreat by British troops, and so the following month Machen wrote an
unashamedly patriotic piece of fiction for the London newspaper the
Evening News, describing how the ghostly intervention of St. George
and his Agincourt archers at the Battle of Mons helped the British.

However, not long after the story first appeared, a significant
number of anecdotes started to emerge from people who claimed
to have really witnessed the ghostly "Angels of Mons." Despite
Machen's continued assertion that the story had no foundation in
fact of any kind, the tale quickly took on the form of an early "urban
legend" that has continued into the present day.

"It was at about this period that variants of my tale began to be
told as authentic histories," recalled Machen. "At first, these tales
betrayed their relation to their original . . . Other versions of the
story appeared in which a cloud interposed between the attacking
Germans and the defending British. In some examples the cloud

served to conceal our men from the advancing enemy; in others, it disclosed shining shapes which frightened the horses of the pursuing German cavalry. St. George, it will he noted, has disappeared—he persisted some time longer in certain Roman Catholic variants—and there are no more bowmen, no more arrows. But so far angels are not mentioned; yet they are ready to appear, and I think that I have detected the machine which brought them into the story.

"I conjecture that the word 'shining' is the link between my tale and the derivative from it," continued Machen. "In the popular view shining and benevolent supernatural beings are angels and nothing else, and must be angels, and so, I believe, the Bowmen of my story have become 'the Angels of Mons.' In this shape they have been received with respect and credence everywhere, or almost everywhere."

IT WAS DURING the Retreat of the Eighty Thousand, and the authority of the Censorship is sufficient excuse for not being more explicit. But it was on the most awful day of that awful time, on the day when ruin and disaster came so near that their shadow fell over London far away; and, without any certain news, the hearts of men failed within them and grew faint; as if the agony of the army in the battlefield had entered into their souls.

On this dreadful day, then, when three hundred thousand men in arms with all their artillery swelled like a flood against the little English company, there was one point above all other points in our battle line that was for a time in awful danger, not merely of defeat, but of utter annihilation. With the permission of the Censorship and of the military expert, this corner may, perhaps, be described as a salient, and if this angle were crushed and broken, then the English force as a whole would be shattered, the Allied left would be turned, and Sedan would inevitably follow.

All the morning the German guns had thundered and shrieked against this corner, and against the thousand or so of men who held it. The men joked at the shells, and found funny names for them, and had bets about them, and greeted them with scraps of music-hall songs. But the shells came on and burst, and tore good Englishmen limb from limb, and tore brother from brother, and as the heat of the day increased so did the fury of that terrific cannonade. There was no help, it seemed. The English artillery was good, but there was not nearly enough of it; it was being steadily battered into scrap iron.

There comes a moment in a storm at sea when people say to one another, "It is at its worst; it can blow no harder," and then there is a blast ten times more fierce than any before it. So it was in these British trenches.

There were no stouter hearts in the whole world than the hearts of these men; but even they were appalled as this seven-times-heated hell of the German cannonade fell upon them and overwhelmed them and destroyed them. And at this very moment they saw from their trenches that a tremendous host was moving against their lines. Five hundred of the thousand remained, and as far as they could see the German infantry was pressing on against them, column upon column, a grey world of men, ten thousand of them, as it appeared afterwards.

There was no hope at all. They shook hands, some of them. One man improvised a new version of the battle-song, "Good-bye, good-bye to Tipperary," ending with "And we shan't get there." And they all went on firing steadily. The officers pointed out that such an opportunity for high-class, fancy shooting might never occur again; the Germans dropped line after line; the Tipperary humorist asked, "What price Sidney Street?" And the few machine guns did their best. But everybody knew it was of no use. The dead grey bodies lay in companies and battalions, as others came on and on and on, and they swarmed and stirred and advanced from beyond and beyond.

"World without end. Amen," said one of the British soldiers with some irrelevance as he took aim and fired. And then he remembered—he says he cannot think why or wherefore—a queer vegetarian restaurant in London where he had once or twice eaten eccentric dishes of cutlets made of lentils and nuts that pretended to be steak. On all the plates in this restaurant there was printed a figure of St. George in blue, with the motto, *Adsit Anglis Sanctus Geogius*—May St. George be a present help to the English. This soldier happened to know Latin and other useless things, and now, as he fired at his man in the grey advancing mass— three hundred yards away—he uttered the pious vegetarian motto. He went on firing to the end, and at last Bill on his right had to clout him cheerfully over the head to make him stop, pointing out as he did so that the King's ammunition cost money and was not lightly to be wasted in drilling funny patterns into dead Germans.

For as the Latin scholar uttered his invocation he felt something between a shudder and an electric shock pass through his body. The roar of the battle died down in his ears to a gentle murmur; instead of it, he says, he heard a great voice and a shout louder than a thunder-peal crying, "Array, array, array!"

His heart grew hot as a burning coal, it grew cold as ice within him, as it seemed to him that a tumult of voices answered to his summons. He heard, or seemed to hear, thousands shouting: "St. George! St. George!"

"Ha! messire; ha! sweet Saint, grant us good deliverance!"

"St. George for merry England!"

"Harow! Harow! Monseigneur St. George, succour us."

"Ha! St. George! Ha! St. George! a long bow and a strong bow."

"Heaven's Knight, aid us!"

And as the soldier heard these voices he saw before him, beyond the trench, a long line of shapes, with a shining about them. They were like men who drew the bow, and with another shout their cloud of arrows flew singing and tingling through the air towards the German hosts.

The other men in the trench were firing all the while. They had no hope; but they aimed just as if they had been shooting at Bisley.

Suddenly one of them lifted up his voice in the plainest English.

"Gawd help us!" he bellowed to the man next to him, "but we're blooming marvels! Look at those grey . . . gentlemen, look at them! D'ye see them? They're not going down in dozens, nor in 'undreds; it's thousands, it is. Look! look! there's a regiment gone while I'm talking to ye."

"Shut it!" the other soldier bellowed, taking aim, "what are ye gassing about!"

But he gulped with astonishment even as he spoke, for, indeed, the grey men were falling by the thousands. The English could hear the guttural scream of the German officers, the crackle of their revolvers as they shot the reluctant; and still line after line crashed to the earth.

All the while the Latin-bred soldier heard the cry:

"Harow! Harow! Monseigneur, dear saint, quick to our aid! St. George help us!"

"High Chevalier, defend us!"

The singing arrows fled so swift and thick that they darkened the air; the heathen horde melted from before them.

"More machine guns!" Bill yelled to Tom.

"Don't hear them," Tom yelled back. "But, thank God, anyway; they've got it in the neck."

In fact, there were ten thousand dead German soldiers left before that salient of the English army, and consequently there was no Sedan. In Germany, a country ruled by scientific principles, the Great General Staff decided that the contemptible English must have employed shells containing an unknown gas of a poisonous nature, as no wounds were discernible on the bodies of the dead German soldiers. But the man who knew what nuts tasted like when they called themselves steak knew also that St. George had brought his Agincourt Bowmen to help the English.

OKAY, MARY

Hugh B. Cave

HUGH B. CAVE (1910–2004) was born in Chester, England, and emigrated with his family to America when he was five. From the late 1920s onward his stories began appearing in such legendary pulp magazines as *Weird Tales*, *Strange Tales*, *Ghost Stories*, *Black Book Detective Magazine*, *Spicy Mystery Stories* and the "weird menace" pulps, *Horror Stories* and *Terror Tales*.

After leaving the horror field in the early 1940s for almost three decades, a volume of the author's best horror tales, *Murgunstrumm and Others*, was published by Karl Edward Wagner in 1977. Cave subsequently returned to the genre with new stories and a string of modern horror novels: *Legion of the Dead*, *The Nebulon Horror*, *The Evil*, *Shades of Evil*, *Disciples of Dread*, *The Lower Deep*, *Lucifer's Eye*, *Isle of the Whisperers*, *The Dawning*, *The Evil Returns* and *The Restless Dead*. His short stories were also collected in a number of volumes, including *The Corpse Maker*, *Death Stalks the Night*, *The Dagger of Tsiang*, *Long Live the Dead: Tales from Black Mask*, *Come Into My Parlor*, *The Door Below* and *Bottled in Blonde*. Milt Thomas' biography, *Cave of a Thousand Tales: The Life & Times of Hugh B. Cave*, was published by Arkham House a week after the author's death.

During his lifetime, Cave received Life Achievement awards from The Horror Writers Association in 1991, The International Horror Guild in 1998 and The World Fantasy Convention in 1999. He was also presented with the Special Convention Award at the 1997 World Fantasy gathering in London, where he was a Special Guest of Honour.

The following story comes from that period when the author had left the pulps and was working for more mainstream and lucrative magazine markets: "In the old days," Cave later recalled, "you could try, say, a *Saturday Evening Post* reject on *Country Gent*, *American*, *Collier's*, *Liberty* and on down the line to, say, *Toronto Star*, where you would still get around $400 for it. But all those slick-paper markets are gone now.

"Those years with the 'slicks' meant writing to editorial formula much of the time. Even the mystery novelettes I did for *Good Housekeeping*—for very fancy money—had to be tailor-made to formula and usually revised at least once to fit the editor's idea of the formula."

HAD YOU ASKED Bill Reavey on Monday morning what he thought of Alaska, he would have grinned and said, "Marvelous!" Quite likely he would have told you that flying freight from rail's end to a wilderness mining camp was the best deal he'd had since the war.

But had you put the same question Monday afternoon, he would have looked at you blankly and said nothing. The mail had arrived and with it a letter from his folks in Indiana. In the letter was a clipping.

Mr. and Mrs. Edgar L. Furbish, the clipping said, *announced yesterday the marriage of their only daughter, Mary, to Mr. Robert Trainer, vice-president of the First Commercial Bank.*

You see, Bill, what happens when a guy stays away too long?

Reavey returned the scrap of newspaper to his pocket just as Matt Murdock, his boss, came into the operations office.

"Your plane ready, Bill?" Murdock asked.

"All ready. We've half an hour yet."

Murdock shook his head. "Not if you're smart. The weather's turning rotten."

Reavey shrugged as he stepped outside. He had been flying supplies to the mine for weeks, and the weather over that wild mass of mountains was almost always bad.

So she married that fellow from the bank, he thought as he trudged on leaden legs across the windswept field. She wouldn't wait . . .

His plane was being warmed up and he approached it, around piles of crated goods and fuel drums, from the rear. His scowl lengthened. One of the boys had given the ship's name a coat of fresh red paint. Quickly he looked away, but in that bleak air the crimson letters danced as though suspended on strings before his face: M-A-R-Y.

Mr. and Mrs. Edgar L. Furbish announced yesterday the marriage of their only daughter, Mary, to . . .

He scanned the sky anxiously as the DC-3 climbed from the barren airstrip. Even in good weather some of the towering peaks along his route were all too ready to trap an unwary pilot. Today not even the glittering crown of McKinley, better than twenty thousand feet high, could be seen through the thickening soup. Head winds buffeted the ship savagely.

Ed Fraser, his co-pilot, glanced at him and grinned crookedly. "Take it easy, boy. Mary never let us down yet."

Bill had no answering smile. He wondered what Ed and the other two would say if they knew about the newspaper clipping in his pocket. Because he knew about the clipping, his vigilance was razor sharp. The plane that he had named for Mary Furbish might not be so lucky now. It, too, might break the faith.

Did you think of that, Mary, when you decided not to wait? Did you give a thought to what it might mean to MacAndrews, Dexter and Fraser, who worship your name on a beat-up old DC-3 and think of you as their guardian angel? That's right, Mary—their guardian angel! Those boys were in the war, too. They believe in that kind of thing . . .

He could not climb high enough to clear the worst of the hidden peaks ahead—not with the plane groaning under such a load. That made it tough.

Joe Dexter came forward to report on the cargo—a nice kid, young but ambitious. "Everything okay," he announced with his small-boy grin. "Bring on your weather!"

"No jitters?" Bill asked.

"No, sir!"

"The front office has priority on jitters," Ed Fraser chuckled. "We've none to spare for you."

"Look, skipper," Dexter said. "Do we stay over at the mine tonight? The reason I ask—MacAndrews and I have a date with two of those nurses we flew in last week for the hospital."

"You'll be able to keep it."

"Oh, boy! Now, if only you'd join us, skipper—that cute little blonde thinks you're really special. But I suppose—" Joe let it drop, knowing that Reavey never went out on dates. The sweetest girl in the world was waiting for the skipper back in Indiana.

At that moment Reavey saw what he'd been looking for and dreading, and the perspiration on his face turned cold. Dead ahead, a torrent of wind-driven snow roared through the haze, swirling, stabbing, weaving like the head of a great white serpent.

On the whole of the run the enemy wind could not have picked a better ambush. The plane was rumbling through a tortuous defile between mountains. Reavey strained to see the ragged peak at its end in time to lift the laden ship over it. There was scant room for maneuvering in that narrow pass. Now the rushing mass of snow was on them, reducing visibility to zero.

Reavey slid the ship on her side, weaving away from the nearer mountain wall. She could be plucked in flight like a butterfly by that howling wind, tunneled in upon them by the gap toward which they struggled. He put her down, saw the tops of the scrub pines below just in time, and flattened out again—so close to the valley floor that the treetops must have been seared.

It was like dodging Jap fighter planes on the trip across the Hump in CBI, he thought wryly. A veteran Hump pilot, he used every maneuver in the book. But that screaming wind, straight from the Arctic icebox, was still engaging him in a dogfight when the valley ended. With a towering wall of rock and ice dead ahead, a ghostly road block in the blizzard, there was but one way to go.

"Angel, baby, stay with us!" Reavey whispered, forgetting for a moment they no longer had a guardian angel.

He hauled the plane's nose up and she thundered skyward. Like a river in full flood the wind crashed against her belly. For one terrible instant she faltered, seemed to lose her nerve, hung fluttering in space. Reavey's face turned dead white.

Beside him Ed Fraser said softly, "Come on, Mary. Do it, baby."

The battered plane stopped shaking. Like a fly buzzing up out of a bottle, she continued her climb.

Ed Fraser let out a stored lung full of breath. "Another two feet," he gasped, "and I could have written my name on that ice wall!"

Reavey was silent. Even when MacAndrews and Joe Dexter came forward to thump his shoulders, he had nothing to say. He knew what the boys were thinking, though. He guessed what they would say.

He was right. When the plane landed at the mine an hour later, they said it: Their adopted angel, the skipper's girlfriend, had brought them through again.

Reavey listened with a scowl on his face. Then, because he had always leveled with these boys, he took the clipping from his pocket and said, "Read this," and walked to the supply shack and found a can of paint and a brush, then sat on the stoop, waiting for the boys to depart. While waiting, he struggled to put his muddled thoughts in order.

Maybe it was his pride that was hurt most. He and Mary Furbish had never seen eye-to-eye on some things, such as the need for flying a beat-up plane in Alaska.

"Skipper." Joe Dexter was standing awkwardly before him. "The boys and I know how you feel and we're sorry as hell. But we think we ought to tell you something. I was elected to come over and put you straight."

Reavey waited, frowning.

"A lot of girls are named Mary, skipper," Joe said. "MacAndrews' mother is. My sister, too." Clumsily Joe stuffed his hands into his pocket and shrugged his shoulders. "Ed Fraser calls his wife Mike, but *her* real name's Mary and their little girl is named after her. We never pushed the point before, skipper—we didn't want to take anything away from you—but we always kind of felt we had more than one guardian angel. The old bus belonged to all of us."

As the skipper stared at him, wordless, Dexter turned to scowl at the paint can. "You—you see what I mean, skipper?"

Reavey stood up. Strangely, he was smiling. Holding the paint can at arm's length, he solemnly poured its contents onto the frozen earth and said, "God love you, Joe—the bunch of you." Then he squared his shoulders. "That nurse, Joe. The little blonde. What's her name?"

"Why don't you ask her?"

"All right," Reavey said. "I will."

PLAGUE ANGEL

Yvonne Navarro

YVONNE NAVARRO lives in southern Arizona with her husband, author Weston Ochse. By day she works on historic Fort Huachuca, and by night she chops her time into little pieces, dividing it among writing, art, college, three rescue Great Danes, two attention-greedy parakeets and family (not necessarily in that order).

She's written seven solo novels about topics ranging from vampires (*AfterAge*) to the end of the world (*Final Impact* and *Red Shadows*). She's also the author of a number of movie tie-ins, including the novelizations of *Ultraviolet*, *Elektra*, *Hellboy* and seven novels—five of them originals—in the *Buffy the Vampire Slayer* universe.

Her work has won the HWA's Bram Stoker Award plus a number of other writing awards. Having completed her latest novel, *Highborn*, she's (always) hammering on the next one in the series, *Concrete Savior*, while waiting to see what the Universe decides to throw at her.

"I wasn't really sure where 'Plague Angel' was going when I started it," Navarro admits, "but I knew that I wanted to set a story in Warwick Castle and put my recent visit there to good use.

"As so many stories do, the tale went in its own direction . . . which turned out to be far beyond the paltry limitations of castle walls built by mere human hands."

THEY KNEW HE WASN'T HUMAN, and they knew they couldn't kill him, that he gained strength more and more as time passed and his skills were noticed and praised, if not truly appreciated. So they drove him down, deeper and deeper, below the rooms in which he had practiced his craft. With swords and hooks and claws and all the grand instruments of torture that he had wielded so well, his own tools, they beat on him and hurt him and pushed him deeper, until finally he could do nothing but fold protectively around his own bleeding body as they walled him solidly within the most unreachable, lightless bowels of the building.

They thought he slept, that he knew nothing. But he knew everything. He knew when the men killed each other, smiled as the Black Death swept through Europe and virtually all of the known world, mourned when the heavy hand of human judgment turned from bloodthirsty to the scales, however tilted, of justice, and wept when the plague ran its course and trickled away to near non-existence.

They had locked him away because they thought he was a monster, an expert at killing and maiming. Only the denizens of the dungeon knew of his existence, that he had gleefully stepped in when fellow torturers, beset by guilt and the fear that God would rain judgment down upon their soggy, weak little souls, faltered in their duties. They thought they knew what he could do, and that they now controlled it, controlled him, and that deprived of food, water and light, he would eventually die. Some believed that if no one spoke of him, ever, he would simply cease to exist.

They had no idea.

It was a fun job, well-paying and year-round, and if it wasn't exactly what Jenelle had in mind two years ago when she'd been handed her college degree in fine arts, that was fine. If nothing else, it let her be near a chunk of history and medieval art while feeding the child within her who had never tired of Halloween.

She'd been pretty desperate when she'd auditioned at Warwick Castle; finding out she could actually act had been a bonus, and then a month later she'd met the man who would later become her fiancé. She'd been there ever since, and now she spent five days a week costumed and made up as a creepy, ill-fated court jester who was on the verge of dying from bubonic plague. She startled the unsuspecting tourists on their way into the dungeon tour, giving her hellish introduction with wheedling little words and hideous giggles as she went through each group, one by one, finding something about each person to single them out, to make them feel special. She woke up happy every morning, looked forward to her future, and went to work with a smile on her face. Life was fantastic.

Until she saw the shadow.

"Look at that," Jenelle said, pointing to the back wall. "I saw it this morning. It's amazing that I didn't catch it before."

They were sitting in a newly opened chamber off one of the main torture rooms. This one had been discovered a couple of months ago when a maintenance worker went to patch a crack in the mortar and found a number of the stones loose; it turned out to be a false wall, although the area beyond it was only six feet deep and empty. There was nothing in it now, but Jenelle was sure that some fun and gruesome exhibit would be erected soon enough.

Robbie peered past her pointing finger. "I don't see anything." Her fiancé—even though they were only two weeks away from their wedding, it still felt amazing to call him that—looked forlornly back at the slightly smashed sandwich on his lap. This morning it had been peanut butter and slices of banana, something he'd seen on television and decided to try because it had been Elvis Presley's favorite. After a morning in his bag, now it looked vaguely like wet wallpaper paste.

"Here," she said. She pulled the unwrapped plastic package off his knee and replaced it with her lunch bag. "Apple, cheese, crackers, a bag of crisps. If you're sweet to me, I'll buy you a chocolate bar."

Robbie squinted at her. "You'd eat this mess?"

"Only for you." To prove it, she unwrapped an edge and bit into the gooey sandwich. It was actually pretty good. "Now back to that shadow on the wall."

"I don't see it," he said again. "It's just a wall."

Jenelle levered herself to her feet, glad to be up and off the drafty stone floor. No matter how heavy the blanket they used, it never seemed to do any good. "Look here." She drew the tip of her finger in a pattern from top to bottom on the left. "This is a profile of sorts. "And here—" She did it again, this time in a sort of jagged pattern on the right side. The temporary low-light bulb strung overhead gave her arm its own sweeping blackness. "This looks like a wing."

He studied the wall, but she could tell by his face that it wasn't there for him. "It must be your artistic eye," he said. "It's like cloud-watching. You always spot the coolest things and I just see . . . clouds."

Jenelle didn't say anything else as Robbie changed the subject, talking about the people in the marketing office and some big project he had coming up. Normally she would have been interested in everything he said, but today she just couldn't focus on his words. Her gaze kept going back to that shadow, the one he couldn't see but which seemed so clear to her that it looked ready to tear itself from the stones. He was right, of course—she'd studied painting in all mediums, drawing, sculpting, and all of that had taught her to look for the details, the story behind the obvious. And on that back wall, to her, was definitely something worth more study.

One of the barriers has been broken down, and he can sense the presence of humans. They scurry back and forth like insects, carving and moving and cleaning, talking to each other in excited voices about their discovery and what it might mean. He can hear the voices clearly, but he understands so much more than that—their wants, their fears, their most inner secrets. Their enthusiasm over the ruptured wall, the potential for greed—these humans, they never change.

The work progresses and they ask each other if this will ultimately lead to a passageway to a secret chamber, a room in which someone in the castle's dark and bloody history hid treasures beyond imagining. Will what they eventually expose be worth all their effort, or will it be for nothing more than ancient, empty air?

But air is never empty.

Jenelle could swear that the shadow was getting darker, more . . . intense. She'd checked it out every day since the room had been opened to employees and she and Robbie had lunched in it that first time. He hadn't wanted to come back, and she couldn't blame him. She wasn't supposed to eat in the public cafeteria in costume and the employee break room was all the way across the grounds; at least in the courtroom, they could take their breaks between tours and sit on the benches instead of the floor. Today he'd been too busy to meet her for the midday meal, so she stood in the tiny alcove by herself, chewing on her apple and thinking that the area on the wall no longer seemed so much a shadow as an actual image.

And yes. She was certain that was the edge of a wing on the right side.

"So what exactly were you?" she murmured. "A painting? Or should I say, what *are* you?" Jenelle started to trace the edge on the left, where it almost looked like the contour of a face, then paused. Was the stone warm to the touch? No . . . yes. She was sure of it. Even so, she glanced over her shoulder self-consciously then leaned forward and pressed her face against the wall. It was always cold in the dungeon, but today more so than usual because of a bitter, early fall rainstorm; because her skin was still chilled from being outside, the deep warm surface of the rock shocked her so much that she jerked backwards, lost her footing and fell.

• • • • •

In his memories, the darkness is dissected by the flicker of flames from the torches and the glowing braziers. The single, tiny fireplace recessed into the far wall serves as nothing more than a space for him to heat a few more implements—it gives no warmth to the room or to his many, many victims, and he certainly shares none of his own eternal heat. Comfort comes to him not from the fire's non-existent cheer but from the screams of those who writhe beneath the clamps and the claw and the hook, from the sweet, heavy smell of decay and the sticky thickness of blood on the tongue.

He can't wait to bathe in that scent, and so many others, yet again.

"It'll be fine," Jenelle said. "It'll just look like part of the make-up."

Robbie squinted at the knot on her forehead. It was the size of a robin's egg, purple and bluish-grey, with a nasty split in the middle that had still been weeping blood ten minutes after she came to on the dirty, cold floor of the dungeon. Her head had throbbed for the rest of the afternoon and she'd felt feverish with the pain, wincing every time the edge of her purple jester's hat scraped the upper part of the lump. To really top off her afternoon, when she'd opened her eyes after her tumble, she'd had dirt in her mouth and a damned rat—a *rat*, for God's sake—had been mere inches from her face. She'd reported it to maintenance, but even so, every time she thought of that creature, she started to itch and get sick to her stomach.

"I think you ought to see a doctor," he said. "It looks infected."

Jenelle pushed his hand away and leaned closer to the mirror, checking out the freshly washed wound. "Don't be silly. It only happened a couple of hours ago and we've disinfected it. It'll be gone by the day after tomorrow."

When she backed away from the sink, Robbie followed her out of the bathroom. "Maybe I should stay the night. They say people with head injuries should be monitored for twenty-four hours."

"No way. We agreed, remember? Old-fashioned for the final week before the wedding. No sleeping in the same bed. No exceptions."

"But your head—"

"I wasn't knocked out," she lied. "Time for you to head home."

He hesitated and Jenelle saw on his face that he really was concerned about her rather than just horny. "All right. But you call me if you don't feel well, or if you get a headache."

"Of course." To mollify him, she stepped close and put her arms around him. After a moment, he returned her hug, but gingerly. "I'm fine," she repeated. To prove it, she lifted her face and pressed her lips against his, slipping the tip of her tongue into his mouth when he still held back. She felt him respond and let him pull her closer, ignoring the sting from the sore place on her forehead when it bumped lightly against his eyebrow. As the kiss intensified, she finally had to push him away. "Huh-uh," she said. Then, "Oh, for crying out loud. I've gotten blood on you. Wait a sec."

Robbie swiped at the droplets, effectively smearing red down the side of his eye socket as he tried to rub it away. "You're making it worse," Jenelle said as she came back with a tissue.

He took it from her and rubbed at his face. "Did I get it all?"

She shook her head. "You need a mirror."

"Nah. I need to get out of here before I jump you." He grinned, spit on the tissue and daubed again. "Now?"

"You've pushed it into the corner of your eye, silly."

He wadded up the dirty tissue and shoved it in his pocket. "I'm going home and take a cold shower, then go over my presentation. Big meeting tomorrow with some investors from America." He touched her briefly on the cheek, then he was out the door.

Jenelle's smile faded as she turned the lock. She'd never lied to Robbie about anything, but according to her watch, she'd definitely lost consciousness in the dungeon for almost a quarter of an hour. Why now?

"Because I don't want to screw everything up," she said out loud. She went to the spare bedroom—the one that would be turned into

Robbie's office when he moved in—and pulled open the closet door, then just stood there and gazed at her wedding dress for a couple of minutes. That was the crux of it, all right. The wedding was Saturday, only three days away; and tomorrow was her last day of work until she and Robbie returned from their honeymoon. There were treasured friends and relatives from both sides coming in from all over the world—one guy, someone she'd never met, had been in the military with Robbie and was flying in from China. Her parents were coming from Canada, Robbie's birth father from Australia, on and on. How could she dare put even a wrinkle in all these plans just because of a stupid, crazy fall in the dungeon?

Jenelle closed the door and went back into the bathroom, digging in the medicine cabinet until she found some aspirin and a bottle of Pepto-Bismol. She swallowed three of the chalky tablets, followed it with a couple of swigs of the pink liquid, then went to sit in the living room. She'd decorated it so carefully, in muted blue and white—the colors of the Wedgwood china that her mother so loved. Along with the rest of her flat, it was just the way she wanted it, the perfect little place for her and her husband to start their lives together.

She turned off the lights when they began to hurt her eyes.

Soon.

The centuries of darkness and isolation had weakened him further and forced his essence to withdraw, first into his thoughts, then into his own battered form, and finally into the very walls of the castle itself. The stone welcomed him, became his cold and cruel confidant. He felt its coarse surface, the uneven bite of its ragged edges; he welcomed the sensation and caressed the stones like a deathless lover, finding not a single opening through which escape might be accomplished. Even the rats, those chittering, filthy purveyors of his gifts, could not reach him.

But finally, a fracture in the wall that separated his chamber from the castle proper. A loose stone that invited investigation, the tearing down of a barrier that no one, nearly a thousand years later, knew should never be breached.

Then came the woman. So young, so beautiful, so artistic and curious. She could see the shroud, just that, of what he had once been, and she had been drawn to it, drawn to him.

Inexorably pulled by his heat as it revitalized, the same hellfire that she couldn't resist touching. She'd had to get close to it, more than just fingertips. Human flesh against his stone façade, in exactly the way he needed. And he had thanked her, in his own very special way.

The last tour of the day turned out to be a group of kids on a history field trip. They were from some private and moneyed school in London, and Jenelle could tell by their expensive uniforms, iPods and attitude that they were going to be noisy and hard to control, and that their two chaperones were concerned only that they didn't tick any of them off so badly they'd complain to Mummy and Daddy. There were enough diamond earrings, glittering rings and pricey watches that the parents were probably lawyers, doctors and stockbrokers with the same kind of global connections as the people Robbie was even now sitting down with at his meeting.

One more day of this, she told herself. Only a matter of hours. She gave them her introductory spiel and threw in plenty of macabre giggling and as many personalized quips as she could think of, but she wasn't at the top of her game. She felt like hell, but this went way beyond the lousy headache that, were it a living thing, was surely doing nothing but sneering at the puny aspirins she kept taking. At least she'd been right about the lump looking like part of the makeup. Every now and then the tip of it, where she'd actually split the skin, would leak a drop of thin, reddish liquid. That was disgusting, but not a huge problem here—she was supposed to look like she had the plague—but she was going to have to bandage it tightly beneath her headdress and veil on Saturday. Surely by then she'd feel better and this damned headache would dissipate.

"Step this way, my pretties," she wheedled. Her own voice felt like a spike digging through the pain in her skull. "Mind your heads, now. We wouldn't want them to be damaged before the torturers have their chance!" Some of them grinned nervously at her high-pitched laugh while the rest barely noticed her. All this effort to speak around an odd heaviness in her chest, and for what? To stand in an ancient corridor that was chilling her to her very bones as she tried to entertain these unappreciative teenagers.

Jenelle grimaced, then turned that into a twisted smile that ended in a cough, another one she couldn't cover because it would be out of role for her character. Damn it—something down here was irritating her throat, making her cough every few seconds. Mortar dust, probably, kicked up by the never-ending work on the castle's interior walls. Another fifteen minutes and she'd be done with this group; after that, she could change out of this scratchy costume and dump the painful jester's hat, and forget about it all for a little over two weeks. Her wedding was the day after tomorrow, her Mum and Dad would arrive tomorrow afternoon to help her get ready, and her life—her entire world—was on the verge of changing.

She couldn't wait.

In the small dungeon room, in the early morning hours, he was almost complete again. Almost strong enough to pull free of the stone bonds that had held him for so very, very long.

The dark energy that he needed to reshape himself had always existed, but his imprisonment in this man-made structure had severed his ties to it and left him unable to nourish and love it. Like an infant wrenched from its mother and abandoned, after a time it had finally perished.

But like him, it would never truly die. It gained strength from him, and he from it.

And together again, they would flourish.

• • • • •

"Can I help you in there, dear?"

Jenelle clutched at the edge of the sink for an overlong moment before she finally found her voice. "No, Mum—I'm fine. Just a case of nerves, that's all."

"How about a cup of tea, then? It will help calm you."

"Sure," she said automatically. "That would be nice." Her mother had barely moved away from the other side of the door before Jenelle coughed again. When she looked down at her palm, there were tiny droplets of blood in it. "What the hell," she said. A sinus infection? More like pneumonia—she felt like something huge and painful had taken up residence in her lungs. She flinched when her mother knocked on the door again.

"Tea's on, just a few minutes. You only have an hour before we have to leave for the church. Are you sure I can't help?"

"Yes, I'm sure. I'm almost ready to put on the dress."

The dress—her *wedding* dress. For God's sake, of all the times to feel like crap, why her wedding day? She bent and rinsed her mouth and hands, then wiped at the splatters on the sink with a tissue. She tried to smile at her image but she looked ghastly; despite her well-learned skills with make-up, her skin was chalk-pale and she'd been unable to wipe out the blue shadows beneath her eyes. Her chest felt sore, and she had a painful lump beneath one arm. The horrid knot on her forehead was still there, too, but at least she'd been able to seal the split flesh with super glue and cover it tightly with a small, clean bandage. The headdress on her veil would hide it. In the meantime, she opened the medicine cabinet and found the aspirin bottle. These would help—they *had* to, just long enough to get her through the ceremony and a couple of hours at the reception. Then, when she and Robbie could finally slip away in their limousine, she'd tell him she needed to see a doctor instead, have an exam and get some medication before they left for Hawaii in the morning.

Jenelle drew her breath in and fought off another cough as she stood up straight. They were expecting over a hundred people at the wedding, and half again that at the reception. She could get through this. She *had* to.

Time to put on her wedding gown.

He was whole again.

After so many centuries, it took him awhile to stand upright. When he finally could, he stretched his arms and his muscles, feeling them swell with life once more as he dragged the damp, dungeon air into his lungs. He looked around the tiny room that had held him captive and sneered at its ultimate uselessness, at its inability to contain the great thing that he was.

Voices filtered to his sensitive ears, moving through the primitive corridors, and he knew immediately what that meant. A tour, like the one that young woman had led. The first group of the day. Excellent.

He had taken many disguises during his existence as he'd passed from place to place. This would be the first of many more to come.

"I wish I could say I've never seen you so beautiful, love," Robbie said in a low voice as everyone at the reception clapped madly and he led her to the table where the cake waited to be cut. "But you look just as rotten as I feel."

"I could tell you're sick, too," she whispered back. "What's wrong with us?"

He squeezed her hand. "Lousy cold, that's all. Maybe bronchitis. The timing sucks, but what can you do?"

Jenelle managed to smile at him, then coughed into her hand, fighting to keep the brunt of it inside so no one would notice. Her chest still hurt. "Recuperate on the beach, that's what. With margaritas and sunshine."

"Great idea," he agreed. He stepped into place beside her, and when she picked up the silver-coated cake server, he put his hand over hers. With forced smiles, they cut the first piece, then fed each other the requisite bite for the cameras. When that was finally done, she and Robbie made their way back to the head table, foregoing the dance floor in favor of watching dully as the celebration continued.

At the cake table, one black-clad waitress picked up the cake server and quickly cut the rest of the beautiful three-tiered cake into small, neat pieces, using her thumb and forefinger to push each one onto the plates so the other staff could distribute the slices among the rest of the guests.

He slipped into step behind the tour group as they passed the roped-off corridor leading to the room he was leaving behind. A couple of steps more and the woman in front of him turned, realizing suddenly that someone was behind her. She stumbled when she saw him and he took her bare hand to steady her, rubbing a part of himself into the soft skin by her thumb. She started to say something—"Thank you," perhaps—but instead she shuddered and yanked her hand free before hurrying forward, afraid to her soul but not knowing why. He watched her go, hoping she was a visitor from a foreign land and would carry his gift far.

Mankind had taken to the skies in his absence, a realm once reserved only for him and his dark and light brethren. This would prove to be their undoing.

At the exit, as he saw his first daylight in far too long to remember, and a young man in a costume—really hardly more than a teenager—looked at him, then hurried over and blocked his path before he could leave. "Hey," he said, "I don't remember you at the entrance. You didn't pay."

He cleared his throat, letting his essence reach out and adapt to the current times before using his voice. "But I have no money," he said.

The young man scowled. "I don't know how you got past me," he said, "but don't you ever come back here again."

Before the other man could pull out of range, he touched the teen ever-so-lightly on the cheek. "Not to worry," he said gently. The smile he gave the costumed worker was a grotesque mask of black gums and bloody teeth.

"I won't have to."

SCENT OF THE GREEN CATHEDRAL

Jay Lake

YOU THOUGHT YOU KNEW the way. There was a path, broad and brightly-lit at the first, seducing you through tangled thickets and along narrowing alleys between the boles until there was nothing left but the ache of your feet and a cathedral-green darkness all around you. The forest had become thick and treacherous, wolves in every shadow, brigands hidden in each tree.

Behind? You saw nothing. No evidence of your passage. No backward path. It was as if you had been born in this place, child of leaf and branch.

Before? Everything, leading nowhere. Just the forest's endless sheltering shadow. It was as if you had come to die in this place, a rough beast who would slouch no further.

Then you saw the light, flickering among the branches, a star descending. Stories came to your mind, fairies of old, time stretched to taffy Under the Hill. You had never believed in them.

The light had wings, making a promise of the spark. It sailed toward you, path as smooth and sure as any river's, to spin around your head until the very gleaming made you dizzy and you fell to the leafy loam.

"I am lost," you croaked. "My way is gone."

The wings spread wide then, golden pinions glowing with dawn's rich light. Her face was beauty, a brilliant scarab frozen in the bubbling amber of God's handiwork. Her body was a temple, desirable beyond lust. "There is always a way," she said. "You only need ask."

Your mouth opened, words on your tongue, breath caught in your throat, but the words would not come. Your lungs worked like bellows, creaking in your chest, but no air would move. The amber flowed from her to you, an examination by the lidless green eye of God.

Only those without sin could be saved. Only those with sin would desire salvation. To ask was error, silence a worse failing.

"I . . ." you finally choked the word from your lips, the sound a fishbone gone wrong, but she had already departed.

You were left with only memories of golden light and her ivory-skinned glory. Newfound beads of amber in your fist, you stumbled around a corner into sunlight and traffic. The scent of the green cathedral has never left you.

SNOW ANGELS

Sarah Pinborough

SARAH PINBOROUGH is the author of six horror novels from Leisure Books. Her debut thriller, *A Matter of Blood*, was recently published by Gollancz, and is the first in The Dog-Faced Gods trilogy. She also has a young-adult novel, *The Double-Edged Sword*, out from the same imprint under the name "Sarah Silverwood."

She was the winner of the 2009 British Fantasy Award for Best Short Story, the 2010 award for Best Novella and has been short-listed three times for Best Novel. She has also been short-listed for the World Fantasy Award and for the Shirley Jackson Award.

"The idea for 'Snow Angels' came about in the really cold snap of February 2009," explains Pinborough, "when I was walking my mum's dog for her down by the river.

"The paths were iced over and the grass was crisp and there was never anyone around because it was just too frozen and slippy, and the whole world seemed to have become simply magical shades of white and grey—the habitat of things that didn't perhaps belong entirely with the rest of us.

"I'm a sunshine girl, though, so for me, anything that lived in the frozen wasteland was never going to be entirely friendly . . ."

IT WAS FEBRUARY when the snow fell—the same day the nurses moved Will from his bed at the far end of the dormitory and into the smaller, private sanatorium on a different floor of The House. I was eleven years old. I hadn't seen the sanatorium and I didn't want to. No one that was taken from the bedrooms ever came back, and even as children we knew why. Death lived that way. Dying was, after all, the business of The House; it was what we'd gone there to do. None of us who were left watched as they took Will away. It was better to imagine that he'd never been there in the first place—just a vague shadow or shape, or a ghost of a boy who'd once lived.

The world outside the window had been smothered in grey for days and, as the temperature dropped, frost cracked across the glass and breathed its white onto the lawns where the nurses would let us go out and sit or play if we were feeling well enough and the weather was mild. Finally, as Will was ushered away to die somewhere "other," stillness trickled through The House and thick white flakes drifted in clouds from the sky. Poor, yellow, Will was forgotten in the glory of that sight.

According to Sam, who'd been considered something of a math and science prodigy before cancer had gripped him and squeezed his difference into a less acceptable shape, it hadn't snowed in England for more than thirty years. Sam was fourteen and had been a broad and handsome boy with an easy grin when he first arrived. Now his glasses slid too often down his thin face, as if the tumor in his head was somehow hollowing out his cheeks as it ate up his clever brain.

"At least I think it hasn't," he said. Small frown lines furrowed across his forehead under his sandy hair. By the time the snow came I'd been at The House for more than a year and I'd stopped talking to Sam so much. His smile was too often lop-sided and his sentences drifted away unfinished or suddenly ended with a burst of expletives. It didn't really matter whether he was right or wrong—although an idly curious check years later proved him right—what mattered was that none of us had seen such a thing beyond old photographs and films when we'd had our brief flirtations with normality, and been healthy and at school and had families that weren't ashamed of us. In our short, dark and over-shadowed lives, the arriving snow was something of a gift. A miracle that changed the world into something new—something in which perhaps we belonged as much as everybody else.

There were twelve children in The House that day, and in both the girls' and the boys' dorm thin fingers clutched at the windowsills and wide eyes stared outside. Our breaths coated the glass with rotten steam as we watched, afraid that if we looked away for even a precious second the sky would suck the white treasure back.

We needn't have worried. Over the next few days the cold snap showed no sign of relenting. More freezing snow was driven our way from the Arctic, carried on angry blasts of icy winds that howled across the stretches of water that divided the warm from the cold. The world had changed outside the window. Everything was white.

Even the nurses showed vague signs of humanity beneath their clinically efficient exteriors. They smiled without stopping themselves mid-expression and their eyes twinkled and cheeks flushed with the glow and excitement of the chill. Perhaps it gave them a small lift in the deathly monotony of the duty they had been given. The nurses shared The House with us, but we were two separate tribes and I'm not sure either really "saw" the other—the dying children and the healthy adults. Only when the snow came was there any sense that the blood that flowed through their veins was barely different to our own.

On the morning the nurses came to clear Will's possessions away, I found Amelie in the playroom. She was kneeling on an old couch and peering out across its back through the chipped sash window. She looked thinner. Her large red sweater swallowed her tiny frame and my heart ached. My world had changed when Amelie arrived with her long, blonde hair and sharp blue eyes. Her laughter was infectious and alive, and even as she rapidly got sicker, that laugh never lost its vibrancy. Dying with Amelie made dying easier, even with the knowledge of the tears, the sleeping, the pain and the fear that came before the final move to the sanatorium. I loved Amelie Parker with the whole of my damaged being and, in all the years that have passed since. I don't think that love has ever really let me go.

"Isn't it beautiful?" Her cheekbones cut lines through her skin as she smiled. "We should go outside."

"To the garden?" I looked out at the sea of white and grey. It was cold and my back ached where my kidney was eating itself, but my feet itched to find out what the snow felt like beneath them.

"No," she shook her head. "Past the garden. Lets go out and walk along the river and around the park." Her eyes sparkled. "What do you think?"

"Yeah." I grinned. "Let's do it. Just us."

"Of course just us." She tossed her hair over one shoulder in a gesture that had first made my stomach flip two months earlier on the day she'd climbed out of the back of the ambulance. Now my stomach just tightened. The spun gold had slipped away over the intervening weeks and although she washed and brushed it every day she felt well enough, Amelie's glory was now dull, lank and lifeless. Sometimes she would hold the ends and stare at it sadly, but mostly she smiled defiantly at the world, and I'm sure that in her mind her hair was always the color of the sun.

"Let's do it." She climbed down from the couch and took my hand. "While we still can."

Her palm was dry, as if the skin was flaking away, and although I know that in that moment Amelie was simply referring to the fleeting life the snow and ice was likely to have rather than our own predicaments, those words still haunt me.

We were both sick—Amelie had spent the three days of the snowfall in bed with a hacking cough—but neither of us was in any hurry to die, and so we layered ourselves up in all the warm clothes we could muster. With our coats done up tight, we ventured outside. We weren't the first to explore the snow, but I was the healthiest amongst the children and Amelie the most determined, and we were the first to go beyond the confines of the small garden and the safety of The House's proximity.

We shuffled past the snowman Sam had attempted the day before. It was barely more than a ball of compact white, scarred with dirty streaks. The older boy had drifted back inside within ten minutes of being out, his mind confused and stabbing pains attacking his eyes. It wouldn't be too long before Sam was headed to the sanatorium. He was becoming too erratic and unpredictable. He was nearly just another empty bed to haunt my dreams. Our numbers were dwindling, and by rights I should have had my turn in the sanatorium months before, but my body just kept on living despite the fire in my back.

Amelie coughed once, a long and loud sound that racked her chest, and then as her fragile lungs adjusted to the icy air we stepped through the small gate that separated our world from the one beyond. Somewhere behind us a nurse or two probably stared disapprovingly out of the windows, but none would come and fetch us back in. We were here to die. No one treated us; they just medicated our pain and waited. It didn't matter much to that other tribe at The House whether we did our best to stay alive or otherwise.

We stood at the start of the path that wound a circuit along the river and around the field and simply stared. Before us was an ocean of white that met with grey on the horizon, the colors so similar that it was hard to see where the land ended and the sky began. I squinted against the harsh gleam that glared from the powdery surface and beside me Amelie lifted one hand to her forehead as if we truly were adventurers peering out over alien lands.

"Come on." Her giggle cut into the empty silence, and we trudged carefully forward. The snow had compacted into ice and I could see echoes of the footprints that had beaten it down trapped like fossils in the glistening surface. The ice glittered and, as I looked, the more colors I could see hiding in its shards—purples and blues and pinks and hints at shades in-between. I sniffed, and so did Amelie. It was the only sound other than our crunching feet and the occasional twisting whistle of the wind. My ears stung with the cold, but my heart was lifted by the quiet.

With the ice in places too slick to keep our unsteady feet gripped, we slowly made our way to the edge of the field, arms held out slightly for balance, and then stepped onto the snow. Amelie gasped. Her face shone, and for a second it was almost as if she had a whole lifetime ahead of her.

"It's so soft!"

My feet sunk through the cold white that crumpled beneath my weight, and I pulled my gloves off to slide my fingers into the wet surface. Beside me, Amelie crouched down, so that the hem of her coat was dipping into the snow, and scooped a small handful into her mouth. She grinned and poked her tongue out, and I watched the white dissolve into the hot pink before doing the same back.

We didn't speak but giggled and gasped and held the almost-whole-almost-nothing substance in our fingers until our hands were red and raw. We didn't play with it, or roll it into balls and throw it at each other. Those things didn't come to mind as perhaps they would have with other children. Maybe because it had been a long time since we'd run and laughed and played, and to do that again might break us from the inside out with the memories of all that was lost; or perhaps it was just because our bodies were too tired from the simple fight to stay alive. Whichever, we simply touched the snow and tasted it and smelled it. Our wide eyes drunk in the strange grey view as if it were something to be savored and stored safely away for reliving in the terrible days ahead.

In the distance a blot of darkness came through the gate from the far field and started on the slow walk around the path, a dog bounding ahead. Amelie stood up and we both smiled, willing the animal with its soft fur and wet tongue to come our way. The taller figure paused, and even from the hundreds of yards between us, I was sure I could see the person stiffen. A whistle sliced through the air, and the sheepdog immediately turned and headed back to its master. Together they disappeared back through the gate, as if even from this distance our diseases would somehow be catching. We watched them go and Amelie's smile fell.

"Let's go and look at the river," she said, eventually.

The grey shifted to a deeper hue and shrunk closer to frozen earth, as if the sky above had felt the darkening of our moods. We turned and headed to the river bank where trees rose up like the bones of ancient hands, gnarled and greedy and keen to grasp at anything that would stop the cold ground from dragging them down to be forgotten forever. Barely any hint of brown gasped from the empty branches lost beneath the snow and frost. The temperature dropped and my hot breath turned from steam to almost crystal as we crossed the path to stand overlooking the uneven river and the empty tundra that days before had simply been English fields. My lungs felt raw in the sudden cold.

A few feet from the steep bank Amelie paused, and we stood in silence as the snow began to fall again. Heavy flakes appeared directly above us. They winked into existence at the edge of the grey, and within seconds the sky was falling towards us like drifting ash. I tilted my head up and felt each one land like the kisses of the dead brushing against my skin. More and more tumbled down until the wind caught the excitement and sent the storm whirling in a frenzy across the open spaces. I gasped, the snow and cold air fighting to fill my mouth and lungs first.

Amelie simply smiled, and as the increasing flakes settled quickly on her head and coat, I thought she would be lost in the blizzard that gathered force around us. The wind bit at my exposed ears and cheeks and I stepped up beside Amelie in the small protection of a naked tree. Amelie stared at the river, ignoring the flakes that sat like glitter on her long eyelashes and clung to her skin. I followed her gaze, squinting against the snow that blew in every direction as if we were the center of a maelstrom.

The river hadn't frozen entirely but was covered in a slick sheen as ice fought to conquer the surface. The dark fluid beneath maintained supremacy over the white that had usurped the rest of the surrounding world, the water like a gash across the pale skin of the land. Amelie looked up, her eyes widening. She dropped her head, a flush blazing from her cheeks, and stared at the river again.

"Can you see it? Can you see them?" she laughed, but both the sound and the words were muffled by the heavy air as if the blizzard were trying to create a void in the small space between her and myself. I frowned and stared. My eyes stung, and for a fleeting second I thought I may have seen a flash of purples and blues dancing brightly on the dark, freezing surface—a swirl of colors that were almost shapes in their own right, casting black shadows behind them. I blinked and looked up, forcing my eyes to stay open. All I could see was the tumbling snow.

Amelie laughed again, and jumped slightly with excitement. "But they're beautiful! Aren't they beautiful?" She turned and grabbed my frozen hand with her own. The heat in it burned.

"I can't see. What are you looking at?"

Her eyes shone, the blue so sharp it was as if all the ice in the field had been condensed into those tiny irises. Her cheeks were too flushed for our surroundings, too red against the absence of color.

She gasped again and her eyes darted this way and that, following something beyond my sight and hidden by the falling snow. I wondered which of us the storm was mocking and decided maybe both. I shivered, suddenly aware of the deep chill that had sunk into my bones as fingers of pain squeezed at my spine.

"Let's go inside." Over my shoulder, even the forbidding structure of The House was almost lost in the grip of the blizzard. The snow consumed everything it touched in the relentless onslaught, and I knew with a shiver that if we stayed out here much longer, it would devour us, too, and we would be lost forever. My feet were numb in my shoes and I stepped back slightly, pulling Amelie with me.

"It's too cold. I'm tired."

Her feet stayed planted as she stared, but her thin frame swayed.

"Just two more minutes," she whispered, a beatific smile on her beautiful face. "Please."

As it was, a quarter of an hour passed before the energy slumped from her shoulders and she turned to me with sad eyes and let me lead her back across the field and through the gate to the safety of our world, where children politely waited to die. We didn't speak but went to our separate dormitories, dazed and blinded by the blizzard that had held us in a white embrace for most of the afternoon.

Back in the brightness and warmth of the building my teeth rattled, shaking barely a flicker of warmth into my thin face and it took an hour soaking in a bath before the jaws of the freezing cold released their grip on me. The nurses glared balefully as I shuffled past in my dressing gown but said nothing. I didn't expect them to.

It was still snowing when night finally swallowed what little muted light the day had held. As The House slipped into slumber and took me with it, I dreamed that Death came in a white coat and smothered me while his black eyes glittered purple and blue reflections of something beautiful and terrible that was out of sight. I screamed in my nightmare, but his unflinching fingers burned and then froze my skin as he pulled me upwards, out of the mess of sheets and blankets. Behind him, two nurses waited patiently by the door, one pointing towards the corridor where the elevators were and the other holding a small cardboard box. I struggled, desperate to stay in my bed, not to be dragged to the sanatorium, and around me Death's hands stretched and twisted, each digit hardening into wood until the sharp branches of the skeletal tree by the river had grown from his pale wrists and entangled me.

I woke up scratching madly at my own hot, wet skin.

The shivers and cold sweats grew worse, and by the morning my fever was raging and my throat burned as if every snowflake I had allowed to land on my tongue was a shard of glass embedded there.

The nurses brought pills and hot drinks, and muttered quietly amongst themselves about the *stupid boy and girl and what had they been thinking, especially her being so close to the* . . . and then they'd glance around and down at me, and from behind my haze I could see them wondering if I'd heard and the shutters would close over the parts of their eyes that mattered.

I slept most of the day, and then forced some soup through the barbed wire of my insides and took more aspirin that would ease the flu that the nurses were allowed to treat, but give my ailing kidneys more to worry about.

No one spoke to me, but in my more lucid moments, while the heat and infection raged through my body, I could see curious glances darted my way. I knew then how Will and all the others before him had felt as the slow isolation began. I knew what the quiet watchers were thinking. They thought the sanatorium would be welcoming me next and there was a relief in each of them—even poor confused Sam—that it wasn't their turn quite yet.

They stayed well back and flinched each time I coughed germs out at them. I knew these things without looking because I would have done the same. When I closed my eyes all I could see was falling snow against the crimson dark backdrop. Finally I slept.

The House was still when Amelie woke me. Her face shone in the half-light like the glaze that had been forming on the river, and her long hair hung in lank matted strands. There was barely a hint of blonde left. Her hand was hot on mine.

"I want to go out," she whispered. "I want you to see. *I want to see.*"

She licked her lips and her mouth trembled.

"It's the middle of the night."

"It's nearly dawn. I can't sleep. Please."

"Amelie . . ." I let my sentence drift off. I didn't want to get up. I didn't want to go out. The snow still held a mystery in it, but the cruel cold frightened me. Across the room, Sam stirred in his sleep and barked out a word that meant nothing but was spat fresh into the world with a vehemence I'd never heard from the boy with the easy grin. At night, the cancers ruled our sleep. I looked at Amelie's burning face and knew that I loved her more than I feared the cold grip of the blizzard.

"Okay."

Her fragile smile was almost worth it. I pushed back the covers and shivered, but my skin was cooling. Unlike Amelie's, my fever had begun to break somewhere between dusk and now, and although my limbs ached and my back was on fire, I knew the worst of that particular illness was over.

We moved like silent ghosts through the dark house, and wrapped ourselves up in coats and scarves housed in the rarely used cloakroom and turned the old-fashioned key in the back door. The lock clicked loudly. For a second the falling snow paused as if to welcome us. The cold air crept into the house carrying a handful of flakes on its wings, and as they came in to melt and die on the stone floor, we pulled the door closed and stepped out into the drift.

This time Amelie didn't hesitate or waste time giggling and laughing and clutching at handfuls of the elusive white that now sat several inches high over the frozen ground. Instead, she took my hand and led me out through the garden and across the field to the riverbank. By the time we reached it, The House was a lifetime away and looked like a dark dead thing pasted against the night. My hair was soaked from the relentless snow, and my shins were damp from where the icy wetness had crawled up my jeans above my shoes. My skin tingled with the cold and I flinched with every breath drawn in against my ragged throat.

Equally wet and surely as cold as I, Amelie simply smiled as we reached the slope and stood in the shelter of the frost-gripped tree that had plagued my dreams. The sky was slowly creeping from black to midnight blue, and the snow fell like stars or diamonds forever tumbling against it. I looked at the river. It had lost the battle with the ice since our last visit, and streaks and lines of crystals cut like fractures across the hard sheet of the surface.

"They'll come," Amelie whispered. "I know it."

We stood like that as the sky shifted above us, the blue fading to grey as dawn broke. My body numbed and my skin burned with outrage as the cold tortured it with bitter kisses, but I stayed staring at the river and wondering what I was doing here, knowing in my heart it was simply for the love of the dying, feverish girl beside me.

When the sky and the horizon blended into the same shade, becoming one endless vision of deathly grey, Amelie suddenly laughed and clapped her hands to her mouth.

"They're here!" she said, and jumped up and down on the spot where she stood while my own legs screamed if I even tried to bend them.

"They're here," she repeated, and her whisper escaped in a mist. As she looked upwards, I stared at the river. At the center of the frozen water streams of purples and blues twisted on the surface. Flashes of sparkling lights came simultaneously from the air above and the water below, as if the colors were reflecting from within the ice rather than on the crackled surface. The snow paused, hesitant, as the unnaturally bright colors grew denser. They spiraled and flashed too vividly against the grey that had swallowed the world to be part of it, and yet each of the mad hues had been distilled from the ghosts of colors that lived at the edge of each flake of snow, just out of sight, but held fast in the molecules.

My breath stopped. I was aware of Amelie's joy beside me, but my own moment had locked me in so completely that she might have been miles away. I slowly looked up, dragging my eyes from the dazzling array on the river to the sharp white of the endless horizon.

I gasped. Hazes of colors stretched across the sky right above our heads, their purity made clearer against the backdrop of emptiness and I wondered if somehow these were the Northern Lights dragged to us upon the wind. The numbness in my feet crept away. With an imperceptible sigh the blizzard came again, and as the snow launched itself around us, whipping around our slim frames, the colors pulled in on themselves. Faces formed in the flying streams, sharp eyes and beautiful smiles that danced and flew in the wind.

"Aren't they beautiful?" Amelie's dull hair rose up around her head as the cold air rushed through it, fingers made from icy flakes curiously teasing each strand. Her words barely reached me, the snow thick between us as the creatures in the sky whirled around, examining us. The snow felt like butterfly wings on my skin despite the urgent power of the breeze. For a moment, I thought she was right. They were beautiful. They were angels—snow angels, come to share something wonderful with us. I stared in awe until the air shifted and the moment changed. The angels separated, darting this way and that across the sky before coming back.

Amelie continued to laugh with delight beside me, but my heart froze. The lights in the angels' eyes hardened. The glittering smiles stretched and yawned wide, and I was sure that sharp teeth of black ice flashed from within. And then they rushed at me.

The blizzard was suddenly hard against my skin and snow stung my eyes. I flinched. The wings that beat at me were sticks, not feathers, and as I raised one arm to protect my face the wind forced it down. I squeezed my eyes almost shut, but even through the haze of attacking white I could see the cruel laughter in their eyes and feel their cold breath burning my skin—rotten water dragged from the pit of a stagnant frozen well. Tears streamed from the corners of my battered eyes and the monstrous creatures licked them away.

My feet tried to pull me backwards, but I was stuck on the riverbed, held in place by the snow and the wind and the whirling beings that tore at my skin with greedy fingers. They spoke in whispers that I couldn't quite make out, the words like freezing water in my ears. They sucked the air from my lungs, leaving only an icy void inside me, and through the madness I thought I saw something terrible and dark waiting just behind them—a creature hungrier and meaner and with no mercy, that lived in the blackness hidden just beyond the light.

I don't know how long I stood there. When the wind eventually fell, letting the lifeless snow simply drift to the ground, every inch of my being stung. My fingers and face tingled. My insides were made of ice. Amelie turned and half-collapsed on me, but the smile stayed stretched across her thin, pale face. It was only as we reached half-way across the blanketed field back to The House, my legs barely carrying me, and with Amelie leaning weakly on my arm, that I realized my back no longer hurt. It ached, yes, but it didn't burn. Something had changed.

I think I knew what would happen. It snowed for a further two days, during which time Amelie's fever grew worse. There were unspoken whispers about the sanatorium as she lay listless and sweating in her bed. For my own part, my throat raged and my voice died, but even though the nurses kept me confined to the dormitory and filled me with hot drinks, I could see their immediate concern for me had passed. The boys drifted back over to my side of the room, even poor Sam who would barely see the thaw before they wheeled him upstairs with blood pouring from his nose and his eyes gazing in two different directions.

It was on the second morning that the alarm went up. As with everything in The House, it happened quietly. There were no screams or shouts, simply a shift in the atmosphere. A hurriedness in the nurses' movements. It was seven o'clock in the morning. Amelie's bed was empty, only her thin pathetic outline left in the damp sheet.

I knew where she was. I let them search The House before squeezing the painful words "the river" out from my swollen throat. The snow had stopped, and when I stepped outside the sun shone bright against an azure blue sky, promising a return to normality. We crunched across the field, my small boots following in the remains of

Amelie's last footsteps, their outline barely visible unless you'd known where to look.

She sat frozen on the side of the riverbank. Her hands were wrapped around her knees, and she wore only her nightdress. Her feet were bare. The nurses and I paused a short distance away, and I'm sure I heard one of them let out a tiny gasp. It wasn't that she was dead. We were all used to death, and seeing her sitting there in the thin cotton I knew it couldn't have taken her very long to slip from one state to the other, and for that my breaking heart was glad. Her death we had all been expecting ever since we'd stepped into the cold February air. That didn't make the nurse pause, or my mouth fall open.

It was her hair.

It hung like spun gold down her back, glorious and healthy, the color it must have been before she started dying in earnest and The House claimed her. It was beautiful. Magical. And by all rights, it just couldn't *be*. Her head was tilted backwards, as if she'd been staring at the sky when she died, and a smile danced on her mouth, her lips pink against cheeks that had lost their pallor and become fuller and flushed. She looked radiant but, as I stepped closer, I thought I saw crystals of blue and purple fear at the edges of her eyes, and there was the shadow of something dark behind them as if in the final breath she'd seen something unpleasant and unexpected.

All the children in The House died apart from me. I watched them go in turn and saw how they hated me as my body grew stronger as theirs weakened. After a year, the doctor's ran more tests and found the tumors on my kidneys had shrunk to nothing. They could do nothing but let me out. My childhood, such as it was, continued in foster care. My parents didn't want me back. I had been defective once, and could be again. They weren't prepared to take the risk.

As it turns out, they were right. Six months ago, just after I turned thirty-five, the pain came back. Governments had changed and cancer treatment was back on the menu. Not for me, though. Too aggressive, is what the doctors said. In their eyes I saw the ghosts of the nurses and the elevators to the sanatorium.

Most days now I'm too weak to get out of bed. At best, I sit in the chair by the window and gaze out over the fields and countryside. I thought I was ready. I thought I'd made my peace. But last night the first blizzard in twenty-three years came across from the cold lands. By this morning the world had faded to grey.

The snow still falls. I can feel its purpose, and I think that if I close my eyes a little, I'll see the colors hiding in it. It's beating at the door and sounds like wings, sometimes butterfly, and sometimes something heavier and meaner, and they fill me with fear and make me wish for Amelie in equal measure.

I think I'll go outside. Maybe take a seat. And perhaps I'll see a hint of spun gold before the darkness comes for me.

NEPHILIM

Mark Samuels

MARK SAMUELS is the author of four short story collections: *The White Hands and Other Weird Tales* (Tartarus Press, 2003), *Black Altars* (Rainfall Books, 2003), *Glyphotech & Other Macabre Processes* (PS Publishing, 2008) and *The Man Who Collected Machen & Other Stories* (Ex Occidente, 2010), as well as the short novel *The Face of Twilight* (PS Publishing, 2006). His tales have appeared in both *The Mammoth Book of Best New Horror* and *Year's Best Fantasy and Horror*.

"The Nephilim are a race of fallen angels, the name deriving from Hebrew, and mentioned in the Bible," explains the author. "Some sources translate the word as merely 'giants,' and there are a multitude of weird claims made about their nature.

"Some believe they are the originals of the demons that dwell in Hell, while others believe they were, in fact, ancient astronauts. Whatever they were, and whether or not they ever existed except in the imagination, the thought of them exercised a fascination over me that produced the following tale."

THE ALARM CLOCK WENT OFF at 7:30 a.m. and he awoke. In the immediate hours that followed he had no idea what he was, where he was or even what it meant to be awake. His body was drenched in sweat and he lay staring at the ceiling. He traced the cracks and flaking paint as if charting the geography of an undiscovered land. He did not remember how to move and it was a shock when one of his feet twitched involuntarily. Then he began to look around the room, observing the unfamiliar objects with awe. But as the hours wore on he got further away from the dream that paralyzed his mental processes and started to recover his waking mind.

He tried to speak and croaked out the words, "I am Gregory Myers. I am Gregory Myers." Then he pulled himself to the side of the bed and sat on the edge breathing deeply. He looked at the clock. It was 2:00 p.m. His waking life was returning to him rapidly now.

He finally stood up, put on a dressing gown and went into the bathroom. When he looked into the mirror he felt dumb amazement and horror. His hair had turned white. His skin was deathly white. He looked like an albino.

"I'm sorry but the doctor's fully booked today," the receptionist said without looking up.

"This is an emergency—I've got to see him and I'm not leaving until I do," Myers responded, his voice trembling with emotion.

"What's the emergency?" she persisted, in-between shuffling some patient cards.

"Look at me, will you?" he cried.

She put him to the front of the queue.

"Well," the doctor said, after he had examined Myers, "I really don't know what to say. Obviously I'd like you to see a specialist."

"Is it connected with the dream I told you about?" Myers replied.

"Possibly, though the idea that extreme fright can turn a man's hair white is false, you realize. An old wife's tale that one."

"You don't think it's permanent then?"

"I don't know. To be frank, I'd hope it isn't. But your case is, in my experience, unprecedented. I think that you should certainly . . ."

But Myers had ceased to listen to him. There was another place he wanted to visit immediately.

Myers' favored Catholic church was a huge Gothic pile just over the north side of Stamford Hill. It was only a short bus ride away from his flat in Stoke Newington and was large enough so that he retained his anonymity. He only attended Mass four or five times a year. He was not quite lapsed, for the attractions of the faith held his imagination too tightly, but he was not devout. His confessions invariably included references to his failure to attend Mass regularly. Yet at times, when life overwhelmed him, he turned to the church instinctively and would spend hours at prayer alone in one of the chapels.

There were several penitents sitting patiently and awaiting their turn for confession. The majority of them were elderly women, possibly Irish, he guessed, and they ran the beads of their rosaries between their forefingers and thumbs as if acting in unison.

Myers waited until his time came and then made his confession quickly but with a heartfelt repentance that took him back to his first, many years before. He felt as if this should be his last. Once he was given absolution and his penance he asked the priest for advice concerning his dream and its horrible aftermath. He was terrified of the great black void. Where, he wondered, had been God?

The priest listened sympathetically and told him that perhaps he had only been lost in his own mind, lost in the dream, and that God waited until release from the bondage of sin was attained.

When he returned to his flat he found a message on the answer phone from his employer. Myers phoned him back, just before the office closed, and tried to explain the situation, promising to return to work within a few days.

Myers resolved not to sleep that night, such was his terror of the dream. Strong coffee kept him awake and he found that he had to eat at about 4:00 a.m. Tiredness was a minor inconvenience. The thought of falling back into the black void haunted him much more than the feeling of fatigue. He found, however, when he was not on his guard, that his eyes began to close and that waking consciousness threatened to slip away. The gulf opened up before him and he started awake with a cry of fear.

At dawn he was shivering with cold and staring blankly into the distance.

By the fourth night without sleep he was continuously tired and found it almost impossible to concentrate. But as his body weakened, the terror of sleep only increased. He felt like a man drawn closer and closer to the edge of a crevasse, the movement forwards inexorable and the drop opening out ever more clearly before him.

When he looked at his reflection in the mirror it was to confirm that he had undergone no further changes. He would stand in the bathroom, lean over the sink and peer deeply into the glass. Before the transformation his face was not one that was easily remembered. His hair was thinning and a watery pair of eyes gazed, with no intensity, from behind a pair of rimless glasses. He had a weak chin that seemed continuously a day overdue for a shave. He ran his fingers over the now-white stubble and thought, amusedly, that his five o'clock shadow was less noticeable because of the lack of pigmentation. Before the alteration his face had been ordinary, unremarkable. But now his skin was the color of milk. People turned to look at him for a second time.

As he examined his features, his face appeared, momentarily, to become insubstantial—as if it was not real at all, but an image only half-remembered.

He pulled back his shirt cuff and looked at his watch. Just time for a shave before setting off for Sunday evening Mass.

He sat and watched the first of the communicants leave their places and file silently up towards the altar. His gaze wandered around the church and rested on a plaster statue of Our Lady surrounded by dozens of candles. Shadows flickered to and fro across the statue's upturned face and its hands clasped together in an arch. Then he looked down at the old Roman missal he held. He opened the page marked with a silk ribbon and recited a prayer before communion by St. Ambrose:

"O Gracious Lord Jesus Christ, I, a sinner, presuming not on my own merits, but trusting to Thy mercy and goodness, fear and tremble in drawing near to the Table on which is spread Thy banquet of all delights. For I have defiled both my heart and body with many sins . . ."

A wave of exhaustion swept over him suddenly. His eyes ached at the light and he wondered whether, in this place at least, if he slept he might escape from the hideous dream that haunted him.

By the time he had finished the prayer and resisted drifting off to sleep he saw that he should take his place at the end of the queue. He stood up and edged past the kneeling post-communicants, trying not to disturb them.

He found that his whole body was trembling and he almost tottered as he made his way forward.

One by one his fellow Catholics before him took the wafer on to their tongues and he heard the familiar words being repeated, like a chant: "Body of Christ" and the response "Amen." At last Myers himself stood before the priest, who was clad all in white, with the sacred wafer held outstretched between forefinger and thumb.

But the priest seemed not to see Myers and stood there rigidly, looking right through him as if through glass. Myers persisted, his hands still clasped together and his mouth open, the tongue ever so slightly pushed forward to receive the sacrament.

The priest continued to make no motion towards him and now

had a puzzled expression on his face, as if trying to work out why the person directly behind Myers was hesitating. The hiatus appeared, for Myers, to last for hours and finally he turned away—too afraid to even attempt to receive the communion wine that was being distributed by a deacon close at hand in case the scene should be repeated.

He made his way back to his pew in a state of utter confusion and wondered if those around him regarded him with curiosity. To be refused the Blessed Sacrament! But no one took any notice of him. There were no concealed glances, no furtive and puzzled frowns, and no atmosphere of interest or discomfort. It was as if the incident had simply not occurred.

"The Lord be with you," the priest intoned.

"And also with you," came the response.

"May almighty God bless you, the Father, and the Son, and the Holy Spirit . . . The Mass is ended, go in peace."

Myers' eyes rolled upwards in their sockets. His eyelids tried to shut themselves. He grasped the back of the pew before him for support. He felt that, once he had taken communion, he would risk sleep, but not now. Not without grace. He could not confront the nightmare without grace.

And then, once the priest and the others had filed solemnly away, the congregation stirred themselves and began to leave.

Myers just sat there, clutching his black missal in his hand and gazing at the statue of Our Lady with an expression of hopelessness. It was as if he were seeking comfort from someone in whom he had great trust. He seemed to be seeking confirmation that he had, indeed, been treated very poorly. Finally he got to his feet and left the church, forgetting to cross himself as he did so.

He slunk away from the church as quickly as he could. It was very dark outside and the white, full moon had risen behind the Gothic pile. Its twin towers cast a vast shadow across the street. So pale was his skin that he imagined himself as the offspring of the moon and not akin to his fellow men at all. He seemed only to move amongst them.

He had the idea of paying a visit to a drug-dealing youth and he returned to his flat after that detour. The journey had taken longer than he'd expected. Two buses driving past him punctuated his wait at a request stop, although he had clearly signaled at their drivers to halt.

He attempted to distract his thoughts from the events that were overwhelming him by going over his papers. These were the sum total of his literary output over the last fifteen years. In the early days he had harbored an inflated idea as to the merit of his work and had even enjoyed publication in magazines that nobody read. It was only later that he discovered he preferred to write for himself alone and not for the dubious pleasure of seeing his strange works in print. He liked to dream over them, writing only when inspiration came to him, which was infrequently, and the half-formed pieces and the false starts were either destroyed or subsumed into longer writings—of which there were few. He enjoyed destroying the work that did not satisfy him. Sometimes he even wondered if he actually wrote just so he could obliterate the results.

Although he tried to concentrate on the sheets of paper that were spread out before him, Myers soon found that his eyelids were becoming heavier and heavier. The myriad words held no meaning for him and were like an alien text that he could not decipher. He had the strange feeling that the writings were protecting themselves from him (that it was not just his exhaustion that rendered the words illegible) in order that they might not suffer the annihilation that had met so much else of his writing. The thought distressed him. He began to draw random pages aside and then carefully burned them in the kitchen sink. He crumbled the blackened and charred remains between his fingers before washing the debris away.

Then he decided to sample his new means of staying awake. During his detour after Mass he had bought some pills from a thin and spotty youth who was invariably to be found skulking in the corner of a pub off Stamford Hill. Myers only knew him by sight and reputation, but he had known others who had made deals with him, and the mention of their names and the sight of ready cash smoothed over the youth's reservations.

Gaining his trust seemed to have been made easier by the alteration in Myers' appearance. Now that he resembled an extra from a cheap zombie film, the doomed and the dissolute acknowledged an unspoken kinship that bade him welcome as one of them.

He took two of the pills he had been given. After a short time his mind began to race and he felt his heartbeat increase dramatically. His skin was cold and clammy and he heard a buzzing noise in his ears. The need for sleep gradually ebbed to the back of his mind like the tide going out.

He lay back on his bed and stared at the ceiling, letting the hours pass, though they seemed like days, while his thoughts moved in a frenzied dance. Even this form of debased consciousness was a relief, for it kept the terror of sleep from him.

After dawn he watched the hands of the alarm clock move inexorably around to eight in the morning. He rose, washed and dressed, took two more of the pills and drank two cups of black coffee before setting off for work. The air outside was bitterly cold and a foggy haze, white as he, had wrapped itself around the city during the night.

He caught the train from Stoke Newington to Liverpool Street and it was boarded one station down the line by a ticket inspector. The official made his way along the carriage slowly, examining each passenger's ticket with great care. Myers instinctively looked at his pass prior to the official's arrival. It was out of date. He'd forgotten to renew it. He began to turn over excuses in his mind.

When finally his turn came to have his ticket checked, the inspector totally ignored him. He glanced at Myers' seat as if it were vacant. The man's eyes did not register his existence. He passed by without a pause, continuing his careful scrutiny of the other passengers' tickets as normal. Was he, Myers thought, utterly terrified by the pale and outlandish apparition and determined to avoid any contact with it? No, it wasn't that at all. Even his fellow passengers, he realized, had not reacted in any way when the ticket inspector had passed him by. Surely there would have been some curiosity. Then he did something that was bound to elicit a response. He got to his feet and screamed at the top of his voice. It was true that a few people stirred in their seats. One even got up to close the top section of a window as if a draught had blown through the carriage. But there was no other reaction.

He ran up and down the carriage staring into the other passengers' faces. Again, nothing. He even tried to pull one of them from their seat, but his strength had dissipated and his fingers felt soft and yielding like wet putty.

The train arrived at Liverpool Street and the crowd carried him along as it flowed down the platform. No one saw him and he was constantly jostled and barged by people who turned to look in confusion at something that was apparently not there. But now he noticed a new development, their expressions of fear. Contact with him produced momentary recoil and loathing.

There was surely no doubt now. He must have lost his mind. Too much solitude. Too much brooding. The thought brought back a painful memory that seemed pertinent: Years earlier his late grandfather had written to him only a few weeks after his grandmother had died. The old man had responded to a rare letter from his grandson with just ten words, scrawled in a pitiful way across a sheet of paper:

IT IS NOT GOOD FOR A MAN TO BE ALONE.

Nothing more. By the time Myers received the letter the old man was dead. They found his body washed up on a pebble beach, his face grey and half-devoured by crabs. He had lain there for hours in the early morning sunlight, lolling to and fro in the surf until someone had taken the trouble to look at him more closely.

Something else had changed. He felt utterly numb. There was no sense of distress at this memory as before. The only feeling he had was one of complete desolation, of hopeless futility. Most incredible of all, he no longer dreaded the thought of falling asleep and re-entering the black void. Part of him even welcomed the prospect. For this time he knew that there would be no awakening and that his mind would return permanently to the state from which it had been momentarily snatched.

He began to wander aimlessly towards the Underground system and traveled on the trains at random, taking a last opportunity to examine his fellow men before taking his leave of them. He watched them in their activities, in their haste and self-importance, and as it all fell away from him he passed wraith-like through the crowds, leaving a trail of fearful and uncomprehending expressions in his wake.

Finally, he felt the dream intruding into his waking mind and the states of consciousness and sleeping became intertwined. The vast black void loomed up and he found himself savoring the destruction of his meaningless thoughts. One by one they disappeared, like spent candles.

The universe had become a tomb. Across its intolerable immensity everything was dead and black. The stars had gone out, their fuel having been spent long ago. No planets rolled in the illimitable darkness. They had turned to dust. Eternal night had conquered everything. There were no sounds, for all energy had been exhausted. Only an utter silence remained. Time itself ceased to have any meaning. The universe had been dead for the infinitely greater part of its existence, the period of activity being only a moment at the beginning. The cosmos was cold, bleak and black. But it was not empty. There were ghosts haunting it, deathly white apparitions screaming silently in the black void. At the end, in dust and darkness, in infinite and eternal desolation, these dead souls prowled its edges and were lost forever.

As one they drew near to him. Their hair was white and their skins were fixed in a state of permanent corruption. Pulpy fingers groped towards him in an idiot embrace. He joined them in the eternity of horror, in their manic dance, and tormented clawing at each other. There were billions of them, scattered across the cosmos—and he finally become one with all the other ghosts of dead angels.

THY SPINNING WHEEL COMPLEAT

Chelsea Quinn Yarbro

CHELSEA QUINN YARBRO lives in Richmond, California, with three autocratic cats, and has been an award-winning professional writer for more than forty years. During that time she has sold more than eighty books, including twenty-three volumes in her Saint-Germain historical vampire series. She has published numerous works of short fiction, essays and reviews, and also composes serious music.

A recipient of the 2003 World Horror Convention Grand Master Award, she also received the Fine Foundation Award for Literary Achievement in 1993 and (along with Fred Saberhagen) was presented with the Knightly Order of the Brasov Citadel by the Transylvanian Society of Dracula in 1997.

"Back in the 1940s and '50s, on my occasional visits to my grandmother who lived in the Sacramento Valley, I often noticed a large farm a couple of miles away from her farm," remembers Yarbro. "It was run by a religious community and was known for quality produce of all kinds.

"The women all wore white bonnets and long skirts and rarely left the place; the men wore loose trousers, long smocks, and short, square beards. They were very strict, and their leader was of the fire-and-brimstone variety. I used to wonder what their lives were like.

"One of the possibilities became this story."

Make me, O Lord, Thy spinning wheel compleat
Thy Word my holy distaff make for me . . .
                                        —*Huswuffery*

CHARITY BLAINE STOOD AT THE WINDOW, staring eastward at the long freight train rolling past, a half-mile away, bound north. She counted the cars—one hundred four, one hundred five, one hundred six—and wondered where they would all end up. There were places between here and Canada where the trains could be shifted in other directions, so the cars passing by might end up in Seattle, or Boise, or maybe Saskatoon. Even at this distance she could see the large HAZARDOUS MATERIALS stickers on the tank cars, but could not read what they were carrying. Something poisonous, no doubt.

She shuddered and began to pull at the ties on her apron, suddenly aware that she should be on the back porch where two chickens in buckets of scalding water were waiting for plucking. The caboose, at the end of one hundred nineteen cars, was just sliding into view as she turned away from the window; she was secretly—and sinfully— pleased that out here at the edge of the compound, she could see traffic and trains: not at all like most of the other twenty-three houses, the majority of which were situated to keep the corrupt, wasteful, modern world away from the ninety-six residents of the Brethren of the Word commune.

Passing through the kitchen, she saw her younger sister working the churn, and her grandmother shucking peas. Poor Grace wasn't right in the head, Charity thought as she watched the vacant way the seven-year-old cranked the rotary handle—Grandmother always said that if muscle can do it as well as electricity could, muscle should—

and wondered again what God had intended when He had given Grace the fever two years ago that robbed her of all her brightness and charm, leaving only this blank husk of a girl. Not that she was questioning God's Will, she added inwardly with a quick glance over her shoulder as if to reassure herself that this lapse of hers had gone unnoticed. Such lapses on the part of one of the appointed angels would not be tolerated.

"What were you doing out front?" their grandmother asked sharply.

"Watching the train," said Charity, knowing it was wrong, and useless, to lie.

"Ten's too old for such idleness," said their grandmother. "Remember to ask God to forgive you for your backslide while you attend to your chores. You disobey like that, and Brother Whitelaw will not let you remain an angel in the Daughters of Esther."

"Yes'm," said Charity, and went onto the back porch, taking care to close the kitchen door tightly so no flies could get into the house; it might be autumn, but the flies were still about in quantity, and Grandmother would have a fit if any got into the kitchen: Beelzebub was known to be Lord of the Flies, and so it was doubly important to keep the pests out.

The two headless chickens were upside down in a pair of three-gallon buckets, their russet feather sodden with red-stained water that still steamed faintly in the warm air; Grandmother had removed the giblets and the rest of the innards, so at least she was spared that messy chore, and Grandmother would attend to the singeing when Charity finished her work. Charity drew up a three-legged stool and sat down to her unpleasant task, seizing handfuls of feathers and pulling them against the grain to expose patches of pale skin that reminded her of the look of her grandmother's arms. She put the feathers into a net bag to dry them, and soon bits of fluffy down hung in the air, as bothersome as insects in every way but noise. She tried to pray as she worked, as Brother Whitelaw commanded all his angels do, but her thoughts kept drifting, and the prayers eluded her.

Knowing her grandmother would be listening, instead of praying, she recited part of the old Puritan poem that she had learned before she started at the compound school. " . . . *My conversation make to be Thy reel, And reel thereon the yarn spun of Thy wheel. Make me Thy loom and knit therein this twine, And make Thy Holy Spirit, Lord, wind quills . . ."* The recitation became a chant, and earned a sharp rap of disapproval from Grandmother on the kitchen wall. Charity bit her lower lip and continued to pluck in silence.

When both chickens were fletched, she went to get the tweezers to pull out the pin-feathers still left under the chickens' skins. This was demanding work, made more difficult by the day's heat. Every few minutes, she had to wipe the tendrils of hair that had strayed out of her two long, light-brown plaits out of her eyes. *"Then dye the same in Heavenly colors choice, All pinked with varnished flowers of Paradise."* The old words rang in her ears, their outmoded form giving her comfort, for it helped her to realize that what she did was part of a long, long line of women's devotion to God's work. Continuing to recite the poem, she kept on with the tweezers, her work timed to the pace of the meter.

Those words she did not completely understand she invented meanings for: *"And make my soul Thy Holy rule to be,"* she now understood to mean more Holy Rood, or Rod, than it meant reign; so *make my soul Thy Holy Cross,* not *my soul Thy Holy Reign.* Holy Cross made sense—Holy Reign did not; and the measuring kind of rule, as Ruth Bradley had suggested, they were told was a heretical notion, but she did not know why. And *"Thine ordinances make my fulling mills,"* now that had been a puzzler. She had concluded that it had something to do with getting a word wrong, and that *fulling* was probably *pulling,* and had to do with blocking, as she had been taught to do with new cloth and knitted garments; she still had no idea what mills had to do with it, but that would have to be for a later explanation. She liked the end, though: *"Then clothe therewith Thine understanding, will, affections, judgment, conscience, memory, My words and actions that their shine may fill Thy way with glory, and Thee glorify.*" The images seemed to go with the earlier parts of the poem and it fit with the last lines: "*Then mine apparel shall display before Thee That I am clothed in holy robes for glory.*"

All the angels in the Daughters of Esther knew the poem, and all of them were taught to adhere to its principles: to do the work of angels was to be one with the angels.

The afternoon had advanced more than an hour by the time she was through with the chickens. She removed them from the buckets, carried them into the kitchen and put them in the smaller of two sinks, then went to dispose of the bloody water and to hang up the feather-nets out in the breeze. On her way, she stopped next to Grace, who was pressing the new-made butter into molds. "You're doing a good job there, Grace," she said, because Grandmother said Grace needed more encouragement than most children did.

"Good job," Grace repeated; there was no way to know if she comprehended what she was being told.

"See you don't get any of that blood-water on the melons. Only on the green-leafies," Grandmother reminded Charity. "And follow it up with a good watering, so it gets deep into the roots."

"Yes'm," said Charity, and went to take up her buckets to carry them outside. The back-steps were narrow and creaky, but made to be sturdy. Charity crossed the small parking area where the tractor stood during the good weather, and the pick-up was left at night. She let herself into the vegetable garden through the gate in the high, chain-link fence. The green-leafies were on the left, so she turned that way, trying not to spill any of the bloody water. Her arms were getting a bit sore from all she had done, and she had an instant of annoyance as she realized that she had more Women's Work instruction to attend that evening at the meeting of the Daughters of Esther.

Reaching the kale and spinach rows, she poured the contents of one bucket into the watering declivity that ran between the rows of plants. As she watched the liquid start to sink into the earth, she went to get the hose to make sure all the bed got some of the water. Blood was good for these plants, she knew. When she was finished, she went on to the cabbages, celery and kohlrabi, and repeated the process there. She stared at the bulbous kohlrabis with their absurd, plumey fronds poking out of the globular plant; they always seemed weird to her, but she made sure they, too, were nourished with bloody water and soaked before she returned to the house. As she climbed the back-stairs she looked up and saw a large Northwest jet lunging into the sky from the nearby Tri-County International Airport. "Wonder where they're going?" she asked in a whisper as she watched it until it was nothing more than a silver sliver against the blue.

"What are we to say about the virtue of Esther?" Brother Whitelaw asked the group of ten girls, all between the ages of nine and fifteen. He held his hands up as if he expected to be struck by divine lightning, and waited for an answer; the girls sat around him in sturdy wooden chairs at the edge of the gymnasium floor in the central commune building where the Brethren had their offices and school.

Tirzah Flemming raised her hand first, as she always did, and Brother Whitelaw called on her automatically: Tirzah was fourteen and the oldest daughter of their founder, Joshua Breedon, and his second wife, Naomi Flemming; everyone had high hopes for Tirzah, who was taken in faith more often than any other girl in the commune, and was the fourth angel of the Daughter of Esther—Charity was the ninth. "She was obedient to God's Will, and loyal to the land of Israel. She risked her life and soul for God."

"To the exclusion of her own thoughts," added Brother Whitelaw, his reproach given with a look of sorrow.

Coloring to the roots of her russet hair, Tirzah added sheepishly, "To the exclusion of her own thoughts."

"And what does that teach you to do?" Brother Whitelaw asked of the other girls. "What can you learn from Esther?"

Charity raised her hand, "That females owe more allegiance and devotion to God than males, for the transgression of Eve, and must be prepared to put His Will before our own in all things. That is the creed of the angels, and those who do the work of the angels."

Brother Whitelaw smiled. "Very good, Charity."

"My mother told me that, before she left on her mission," said Charity, trying not to sound proud of her mother, although she was. Her mother was the second angel. "I've remembered it to honor her, and to keep her faith."

"Your mother is an inspiration to all women," said Brother Whitelaw. "Would that more were as devout as she."

Tirzah smiled with mendacious sweetness. "How much longer is she going to be in prison, your mother?"

"A while yet," said Charity, knowing that the earliest she could get out—presuming she lost her appeal—was in twenty-eight years.

Brother Whitelaw stopped the sniping with a few sharp questions. "How many of you can think back to the day Salome Blaine left here to undertake her mission? Do you know how much of it she accomplished before she was caught and tried?"

Martha Hill, the oldest of the nine, spoke up. "She left here in August, four years ago. She was twenty-five, when it was revealed to Brother Breedom that mission should begin—"

"As revealed in Scripture," Brother Whitelaw interjected.

Ruth Bradley coughed but said nothing.

"Yes," said Martha, going on crisply, "She was caught ten months later by the federal agents of Satan, having killed thirty-eight people and injured another ninety-two, all unbelievers and idolaters. Her sentence is being appealed. She is our second angel, and so far, the most successful of all of those who have been sent on missions."

"Salome was one of our most devoted operatives, and she deserves our thanks and emulation. She chose her targets with great care: theaters showing un-Godly films, malls praising Mammon, arcades of games given over to the lure of false achievements and unholy adulation, schools where science is advanced over religion. All of you girls should ask God to make you as staunch as Salome Blaine has been, especially those of you who are not yet doing the work of angels. She never flinched from her task, though she risked her freedom and her life to do so, and has accepted her martyrdom without complaint." He nodded to Charity. "You have a great deal to live up to, Charity."

"I know," said Charity. "I pray for my mother every night, and I hope I'll do as well when my time comes."

"She was a sniper, wasn't she?" Ruth Bradley asked.

"A very good one," said Charity, with a satisfaction she knew was wrong. "I hope I can do as well, when my mission comes."

"If she was so good, why was she caught?" Tirzah challenged.

"God wanted her as a martyr as well as an angel," said Ruth.

"She had no way to depart from her position," said Charity.

"First things first," said Brother Whitelaw, calling them to order before the girls got to bickering. "No matter which path of redemption you choose, you will have to give us Brethren at least one child before you depart on your mission—no child, no mission: so our founder has taught."

"I intend to have two children at least before I go out to kill," said Tirzah, smiling smugly at her own ambitions.

"If you do this for yourself in order to advance yourself, God will be displeased," said Delilah Marsh, who was twelve and just beginning to show real promise. "You must not ask God to smile upon what you do if you aren't doing it completely for Him, without expectation of praise or distinction. *Make me, O Lord, Thy spinning wheel compleat.*"

"I will have them for God, and for our faith," said Tirzah with a pious expression.

"As will you all," said Brother Whitelaw, again quashing an argument. "Your lives are to be an expression of your faith; you will give an untainted life to the Brethren, as a pledge of salvation, and you shall remove sinners from the world, for the glory of God. It is your honor to avenge the honor of God. You will offer all those lives in expiation for the sins of Eve, and you will humbly thank God for allowing you this opportunity. That is what you are here to learn to do—to deliver the world from the—"

"—The sins of the world, to return to Eden," said Ruth. "We will restore the Grace lost to us by our Mother Eve."

"And then we will have a choice of how we are to show our devotion," said Martha, her serious young face brightening. "We can be snipers, or poisoners, or explosives' handlers, or arsonists, or garotters, so long as we bring down those who have turned away from God, we do Him service."

"Very good, Martha," said Brother Whitelaw.

"I seek to serve God with my life," said Martha, giving Tirzah a sidelong glance.

"We should all do that, I hope," said Tirzah, a bit huffily.

"With humility and a grateful heart: *Make me Thy loom and knit therein this twine, and make Thy Holy Spirit, Lord, wind quills*," Brother Whitelaw reminded them, his voice going stern. "You have a chance to redeem Eve if you can do your work without pride and without expectation of divine favor."

The girls all exchanged uneasy looks, and finally Selah Wilkins, the most devout of the girls, said, "We deplore our sins, and ask only that God allows us to please Him in whatever way His purpose is best-served."

"Amen," said Charity with the others as she thought of her mother in her prison cell, and how God had rewarded her for her dedication to Him.

Grandmother was ailing; she lay propped up in her bed, half-a-dozen pillows supporting her; her breath was wheezy and she had turned the color of washed curds. Her hair was tucked under her cap, but the few, iron-grey tendrils that had escaped were lank. She had been fine until word had come, three days ago, that her daughter's appeal had been denied, and that Salome would be in prison for another twenty-three years, barring any new legal maneuvers. Grandmother had not been herself since she had heard; she had retreated into illness and prayer, attempting to surrender her will to God, to embrace the martyrdom He had decreed for her daughter. Even now, she was whispering her penitent entreaty to God, to make her acquiescent to His Will.

"Do you want anything?" Charity asked as she adjusted the blankets around her grandmother's torso. She, too, was feeling shocked, caught up in disbelief that her mother was being treated as if she were a dangerous serial killer. By caring for her grandmother, she hoped to ease the pain that gnawed at her. "I've got chicken broth on the stove, and both Missus Wilkinses brought over food for you. Lewanna Wilkins has taken Grace for the time being, so I can devote myself to you."

"*In the footsteps of saints and of martyrs I tread,*" muttered Grandmother, reciting one of the Brethrens' favorite hymns.

"That you do, Grandmother," said Charity, doing her best to soothe the old woman. "You have always followed the saints and martyrs."

"*Let nothing stay me now from Thy Word fulfilled,*" she continued, her eyes fixed on the middle distance.

"Grandmother," said Charity, a bit more forcefully. "Do you want something to eat? Is there anything I can do for you?"

"You can take your oath as an angel, and make way for God to bring Paradise to earth," said the old woman in sudden fierceness.

"Anything else? Is there anything I can do for you—right now?"

Grandmother blinked, then said, "Bathroom."

Of all the services she had to render her grandmother, this was the one that Charity liked the least, but she nodded. "Let me help you." She sighed as she turned back the covers, then positioned herself to wedge her shoulder under her grandmother's arm so she could support her through the living room and across the little hallway into the bathroom, where she maneuvered her grandmother onto the toilet, then left her to do what she had to do, returning to assist her grandmother back to bed.

"Your father . . . your father," said Grandmother as Charity eased her back onto her pillows.

"What about my father?" Charity asked, not truly interested, for she had heard the same stories about him for years.

"He spoke against your mother, against the Brethren, so Brother Breedon told me." She sounded stronger now, but also deeply ashamed. "He spoke in court against us all."

"Spoke against?" Charity was baffled. "How could he? When?"

"Before the court that reviewed your mother's conviction," said Grandmother, and lowered her head in prayer. "Brother Breedon says that it was his testimony that accounts for the severity of her sentence. He told the unbelievers that Salome was falsely called an angel, one devoted to the expiation of the Sins of Eve."

"But how is that possible? My father's been dead for five years," said Charity. "I put flowers on his grave last Sunday."

"Oh, yes, dead. Dead." Grandmother coughed and began to pray.

"If he's dead, how could he—?" She stopped as she encountered the quelling stare her grandmother gave her.

"You go pray for his soul, girl; he's dead as if he were in the grave. And bring me a bowl of broth and rice."

Relieved that Grandmother was seeming more like herself, Charity adjusted the coverlet before hastening off to the kitchen, murmuring as she went, "*Make me, O Lord, Thy spinning wheel compleat . . .*"

"*The Lord bless her and keep her, the Lord make His Face to shine upon her and give her peace; the Lord be gracious unto her. Amen,*" Joshua Breedon said as Grandmother's coffin was lowered into the grave; the October day was cool and blustery, and there was a promise of rain in the scudding clouds. "Ten months an invalid, then God relieved her suffering." Brother Breedon tossed the ritual handful of earth onto the unfinished pine box.

"Amen," echoed all the Brethren; the entire commune had attended Grandmother's funeral, a rare distinction among the Brethren.

"She has gone before her daughter, to make the way ready for Salome's coming to glory as an angel of the Daughter of Esther," Breedon continued, his stirring, musical voice as persuasive as the deep notes of an organ. "When she enters before God, the angels in Heaven will know her as one of their own. The heavenly hosts will salute her with trumpets and cymbals, and she will be given wings and a robe of white. Evangeline Milcah Blaine devoted her life to the tasks of faith. She prepared her daughter for the rigors of her mission, she sheltered her granddaughters, and provided an example for her granddaughter Charity. Hers was a path of humility and service, her devotion an example for all of us. Although she never went on a mission herself, she was prepared to do all that she, as a woman, could to open the way of salvation. As a distaff Elder of the Brethren, she was a living example of sanctity. We will honor her memory by naming the next mission for her, and the retribution we deliver will shine more brightly for her Grace."

Another chorus of "Amens" endorsed this last, and a few of the men took shovels to begin to cover Charity's grandmother's coffin with dirt.

Tirzah Flemming, standing next to her father, looked over at Charity, her manner prim but satisfied. "The Brethren will decide about your grandmother's house tonight," she said just above a whisper.

"I know," Charity whispered back as she held Grace's hand tightly so her sister would not try to play in the earth being piled on Grandmother's grave.

"They'll probably assign someone to live with you," Tirzah said, speaking a little more loudly, a hint of smugness in her pious smile. "It wouldn't be right to let you live alone."

"I am old enough to manage," said Charity, raising her voice to be heard over the sound of the two panel trucks lumbering out of the main drive, carrying off commune honey to the organic markets in the nearest cities. In a few days there would be more trucks, and they would take pickles and preserved fruits to market.

Joshua Breedon held up his hand for silence. "There is much to do. Go about your tasks with watchful hearts, so you do not encounter snares left for you by Satan."

"Yes, Father," said Tirzah, staring at Charity.

Ruth Bradley glanced at Charity, her face so guarded that there was almost no trace of her thoughts showing there. She nodded once and followed her stepfather away from the grave; she never looked back.

"What do you think will happen now?" The question came from Isaiah Breedon, who was fourteen and becoming restive.

"I'm going back to my grandmother's house," said Charity, and started to walk away.

"But you will have to send your sister to someone who can care for her."

Charity kept on walking.

The year faded into winter; at Christmas Brother Breedon announced the betrothal of Charity Blaine to Noah Whitelaw; he moved into her grandmother's house with her the day they were married. She tried to esteem him, but secretly found his habits disgusting, though she said nothing to anyone. Her pregnancy was confirmed at the start of June, and her training for her angelic mission began in earnest.

"You will need to make a practice journey into the city," Brother Breedon announced to Charity in August.

"But—" She indicated her expanded abdomen. "I can't move quickly, and I'll attract attention."

"It doesn't matter. We'll give you instructions to find the place you are to go. People will help you, seeing that you're with child, and a young woman. If you tell them you are lost, they will help you more." He beamed at her, laying his hand on her shoulder. "Your marksmanship is improving quite satisfactorily, and it is time you learned the targets you will be searching out. You will not only punish the ungodly for their faithlessness, you will be revenged for your mother's incarceration."

"I'll try to do what God wishes me to do."

"As angels will do," approved Brother Breedon.

• • • • •

As eager and curious as Charity had been about seeing the huge, sinful city where her mother had been tried, she found herself developing a knot in her belly almost as large as her growing baby. The streets were so crowded, the people so unfamiliar that when the truck driver hauling pickles and preserves from the commune dropped her off in front of the court house, Charity wanted to climb back into the cab and hide there until they were once again out of the city and back at the commune.

"Angels persevere in God's work: *My words and actions that their shine will fill Thy way with Glory, and Thee Glorify,*" she said aloud, repeating the lesson Brother Breedon had told her before she left. "God will not look lightly on those who fail to avenge His Cause."

She stood facing the Franklin County Court House, tempted to cross the street and go inside, though her orders had told her to go into the small park behind her and find a place from which she could shoot when she came back with her rifle. It took her a few minutes to select a crosswalk; by the time the light changed to allow her to walk, she had turned all her thoughts to the Judgment and how she would do God's work in bringing it about through the deaths of those who had turned away from God.

The park occupied half a city block, with a fenced playground at the far end. Charity went in that direction, looking up into the branches of the old oaks that clustered along the east side of the park. She realized that she would be able to climb up the playground fence and get into the branches of one of the trees, and her heart leaped in anticipation. After her child came, she could do the climb. On the day of her mission, if she arrived before dawn, she could be in the branches with no one the wiser. Satisfied that she would be able to fulfill the task set for her as an angel, she made her way to the supermarket that the truck driver had pointed out to her.

"So there you are," the driver called out. "Do you want to see where your fruits and vegetables and honey end up? I can wait if you want to take a look around inside."

Charity thought of her father, lured away from God by such things as the worldly luxuries offered inside the store, and shook her head. "No, thank you. I don't want us to be late, getting back to the . . . farm." She had been told not to call her home a commune or a compound, and was relieved that she remembered.

"Did you find out what you wanted to know?" The truck driver started the engine and eased the gears into place; the truck rolled forward.

"Yes, I did." She beamed at him, knowing that when she returned, she would be cleansing the earth of sin and restoring Eden in all its goodness and simplicity.

The truck was moving faster and the driver changed gears again, making his way through the traffic with ease. "You ever been to the city before?"

"No," said Charity. "But now I've seen it, I know I'll be back," she added as the truck bore her back to the compound and her final preparations for her angelic mission.

OLD MR. BOUDREAUX

Lisa Tuttle

LISA TUTTLE was born in the United States, but has been resident in Britain for almost thirty years. She began writing while still at school, sold her first stories while attending university, and won the John W. Campbell Award for Best New Science Fiction Writer of the year in 1974.

She is the author of eight novels (most recently the contemporary fantasy *The Silver Bough*) and numerous short stories, in addition to several books for children. She edited *Skin of the Soul*, an anthology of horror stories by women, and Ash-Tree Press is publishing a multivolume collection of her short fiction, beginning with *Stranger in the House: The Collected Short Supernatural Fiction, Volume One*.

"When I was growing up in Houston I loved to go exploring along the banks of Buffalo Bayou, in the hidden no-man's-land that existed just beyond the end of our street," remembers Tuttle.

"I was reminded of this a few years ago when, on a visit to Houston, some friends took me to their local hike-and-bike trail, and once again I saw the slow brown water glittering in the sunlight, the turtles on rocks and snakes disappearing into the undergrowth beside the bayou, and realized that this patch of wilderness still existed inside the modern city—and wondered what other impossible things might be out there that an adult might dismiss as a childish fantasy. That's when I had the idea for this story."

SOME THINGS DON'T CHANGE, but feelings do.

I was tense and unhappy, my mind on death, as I crossed the Atlantic, but back on the ground again I suddenly relaxed. Around me people spoke English or Spanish instead of French, and the familiar cadences of Texas carried me back to infancy. Even in the impersonal setting of the airport I felt oddly comfortable, and when I stepped outside the air-conditioned interior and the moist, hot, living air of Houston licked my skin, I could have been a baby in my mother's arms. For the first time since I'd heard that my mother was dying, I relaxed and just accepted it. Maybe, after ninety-six years on the face of the earth, she was ready to go home.

When I reached the hospital downtown, I found her unconscious, but alive. Maybe she slept, I don't know, but behind their shut lids her eyes did not move, and there was no response from her when I spoke. Her breath sounded scarily loud and rasping but scarcely stirred the white sheet stretched above her thin chest. I didn't need the nurse to tell me how little time was left.

I sank into the molded plastic chair at her bedside, and gathered her cool little hand into both of mine where it lay, relaxed and empty.

Tears pricked my eyes and I felt a swirl of panic behind my ribs. Fifty-eight years old—nearly an old woman myself—I was scared and helpless as a child about to be orphaned. What could I do?

I leaned over and kissed her soft, withered cheek. Pulling back, I blurted, "I love you." It wasn't the way we'd been used to talk to each other, but maybe I shouldn't have taken so much for granted. So I stumbled on, trying to cram into a few minutes the appreciation I should have expressed hundreds of times over the years, saying sorry for all my sins and omissions. Such talk would have embarrassed her,

I knew, if she'd heard me, and made her worry that I was unhappy, so she would have struggled to reassure me, and we'd have ended up in a welter of awkward misunderstanding—I could only make things worse at this late stage by apologizing for things I could not, and did not deeply even *want* to change—so I shut up as abruptly as I'd begun.

Still not a flicker from her; only her breathing continued, painful-sounding and slow.

After awhile, unable to bear the silence, I whispered, "I wish I could do something." She had done so much for me. She had always been the one to give, and I had simply taken. My mother was one of those old-fashioned women—I believe a few still exist, somewhere—who defined herself by her relationship to others. She lived through her family and the people who needed her help, and for her the reward was in the doing. She never resented the demands of others, yet found it difficult to ask for anything for herself. She would have liked half-a-dozen children but had to make do with me, the only baby she managed to carry to term, and at an age when she'd nearly given up hope. She'd cared for my father's brain-damaged younger sister for many years, and had nursed her own mother through her final illness—she'd actually moved into my grandmother's house when she could no longer cope on her own. The move itself was no sacrifice—my father was still alive then and went along with her quite happily to live in the bigger house—and my grandmother was of a generation and social standing who'd hired servants as a matter of course, so it wasn't like my mother became a drudge tied down to household chores—but, to me, such a life, such an obligation was unthinkable. I had always been free in my life and my loves, free to come and go as I chose and follow my own personal star. As long as I made enough to support myself—and, somehow, I'd always managed—there were no restraints on my freedom.

Since my father's death I was the only family my mother had left. At any time in the past six years I might have received the call I dreaded, the summons to Houston to decide her fate, supervise her care, put

her into a home, take responsibility for someone sadly broken by age . . .
I had dreaded it, but it had never happened. She'd remained *compos
mentis* and physically fit despite increasing frailness. She'd gone on
living alone in that big house with the aid of a housekeeper and a few
younger friends, and I'd never been put to the test.

A worm of doubt twisted in my gut. Not just chance, was it? Not
just good luck for both of us. She knew what I was like. Of course she
wouldn't ask. She would sacrifice herself rather than become a burden
to me.

I shouldn't have waited to be asked.

My throat ached. I wanted to cry now that it was too late for
anything but self-pity.

She opened her eyes and gazed vaguely in my direction. My heart
gave a lurch. I swallowed my regrets and leaned forward. "Ma." I
squeezed her hand gently. "How do you feel?"

"Not much . . . not much longer."

I shivered. "Can I get you anything? Do anything for you?"

The faintest of smiles moved her mouth and I felt her fingers stir in
my grasp. She was stroking my hand. Even at the last, she was more
concerned about me.

"I mean it. Anything. If there's anything I can do. I know it's too
little, too late, but . . . I love you. You know that? And I'm sorry
. . ." I took a shaky breath, mastered myself. "Sorry if I've been a
disappointment to you. You know, never giving you a grandchild, my
crazy lifestyle, living so far away and all . . ."

"Shhh, shhh." The gentle hushing sound reminded me of all the
times she'd soothed me when I was feverish or scared, over-tired, or
simply in a temper.

"I just wanted you to know. And I wish I'd done more to show you
I love you. I wish there was something I could do *now*."

Then I shut my mouth, aware that I was doing it again, turning it
around, making it all about *me*. I wanted her to give me her blessing;
that's what this was really about.

She didn't answer right away, and an expression I couldn't interpret flickered across her face, and then she sighed very faintly. "I don't like to ask . . ."

My heart gave a startled leap. "Ma! Anything. What is it?"

"The house is yours. I left it to you."

I didn't know what to say. I had assumed I'd inherit everything she left, but I'd never asked about her will. If she'd decided to divide her property among several deserving charities, or give it to her church, that was her right. I wouldn't take it to court.

Her voice came out dry and whispery. "But you don't want it, you'll sell it. Won't you?"

I shrugged, equivocating, but of course I meant to sell. What else? She was my only remaining link to this city; I'd returned over the years only for her sake. The house was lovely, but I wasn't going to live in it, whereas I could live on the proceeds for years; maybe, with wise investments, forever. "Maybe . . . if you don't mind."

She closed her eyes. "I can't ask . . ."

My pulse pounded. What was it, this sacrifice? Something to prove my love? Did she want me to give up my claim to her property? "Yes, you can," I said, and hated the tremor in my voice. "Ask. I'll do whatever you want."

She opened her eyes. "He needs to be looked after. He won't have anyone after I'm gone."

That wasn't what I'd expected at all. "You want me to give the house to someone?"

Her brow furrowed. "No—of course not. He doesn't need it. The house is yours. He's used to it, but I don't think it matters where he lives."

"Ma, I'm not with you. I don't understand what you want me to do."

She sighed. "I want you to take care of him. He needs someone. And you . . ."

"Who are you talking about?"

Her pale eyebrows rose in astonishment. "Mr. Boudreaux, of course."

That was a name I hadn't heard in years.

Old Mr. Boudreaux was my grandmother's fancy man.

I'm not sure where I picked up that expression, but as a child it appealed to me, and it seemed an appropriate label for the little old man who shared Nanny's house. He was someone who had caught her fancy, someone she was sweet on, someone sweet and desirable like those tiny little cakes called fancies, covered in thick, sweet icing in appealing pastel colors.

Of course it caused a scandal when Nanny came back from a trip to New Orleans with a strange man on her arm and then, without a word of explanation, without the slightest attempt to give a veneer of social acceptability to their relationship, set up home with him. She sold the house in River Oaks and moved the two of them into the mansion her late husband had commissioned but never lived to see finished. This was a shocking thing in the social circles she'd previously presided over, and she was never allowed to forget it.

"Why don't you and Mr. Boudreaux get married?" I remember asking my grandmother once. Children tend to accept whatever happens in their family as the norm, but I knew this wasn't right because my parents were disturbed by Nanny's behavior.

"Marriage is for younger folks, Darlin'," she replied. "I don't need to get married again, and Mr. Boudreaux is *far* too old for that kind of carry-on."

I never knew the man's first name, or anything about his existence before he took up with my grandmother. It wasn't like there was some big mystery about it; simply, I'd never cared enough to ask. Adult relationships had been of no interest to me as a child, and when I was grown up I was too absorbed in my own relationships with contemporaries to spare much thought for older generations. I imagined he'd passed away within weeks or months of my grandmother's death, if not several years before.

Certainly, I believed he was dead when I promised my dying mother that I would look after him. Yes, truly, for as long as he needed me. Of course I didn't mind! I'd be happy to do it. It was like reassuring a child who still believed in Santa Claus, and although I didn't think there was any harm in it, I was sorry to have to lie to her, saddened that my mother, who had been so alert and engaged with the world all her life should, at the last, have slipped into a muddled dream of times past.

But how like my mother it was: even on her deathbed she was worrying about other people.

Peace settled on her after I gave my promise. She did not say another word. She died, perhaps an hour later, with me still holding her hand.

Nanny's house—that was how I still thought of it—had been built on ten acres of uncultivated woodland, well outside the city limits when my grandfather bought it back in the 1940s. Since then, Houston had grown like a ravenous amoeba, spreading in all directions. The freeway system had expanded and new neighborhoods had popped up with all the accompanying services, schools and shopping malls a modern family could want. What had been a rural area even in my childhood was now suburban, and much in demand. At any time since Nanny's death my parents could have sold some or all of the surrounding acres for a pot of money, but they hadn't. I know they liked the privacy and quiet, the sensation of being deep in the country, when they were actually just a short drive away from a particularly nice shopping center, and everything else the city could offer.

Getting away from the hospital complex took me some time, and navigating the freeways was a nerve-wracking experience, but once I'd managed, more by luck than skill, to force my way across four lanes to the necessary exit, the rest of the route was a piece of cake. As I drove along the winding, tree-lined residential streets I relaxed, comfortable here in a way I could not understand. I thought of myself as European—by choice, sensibility and heritage, if not actual birthright—and I had lived abroad for nearly four decades. I'd tell anyone who asked that Houston's climate was inhuman, unbearable for most of the year, and the social-political climate was no better. I'd left as soon as I could, never wanted to live there again, and yet . . . and yet . . . Being here was something else. The physical atmosphere acted upon me like some terrifying truth serum, forcing me to admit that, like it or not, on some level, here was where I belonged.

I eased up on the gas. Even before I saw the old metal mailbox, still leaning at a slight angle, I'd anticipated it, and was slowing to take the turn. As the car moved, bumping and swaying on the uneven, pot-holed driveway into the mysteriously cool, shadowy, pine-scented tunnel created by the trees that so closely lined it, I imagined it was carrying me into a lost world, like Conan Doyle's, a primeval pocket universe out of time. It was a fantasy I used to savor on every visit, well into my teens. Memories bubbled up from my past, mostly the books: *The Lost World*, *Dwellers in the Mirage*, *Fu Manchu*, *She*, old hardbacks by Talbot Mundy, P.C. Wren, Louise Gerard, E.M. Hull and Richard Halliburton. Nanny's bookshelves were full of exotic delights, adventure stories, romances and travel books from long ago. I was happy to read while the grown-ups talked or played cards, and when, inevitably, I was ordered to stop ruining my eyes and go outside to get some fresh air I'd smuggle a book out with me. The best place to read about lost worlds and adventurers hacking their way through the Matto Grosso was in some private corner of the mysterious uncharted wilderness all around me.

The house finally came into view, familiar as my mother's face. It was a handsome building modeled on some New Orleans mansion, and back when it was built it was considered awfully grand, especially for its primitive setting, too far from the city for convenience. But times had changed. While I continued to inhabit a cramped little apartment in Paris, most Americans lived, and built, on an increasingly grandiose scale. It was no longer unusual for bathrooms to outnumber the bedrooms in a house, and while the house had come to seem more ordinary (would anyone call it a "mansion" today?) the undeveloped acres all around it constituted prime real estate.

I parked the car on the turning circle and tried to look at the house objectively. It was over sixty years old, there might be structural problems, very likely the central heating and air conditioning systems needed replacing. But it would sell. Someone would buy it, whatever the drawbacks, if only for the land it stood on.

I got out of the car and inhaled the scent of dry earth and pine-needles that could not cover the swampy, fecund odor of the bayou underneath. A mosquito whined past my ear. I felt the sweat gluing my clothes to my skin, and I turned my back on the forest and went indoors.

It was much cooler there, even though the air conditioning had been set to the lowest level. The cold bare marble floor in the front hall had something to do with the almost chilly atmosphere, I suppose. Pale wooden shutters—my mother's improvement on Nanny's dust-gathering drapes—filtered out the harshest rays of the sun. I went into the big living room where the atmosphere, the subtle ambient scents of furniture polish, flowers, room freshener, whatever it was, spoke to me so immediately and intimately of home that I was put at my ease. It had always been like that, I'd always loved coming here. It didn't seem possible that my mother was dead, and this house was mine alone.

The house did not feel empty. I shivered as the sweat dried on my skin, and I recalled the promise I'd made to my dying mother. I couldn't remember when Mr. Boudreaux had died. Surely I would have been told. I didn't think he'd been present at Nanny's funeral. He must have predeceased her. Although I'd never known much about him, I'd had the impression that he was a good deal older than my grandmother, and she'd been over ninety when she died. But even if he'd been a few years younger—even a decade younger—it was now twenty years on . . .

My skin crawled as I imagined a shriveled, dehydrated old man lying in his own filth in one of the bedrooms upstairs.

I'd promised my mother I'd take care of him.

I forced myself up the stairs before I could chicken out. My ears straining for a faint moan or whimper, I checked out each and every room.

Finally I managed to calm down, reassured that I really was alone in the big house. I felt a bit sheepish. Just because my mother had slipped into the past for a few moments at the end of her life was no reason for me to get crazy.

Every room was clean and tidy, kept that way by the housekeeper, and lack of use. The only bedroom showing any sign of recent occupation was my mother's: there was an empty water glass on the bedside table along with a little tin of Altoids and a book-marked paperback of *The Joy Luck Club*. The bed was made up, but there was an indentation visible in the cotton coverlet, showing where someone had sat down on it.

I sat down there, where my mother had been, and suddenly felt dizzy with grief and exhaustion. I lay back, my head on the pillow, and the faintest whiff of her perfume (Chamade) brought the tears stinging my eyes. For distraction, I thought about Mr. Boudreaux, dredging my memory for some solid facts about him. How had he managed to remain such a stranger? He'd always been around throughout my childhood, the quiet, little old man who lived in my grandmother's house. He rarely spoke to me that I could recall; we certainly never bonded; I don't think I'd ever spent time with him alone. Why would I? A closer friendship between us was not forbidden, simply unattractive. We weren't even related.

I could barely remember him now, although I'd seen him several times a month for the whole of my childhood and adolescence. No matter how I searched my memory, his face refused to come back to me. His only significance was due to the scandalous cloud that hung over his long and apparently contented relationship with my grandmother. It was generally assumed that they never married because of some legal obstacle: he had a wife already, who would not allow his remarriage. Or else there was something in my grandfather's will that prohibited it. Both these "reasons" seemed unlikely to me.

Nanny had loved Mr. Boudreaux; she was rich and he had nothing but her. How would he manage if she died first? Had Nanny invoked a promise from her daughter like the one I'd just made my mother? Who was Mr. Boudreaux, and what had happened to him?

When I opened my eyes again the room was dark, and I was well-rested. Checking the clock, I figured out it must be nearly dawn, and that I'd slept for over ten hours. After washing, I went downstairs and drank a cup of instant coffee as I watched the sun come up through the trees.

When I went outside to get my bag out of the car, I was surprised by how pleasantly fresh the air felt. Since I'd left, I'd come to believe Houston outdoors was unfit for human habitation except in winter. It was now high summer, and my body responded to the ambient temperature with a greedy desire that took me by surprise. The heat would be unbearable later, so I decided to make the most of it, and set off for a walk right away, leaving my bag beside the car.

As soon as I left the driveway I plunged into the murk of the pine woods. Nostalgia rose, powerful as sickness, when I breathed in the familiar scent of the land. It was strong and contradictory, mixing fresh and foul odors. One part was the clean, resinous scent of pine, along with the subtle, baked smell of the earth, but mingling and merging with this goodness was the fetid reek of rotting vegetation and stagnant water. It was an odor more distinctive than that of any of the cities I'd known—Paris, London, Amsterdam, Hong Kong—and it stirred old emotions.

Not until that moment had I realized how much I missed it. Or how primal the feeling for a place could be.

It was like the smell of a living body, like catching the whiff of another person—not always repellent, whatever deodorant manufacturers would have you believe. Especially not when it's someone dear to you.

I was suddenly as thrilled and eager as I'd ever been as a child embarking on exploration.

Houston was originally settled on the banks of Buffalo Bayou, but most people, locals or visitors, seemed barely aware of it as a waterway. The bayou wasn't at the heart of the city, intrinsic to it the way the Thames was to London, or the Seine to Paris. Of course, it wasn't a river. I still remembered the definition I'd copied down in Texas History class for "bayou": "a slow-moving creek or stream." To me, it was much more than that.

I had grown up in a very ordinary, very boring residential subdivision of the city, full of little brick boxes built not long after the war. Even the trees were the same age as the houses, all planted a regulation distance apart—there wasn't a scrap of nature or wildness in the neighborhood, not so much as a tangled, overgrown garden or an abandoned house that could have been haunted. My family didn't travel or go on exotic vacations. My only taste of something different, of a bigger, more primitive world, apart from the books I read incessantly, came from our regular visits to my grandmother. Her house occupied a mysterious borderland between the ordinary suburban world I lived in and The Wilderness. Inside the woods, which began just a few yards beyond her house and encompassed a stretch of bayou, there existed countless other worlds. I could find anything there: dinosaur tracks, a magic playhouse, an Aztec temple, a lost civilization, buried treasure, warring tribes, magical talking beasts, the fountain of youth or the source of the Amazon . . . nothing seemed impossible.

Most of my memories of the adventures I'd had here in this ten-acre patch of scrubby woodland originated in someone else's imagination. They were my personal take on whatever book I happened to be reading, and if I could recall them with any degree of accuracy I was sure they would only embarrass me. What mattered was the emotion, the happiness I'd known in this place—that's what I was so eager to recapture.

What added to the charm, I'm sure, was that it was so private. I didn't share it with anyone. I had no brothers, sisters or cousins, and never took any friends along on these family visits. I learned early not to talk to the adults about what I got up to. To them, the bayou was a source of danger and contamination. It was polluted with sewage and industrial waste, it was a source of disease-carrying mosquitoes and the home for at least three different varieties of poisonous snakes. I was strictly forbidden from swimming in it, and although I always kept to the rule about not swimming alone, I did sometimes just wade in the clear-running shallows. Afraid that if they were reminded of it too often they might eventually forbid me to play there at all, I kept quiet about it.

Now, as I plunged deeper into the woods, eager to return to the bayou, the old passion rose up again, making me forget my age. I'd never forgotten this part of my childhood; it was too basic to who I was, but for the first time it seemed strange to me that I'd never tried to go back, to make my way through the familiar woods and look upon the bayou again. It was as inexplicable as if I'd stopped visiting some close relative. After all, I'd kept coming back to Houston—in the last decade I'd managed a visit every year to see my parents.

I had to stop to disentangle myself from a bush. I paused, wiped the sweat out of my eyes, and fanned my face ineffectually with one hand, knowing it was probably blotched with red. Although I hadn't gone very far, I was already breathless and much too hot. Insects buzzed and whined about my head, and my right arm was stinging: I saw a blood-beaded line where a thorny branch must have caught me.

Where was the path?

In my memory, there were several distinct trails I could take down to the bayou. But now that I considered it, unless my grandmother used to give her yard man special instructions, the only person who could have cleared a trail was either me or Mr. Boudreaux. Whatever existed back in the 1960s would have disappeared long ago.

For a moment, I thought about giving up.

There was a very good reason for not returning to a childhood playground, and that was that I was no longer a child. I was one of the grown-ups now, aware there was more chance of picking up a tick (which might give me Lyme disease) or stepping on a copperhead (whose bite might *kill* me) than there was of discovering something truly wonderful in these woods. I no longer believed in magic, and knew too much about geography and history to imagine I might stumble across the ruins of an old Aztec or Mayan temple.

But when I looked around behind me I couldn't see the house. Reasoning that it might take me just as long to struggle back to it as it would to press on and be rewarded by the sight of the bayou, I decided to continue.

With an effort, trying not to think of snakes or worry about poison ivy or biting insects among the mass of undergrowth surrounding me, I forced my way ahead and eventually—probably no more than five minutes later—the forest thinned, and I found myself standing on a sand-and-clay bank, a few feet above a wide, gleaming stretch of brown water.

I was amazed at how well this peaceful vision matched my memory. The bayou, winding away into woodland, overhung by trees, was beautiful and mysterious and roused a feeling in my heart that I'd class somewhere between aesthetic pleasure and religious awe. Although I'm very much a city person—or maybe because of it—my occasional encounters with nature produce a powerful impact, making me realize there's a lot more to the world than I know. Of course, I usually forget this insight a moment after I've had it. Or at least I continue to live as if I had.

I looked down at the darkly glinting water and wondered about its depth. A stone at the water's edge moved, and I caught my breath, imagining I'd seen something impossible, then recognized it as a turtle, one of four, basking in the early sun. I heard the sharp, impatient hammer of a woodpecker in the woods behind me. More distantly came the unending, windy rushing sound I knew must be the freeway traffic, but apart from that, which was easily ignored, it was quiet. It was almost impossible to believe this land actually existed, unknown and unspoiled, *inside* a big city. I felt as if I'd stepped back in time, or been transported in space—like a child again.

I didn't want to leave.

The heat, the scratch on my arm, worries about tick bites and snakes—they no longer bothered me. I made my way along the embankment. With the bayou to follow, I didn't need a path. My old passion for exploring had hold of me again.

The scenery became more and more familiar; a feeling I distrusted. I had to be kidding myself. It was forty years since I'd roamed these woods, and even the natural course of the stream had probably changed in that time.

But it was more than a vague sense of *déjà vu*—I knew this place. Gradually, the banks rose higher from the water, and the sandy strand on this side widened out into a beach, which I remembered well as a favorite place to play. And there, where the bank rose up especially steeply, showing a pale, pitted face where nothing grew, that was "the cliff," and I'd practiced my mountaineering skills there. (Pathetic, yes, but the best I could do on this flat, coastal plain.) A little further along—my pace picked up as I remembered—there was a natural hollow that I'd managed to enlarge. I'd made it into "my cave" and it was a great place to escape the heat of the sun and curl up and read. And it was still there. After all this time, natural forces had not eroded it away. My little hidey-hole was still a snug retreat.

For a moment I regretted not having brought a book along, for old time's sake. And then I saw that somebody was there before me.

No. My heart gave a lurch, and I stopped and stared. There was something inside the "cave"—some blankets and maybe a cushion . . . ?

Were they mine? I remembered the trouble I'd gotten into when a couple of my grandmother's cushions went missing . . . how was I to know they were so special? But whatever was out here now, it could not be my grandmother's cushions. I'd returned my makeshift bed to the house, and my allowance had been docked for several months, to pay for specialist dry-cleaning.

It was the wrong color, anyway; not elegant cushions but something lumpy, off-white, beige, khaki . . . maybe a pile of old clothes. Some other children might have found their way to this hideout, or else it was only litter, deposited there when the waters rose above flood level.

I went closer, and then closer still, picking my way along the water's edge far more slowly and cautiously than I would have as a child, because there was a prickling, crawling sensation all down my back as I began to suspect it was something more, and worse, than a pile of rags.

It was a body. I stopped and fought the urge to turn and run away. Stupid to go running for help only to find out my deteriorating eyesight had tricked me. I made myself go closer, until I was absolutely sure. Yes, it was a body, small as a child.

Strangely, now that I was sure, I wasn't afraid. I wasn't even horrified. It was like a discovery made in a dream, where normal reactions are inappropriate.

Not so much calm as detached I went closer for a better look. It was not a child's body after all, but an old man's, and I wasn't sure he was dead.

"Mr. Boudreaux?"

I spoke on impulse, not because I recognized him, but simply because that was the name of the old man whose fate I'd been wondering about. And yet as soon as I spoke, everything changed. I saw for sure that he was still breathing, and as I gazed so intently at his face, trying to match it to one already in my memory, the waxy stillness of it softened beneath my gaze, almost as if my attention had brought him back to life. I looked from that ancient, sleeping face, to the hand I could see curled against his side, tiny and claw-like. If he wasn't Mr. Boudreaux, his presence here on my property became even more mysterious.

I looked around. There was no sound, as if the whole world held its breath. Sunlight lanced off the water below, unbearably bright.

"Mr. Boudreaux?" My voice trembled. "Mr. Boudreaux, is that really you?"

I stared down at the wizened figure curled into the hollowed-out space in the earth and saw his eyes were moving behind their closed lids. His breathing was so shallow that it scarcely lifted his sunken chest, but there was no doubt about it: he was breathing, was dreaming. Alive, but for how much longer?

I took a deep breath and spoke with determination. "I'm going to get help. I don't have a phone with me, so I'll have to go back to the house and call from there. I won't be long, I promise—"

His eyes flashed open. For a moment they seemed like a new baby's, unable to focus, but then they fastened on to my face, and he smiled with recognition. He tried to speak—the dry, cracked lips parted slightly, and I saw his tongue moving—but he made no sound.

"It's all right," I said gently. "I've found you, and I'm just going to get help."

I hadn't finished speaking when he put his arms out to me, and I realized that, of course, the simplest, quickest way to rescue him was to carry him back to the house myself. Once I'd given him some water and he'd had a chance to recover, he could tell me who to call. So I took hold of him, bracing myself for a weight that wasn't there. To my astonishment, he was lighter than a baby. I'd carried luggage that weighed more than him across half of Europe, not to mention up and down the steps of the Métro. And, unlike most burdens, he wasn't a dead weight. He wrapped his arms around my neck and pulled his legs up out of the way, to make it easier for me to carry him.

And it *was* easy—more than just easy, it was a pleasure. And this time I found the path right away, so had no problem in getting back to the house.

Inside, I put him down gently on the bigger of the two couches in the living room, propped him up among cushions, and fetched him a glass of water from the kitchen. I made sure it was lukewarm, and warned him not to drink too much or too quickly or he might make himself sick.

He smiled at me as if to say he'd been around long enough to know all about that, and took a careful sip. I watched in peaceful silence as he slowly drank the water. I had a lot of questions, of course, but they could wait.

He didn't want anything to eat, and he shook his head, a look of sadness on his face, when I asked if there was anyone I should call.

"Don't you have any family?"

Another slow, mournful turning of his head. Like me, he was all alone in the world. Maybe whoever had been taking care of him had gotten fed up and dumped him in the wilderness, or maybe he'd wandered off. I didn't know if he could speak or how well his thought processes worked. He seemed to understand everything I said perfectly well, but when I asked him his name he gave me a puzzled yet hopeful look, as if expecting me to supply it.

"Mr. Boudreaux?"

He gave me the same uncertain look. He couldn't remember, it said, but if that's what I wanted to call him . . . I sighed. "How about a bath?"

He brightened up at that, nodded, and held out his arms to be lifted with the perfect simplicity and trust of a young child.

This time, as I gathered him into my arms again, I recognized the feeling that flowed through me as love: not desire, not gratification, not as I'd ever felt it before, but something pure and strong and deep, the way I think a mother must love her child.

I carried him upstairs to the master bathroom, and settled him into a comfortably cushioned wicker basket chair to wait while I ran the bath. When I turned back to look at him and saw that he had not moved, he was waiting for me to undress him, I knew a little flicker of unease. I'd never undressed another person except erotically; I had no experience as a caregiver. But I think I managed to avoid any hesitation, even the slightest sign that I was uncomfortable.

I unbuttoned his shirt, and gestured for him to lean forward so I could slip it off. As I did so, I saw the scars on his back. Alongside his shoulder blades were two dark, curving lines, a parenthesis carved into his flesh. No accident had put them there; they spoke of ancient surgery, of an excision long ago.

I understood. He had been born—perhaps *created* is the better word—with wings. I could see them in my mind's eye, magnificently large and strong, bigger than a swan's, and covered entirely in glossy dark feathers, perhaps reddish brown, perhaps sable. Or maybe the feathers never had a chance to sprout; maybe the operation took place soon after his birth. However it was, it must have been traumatic for him. He was fearful, I could see, that having discovered his difference I would turn on him. Although it seemed impossible to me, I knew it must have happened before.

Carefully, with infinite tenderness, I embraced him.

"Welcome home," I whispered, and might have been speaking to myself.

A FEAST OF ANGELS

Jay Lake

ST. PETER MADE FRIEDRICH NIETZSCHE coroner of Heaven. Though Heaven stands outside time, all things there both concurrent and infinite, being human Nietzsche's perceptions were perforce more or less sequential. Heaven's coroner was a stultifying job, as death was unknown there.

"I am convinced," Nietzsche told Origen of Alexandria over a six-pack of Stroh's, "that this is my punishment." They sat at a picnic table on a small, isolated cloud.

The little Egyptian's hand spasmed, crinkling his own can of beer. "This is hell," he whispered. Lately they spoke American English, equally foreign to both. Also equally offensive in its colloquial imprecision. "The Adversary has crafted this eternity for such as us."

"Could be worse." Nietzsche stared down off their cloud at a bus loaded with joyful Charismatics bound for Branson, Missouri, on a three-day pass. "We could be with *them*."

"Though all days in Heaven are the same, still I have been here a very long time." Origen tugged another Stroh's off the six-pack. "There *have* been worse things. Old Hermes Trimegistus got it wrong. As below, so above."

Nietzsche shuddered, imagining the Heaven of the Inquisition, or John Calvin. Origen had lived through them both. Aimee Semple McPherson had been bad enough for him.

St. Peter appeared, pot-bellied and irritated. His robes were askew and his halo appeared to have developed a crack. "We've got a problem."

"This is Heaven," said Nietzsche. "There are no problems."

Origen burped for emphasis, the yeasty odor of recycled Stroh's disturbing Heaven's usual pine-scented freshness.

Peter frowned, obviously picking his words with care. "This problem has always existed, but now I wish to address it."

"Sh-sh-shimultaneity," said Origen, who had been talking to Einstein lately. "No shuch thing."

Nietzsche shot Origen a hard glare. "What kind of trouble?"

"Coroner trouble," said Peter.

"In *Heaven*? I thought you were just yanking my chain."

"Consider yourself yanked," said Peter darkly. "We need you now."

"Now is the same as then in Heaven," muttered Nietzsche, disentangling himself from the picnic table. "Where are we going?"

"Other end of time," said Peter.

"Hot dog," Origen shouted. He vaulted over the table after Nietzsche and St. Peter. "I always wanted to see Creation."

They stood on nothing, slightly above a rough-textured plain receding into darkness. Scattered vegetation struggled from the surface; thin, sword-like plants. The only light was from St. Peter's Heavenly effulgence. Somewhere nearby, water lapped against an unseen shore. Unlike the rest of Heaven, this place stank of mold and rust and an odor of damp rock.

"I'm impressed," observed Nietzsche. "What is this? The root cellar?"

"Foundations, more like it," Peter said.

They both glanced at Origen, who looked intently into the darkness. Peter waved his staff and the three of them, still standing on nothing, began to cruise over the landscape. Nietzsche found this far more unnerving than Heaven's usual cloudscape.

"Clouds," said Peter, "simply hide the unsettling reality."

Nietzsche stared at him.

Peter shrugged. "This close to the source, thoughts are words."

"Mind your soul." Origen spoke quietly. He sounded very sober.

There was a glimmering of light ahead, a false dawn that grew into a constellation of fireflies as they approached.

"This is the problem." Peter's voice was stony and grim. "This has always been the problem."

The fireflies became bonfires, and the bonfires became a sky full of light, and the sky full of light became a host of angels, in their naked majesty all swords and pinions and flames and power, burrowing amongst ribs larger than rivers.

Angels feasting on the corpse of God.

Like maggots eating Leviathan.

"His bones are the world's," Origen said quietly. "His flesh is the world's. I was right. The Adversary did create Earth to torment us."

"Heaven stands outside time," Peter declared. "The world is made, for the first time and anew, over and over. For ever and ever."

"So what do we do?" Nietzsche asked. "Is this the beginning, or the end?"

Peter turned to Nietzsche, laid one trembling hand on his shoulder. "Make it different this time. You have free will. He made you so. Break the cycle and create us a better world."

"I have no power here."

"You are Heaven's coroner."

"God is dead," Nietzsche whispered.

"Long live God," Peter echoed.

"The Earth was without form and void," said Origen.

Though it took time beyond measure for them to see the difference, mountains rose from His bones, while the terrible angels birthed snakes who would someday be teachers of men in their innocence.

TRANSFIGURATION
Richard Christian Matheson

RICHARD CHRISTIAN MATHESON is a film and television writer, producer and director. He has worked with Bryan Singer, Steven Spielberg and Roger Corman, among others; he has also written and/or produced three mini-series, eight feature films and thirty pilots, plus hundreds of comedic/dramatic television series episodes for HBO, TNT, NBC, CBS, ABC, Showtime Networks, Fox Network and Syfy.

He has also published two short story collections and a novel. Matheson is a studio musician who studied with Ginger Baker of Cream and has played drums with the Smithereens and Rock Bottom Remainders. He has worked as a paranormal investigator for UCLA and is considered an expert in parapsychology. He runs his own production company in Los Angeles and The Matheson Company with his father, famed fantasy writer Richard Matheson.

Describing the original story that follows, the author is typically succinct: "The North Slope of Alaska is an oblivion. To those who risk passage, death is always near, and I wanted to somehow capture its anonymity and haunted lure. Which lead me to the road that slashes it; a two-lane, in arctic void, where ugly secrets and desolation dwell. A man could go mad."

IT IS EASY TO BECOME disoriented here. Snow is everywhere and the corners of the world soften and vanish. Sometimes when I dream, I watch myself drilling the thick, blue ice. I bore a large opening and stand over it, then slip through. I slide into the ancient sea beneath and, as currents gently sweep me away, my pained thoughts ease. I look up, through the ice, to see a place I never belonged, that never wanted me. Then, I close my eyes and fall asleep. I am finally home.

Angels come out at night, restless and far from Heaven.

We like to move about when the sun dies and we can more easily pass for human. The night hides our secret and our tasks. It is not known where we dwell—whether in the air, the void or the planets, as some have noted, but whether by thrones or dominions, we were created to convey His will to men. We like cold places and are not subject to death, or any form of extinction, extradition or censure. As divine soldiers, we keep order in an impure, Godless world, and I do what I must to serve Him. No matter the cost.

I am seventy miles north of Fairbanks, where pavement dead-ends and the Alaskan Highway turns into Dalton Highway; a hypnotic, gravel throat that stretches 414 miles across vast, plains of snow, all the way to Deadhorse, on the remote North Slope oil fields, at Prudhoe Bay. Bluish ice and dry snow surround the two-lane I'm on, as if infinite square miles of suffocated flesh and, on indefinable horizon, it collides with white-capped peaks that rise up from the bleakness like paralyzed waves.

Dalton is the "haul road" for eighteen-wheelers like mine and when it isn't trying to kill you, the road takes you straight to where North America, for good or bad, finally runs out of land and surrenders to frigid sea. Along the way, I pass "Coldfoot" and "Beaver Slide" and, at mile 75, "Roller Coaster," where the icy, two-lane goes down steep, fast, then up steeper, making big rigs like mine slip and lose their grip. They'll tumble sideways, over and over, crushing the cab and driver, and when you come upon the mangle it makes you sick. People should die for a better reason.

These plains are violent and primitive and it's a killing field when winter hits. I've seen bad ones at Avalanche Alley, near mid-point; a man-eating gust of winter flipped a married couple's rig and shoved them through the windshield onto hard ice. Wolves finished them off. The weather's usually out to get you, so freezing to death is the easy way out. You can feel it. Arctic skies stare down at you, on the two-lane, where spruces huddle and the frozen Yukon River is still as sculpted glass. When I drive beside it, I imagine fish, posed motionlessly in the frozen river like you see them sometimes in modern paintings. There is an incompleteness to this place that makes your mind fill things in. A gloom and need. But that isn't why I come.

To get to Deadhorse, I tank up a grand of diesel, two big thermoses of black coffee and some candy bars. Sugar and caffeine wind me just right. I always have my notebook, too. I like to keep track. Dates; descriptions. My ride is a thirteen-speed, dual-stack, diesel Kenworth. Whole shebang grosses out at 88,000 pounds fully packed. 475 horsepower, eighteen aluminum wheels, tandem axles, Ultra-Shift, Air-Suspension. Sleeper, too. Only home I ever had and a hell of lot better than what I was born into. But even when a man dies inside, it's only the beginning. *Hebrews 12:22–23* says that when we get to Heaven we will be met by a myriad of angels, and spirits of righteous men will be made perfect. Myths of hopelessness are just that and do no one good.

My twin, thirty-foot trailers get filled with groceries, medicine, cars; anything you can't get where it drops to fifty below. Deadhorse trucks in everything life in a lifeless place needs, maybe some it doesn't. Truckers are a transfusion for the isolated workers of the Conoco

Philips North Slope facility, every one of them trapped like cubes in an ice tray. As for the road, the Dalton has strict rules:

1) ALWAYS DRIVE WITH HEADLIGHTS ON.
2) WATCH THE ROAD AHEAD AND BEHIND FOR PLUMES OF DUST OR SNOW SIGNALING ANOTHER VEHICLE.
3) BEFORE PASSING, MAKE SURE OPERATORS OF OTHER VEHICLES KNOW YOU'RE THERE.
4) DO NOT STOP ON THE ROAD. IF YOU CAN'T GET OFF THE ROAD, PULL FAR TO THE RIGHT AND ACTIVATE YOUR HAZARD LIGHTS.
5) RESPECT THE SPEED LIMIT BECAUSE IF A RIG GOES TOO FAST, ITS WEIGHT WILL CREATE WAVES UNDER THE ICE THAT WILL MAKE THE ROAD BUCKLE AND COLLAPSE.

Now and then, overweight rigs driving over the limit drop through the cracking road, where it thins, and disappear like they were never there; I've seen huge carriers devoured by a big, jagged mouth in the road, the sloshing, polar sea beneath. Sometimes God needs a sacrifice. Sometimes the road is complicit. No life is sacrosanct.

Visibility is always an issue out here and when reflector posts vanish in white-outs, we chain our rigs together and ride it out, sitting in our cabs, listening to starved winds trying to get in. Snow can fill up the air intakes and choke you to death, so I keep my engine running even though the truck heater doesn't keep me warm. In bone-deep cold, blood slows and you can hear it throb in your ears like a dying heart.

Out here, no one knows you, no one cares, no one takes an interest. We come, we go. There's no cameras, no checkpoints. I could be anybody. Do anything. God's work requires the clandestine and though angels may have flesh which resembles polished metal or faces like lightning, I wander free of such telling detail.

During the '74 oil crisis, the Dalton got carved in six months, borne of lies and avarice. It was clawed from denuded nowhere and runs alongside the massive veins of the 800-mile Trans Alaska Pipeline that runs from Deadhorse to the port at Valdez. Long-haulers do the four hundred miles, but they all know it's a bad road, a bad bet. Some don't make it. The oil company doesn't care. There's always vultures. Ask me, people like that don't deserve to live. Add them to the fucking list.

Driving the ice-road seems to go on forever; like being lost at sea. You can't get a cell phone to work past mile 28, but there's no one I want to talk to. People waste my time. Exploit my best intentions. I prefer being alone, in my rig, not having to talk or listen. I've heard it all. Lies disguised as prayers, lust masqueraded as faith. We live in dire times and I am sanctioned by our Father to do something about it. All things have been created by Him and for Him. And He is before all things, and in Him all things hold together. For He shall give His angels charge over earth.

Those who forget that cannot die enough times.

Going down a slope, my dual stacks belch scarves of exhaust and when weather's decent, I get lost in the locomotive hum of my tires on gravel. It puts me in a trance and lets me forget bad things; at least try. The worst nights, you come across accidents. Agonized faces, pinned under steel, begging for relief. Jack-knifes, rear-enders, head-ons. I kneel and calm them as life seeps from their scared eyes.

At the three-quarter mark, my rig strains through Atigun Pass, at 4,752 feet. Air gets thin and birds and animals don't come out much. The tundra is a sheet of uncrumpled, white paper as I stare at amber halogens, drink my fourth cup of black. Long-haul truckers are ants who never looked up, escorting cargo through frozen wasteland, and they don't realize that angels can take on the appearance of men when the occasion demands and so they are imprisoned. It is said a book must be "the ax for the frozen sea within us" referring certainly to the Scriptures. Half-frozen seas surround any life, threatening to wash people away. Life is a condemned promise and someone must pay.

They say drivers see things out here.

Apparitions or ghosts or the lingering energy of those who have died or whatever word you can live with. Once, on a brutal run, when I hadn't slept in almost forty hours, I saw my dead father standing bloodied in the middle of the road, grinning in that hateful way he did the day he was taken from this world. But he was one of those people who never totally die because they leave a terrible dent inside you and your mind can't let go.

The aboriginal people up here say the dead seek salvation, but it is not because they are spirits that they might be angels; they become angels when they are chosen. And only the chosen are raised up. The rest burn; their debased souls punished, their flesh disemboweled.

Last month, snow flurries were hammering me from all directions, and I swore I saw my brother beside the road in the white mayhem, screaming and running from something that terrified him, his long legs getting stuck in the deep drifts as he looked over at me with pleading eyes. He mouthed my name though I couldn't hear it with my windows up. But the way he died all came back. Another day I'd like to forget. But those are the days you can't.

Out here, wait long enough, everything comes back.

I've seen other people, too, in the hungry, falling snow, even though I know they're long gone. They stare at me, helplessly, as they dart in front of my headlights and the grille smashes their flesh and bones and they're swept under the truck. I know they were just mirages.

The Big Blank.

That's what long-haulers call it up here. It's when the outside world and your thoughts merge, a perilous weave that undermines sanity. Sometimes the soft powder takes on human shape. Milky silhouettes, without detail, who somehow want something. Fatigue breeds dark thoughts; every big-rigger and long-hauler knows it. The mind is a complicated thing and a childhood like mine is no help. Even angels suffer. God sees to that for his own reasons.

Things do bother me.

When I've been awake for too long, my mind loosens and sometimes I imagine skidding off the road and dying in the crush of my overturning rig. I quietly bleed in the cold, and the snowy shapes circle me until I can't breathe. I fight them, but it is always too late. Angels can't die yet I imagine it.

A psychiatrist at that place once told me it was a *projection*. Like with movies. Light passes through the film and it gets bigger on the screen. I guess he was saying thought and faith have that kind of power. But he had no fucking idea who he was dealing with.

I reach the Ice-Cut grade, a steep climb with sheer drops on both sides, and grip the wheel tightly. When I'm going fast, my tires hiss on the frosted flatness, like a monster's sled, and the tire tracks disappear as ice instantly re-seals. I rumble across the road, bite into a Butterfinger and watch the speedometer. I stay ahead of schedule so I can stop if I need to. Lick chocolate off my fingers and watch for approaching headlights in my rear-views and ahead. Scan for plumes of white, jutting and hovering over roadway, see none and finally know I'm alone.

I slowly pull over in the solitude.

There is something sad out here. Sometimes I hear wolves, mourning in the desolation. If I'm very quiet and still, I feel sleepless tides roaming under the ice. Mostly, I hear nothing until the winds anger, shoving my eighteen-wheeler like it's in their way. I glance at my watch and know I must move quickly. I pull on leather gloves, parka and goggles, leave the engine idling and get out.

The air freezes my face, as winds howl and tangle and my amber halogens leave orange-peel streaks on falling flakes. Diesel ghosts from the chrome stacks as I lean down, unlock the storage space under my driver's door, and withdraw my rechargeable ice-fishing drill. I remove it from its case, quickly find a patch of thinner ice beside my rig and trudge toward it. Fifteen miles behind me, headlights flare on a far rise; another rig will be here in ten minutes.

I re-check my watch, grip the drill with both gloved hands, press the five-foot-long bit onto the frozen ground. The high torque and fast rotation allow me to work quickly before the other rig shows. The bladed teeth bite into the hard ice and, as winds rake, I begin to drill a fifteen-inch diameter opening. The grind of the motor makes my arms shake and curlicues of ice cover my waterproof boots. The whirling bit finally reaches the sea, five feet below, and I reverse the drill, pull it out, check the opening. Replace the drill in its case and toss it back in the storage compartment. Then, I grab the cinched canvas bag beside it.

I open it and begin to empty its contents into the hole.

I am at home out here. Angels have authority over the natural world, even when people don't realize their time has come. Hell is a self-inflicted state of mind and people get what they goddamned deserve whether they like it or not.

As I work, I like it best when the snow falls audibly; a hushed downpour. Sometimes, what I drop in goes easily, sliding into the water beneath the ice road. Sometimes, I have to use a knife to cut it to size. Once the bag is empty, I fill the opening back up with snow, kicking it in, and pack it down with my heavy soles. It disappears fast in the cascading white, as if miraculously healed, and I get back in my idling rig.

I watch stars fight for their moment in overcast sky. Thank the Holy Father. In *Genesis 18*, Abraham welcomed angelic guests who appeared to be nothing more than common travelers. Truth disguises itself when necessary.

I flip on the overhead fog lights and they cast sick glow as the other truck finally passes with a high-beam nod and I lower my visor to block the glare. But I never look at myself in the hinge-down mirror. Prayer cannot repair flesh so ravaged. I have learned to accept shame and rage. There have always been sightings of angels who appear to be a man with unusual features. But I hate God for allowing this to fucking happen to me.

My tires leave grimy waffle marks on the road and snow carpets the ground behind me like I was never there. Snow is like time. It covers whatever it touches with a new layer of meaning that replaces the previous one and the one before that. Out here, it paints over everything and this 414 mile, barren forever is a place of temporary fact, of evidence erased.

Except for more headlights that approach from miles ahead, the Big Blank is shiny and black now, drawing me to Prudhoe Bay. I stare at the wide beams, the rushing dotted line. Long-haulers call it the *Zipper* and swear if you look at it too long, it gets inside you; does bad things. As I near Deadhorse, it's 3:36 a.m. and seventeen below. Tall, sodium-vapor lights spill on the road and there are no trees, only machines, mechanical shadows. There isn't even a church. It tells you everything. Where there is no God, impulse and pain rule. I have seen it.

Steam blasts from industrial structures and workers are up, walking around in parkas; shifts that come and go twenty-four hours a day, an exhausted army of detached, clock-less zombies, deserted by friends and families who loathe them. Most are liars. None can love. Thousands come and go, less than twenty-five live here. It is a soulless, transient dungeon and if they knew who I was, they would fall to their knees, ask for forgiveness.

Let them die for sins they relish.

I drop my haul at the transportation yard, get paid, buy a hot meal at the diner, check into the Prudhoe Bay Hotel, a one-story outcropping that squats in this gulag.

The frozen Atlantic Ocean nearby is mostly slush without visible tide and the local hardware store operates out of a thrashed doublewide. It's open 24/7, even during white-outs, and their policy is if they don't have it, you don't need it. I drop in to buy replacement gloves, hacksaw blades. Go back to my room.

Try to sleep.

Snowdrifts are up to the windows, and I drink scotch and watch the septic swirls of smoke from the refineries. Listen to arguments in the street spilling from bars. The laughter and alcohol madness. The frantic despair of the voices, their pathetic, greedy noise. They are all damned.

They will get sick and become empty and agony will ravage them.

Poison seeks itself.

From my window, I stare at the anemic expanse that leads back to Fairbanks. I measure the numbing monotony with bloodshot eyes. The undetected things beneath. Terrified expressions, twisted limbs, torn flesh. The couples and the ones who were alone. I imagine them all under the vast ice, finally where they should be. Here, they will always look the same, forever preserved, unable to make bad decisions, demolish lives. I saved them. If they could, they would spiral from the countless openings I drilled, vaporous and sorrowful, wanting to be forgiven. But it's too late. Salvation is not given to the irredeemable.

I can feel the scotch and my skin hurts where scars seam my scathed features.

Sometimes when I dream, I watch myself drilling the thick blue ice. I make a large opening and stand over it, then step into it and slip through. I slide through the narrow opening and into the ancient sea underneath and, as currents gently sweep me away, I finally relax. My bad thoughts and fears stop and I look up through the ice and see a world I never belonged in, that never wanted me.

People don't care.

They do what they want. They ruin their life. They ruin yours. They take and take. Smother everything good, give nothing back. Like my family did. It's the same everywhere I go. Every other truck route across this fucked-up country. I bring them here, where no one will find them. But none are missed. When I give them back to the sea, maybe there is some balance in this damaged, indifferent world.

I remember the one from last week. Refinery worker. Nervous. On his way to Deadhorse. Black oil under his fingernails, unslept eyes. We pulled out of Fairbanks as the weather got bad. The windshield iced over and my rig's steel wipers ground at it. He glanced over at me, thanked me for the lift. I offered him coffee from my thermos and he said yes, in a polite voice. But I could tell he was a person who hurt others and derived pleasure when they begged. I could detect in his casual conversation that he cared only for himself and that anyone stupid enough to get close to him would suffer. As he sipped, he glanced at my pistol mounted on my door bracket. Looked back at me. We hit a rut, duct tape rolled from under the seat and the blizzard swallowed us whole.

That was that.

Just like the ones I met in San Diego. And down south. Back east. Tulsa. So many voices and faces. I get people talking while we drink coffee so I can write down the details later. Otherwise, I lose track. They're all narcissists. Bullies. All 361 of them talked about themselves, only a handful ever asked me a question about myself or faith or where their soul might be bound. Vain, worthless assholes.

The longest recorded night in Prudhoe was fifty-four days. The shortest was twenty-six minutes. No matter where you are, it is a world of extremes. Each must make peace with that somehow, each in their own way. Heaven and Hell are not so different. Sometimes, in summer, when mosquitoes swarm, it gets warm here and the Aurora Borealis makes you swear you can see your whole life in its randomness. Time and places. Hurts. The faces of people who never cared. The strangers who did you wrong. The rape and torture.

The world is a diseased zoo.

As I listen to them laughing like banshees, on the icy street outside, I'm exhausted and sore. When generators die, and lights go out and my room turns black, I stumble hard against the small dresser and hear its mirror fall and shatter. I always turn mirrors around in my motel rooms, even tape blankets over them so I never have to see. But after a minute, the generator starts back up, the lights flicker and I glance down, without thinking, to avoid shards in my bare feet.

As the bulbs twitch, I see splinters of a terrible face I had forgotten. A scarred mosaic of every face in my family, the mouth an ugly slash like my father's, the eyes filled with sick contempt and futility like my mother's. The nose crammed and broad and common like my brother's. I stare at myself, reflected in vicious jigsaw fragments, and weep.

And though I fight its truth, I understand, at that instant, that I am guilty and damned. I am not of Heaven but Earth. I take. Give nothing back. I am no better than anyone. Sadism and suffering is all I know; I was raised with it. I am one of them. My heart is an Inquisition, my thoughts are vile and filthy. God has abandoned me and I am forsaken.

I have been drinking sand.

When day breaks in Deadhorse, I am broken. Betrayed. I dress and shower and I tell the front-desk man I will pay for the mirror and he tells me it is seven years of bad luck. He smiles like a lizard and I want to put a bullet in his head. Outside, engines are freezing up and plans changing. Workers need to get across the Big Blank, some with no means. I walk to the diner for coffee and a young woman with willing eyes asks me for a lift to Fairbanks. I refuse and tell her I'm not going all the way through. She doesn't know what I mean since the road ends where it ends and nowhere else.

Fuck her. Fuck everyone. Fuck God most of all. For his lies; for making me believe them.

I get in my rig and head toward Fairbanks, thinking about how the world is worthless and can never be saved. Like my family. Like me. The psychiatrist was right but I couldn't understand. He came to my ward and led me out into the garden and tried to help me. I thought he was evil, trying to cure an angel. I cut out his tongue with shears, got out of that place and moved on. We all have regrets.

The falling snow starts to wall me in and I drive faster, ignoring the speed limit. I reach a stretch of the Dalton with thin ice and push the engine harder, speeding over the slick surface. My steering wheel shakes as the rig starts to create waves under the road that will make it buckle ahead, the undulations like a massive blanket slowly shaken in the wind.

As my tires wobble, I look over and see my brother on hillocks of white, with the sawed neck I gave him; a gory joker's collar. Beside him is my murdering father and my sadistic mother. Both staring, unblinking, waiting for me because they know I am no better than they are and never will be, and that I belong in the icy water with them for what I did.

I feel the sea shuddering below the road as the waves roll thicker and begin to break the ice and the two-lane starts to crack under the weight of my truck. It suddenly ruptures like a pane of broken glass and my engine is a roaring, wounded creature as a wide crack races toward me. Then, another. Then, more, wider and faster, the erupting waves tearing the road open.

The tires spin and I downshift, and my rig abruptly stops and hitches into the dark slush. My seat belt holds me tight against the sudden lurch and my fog lights shine on the collapsing road as it cracks apart, the water churning beneath, leaking upward. The rig begins to make hideous, scraping noises and the huge front tires and grille nose into the shattered roadway as the massive engine slowly dies and sea sloshes up to my doors, wanting me. I watch it without reaction and know I deserve this.

I slowly open my windows.

The freezing water gushes in, lapping at me, and I gasp at the aching cold, drinking in icy saltiness that fills me. I watch my belongings move, in slow motion, in the inundated cab, the inked pages in my notebook running, details and names washed off the paper; my pious, repellent spree. The truck creaks and tilts, huge trailers wrenched and twisting, and I look up through the windshield as sea submerges us and we slowly descend into green-black Ocean.

My dreams were premonitions. But they were wrong.

As we drown, I see murky images, drifting closer.

I can just make them out and am afraid as they move toward me with gunshot faces, slashed throats, many without legs or arms, mouths duct-taped. Pale crowds of them emerge through kelp, mutilations fresh, bloody clothes billowing. Wanting to hurt me as I hurt them.

They tear at me and I look up to see a place I never belonged; that never wanted me.

The sea goes red and I am finally home.

EVIDENCE OF ANGELS

Graham Masterton

GRAHAM MASTERTON was born in Edinburgh, Scotland, where his story "Evidence of Angels" is set. His career as a horror writer began almost accidentally in 1975. Up until then, as the editor of both *Penthouse* and *Forum* magazines, he had been making his name as the writer of hugely successful sex-instruction manuals, such as *How to Drive Your Man Wild in Bed*. When the bottom fell out of that particular market, he offered his publishers *The Manitou*, a story about a Native American medicine man who was reborn in the present day to take his revenge. It was subsequently turned into a movie starring Tony Curtis.

He has followed it with more than 100 horror novels and stories, many of which have been adapted for television and graphic novels. His latest books include *Blind Panic* (the fifth and final Manitou novel), *Fire Spirit, Ghost Music*, *Descendant* and *Demon's Door*, the latest in the Jim Rook series.

Masterton was the first Western horror novelist to be published in Poland, and he and his wife, Wiescka, are frequent visitors to Warsaw, Poznan and Wroclaw.

"I was given the idea for 'Evidence of Angels' by a friend in the Human Development department at the University of Wisconsin in Madison," remembers the author. "His friend had filmed small children taking their first steps and concluded that they could only be walking with the help of some invisible support. That support, those helping hands, could only be those of some unseen guardian.

"In other words, an angel."

BEFORE HE WAS BORN she loved him with a fierce and sisterly love, and called him Alice. Her mother let her rest her head against her stomach to hear his heart beating inside her, and sometimes she felt the strong fleshy ripple of his kicking. With some of the money that her parents had given her for her thirteenth birthday, she went to Jenner's and bought him a little lace-collared dress in the Stewart tartan, and kept it hidden to surprise him on the day that he was due to be born.

She was so sure that he was going to be a girl that she played out imaginary scenes in her head, in which she taught Alice her first ballet steps; and in which they danced the opening scenes of *La Fille Mal Gardée* to amuse their mother and father. And she imagined taking her for walks on winter mornings up to the Castle Mound, where strangers would stop and coo at Alice and think that Gillie was Alice's mother, instead of her older sister.

But one January morning she heard her mother crying out; and there was a lot of running up and downstairs. And father drove mother off to the Morningside Clinic, while the snow swarmed around them like white bees, and eventually swallowed them up.

She spent the day with Mrs. McPhail, who was their cleaner, in her neat cold house in Rankeillor Street, with its ticking clocks and its strong smell of lavender polish. Mrs. McPhail was tiny and disagreeable, and kept twitching her head like a chicken. She gave Gillie a bowl of greyish stew for lunch, with onions in it, and watched and twitched while Gillie miserably pushed it around and around, and the snow on the kitchen windowsill heaped higher and higher.

Mrs. McPhail's rotary washing line stood at an angle in the center of her backyard, and that was clogged up with snow, too. It looked to

Gillie like a seraph, with its wings spread; and as she looked, the sun suddenly broke out from behind the clouds, and the seraph shone, dazzling and stately, yet tragic, too, because it was earthbound now, and now could never hope to return to Heaven.

"Do you no care for your dinner?" asked Mrs. McPhail. She wore a beige sweater covered with pills of worn wool, and a brown beret, even indoors. Her face made Gillie think of a plate of lukewarm porage, with skin on, into which somebody had dropped two raisins for eyes, and drawn a downward curve with the edge of their spoon, for a mouth.

"I'm sorry, Mrs. McPhail. I suppose I'm not very hungry."

"Good food going to waste. That's best lamb, and barley."

"I'm sorry," she said.

But then, unexpectedly, the disagreeable Mrs. McPhail smiled at her, and said, "Don't fash yourself, darling. It's not every day that you get a new baby, now, is it? Now what do you think it'll be? A boy or a girl?"

The thought of it being a boy had never entered Gillie's head. "We're going to call her Alice," she said.

"But what if she's a he?"

Gillie put down her fork. The surface of her stew was floating with small globules of fat. But it wasn't the stew that made her feel nauseous. It was the unexpected idea that her mother might have been harboring a brother, instead of a sister. A brother! A son and heir! Wasn't that what grandma had always complained about, every time that they visited her? "Such a pity you never had a son and heir, Donald, to carry on your father's name."

A son and heir wouldn't want to learn ballet steps. A son and heir wouldn't want to play with her doll's house, which she had carefully brought down from the attic, and fitted with new carpets, and a dining table, and three plates of tiny plaster-cast meals with sausages and fried eggs.

She had saved for so long for that tartan dress. Supposing the baby was a boy? She flushed at her own stupidity.

"You look feverish, pet," said Mrs. McPhail. "Don't eat your dinner if you don't feel like it. I'll warm it up for later. How about some nice pandowdie?"

Gillie shook her head. "No, thank you," she whispered, and tried to smile. In the backyard, the sun had vanished, and the sky was growing grim; but the rotary clothesline looked more like a wrecked angel than ever. She could hardly bear to think of it standing there, throughout the night, unloved, and abandoned, and unable to fly.

"Let's watch telly," said Mrs. McPhail. "I can't miss *Take the High Road*. I wouldnie have a thing to talk about tomorrow, doon the bingo."

They sat on the clumpy brown sofa and watched television on Mrs. McPhail's blurry ex-rental television set. But every now and then, Gillie would look over her shoulder at the seraph in the backyard, watching his wings grow larger and thicker as the snow fell faster still. Perhaps he would fly, after all.

Mrs. McPhail was noisily sucking a humbug. "What do you keep keekin' at, pet?"

Gillie was embarrassed at first. But somehow she felt that she could tell Mrs. McPhail almost anything, and it wouldn't matter. It wouldn't get "reported back," the way that her grandma had once reported her comments about school back to her mother and father.

"It's your clothesline. It looks like an angel."

Mrs. McPhail twisted herself around and stared at it. "With wings, you mean?"

"It's only the snow."

"But you're right, pet. That's just what it looks like. An angel. Seraphim and cherubim. But they always arrive, don't you know, when a baby arrives. It's their duty to take good care of them, those little ones, until they can stand on their own two feet."

Gillie smiled and shook her head. She didn't understand what Mrs. McPhail was talking about, although she didn't like to say so.

"Every child has a guardian angel. You have yours; your new baby has hers. Or his. Whatever it's turned to be."

It has to be Alice, thought Gillie, desperately. *It can't be a son and heir*.

"Would you like a sweetie?" asked Mrs. McPhail, and offered her the sticky, crumpled bag.

Gillie shook her head. She was trying to give up sweeties. If she couldn't make the grade as a ballerina, she wanted to be a supermodel.

By four o'clock it was dark. Her father came at five o'clock and stood in the porch of Mrs. McPhail's house with snow on his shoulders and whisky on his breath. He was very tall and thin, with a tiny sandy moustache and bright grey eyes like the shells you could find on Portobello Beach before they went dry. His hair was thinning on top and it was all sprigged up.

"I've come to take you home," he said. "Your mum's well and the baby's well and everything's fine."

"You've been celebrating, Mr. Drummond," said Mrs. McPhail, with mock disapproval. "But you've every right. Now tell us what it was and how much it weighed."

Dad laid both his hands on Gillie's shoulders and looked right into her eyes. "You've a baby brother, Gillie. He weighed seven pounds, six ounces and we're going to call him Toby."

Gillie opened her mouth but she couldn't speak. Toby? Who was Toby? And what had happened to Alice? She felt as if Alice had been secretly spirited away, and her warm place in her mother's womb given to some strange and awful boy-baby whom she didn't know at all, the human equivalent of a cuckoo.

"That's grand!" said Mrs. McPhail. "No wonder you've been taking the malt, Mr. Drummond! And a cigar, too, I shouldn't be surprised!"

"Well, Gillie?" asked her father. "Isn't it exciting! Think of all the fun you'll be able to have, with a baby brother!"

Gillie was shaking with a genuine feeling of grief. Her eyes filled with tears and they ran down her cheeks into her tartan scarf. *Alice! They've taken you away! They never let you live!* She had thought of Alice so often that she even knew what she looked like, and what they were going to play together, and what they would talk about. But now there was no Alice, and there never would be.

"Gillie, what's the matter?" her father asked her. "Are you feeling all right?"

Gillie's throat felt as if she'd swallowed one of Mrs. McPhail's humbugs without sucking it. "I bought—" she began, and then she had to stop because her lungs hurt and every breath was a painful sob. "I bought—I bought her a dress! I spent my birthday money on it!"

Her father laughed and gave her a hug. 'There now, don't you go worrying your wee head about that! We'll go back to the shop and swap it for a romper-suit, or maybe some trews! How about that? Come on now, this is such a happy day! No more greeting now, you promise?"

Gillie sniffed and sniffed again and wiped her eyes with her woolly gloves.

"Girls of that age," said Mrs. McPhail, sagely. "She's been good today, though. She didn't eat much of her lunch, but she's an angel."

They crossed Clerk Street in the whirling snow. Her father had parked outside the Odeon Cinema and already the car was beginning to look like an igloo on wheels. The Odeon was showing *Alice in Wonderland* and Gillie could almost believe that it wasn't a coincidence at all, but that the cinema management had arranged it with her parents in order to mock her.

They drove back toward the center of the city. Above Princes Street, the castle rock was scarcely visible through the blizzard, and last-minute shoppers trudged along the gritty, salted pavements like lost souls struggling through a dream from which they could never wake up.

A year passed and it was winter again. She sat in front of her dressing table mirror with a tablecloth on her head and wondered what it would be like to be a nun. She liked the look of herself as a nun. She was very thin, very small-boned for fourteen, with a pale complexion and large dark eyes—eyes that were rather soulful and droopy the way that some Scottish eyes are. She could work among the sick and homeless, selflessly bandaging their sores and giving them drinks of water.

The only trouble was, nuns had to give up men and she was very keen on John McLeod in the lower sixth, even though he had never noticed her (as far as she knew, anyway). John McLeod was very tall with raging red hair and he was the captain of curling. She had gone to watch him play and once she had given him a winter-warmer. He had popped it in his mouth and said, "Ta."

The other trouble was that becoming a nun was a very Roman Catholic sort of thing to do and the Drummond family were Church of Scotland through and through.

She stood up and went to the window. The sky was the color of pale gum, and the gardens of Charlotte Square were filled with snow.

"What do you think, Alice?" she asked. Alice was still alive, somewhere in the back of Gillie's mind, somewhere dark and well-protected. She knew that if she ever forgot about Alice, then Alice would cease to exist, completely, as if she had never been thought of.

You want to become a nun? Alice replied. *Do it secretly. Take your holy orders without telling anybody.*

"But what's the point of that? What's the point of becoming a nun if nobody else knows?"

God will know. Devote your life to serving God and honoring the Virgin Mary, and to helping your fellow human beings even if they're drunk in doorways, and you will be rewarded in Heaven.

"But what if John McCleod asks me to the pictures?"

In that case you may renounce your nunly vow, at least for one night.

She was still looking out of the window with the tablecloth on her head when her father unexpectedly came into her bedroom. "What's up with you?" he asked. "Are you playing at ghosts?"

Gillie dragged off the tablecloth and blushed.

"Your mother wants you to feed Toby his lunch while she gets the washing done."

"Do I have to? I'm supposing to be finishing my homework."

"Where? What homework? I don't see any homework. Come on. Gillie, mum's awful busy with the house to keep and Toby to take care of. I do expect you to lend a hand."

Gillie reluctantly followed her father downstairs. They lived in a large four-story house in Charlotte Square which they had inherited from mum's parents when they died and which they could barely afford to keep up. Most of the decorations were still unchanged from granny and grandfather's day: brown floral wallpaper and brown velvet curtains, and large gloomy paintings of stags at bay. About the most cheerful picture was a view of Ben Buie in a thunderstorm.

Her mother was in the large, yellow-tiled kitchen, strapping Toby into his highchair. She was slender and slight, like Gillie, but she was fair-haired rather than dark, with very sharp blue eyes. Toby had inherited her fairness and her eyes, and he had a mop of curly blond hair as fine as cornsilk, which her mother refused to have cut. Daddy didn't like it much because he thought it made Toby look like a girl; but Gillie knew better. Alice would have been gentle and dark, like her, and they would have spoken together in giggles and whispers.

"His hotpot's ready," said mum, and gave Gillie the open jar, wrapped in a cloth because it was hot. Gillie drew up a chair at the large pine kitchen table and stirred the jar with a teaspoon, Toby smacked his fat little hands together and bounced up and down on his bottom. He was always trying to attract Gillie's attention but Gillie knew who he was and she didn't take any notice. He was a cuckoo. Dear dark Alice had never been allowed to see the light of day, and here was this fat curly *thing* sitting in her place. He even slept in Alice's crib.

Gillie spooned up pureed hotpot and put it up against Toby's lips. The instant Toby tasted it he turned his head away. Gillie tried again, and managed to push a little bit into his mouth, but he promptly spat it out again, all down his clean bib.

"Mum, he doesn't like it."

"Well, he has to eat it. There's nothing else."

"Come on, cuckoo," Gillie cajoled him, trying another spoonful. She held his head so that he wouldn't turn away, and squeezed his fat little cheeks together so that he *had* to open his mouth. Then she pushed the whole spoonful onto his tongue.

There was a long moment of indignant spluttering, while Toby grew redder and redder in the face. Then he let out a scream of protest, and hotpot poured out of his mouth and sprayed all over the sleeve of Gillie's jumper.

Gillie threw down the spoon in fury. "You cuckoo!" she screamed at him. "You horrible fat cuckoo! You're disgusting and I hate you!"

"*Gillie!*" her mother protested.

"I don't care! I hate him and I'm not feeding him! He can die of starvation for all I care! I don't know why you ever wanted him!"

"Gillie, don't you dare say such a thing!"

"I dare and I don't care!"

Mum unbuckled Toby from his highchair, picked him up and shushed him. "If you don't care you'd better get to your room and stay there for the rest of the day with no tea. Let's see how *you* like a bit of starvation!"

It started to snow again. Thick, tumbling flakes from the Firth of Forth.

"They really believe that I don't know what they did to you, Alice."

You must forgive them, for they know not what they do.

"I don't want to forgive them. I hate them. Most of all I hate them for what they did to you."

But you're a nun now. You've taken holy vows. You must forgive them in the name of the Father, and of the Son and of the Holy Spirit amen.

Gillie spent the afternoon lying on her bed reading *Little Faith*, which was a novel about a nun who started a mission in the South Seas and fell in love with a gun-runner. She had read it twice already, but she still loved the scene where the nun, who has fasted for five days and five nights as a penance for her passionate feelings, is witness to a miraculous vision of St. Theresa, "incandescent as the sun," who forgives her for feeling like a woman.

At five o'clock she heard her mother carrying Toby upstairs for his bath. At half-past five she heard mummy singing to him in his bedroom, across the corridor. She sang him the same lullaby that she always used to sing for Gillie, when she was small, and the sound of it made Gillie feel even more depressed and left out. She turned her face to the wall and stared miserably at the wallpaper. It was supposed to be roses, but it seemed to have a sly hooded face in it, medieval-looking and misshapen, like a leper.

"*Dance to your daddy, my little babby. Dance to your daddy, my little lamb. You shall have a fishy, in a little dishy. You shall have a fishy when the boat comes in . . .*"

Not long after her father opened her door. "Are you ready to say that you're sorry?" he asked her.

Gillie didn't answer. Her father waited at the door for a while, and then came in and sat on the side of the bed. He laid his hand gently on her arm, and said, "This is not like you. Gillie. You're not jealous of Toby, are you? You don't have to be. We love you just as much as ever. I know that mummy's busy with Toby a lot of the time, but she still cares for you, and so do I."

But what about me? said Alice.

"How about saying you're sorry, and coming down for some tea? There's fish fingers tonight."

You never cared about me.

"Come on, Gillie, what do you say?"

"*You never cared about me! You wanted me dead!*"

Her father stared at her in disbelief. "Wanted you dead? What put such a thought into your head? We love you; we wouldn't have had you otherwise; and if you want to know the truth you would have stayed our only child, and we would have been glad of it, if only Toby hadn't been conceived by accident. We didn't mean to have him, but we did, and now he's here, and we love him. Just the same way that we love you."

Gillie sat up in bed with reddened eyes. "Accident?" she said. "Accident? Try telling Alice that Toby was an accident!"

"Alice? Who's Alice?"

"*You killed her!*" Gillie screamed. "*You murdered her! You murdered her and she never lived!*"

Alarmed, angry, her father stood up. "Now, come on, Gillie. I want you to calm down. Let me call mummy and we'll have a wee chat."

"I don't want to talk to either of you! You're horrible! I hate you! Go away!"

Her father hesitated for a moment. Then he said, "The best thing for you to do, my girl, is to have your bath and get yourself to bed. We'll talk some more in the morning."

"I don't want your stupid bath."

"Then go to sleep dirty. It makes no difference to me."

She lay on her bed listening to the noises in the house. She could hear her mother and father talking; and then the bath running. The cistern roared and whistled just above her room. She heard doors opening and closing, and the burbling of the television in her parents' bedroom. Then the door was closed and all the lights were switched off.

Outside the window, the city was so thickly felted in snow that it was totally silent, from Davidson's Mains to Morningside, and Gillie could almost have believed that everyone was dead, except for her.

She was woken by a bright light dancing on the wallpaper. She opened her eyes and frowned at it for a while, not quite sure where she was, or whether she was sleeping or waking. The light quivered and trembled and danced from side to side. Sometimes it was like a wide squiggly line and then it would suddenly tie a knot in itself, so that it formed the shape of a butterfly.

Gillie sat up. She was still fully dressed and her leg had gone dead because she had been sleeping in a funny position. The light was coming from under her door. First of all it was dazzling and then it was dim. It danced and skipped and changed direction. Then it retreated for a while, so that all she could see was a faint reflected glow.

Oh, no! she thought. The house is on fire!

She climbed off her bed and limped dead-legged to the door. She felt the doorknob to see if it was hot. The Fire Brigade had come to the school to give them all a lecture on do's and don'ts, and she knew that she wasn't to open the door if it was hot. Fire feeds on oxygen like a babby feeds on milk.

But the doorknob was cold, and the door panels were cold. Cautiously, Gillie turned the knob, and opened the door, and eased herself into the corridor. Toby's room was directly opposite; and the light was shining from all around Toby's door. At times it was so intense that she could scarcely look at it, and it shone through every crevice, and even through the keyhole.

She sniffed. The odd thing was that she couldn't smell smoke. And there was none of that crackling sound that you normally get with a fire.

She approached Toby's door and dabbed the doorknob with her fingertip. That, too, was quite cold. There was no fire burning in Toby's room. For a moment, she became dreadfully frightened. She had a cold, sliding feeling in her stomach as if she had swallowed something really disgusting and knew that she was going to sick it up again. If it wasn't a fire in Toby's room, what was it?

She was just about to run to her parents' room when she heard an extraordinary noise. A thick, soft, rustling noise; and then the sound of Toby gurgling and giggling.

He's laughing, said Alice. *He must be all right.*

"I wish it had been a fire. I wish he was dead."

No you don't; and neither do I. You're a nun now; you're in holy orders. Nuns forgive everything. Nuns understand everything. Nuns are the brides of Christ.

She opened Toby's door.

And *Holy Mary!* cried Alice.

The sight that met her eyes was so dramatic and so dazzling that she fell to her knees on the carpet, her mouth wide open in disbelief.

In the center of Toby's nursery stood a tall white figure. It was so blindingly bright that Gillie had to shield her eyes with the back of her hand. It was so tall that it almost touched the ceiling, and it was dressed in swathes of brilliant white linen, and it seemed to have huge folded wings on its back. It was impossible for Gillie to tell if it were a man or a woman. It was so bright that she couldn't clearly see its face, but she could vaguely distinguish two eyes, floating in the brilliance like chicken embryos floating in egg-white; and the curve of a smile.

But what made Gillie tremble more than anything else was the fact that Toby was out of his crib, and standing on his cribside rug, *standing*, with this tall, dazzling creature holding his little hands for him.

"Toby," she whispered. "Oh God, Toby."

But all Toby did was turn toward her and smile his cheekiest smile, and take two unsteady steps across the rug, while the dazzling creature helped him to balance.

Gillie slowly rose to her feet. The creature looked at her. Although it was so bright, she could see that it wasn't staring at her aggressively. In fact there was something in its eyes that seemed to be appealing for understanding; or at least for calm. But then it lifted Toby up in its arms, right up in the air in its brilliant, flaring arms, and Gillie's composure fell apart like a jigsaw falling out of its box.

"*Mum!*" she screamed, running up the corridor and beating on her parents' bedroom door. "Mummy there's an angel in Toby's room! Mum, mum, mum, come quick! There's an angel in Toby's room!"

Her father and mother came bursting out of the bedroom ruffled and bleary and hardly knowing where they were going. They ran to Toby's nursery and Gillie ran after them.

And there he was, tucked up in his blue-and-yellow blanket, sucking his thumb. Content, curly and right on the edge of falling to sleep.

Dad turned and looked at Gillie with a serious face.

"I saw an angel," she said. "I'm not making it up, I promise you. It was teaching Toby to walk."

Dr. Vaudrey laced his fingers together and swung himself from side to side in his black leather armchair. Outside his window there was a view of a grey brick wall, streaked with snow. He had a dry pot plant on his desk and a photograph of three plain-looking children in sweaters that were too small for them. He was half-Indian, and he wore very thick black-framed glasses and his black hair was brushed back straight from his forehead. Gillie thought that his nose looked like an aubergine. Same color. Same shape.

"You know something, Gillie, at your age religious delusions are very common. To find a faith and to believe in its manifestations is a very strong desire for adolescent young women."

"I saw an angel," said Gillie. "It was teaching Toby to walk."

"How did you know it was an angel, what you saw? Did it say to you, 'Hallo, excuse me, I am an angel and I have just popped in to make sure that your baby brother doesn't have to scurry about on his hands and knees for the rest of his life?'"

"It didn't say anything. But I knew what it was."

"You say you knew—but how? This is the point that I am trying to make to you."

Gillie lowered her eyes. Her hands were resting in her lap and somehow they didn't even look like hers. "The fact is I'm a nun."

Dr. Vaudrey swung around to face her. "Did I hear what you said correctly? You are a *nun!*"

"In secret, yes."

"An undercover nun, is that what you're saying?"

Gillie nodded.

"May I ask to which order you belong?"

"It doesn't have a name. It's my own order. But I've given my life to God and the Blessed Virgin and to suffering humanity even if they're drunk in doorways."

Dr. Vaudrey slowly took off his spectacles and looked across his desk at her with infinite sympathy, even though her head was lowered and she couldn't see him. "My dear young lady," he said, "you have the most laudable aims in life; and it is not for me to say what you saw or what you didn't see."

"I saw an angel."

Dr. Vaudrey swung himself around in the opposite direction. "Yes, my dear. I believe that you probably did."

The young minister was waiting for her in the library. He was stocky, with thinning hair and fleshy ears, but she thought he was really quite good-looking for a minister. He wore a horrible sweater with reindeer leaping all round it and brown corduroy trousers.

"Sit down," he said, indicating a dilapidated sofa covered with cracked red leather. "Would you care for some coffee? Or maybe some Irn Bru? Mind you I'm fairly sure the Irn Bru's flat. They bought it in two Christmasses ago, and it's been sitting in the sideboard ever since."

Gillie sat pale and demure at the very far end of the sofa and gave the minister nothing more than a quick negative shake of her head.

He sat astride a wheelback chair and propped his arms across the top of it. "I can't say that I blame you. The coffee's no good, either."

There was a long silence between them. The library clock ticked so wearily that Gillie kept expecting it to stop, although it didn't.

"I suppose I ought to introduce myself," said the young minister. "I'm Duncan Callander, but you can call me Duncan if you want. Most of my friends called me Doughnuts. You know—Duncan Doughnuts?"

Another long silence. Then Duncan said, "You've seen an angel, then? In the flesh so to speak?" Gillie nodded.

"This Doctor Vaudrey . . . this psychiatrist . . . he thinks that you've been suffering some stress. It's partly due to your age, you see. Your mind and your body are going through some tremendous changes. It's only natural to look for something more to believe in than your parents and your schoolteachers. With some girls it's a pop group; with other girls it's God. But Doctor Vaudrey thought your case was very interesting. He's had girls with religious visions before. But none like yours. He said he could almost believe that you really saw what you said you saw."

He took out his handkerchief and made an elaborate ritual out of wiping his nose. "That's why he passed you onto your own minister, and why your own minister passed you onto me. I'm a bit of a specialist when it comes to visions."

"I saw an angel," Gillie repeated. She felt that she had to keep on saying it until they believed her. She would go on saying it for the rest of her life, if necessary. "It was helping Toby to walk."

Duncan said, "It was six-and-a-half to seven feet tall, dazzling white, and you could just about make out its eyes and its mouth. It may have had wings but you're not at all sure about that."

Gillie turned around and stared at him. "How did you know that? I haven't told that to anybody."

"You didn't have to. Yours is the twenty-eighth sighting since 1973, and every single one sounds exactly like yours."

Gillie could hardly believe what she was hearing. "You mean—*other* people have seen them—as well as me?"

Duncan reached out and took hold of her hand and squeezed it. "Many other people, apart from you. It's not at all uncommon. The only uncommon thing about *your* seeing an angel is that you're just an ordinary girl, if you can forgive me for saying so. Most of the other manifestations have come to deeply religious people, ministers and missionaries and such, people who have devoted all of their life to their church."

"I have, too," Gillie whispered.

Duncan gave her an encouraging smile. "You have, too?"

"I took holy orders."

"Where did you do this? At St. Agnes?"

Gillie shook her head. "In my bedroom."

Duncan laid his hand on her shoulder. "Then you're a very exceptional novice indeed. And you must be pure of heart, and filled with love, or else you couldn't have seen what you saw."

"Are angels dangerous?" asked Gillie. "Toby won't get hurt, will he?"

"Quite the opposite, as far as I know. In all of the sightings of angels that I've read about, they've been protecting people, particularly children. We don't really know for sure whether they come from Heaven, or whether they're some kind of visible energy that comes out of the human mind. All kinds of people have been trying to prove their existence for years. Physicists, bishops, spiritualists . . . you name them. Just think what a spectacular boost it would be if the Church could prove that they were real, and that they had been sent by God!"

He reached across his desk and picked up a book with several marked pages in it. "You see these pictures? This is the closest that anybody has ever come to proving that angels exist. For forty years, pediatric studies of babies taking their first steps have proved beyond a shadow of doubt that they are technically in defiance of all the laws of physics when they begin to toddle. They don't have the physical strength, they don't have the balance. And yet—miraculously—they do it.

"In 1973 a team of doctors set up an experiment at Brigham & Women's Hospital in Boston, in America, using children who were just on the verge of walking. They took ultraviolet and infra-red photographs . . . and here, you can see the results. In at least five of these pictures, there's a tall shadowy shape which appears to be holding the toddler's hands."

Gillie studied them closely, with a prickling feeling down her back, as if centipedes were crawling inside her jumper. The shapes were very dim, and their eyes were barely visible. But they were just the same as the dazzling figure who had visited Toby's bedroom.

"Why hasn't anybody said anything about this before?" she asked. "If there have been twenty-seven other sightings, apart from mine, why hasn't anybody said so?"

Duncan closed the book. "Church politics. The Roman Catholics didn't want the sightings mentioned in case they prove not to be angels, after all, but simply some sort of human aura. And the Church of Scotland didn't want them mentioned because they frown on miracles and superstition and hocus-pocus. Nobody said anything because they were all monks or nuns or ordained clergy, and they were under strict instructions from their superiors to keep their visions to themselves."

"But I'm not a real nun! I could say something about it, and nobody could stop me!"

Duncan said, "First of all I have to speak to the kirk elders, to see what they think about it. After all, if a statement is made to the effect that one of our parishioners has witnessed an angel, then the church is going to be closely involved in all of the publicity that's bound to follow."

"You do believe me, though, don't you?" said Gillie. "I'm not mad or anything. I really saw it and it was really there."

"I believe you," smiled Duncan. "I'll talk to the elders tomorrow, and then I'll come around to your house and tell you what they've decided to do."

That evening, while they were having supper at the kitchen table, lamb chops and mashed neeps, little Toby came wobble-staggering across the floor and clung to the edge of Gillie's chair. He looked up at her and cooed.

"Go away, cuckoo," she told him. "You'll have your Marmitey fingers all over my skirt." For a split-second, she thought she saw his eyes flash—actually flash—like somebody taking a photograph.

You'd better watch what you say, Alice warned her. *Toby's got a guardian angel, and you don't want to go upsetting* him.

A weak sun was shining through the dishrag clouds when Duncan Callander came to call the next afternoon. He sat in the best room and mum gave him a cup of tea and a plateful of petticoat tails.

"I talked to the kirk elders this morning. We had a special meeting, in fact. I want to tell you that they all extend their warmest best wishes to young Gillie here, and that they very much appreciate her bringing such a delightful story to their attention."

"But it's not a story!" Gillie interrupted.

Duncan raised his hand to silence her. He didn't look her in the eye. He looked instead at the pattern on the carpet and spoke as if he had learned his words from a typewritten sheet of paper.

"As I say, they were very appreciative, and very amused. But they find that there is no evidence at all that what Gillie saw was anything more than an optical illusion; or a delusion brought on by the stress of having a new baby in the household. In other words, the most likely explanation is a little show of harmless attention seeking by an older sister who feels jealous and displaced."

Gillie stared at him. "You said you believed me," she whispered. "You said you believed me."

"Well, yes, I'm afraid that I did, but it was wrong of me. I have a rather mystical turn of mind, I'm afraid, and it's always getting me into hot water. The kirk elders—well, the kirk elders pointed out that nobody has ever produced any conclusive proof that angels actually exist, and until that happens the kirk's official line is that they do not."

He took a breath. "I apologize if I misled you."

"And that's all?" Gillie demanded. "That's all that's going to happen? I saw an angel and you're going to say that I was making it up because I was jealous of Toby?"

"If you want to put it that way, yes," Duncan told her, although he spoke so soft and ashamed that she could hardly hear him.

Mum took hold of Gillie's hand and squeezed it. "Come on, sweetie. You can forget it all now; put it behind you. Why don't I bake you your favorite cake tonight?"

Where are you going to sleep? asked Alice.

"I don't know. I'll find somewhere. Tramps have to."

You're not going to sleep in a doorway on a freezing-cold night like this?
"I'll find a squat. Anywhere's better than home."

Your supper's waiting on you. Mum baked that rich thick chocolate cake. Your warm bed's all turned down.

"I don't care. What's the point of cakes and warm beds if people say you're a liar. Even that minister said I was liar, and who was the one who was doing the lying?"

She had trudged the whole length of Rose Street, between brightly-lit pubs and Indian restaurants, jostled by rowdy teenagers and cackling drunks. Maybe Mrs. McPhail would have her for the night. Mrs. McPhail believed in angels.

By the time she had crossed Princes Street and started the long walk up Waverley Bridge, it had started to snow again. Sir Walter Scott watched her from his Gothic monument as if he understood her predicament. His head, too, had been full of fancies. She was wearing her red duffle coat and her white woolly hat, but all the same she was beginning to feel freezing cold, and her toes had already turned numb.

At the top of the hill the streets were almost deserted. She crossed North Bridge Street but she decided to walk down the back streets to Mrs. McPhail's in case Dad was out looking for her in the car.

She had never felt so desolate in her life. She had known that people would find it difficult to believe her. She hadn't minded that. What had hurt so much was Duncan's betrayal. She couldn't believe that adults could be so cynical—especially an adult whose chosen calling was to uphold truth and righteousness and protect the weak.

She was halfway down Blackfriars Street when she saw a young man walking very quickly toward her. He was wearing a tam and an anorak and a long Rangers scarf. He was coming toward her so fast that she wondered if somebody were chasing him. His face was wreathed in clouds of cold breath.

She tried to step to one side, but instead of passing her he knocked her with his shoulder, so that she fell back against a garden wall.

"What did you do that for?" she squealed at him; but immediately he seized hold of the toggles of her duffle coat and dragged her close to him. In the streetlight she could see that he was foxy-faced and unshaven, with a gold hoop earring in each ear, and skin the color of candle wax.

"Give us your purse!" he demanded.

"I can't!"

"What d'you mean you can't? You have to."

"I'm running away. I've only got six pounds."

"Six pound'll do me. You can always run away again tomorrow. I don't even have anywhere to run away from."

"No!" screamed Gillie, and tried to twist away from him. But he clung onto her duffle coat and wrenched her from side to side.

"Out with your purse or it'll be the worse for you, bonny lass!"

"Please," she swallowed. "Please let me go."

"Then let's have your purse and let's have it quick."

His face was so close to hers that she could smell the stale tobacco on his breath. His eyes were glassy and staring. She reached into her pocket, took out her furry Scottie-dog purse and handed it to him. He glanced down at it in disdain.

"What's this? A dead rat?"

"It's my p-p-p—"

He thrust the purse into his pocket. "Trying to make me look stupid, is it? Well, how about a little souvenir to make *you* look even stupider?"

He dragged off her woolly hat, seized hold of her hair, and wrenched her from side to side. She couldn't scream. She couldn't struggle. All she could do was gag with fear.

But it was then that she felt the pavement vibrating beneath her feet. Vibrating, as if a heavy road-roller were driving past. She heard a deep rumbling noise, that rapidly grew louder and louder, until she was almost deafened. The young man let go of her hair and looked around in alarm.

"What in the name of—" he began. But his words were drowned out by a thunderous blast of sound, and then a dazzling burst of white light. Right in front of them, a tall incandescent figure appeared, crackling with power, a figure with a crown of sizzling static and immense widespread wings.

It was so bright that the entire street was lit up, as if it were daylight. The falling snow fizzed and evaporated against its wings. Gillie stayed with her back to the garden wall, staring at it in disbelief. The young man stood staring at it, too, paralyzed with fear.

The wings flared even wider, and then the figure reached out with one long arm, and laid its hand on top of the young man's hand, as if it were blessing him, or confirming him.

There was a sharp crack which echoed from one side of the street to the other. The young man screamed once; and then smoke started to pour out of his mouth and his nose; and he exploded. Fragments of tattered anorak were strewn all over the pavement, along with smoking ashes and dismembered shoes.

Almost immediately, the figure began to dim. It folded its wings, turned and vanished into the snow, as quickly and completely as if it walked through a door. Gillie was left with nothing but the young man's scattered remains and an empty street, although she could see that curtains were being pulled back, and people were starting to look out of their windows to see what had happened.

She picked up her purse. Next to it, there were six or seven white feathers—huge and soft and fluffy as snow, although some of them were slightly scorched. She picked those up, too, and started to walk quickly back toward North Bridge Street, and then to run. By the time she heard the fire engines she was well on her way home.

She pushed Toby through the kirkyard gate and up between the snow-topped gravestones. Duncan was standing in the porch, pinning up some notices. He gave her an odd look as she approached, although he didn't turn away.

"What have you come for?" he asked her. "An explanation, or an apology? You can have both if you like."

"I don't need either," she said. "I know what I saw was true and I don't need to tell anybody else about it. I know something else, too. Everybody has a guardian angel of their own, especially the young, because everybody has to do something impossible, now and again, like learning to walk, or learning that your parents do care about you, after all."

"You seem to be getting on better with your little brother," Duncan remarked.

Gillie smiled. "God must have wanted him, mustn't he, or else he wouldn't have sent him an angel. And God must have wanted me, too."

Duncan gave her a questioning look. "There's something you're not telling me. You haven't seen another angel, have you?"

"Did you hear about the lad who was struck by lightning last night, in Blackfriars Street?"

"Of course. It was on the news."

"Well, I was there, and it wasn't lightning. Whoever heard of lightning in a snowstorm?"

"If it wasn't lightning, then what?"

Gillie reached into her pocket and took out a handful of scorched feathers, which she placed in Duncan's open hand. "There," she said. "Evidence of angels."

He stood in the porch for a long time, watching her push Toby away down the street. The wintry breeze stirred the feathers in his hand and blew them one by one across the kirkyard. Then he turned around and went inside, and closed the door.

FEATHERWEIGHT

Robert Shearman

ROBERT SHEARMAN is an award-winning writer for stage, television and radio. He was resident playwright at the Northcott Theatre in Exeter, England, and regular writer for Alan Ayckbourn at the Stephen Joseph Theatre in Scarborough. However, he is probably best known for his work on BBC-TV's *Doctor Who*, bringing the Daleks back to the screen in the BAFTA Award–winning first series of the revival in an episode also nominated for a Hugo Award.

Shearman's first volume of short stories, *Tiny Deaths*, was published in 2007. It won the World Fantasy Award for Best Collection, and was also short-listed for the prestigious Edge Hill Short Story Prize and nominated for the Frank O'Connor International Short Story Prize. The author's second collection, *Love Songs for the Shy and Cynical*, won the 2010 British Fantasy Award and was co-winner of the Shirley Jackson Award.

A collection of his stage plays, *Caustic Comedies*, was recently published, with a third story collection, *Everyone's Just So So Special*, forthcoming.

"I don't like writing at home much," Shearman admits. "Home is a place for sleeping and eating and watching afternoon game shows on TV. There are too many distractions. So, years ago, I decided I'd only write first drafts in art galleries.

"And the best of them all is the National Gallery, in London, a pigeon's throw from Nelson's Column. I can walk around there with my notebook, thinking up stories—and if I get bored, there are lots of expensive pictures to look at. Perfect.

"A lot of those paintings, however, have angels in them. They're all over the place, wings raised, halos gleaming—perching on clouds, blowing trumpets, hovering around the Virgin Mary as if they're her strange naked childlike bodyguards. And I began to notice that, whenever the writing is going well, the angels seemed happy, and would smile at me. And whenever the words weren't coming out right, when I felt sluggish, when I thought I'd rather take off and get myself a beer, they'd start to glare.

"I wrote this story in the National Gallery. Accompanied by a lot of glaring angels. Enjoy."

HE THOUGHT AT FIRST that she was dead. And that was terrible, of course—but what shocked him most was how dispassionate that made him feel. There was no anguish, no horror, he should be crying but clearly no tears were fighting to get out—and instead all there was was this almost sick fascination. He'd never seen a corpse before. His mother had asked if he'd wanted to see his grandfather, all laid out for the funeral, and he was only twelve, and he really really didn't—and his father said that was okay, it was probably best Harry remembered Grandad the way he had been, funny and full of life, better not to spoil the memory—and Harry had quickly agreed, yes, that was the reason—but it wasn't that at all, it was a bloody dead body, and he worried that if he got too close it might wake up and say hello.

And now here there *was* a corpse, and it was less than three feet away, in the passenger seat behind him. And it was his *wife*, for God's sake, someone he knew so well—or, at least, better than anyone else in the world could, he could say that at least. And her head was twisted oddly, he'd never seen her quite at that angle before and she looked like someone he'd never really known at all, he'd never seen her face in a profile where her nose looked quite that enormous. And there was all the blood, of course. He wondered whether the tears were starting to come after all, he could sense a pricking at his eyes, and he thought it'd be such a *relief* if he could feel grief or shock or hysteria or something . . . when she swiveled that neck a little towards him, and out from a mouth thick with that blood came "Hello."

He was so astonished that for a moment he didn't reply, just goggled at her. She frowned.

"There's a funny taste in my mouth," she said.

"The blood," he suggested.

"What's that, darling?"

"There's a lot of blood," he said.

"Oh," she said. "Yes, that would make sense. Oh dear. I don't feel I'm in any pain, though. Are you in any pain?"

"No," he said. "I don't think so. I haven't tried to . . . move much, I . . ." He struggled for words. "I didn't get round to trying, actually. Actually, I thought you were dead."

"And I can't see very well, either," she said.

"Oh," he said.

She blinked. Then blinked again. "No, won't go away. It's all very red."

"That'll be the blood," he said. "Again."

"Oh yes," she said. "Of course, the blood." She thought for a moment. "I'd wipe my eyes, but I can't seem to move my arms at all. I have still got arms, haven't I, darling?"

"I think so. I can see the right one, in any case."

"That's good. I do wonder, shouldn't I be a little more scared than this?"

"I was trying to work that out, too. Why I wasn't more scared. Especially when I thought you were dead."

"Right . . . ?"

"And I concluded. That it was probably the shock."

"That could be it." She nodded, and that enormous nose nodded, too, and so did the twisted neck, there they were, all nodding, it looked grotesque—"Still. All that blood! I must look a sight!"

She did, but he didn't care, Harry was just so relieved she was all right after all, and he didn't want to tell her that her little spate of nodding seemed to have left her head somewhat back to front. She yawned. "Well," she said. "I think I might take a little nap."

He wasn't sure that was a good idea, he thought that he should probably persuade her to stay awake. But she yawned again, and look!—she was perfectly all right, wasn't she, there was no pain, there was a lot of *blood*, yes, but no pain. "Just a little nap," she said. "I'll be with you again in a bit." She frowned. "Could you scratch my back for me, darling? It's itchy."

"I can't move."

"Oh, right. Okay. It's itchy, though. I'm allergic to feathers."

"To what, darling?"

"To feathers," she said. "The feathers are tickling me." And she nodded off.

His first plan had been to take her back to Venice. Venice had been where they'd honeymooned. And he thought that would be so romantic, one year on exactly, to return to Venice for their first anniversary. They could do everything they had before—hold hands in St. Mark's Square, hold hands on board the *vaporetti*, toast each other with champagne in one of those restaurants by the Rialto. He was excited by the idea, and he was going to keep it a secret from Esther, surprise her on the day with plane tickets—but he *never* kept secrets from Esther, they told each other everything, it would just have seemed weird.

And thank God he had told her, as it turned out. Because she said that although it was a lovely idea, and yes, it *was* very romantic, she didn't want to go back to Venice at all. Truth to tell, she'd found it a bit smelly, and very crowded, and *very* expensive; they'd done it once, why not see somewhere else? He felt a little hurt at first—hadn't she enjoyed the honeymoon then? She'd never said she hadn't at the time—and she reassured him, she'd *adored* the honeymoon. But not because of Venice, because of him, she'd adore any holiday anywhere, so long as he was part of the package. He liked that. She had a knack for saying the right thing, smoothing everything over.

Indeed, in one year of marriage they'd never yet had an argument.

He sometimes wondered whether this was some kind of a record. He wanted to ask all his other married friends, how often do you argue, do you even argue at all?—just to see whether what he'd got with Esther was something really special. But he never did, he didn't want to rub anyone's noses in how happy he was, and besides, he didn't have the sorts of friends he could be that personal with. He didn't need to, he had Esther. Both he and Esther had developed a way in which they'd avoid confrontation—if a conversation was taking a wrong turning, Esther would usually send it on a detour without any apparent effort.

Yes, he could find her irritating at times, and he was certain then that she must find him irritating, too—and they could both give the odd warning growl if either were tired or stressed—but they'd never had anything close to a full-blown row. That was something to be proud of. He called her his little diplomat! He said that she should be employed by the UN, she'd soon sort out all these conflicts they heard about on the news! And she'd laugh, and say that he clearly hadn't seen what she was like in the shop, she could really snap at some of those customers sometimes—she was only perfect around *him*.

And he'd seen evidence of that, hadn't he? For example—on their wedding morning, when he wanted to see her, and all the bridesmaids were telling him not to go into the bedroom, "*Don't*, Harry, she's in a filthy temper!"—but he went in anyway, and there she was in her dress, she was so beautiful, and she just *beamed* at him, and kissed him, and told him that she loved him, oh, how she loved him. She wasn't angry. She wasn't ever going to be angry with him. And that night they'd flown off to Venice, and they'd had a wonderful time.

So, not Venice then. (Maybe some other year. She nodded at that, said, "Maybe.") Where else should they spend their anniversary then? Esther suggested Scotland. Harry didn't much like the sound of that, it didn't sound particularly romantic, especially not compared to Venice.

But she managed to persuade him. How about a holiday where they properly *explored* somewhere? Just took the car, and *drove*—a different hotel each night, free and easy, and whenever they wanted they could stop off at a little pub, or go for a ramble on the moors, or pop into a stately home? It'd be an adventure. The Watkins family had put their footprints in Italy, she said, and now they could leave them all over the Highlands! That did sound rather fun. He didn't want it to be *too* free and easy, mind you, they might end up with nowhere to stay for the night—but he did a lot of homework, booked them into seven different places in seven different parts of Scotland. The most they'd ever have to drive between them was eighty miles, he was sure they could manage that, and he showed her an itinerary he'd marked out on his atlas. She kissed him and told him how clever he was.

And especially for the holiday he decided to buy a sat nav. He'd always rather fancied one, but couldn't justify it before—he knew his drive into work so well he could have done it with his eyes closed. He tried out the gadget, he put in the postcode of his office, and let it direct him there. It wasn't the route he'd have chosen, he was quite certain it was better to avoid the ring road altogether, but he loved that sat nav voice, so gentle and yet so authoritative: "You have reached your destination," it'd say, and they'd chosen a funny way of getting there, but yes, they certainly had—and all told to him in a voice good enough to be off the telly. The first day of the holiday he set in the postcode to their first Scottish hotel; he packed the car with the suitcases; Esther sat in beside him on the passenger seat, smiled and said, "Let's go."

"The Watkinses are going to leave their footprints all over the Highlands!" he announced, and laughed.

"Happy anniversary," said Esther. "I love you."

On the fourth day they stayed at their fourth stately home of the holiday a little too long, maybe; it was in the middle of nowhere, and their next hotel was also in the middle of nowhere, but it was in a completely different middle of nowhere. It was already getting dark, and there weren't many streetlights on those empty roads. Esther got a little drowsy, and said she was going to take a nap. And the sat nav man hadn't said anything for a good fifteen minutes, so Harry knew he *must* be going in the right direction, and maybe Esther sleeping was making him a little drowsy, too—but suddenly he realized that the smoothness of the road beneath him had gone, this was grass and field and *bushes*, for God's sake, and they were going down, and it was quite steep, and he kept thinking that they had to stop soon surely, he hadn't realized they were so high up in the first place!—and there were now branches whipping past the windows, and actual trees, and the car wasn't slowing down at all, and it only dawned on him then that they might really be in trouble. He had time to say "Esther," because stupidly he thought she might want to be awake to see all this, and then the mass of branches got denser still, and then there was sound, and he hadn't thought there'd been sound before, but suddenly there was an awful lot of it. He was flung forward towards the steering wheel, and then the seat belt flung him right back where he had come from—and that was when he heard a snap, but he wasn't sure if it came from him, or from Esther, or just from the branches outside. And it was dark, but not yet dark enough that he couldn't see Esther still hadn't woken up, and that there was all that blood.

The front of the car had buckled. The sat nav said, "Turn around when possible." Still clinging on to the crushed dashboard. Just the once, then it gave up the ghost.

He couldn't feel his legs. They were trapped under the dashboard. He hoped that was the reason. He tried to open the door, pushed against it hard, and the pain of the attempt nearly made him pass out. The door had been staved in. It was wrecked. He thought about the seat belt. The pain that reaching it would cause. Later. He'd do that later. Getting out the cell phone from his inside jacket pocket— not even the coat pocket, he'd have to bend his arm and get into the coat first and *then* into the jacket . . . Later, later. Once the pain had stopped. Please, God, then.

Harry wished they'd gone to Venice. He was sure Venice had its own dangers. He supposed tourists were always drowning themselves in gondola-related accidents. But there were no roads to drive off in Venice.

He was woken by the sound of tapping at the window.

It wasn't so much the tapping that startled him. He'd assumed they'd be rescued sooner or later—it was true, they hadn't come off a main road, but someone would drive along it sooner or later, wouldn't they? It was on the *sat nav route*, for God's sake.

What startled him was the realization he'd been asleep in the first place. The last thing he remembered was his misgivings about letting Esther nod off. And some valiant decision he'd made that whatever happened *he* wouldn't nod off, he'd watch over her, stand guard over her—*sit* guard over her, he'd protect her as best he could. As best he could when he himself couldn't move, when he hadn't yet dared worry about what damage might have been done to him. What if he'd broken his legs? (What if he'd broken his spine?) And as soon as these thoughts swam into his head, he batted them out again—or at least buried them beneath the guilt (some valiant effort to protect Esther that had been, falling asleep like that!) and the relief that someone was there and he wouldn't need to feel guilt much longer. Someone was out there, tapping away at the window.

"Hey!" he called out. "Yes, we're in here! Yes, we're all right!" Though he didn't really know about that last bit.

It was now pitch black. He couldn't see Esther at all. He couldn't see whether she was even breathing. "It's all right, darling," he told her. "They've found us. We're safe now." Not thinking about that strange twisted neck she'd had, not about spines.

Another tattoo against the glass—*tap, tap, tap*. And he strained his head in the direction of the window, and it hurt, and he thought he heard something pop. But there was no one to be seen. Just a mass of branches, and the overwhelming night. Clearly the tapping was at the passenger window behind him.

It then occurred to him, in a flash of warm fear, that it was *so* dark that maybe their rescuer couldn't see in. That for all his tapping he might think the car was empty. That he might just give up tapping altogether, and disappear into the blackness. "We're in here!" he called out, louder. "We can't move! Don't go! Don't go!"

He knew immediately that he shouldn't have said don't go, have tempted fate like that. Because that's when the tapping stopped. "No!" he shouted. "Come back!" But there was no more; he heard something that might have been a giggle, and that was it.

Maybe there hadn't been tapping at all. Maybe it was just the branches in the wind.

Maybe he was sleeping through the whole thing.

No, he decided forcefully, and he even said it out loud, "No." There had been a *rhythm* to the tapping; it had been someone trying to get his attention. And he wasn't asleep, he was in too much pain for that. His neck still screamed at him because of the strain of turning to the window. He chose to disregard the giggling.

The window tapper had gone to get help. He'd found the car, and couldn't do anything by himself. And quite right, too, this tapper wasn't a doctor, was he? He could now picture who this tapper was, some sort of farmer probably, a Scottish farmer out walking his dog—and good for him, he wasn't trying to be heroic, he was going to call the *experts* in, if he'd tried to pull them out of the car without knowing what he was about he might have done more harm than good. Especially if there *was* something wrong with the spine (forget about the spine). Good for you, farmer, thought Harry, you very sensible Scotsman, you. Before too long there'd be an ambulance, and stretchers, and safety. If Harry closed his eyes now, and blocked out the pain—he could do it, it was just a matter of not *thinking* about it—if he went back to sleep, he wouldn't have to wait so long for them to arrive.

So he closed his eyes, and drifted away. And dreamed about farmers. And why farmers would giggle so shrilly like that.

• • • • •

The next time he opened his eyes there was sunlight. And Esther was awake, and staring straight at him.

He flinched at that. And then winced at his flinching, it sent a tremor of pain right through him. He was glad to see she was alive, of course. And conscious was a bonus. He hadn't just hadn't expected the full ugly reality of it.

He could now see her neck properly. And that in its contorted position all the wrinkles had all bunched up tight against each other, thick and wormy; it looked a little as if she were wearing an Elizabethan ruff. And there was blood, so much of it. It had dried now. He supposed that was a good sign, that the flow had been staunched somehow, that it wasn't still pumping out all over the Mini Metro. The dried blood cracked around her mouth and chin as she spoke.

"Good morning," she said.

"Good morning," he replied, and then automatically, ridiculously, "did you sleep well?"

She smirked at this, treated it as a deliberate joke. "Well, I'm sure the hotel would have been nicer."

"Yes," he said. And then, still being ridiculous, "I think we *nearly* got there, though. The sat nav said we were about three miles off."

She didn't smirk this time. "I'm hungry," she said.

"We'll get out of this soon," he said.

"All right."

"Are you in pain?" he asked.

"No," she said. "Just the itching. The itching is horrible. You know."

"Yes," he said, although he didn't. "I'm in a fair amount of pain," he added, almost as an afterthought. "I don't think I can move."

"Not much point bothering with that hotel now," said Esther. "I say we move right on to the next, put it down as a bad lot."

He smiled. "Yes, all right."

"And I don't think we'll be doing a stately home today. Not like this. Besides, I think I've had my fill of stately homes. They're just houses, aren't they, with better furniture in? I don't care about any of that. I don't need better furniture, so long as I have you. Our own house, as simple as it might be, does me fine, darling. With you in it, darling."

"Yes," he said. "Darling, you do know we've been in a car crash. Don't you?" (And that you're covered in blood.)

"Of course I do," she said, and she sounded a bit testy. "I'm itchy, aren't I? I'm itching all over. The feathers." And then she smiled at him, a confrontation neatly avoided. Everything smoothed over. "You couldn't scratch my back, could you, darling? Really, the itching is *terrible*."

"No," he reminded her. "I can't move, can I?"

"Oh yes," she said.

"And I'm in pain."

"You said," she snapped, and she stuck out her bottom lip in something of a sulk. He wished she hadn't, it distorted her face all the more.

"I'm really sorry about all this," he said. "Driving us off the road. Getting us into all this. Ruining the holiday."

"Oh, darling," she said, and the lip was back in, and the sulk was gone. "I'm sure it wasn't your fault."

"I don't know what happened."

"I'm sure the holiday isn't ruined."

Harry laughed. "Well, it's not going too well! The car's a write-off!" He didn't like laughing. He stopped. "I'll get you out of this. I promise." He decided he wouldn't tell Esther about the rescue attempt, just in case it wasn't real, he couldn't entirely be sure what had actually happened back there in the pitch black. But he couldn't keep anything from Esther, it'd have been wrong, it'd have felt wrong. "Help is on its way. I saw a farmer last night. He went to get an ambulance."

If the Scottish farmer *were* real, then he wouldn't ever need to bend his arm to reach his cell phone. The thought of his cell phone suddenly made him sick with fear. His arm would snap. His arm would snap right off.

"A farmer?" she asked.

"A Scottish farmer," he said. "With a dog," he added.

"Oh."

They didn't say anything for a while. He smiled at her, she smiled at him. He felt a little embarrassed doing this after a minute or two—which was absurd, she was his wife, he shouldn't feel awkward around his wife. After a little while her eyes wandered away, began looking through him, behind him, for something which might be more interesting—and he was stung by that, just a little, as if he'd been dismissed somehow. And he was just about to turn his head away from her anyway, no matter how much it hurt, when he saw her suddenly shudder.

"The itch," she said. "Oh God!" And she tried to rub herself against the back of the seat, but she couldn't really do it, she could barely move. The most she could do was spasm a bit. Like a broken puppet trying to jerk itself into life—she looked pathetic, he actually wanted to laugh at the sight of her writhing there, he nearly did, and yet he felt such a pang of sympathy for her, his heart went out to her at that moment like no other. On her face was such childlike despair, *help me*, it said. And then: "Can't you scratch my fucking back?" she screamed. "What fucking use are you?"

He didn't think he'd ever heard her swear before. Not serious swears. Not "fucking." No. No, he hadn't. "Frigging" a few times. That was it. Oh dear. Oh dear.

She breathed heavily, glaring at him. "Sorry," she said at last. But she didn't seem sorry. And then she closed her eyes.

And at last he could turn from her, without guilt, he *hadn't* looked away, he hadn't given up on her, in spite of everything he was still watching over her. And then he saw what Esther had been looking at behind his shoulder all that time.

Oddly enough, it wasn't the wings that caught his attention at first. Because you'd have thought the wings were the strangest thing. But no, it was the face, just the face. So round, so *perfectly* round, no, like a sphere, the head a complete sphere. You could have cut off that head and played football with it. And there was no blemish to the face, it was like this had come straight from the factory, newly minted, and every other face you had ever seen was like a crude copy of it, some cheap hack knock-off. The eyes were bright and large and very very deep, the nose a cute little pug. The cheeks were full and fat and fleshy, all puffed out.

But then Harry's eyes, of course, *were* drawn to the wings. There was only so long he could deny they were there. Large and white and jutting out of the shoulder blades. They gave occasional little flaps, as the perfect child bobbed about idly outside the car window. Creamy pale skin, a shock of bright yellow hair, and a bright yellow halo hovering above it—there was nothing to keep it there, it tilted independently of the head, sometimes at a rather rakish angle—it looked like someone had hammered a dinner tray into the skull with invisible nails. Little toes. Little fingers. Babies' fingers. And (because, yes, Harry did steal a look) there was nothing between the legs at all, the child's genitals had been smoothed out like it was a naked Action Man toy.

The little child smiled amiably at him. Then raised a knuckle. And tapped three times against the glass.

"What are you?"—which Harry knew was a pointless question, it was pretty bloody obvious what it was—and even the cherub rolled his eyes at that, but then smiled back as if to say, just kidding, no offense, no hard feelings.

The child seemed to imitate Harry's expressions, maybe he was sending him up a little—he'd put his head to one side like he did, he'd frown just the same, blink in astonishment, the whole parade. When Harry put his face close to the window it hurt, but he did it anyway—and the child put its head as close as it could, too. There was just a sheet of glass between them. They could have puckered up, they could almost have kissed had they wanted! And at one point it seemed to Harry the child *did* pucker up those lips, but no, it was just taking in a breath, like a sigh, a hiss. "Can you understand me? Can you hear what I'm saying?" The child blinked in astonishment again, fluttered its wings a bit. "Can you get help?" And what did he expect, that it'd find a phone box and ring the emergency services, that it'd fly into the nearest police station? "Are you here to watch over us?"

And then the cherub opened its mouth. And it wasn't a sigh, it *was* a hiss. Hot breath stained the glass; Harry recoiled from it. And the teeth were so sharp, and there were so many, how could so many teeth fit into such a small mouth? And hiding such a dainty tongue, too, just a little tongue, a *baby's* tongue. The child attacked the window, it gnawed on the glass with its fangs. Desperately, hungrily, the wings now flapping wild. It couldn't break through. It glared, those bright eyes now blazing with fury, and the hissing became seething, and then it was gone—with a screech it had flown away.

There was a scratch left streaked across the pane.

Harry sat back, hard, his heart thumping. It didn't hurt to do so. There *was* pain, but it was something distant now, his body had other things to worry about. And whilst it was still confused, before it could catch up—and before he could change his mind—he was lifting his arm, he was bending it, and *twisting it back on itself* (and it didn't snap, not at all), he was going for his coat, pulling at the zip, pulling it down hard, he was reaching inside the coat, reaching inside the jacket inside the coat, reaching inside the pocket inside the jacket inside the—and he had it, his fingers were brushing it, his fingers were gripping it, the phone, the cell phone.

By the time he pulled it out his body had woken up to what he was trying to do. Oh no, it said, not allowed, and told him off with a flush of hot agony—but he was having none of that, not now. The phone was turned off. Of course it was. He stabbed at the pin number, got it right second time. "Come on, come on," he said. The phone gave a merry little tune as it lit up. He just hoped there was enough battery power.

There was enough battery power. What it didn't have was any network coverage. Not this far out in the Highlands! Not in one of the many middles of nowhere that Scotland seemed to offer. The signal bar was down to zero.

"No," he insisted, "no." And the body really didn't want him to do this, it was telling him it was a *very* bad idea, but Harry began to wave the phone about, trying to pick up any signal he could. By the time a bar showed, he was raising the phone above his head, and he was crying.

He stabbed at 999. The phone was too far away for him to hear whether there was any response. "Hello!" he shouted. "There's been a car crash! We've crashed the car. Help us! We're in . . . I don't know where we are. We're in Scotland. Scotland! Find us! Help!" And his arm was shaking with the pain, and he couldn't hold on any longer, and he dropped it, it clattered behind his seat to the floor. And at last he allowed himself a scream as he lowered his arm, and that scream felt good.

The scream didn't wake Esther. That was a good thing. At least she was sleeping soundly.

For a few minutes he let himself believe his message had been heard. That he'd held on to a signal for long enough. That the police had taken notice if he had. That they'd be able to track his position from the few seconds he'd given them. And then he just cried again, because really, why the hell shouldn't he?

He was interrupted by a voice. "Turn around when possible." His heart thumped again, and then he realized it was the sat nav. It was that nice man from the sat nav, the one who spoke well enough for telly. The display had lit up, and there was some attempt at finding a road, but they weren't on a road, were they? And the sat nav was confused, poor thing, it couldn't work out what on earth was going on. "Turn around when possible," the sat nav suggested again.

Harry had to laugh, really. He spoke to the sat nav. It made him feel better to speak to someone. "I thought I'd heard the last of you!"

And then the sat nav said, "Daddy."

And nothing else. Not for a while.

For the rest of the day he didn't see anything else of the child. He didn't see much else of Esther, either; once in a while she seemed to surface from a sleep, and he'd ask her if she were all right. And sometimes she'd glare at him, and sometimes she'd smile kindly, and most often she wouldn't seem to know who he was at all. And he'd doze fitfully. At one point he jerked bolt upright in the night when he thought he heard tapping against the window—"No, go away!"—but he decided this time it really was the wind, because it soon stopped. Yes, the wind. Or the branches. Or a Scottish farmer this time, who can tell? Who can tell?

In the morning he woke to find, once again, Esther was looking straight at him. She was smiling. This was one of her smiling times.

"Good morning!" she said.

"Good morning," he replied. "How are you feeling?"

"I feel hungry," she said.

"I'm sure," he said. "We haven't eaten in ages."

She nodded at that.

Harry said, "The last time would have been at that stately home. You know, we had the cream tea. You gave me one of your scones."

She nodded at that.

Harry said, "I bet you regret that now. Eh? Giving me one of your scones!"

She nodded at that. Grinned.

"The itching's stopped," she declared. "Do you know, there was a time back there that I really thought it might drive me *mad*. Really, utterly loop the loop. But it's stopped now. Everything's okay."

"That's nice," he said. "I'm going to get you out of here, I promise."

"I don't care about that anymore," she said. "I'm very comfortable, thanks." She grinned again. He saw how puffed her cheeks were. He supposed her face had been bruised; he supposed there was a lot of dried blood in the mouth, distorting her features like that. "In fact," she said, "I feel as light as a feather."

"You're feeling all right?"

She nodded at that.

"Can you open the door?" he asked. She looked at him stupidly. "The door on your side. Can you open it? I can't open mine."

She shrugged, turned a little to the left, pulled at the handle. The door swung open. The air outside was cold and delicious.

"Can you go and get help?" he asked. She turned back to him, frowned. "I can't move," he said. "I can't get out. Can you get out?"

"Why would I want to do that?" she asked.

He didn't know what to say. She tilted her head to one side, waiting for an answer.

"Because you're hungry," he said.

She considered this. Then tutted. "I'm sure I'll find something in here," she said. "If I put my mind to it." And she reached for the door, reached right outside for it, then slammed it shut. And as she did so, Harry saw how his wife's back bulged. That there was a lump underneath her blouse, and it was moving, it *rippled*. And he saw where some of it had pushed a hole through the blouse, and he saw white, he saw feathers.

"Still a bit of growing to do, but the itching has stopped," she said. "But don't you worry about me, *I'll* be fine." She grinned again, and there were lots of teeth, there were too many teeth, weren't there? And then she yawned, and then she went back to sleep.

She didn't stir, not for hours. Not until the child came back. "Daddy," said the sat nav, and it wasn't a child's voice, it was still the cultured man, calm and collected, as if he were about to navigate Harry over a roundabout. And there was the cherub!—all smiles, all teeth, his temper tantrum forgotten, bobbing about the window, even waving at Harry as if greeting an old friend. And, indeed, he'd brought friends with him, a whole party of them! Lots of little cherubs, it was impossible to tell how many, they would keep on bobbing so!—a dozen, maybe two dozen, who knows? And each of them had the same perfect face, the same spherical head, the same halos listing off the same gleaming hair. Tapping at the window for play, beating on the roof, beating at the door—laughing, mostly laughing, they wanted to get in but this was a game, they liked a challenge! *Mostly* laughing, though there was the odd shriek of frustration, the odd hiss, lots more scratches on the glass.

One little cherub did something very bad-tempered with the radio aerial. Another little cherub punched an identical brother in the face in a dispute over the rear-view mirror. They scampered all over the car, but there was no way in. It all reminded Harry of monkeys at a safari park. He'd never taken Esther to a safari park. He never would now. "Daddy Daddy," said the sat nav. "Daddy Daddy," it kept on saying, emotionless, even cold—and the little children danced merrily outside.

"Oh, aren't they beautiful!" cooed Esther. She reached for the door. "Shall we let them in?"

"Please," said Harry. "Please. Don't."

"No. All right." And she closed her eyes again. "Just leaves more for me," she said.

For the first few days he was very hungry. Then one day he found he wasn't hungry at all. He doubted that was a good thing.

He understood that the cherubs were hungry, too. Most of them had flown away, they'd decided that they weren't going to get into this particular sardine tin—but there were always one or two about, tapping away, ever more forlorn. Once in a while a cherub would turn to Harry, and pull its most innocent face, eyes all wide and Disney-dewed, it'd look so *sad*. It'd beg, it'd rub its naked belly with its baby fingers, and it'd cry. "Daddy," the sat nav would say at such moments. But however winning their performance, the cherubs still looked fat and oily, and their puffy cheeks were glowing.

Harry supposed they probably were starving to death. But not before he would.

One day Harry woke up to find Esther was on top of him. "Good morning," she said to him, brightly. It should have been agony she was there, but she was as light as air, as light as a feather.

Her face was so very close to his, it was her hot breath that had roused him. Now unfurled, the wings stretched the breadth of the entire car. Her halo was grazing the roof. The wings twitched a little as she smiled down at him and bared her teeth.

"I love you," she said.

"I know you do."

"I want you to know that."

"I do know it."

"Do you love me, too?"

"Yes," he said.

And she brought that head towards his—that now spherical head, he could still recognize Esther in the features, but this was probably Esther as a child, as a darling baby girl—she brought down that head, and he couldn't move from it, she could do whatever she wanted. She opened her mouth. She kissed the tip of his nose.

She sighed. "I'm so sorry, darling," she said.

"I'm sorry, too."

"All the things we could have done together," she said. "All the places we could have been. Where would we have gone, darling?"

"I was thinking of Venice," said Harry. "We'd probably have gone back there one day."

"Yes," said Esther doubtfully.

"And we never saw Paris. Paris is lovely. We could have gone up the Eiffel Tower. And that's just Europe. We could have gone to America, too."

"I didn't need to go anywhere," Esther told him. "You know that, don't you? I'd have been just as happy at home, so long as you were there with me."

"I know," he said.

"There's so much I wanted to share with you," she said. "My whole life. My whole life. When I was working at the shop, if anything funny happened during the day, I'd store it up to tell you. I'd just think, I can share that now. Share it with my *hubby*. And we've been robbed. We were given one year. Just one year. And I wanted *forever*."

"Safari parks," remembered Harry.

"What?"

"We never did a safari park, either."

"I love you," she said.

"I know," he said.

Her eyes watered, they were all wide and Disney-dewed. "I want you to remember me the right way," she said. "Not covered with blood. Not mangled in a car crash. Remember me the way I was. Funny, I hope. Full of life. I don't want you to spoil the memory."

"Yes."

"I want you to move on. Live your life without me. Have the courage to do that."

"Yes. You're going to kill me, aren't you?"

She didn't deny it. "All the things we could have done together. All the children we could have had." And she gestured towards the single cherub now bobbing weakly against the window. "All the children."

"Our children," said Harry.

"Heaven is *filled* with our unborn children," said Esther. "Yours and mine. Yours and mine. Darling. Didn't you know that?" And her wings quivered at the thought.

She bent her head towards him again—but not yet, still not yet, another kiss, that's all, a loving kiss. "It won't be so bad," she said. "I promise. It itches at first, it itches like hell. But it stops. And then you'll be as light as air. As light as feathers."

She folded her wings with a tight snap. "I'm still getting used to that," she smiled. And she climbed off him, and sprawled back in her seat. The neck twisted, the limbs every which way—really, so ungainly. And she went to sleep. She'd taken to sleeping with her eyes open. Harry really wished she wouldn't, it gave him the creeps.

Another set of tappings at the window. Harry looked around in irritation. There was the last cherub. Mewling at him, rubbing his belly. Harry liked to think it was the same cherub that he'd first seen, that it had been loyal to him somehow. But of course, there was really no way to tell. Tapping again, begging. So hungry. "Daddy," said the sat nav.

"My son," said Harry.

"Daddy."

"My son."

Harry wound down the window a little way. And immediately the little boy got excited, started scrabbling through the gap with his fingers. "Just a minute," said Harry, and he laughed even—and he gave the handle another turn, and the effort made him wince with the pain, but what was that, he was used to that. "Easy does it," he said to the hungry child. "Easy does it." And he stuck his hand out of the car.

The first instinct of his baby son was not to bite, it was to nuzzle. It rubbed its face against Harry's hand, and it even purred, it was something like a purr. It was a good five seconds at least before it sank its fangs into flesh.

And then Harry had his hand around its throat. The cherub gave a little gulp of surprise. "Daddy?" asked the sat nav. It blinked with astonishment, just as it had echoed Harry's own expressions when they'd first met, and Harry thought, I taught him that, *I taught my little boy*. And he squeezed hard. The fat little cheeks bulged even fatter, it looked as if the whole head was now a balloon about to pop. And then he pulled that little child to him as fast as he could—banging his head against the glass, *thump, thump, thump*, and the pain in his arm was appalling, but that was good, he *liked* the pain, he wanted it—*thump* one more time, and there was a crack, something broke, and the sat nav said "Daddy," so calm, so matter-of-fact—and then never spoke again.

He wound the window down further. He pulled in his broken baby boy.

He discovered that its entire back was covered with the same feathers that made up the wings. So for the next half-hour he had to pluck it.

The first bite was the hardest. Then it all got a lot easier.

"Darling," he said to Esther, but she wouldn't wake up. "Darling, I've got dinner for you." He hated the way she slept with her eyes open, just staring out sightless like that. And it wasn't her face any more, it was the face of a cherub, of their dead son. "Please, you must eat this," he said, and put a little of the creamy white meat between her lips; it just fell out on to her chin. "Please," he said again, and this time it worked, it stayed in, she didn't wake up, but it stayed in, she was eating, that was the main thing.

He kissed her then, on the lips. And he tasted what would have been. And yes, they would have gone to a safari park, and no, they wouldn't have gone back to Venice, she'd have talked him out of it, but yes, America would have been all right. And yes, they would have had rows, real rows, once in a while, but that would have been okay, the marriage would have survived, it would all have been okay. And yes, children, yes.

When he pulled his lips from hers she'd been given her old face back. He was so relieved he felt like crying. Then he realized he already was.

The meat had revived him. Raw as it was, it was the best he had ever tasted. He could do anything. Nothing could stop him now.

He forced his legs free from under the dashboard, it hurt a lot. And then he undid his seat belt, and that hurt, too. He climbed his way to Esther's door, he had to climb over Esther. "Sorry, darling," he said, as he accidentally kicked her head. He opened the door. He fell outside. He took in breaths of air.

"I'm not leaving you," he said to Esther. "I can see the life we're going to have together." And yes, her head was on a bit funny, but he could live with that. And she had wings, but he could pluck them. He could pluck them as he had his son's.

He probably had some broken bones, he'd have to find out. So he shouldn't have been able to pick up his wife in his arms. But her wings helped, she was so light.

And it was carrying Esther that he made his way up the embankment, up through the bushes and brambles, up towards the road. And it was easy, it was as if he were floating—he was with the woman he loved, and he always would be, he'd never let her go, and she was so light, she was as light as feathers, she was as light as air.

MOLLY AND THE ANGEL

Brian Stableford

BRIAN STABLEFORD taught sociology for twelve years at the University of Reading before becoming a full-time writer in 1988. He has published more than 100 books, including over sixty novels, sixteen collections, seven anthologies and thirty nonfiction titles.

His recent novels include *Alien Abduction: The Wiltshire Revelations* and *Prelude to Eternity*. He has also completed a five-volume set of translations of the "scientific marvel fiction" of Maurice Renard, and a six-volume set of the scientific romances of J.H. Rosny the elder.

Stableford was the recipient of the 1999 Science Fiction Research Association's Pilgrim Award for contributions to science fiction scholarship, and he has also been presented with the SFRA's Pioneer Award (1996), the Distinguished Scholarship Award of the International Association for the Fantastic in the Arts (1987) and the J. Lloyd Eaton Award (1987).

"'Molly and the Angel' was the first of a series of seven sequels to 'When Molly Met Elvis,'" explains the author, "which I hoped to publish in *Interzone* in the run-up to the Millennium. However, the editor abandoned the series after one more story, without bothering to tell me until the whole set was written, prompting me to cancel my subscription and never read the magazine again. There were no angels involved."

THE FIRST TIME MOLLY SAW THE ANGEL he was standing in the middle of the pedestrianized precinct at the end of Stockwell Road. There was no mistaking what he was. He had wings like a great white eagle, whose pinion feathers were touching the ground although the tops of their great furled arches extended a foot and a half above the circle of light that rimmed his head. It wasn't a comedy halo, like a battery-powered quoit, but a solid disk half as bright as the winter sun. He was dressed in a dazzling-white robe that hung loose from his broad shoulders to his sandaled feet. He looked slightly puzzled, but only in an intellectual sort of way—more curious than alarmed and not in the least discomposed.

No one was paying any attention to the angel, even though the passersby had nothing more pressing to do than was normal for a Tuesday morning in February. The shoppers and the truanting kids saw him all right, but they wouldn't look directly at him and they made detours to avoid passing within arm's reach of him. He couldn't have alienated so much attention if he'd been carrying a clipboard, a blue pencil and a sheaf of questions about sanitary protection.

Molly almost paused—but during the little margin of hesitation that might have realized the *almost* she lost heart and quickened her step, just like everybody else.

Later, she told herself that she'd had to do it. She couldn't afford to get involved in anything dodgy. She'd kept the affair with Elvis secret, of course; if she'd told anyone it would have got back to the social services. Not that she'd have been sectioned again—you practically had to kill someone to get sectioned these days—but it would have come up when the next group meeting considered the possibility of restoring custody of the kids. The only thing likely to have a worse effect on the average group meeting than the news that the client thought she'd had a fling with Elvis—even one that had never got as far as actual penetration—was the news that the client thought she'd been visited by an angel.

The entire audience for *Touched by an Angel* was probably made up of social workers, who presumably figured the show as the ultimate wet dream but couldn't believe a word of it. It was very popular in the States, they said, but so was Elvis; neither played quite as well in Brixton, even on what the local Estate Agents called the "Dulwich fringe."

Even so, she regretted falling into step with everybody else and pretending that the angel wasn't there. It was cowardly. It was no consolation to think that angels' missions were probably supposed to work that way. In all probability, nobody ever stopped to speak to an angel except the person the angel had come to see. There would be a certain propriety in that—and if angels couldn't maintain propriety in this godforsaken world, who could?

When she saw the angel again he was standing outside the old Salvation Army Temple. There was a split second when she didn't quite recognize him, but the face was unmistakable even though everything else about him had changed. His wings were only half the size they had been, and were now patterned like a pigeon's. The nimbus was gone, although his hair was still luxuriant and golden blond. The white robe was gone, too, unless its trailing hem had been tucked up above the knee so that it could remain hidden within the tan-colored raincoat he was wearing—which seemed unlikely, given that the bottoms of a pair of grey flannel trousers were clearly visible, their turn-ups resting on brown suede loafers. He still seemed a trifle bewildered, and discomposure was beginning to creep up on him now.

The benches where the down-and-outs hung out were crowded, but none of the alkies was looking at the angel. They couldn't have treated him with more disdain if he'd been a Tory councilor down from Westminster on a fact-finding tour.

Molly had thought for some months after it closed that the alkies kept returning to the Temple out of habit and sentiment, but Francine had eventually let her in on the secret that it was just round the corner from the lock-up where the local white van man stored the bottles and cans he shipped in from Eastenders three times a week. It was the cheapest source of strong cider for miles around. The white van man was called Lucas but the alkies called him Saint Luke because he allowed them to buy at wholesale prices without a trade card. The local crackheads looked upon the alkies with naked envy, knowing full well that their prices went up as their dependency increased—but their supplier insisted on being known as Saint John anyway, just for form's sake.

Again, Molly almost stopped when she saw the angel, in spite of the fact that he was hanging about in a place where she usually quickened her paces in order to minimize the deluge of cackling abuse. Again, she couldn't quite bring herself to interrupt her stride.

The down-and-outs weren't in the least bothered by the fact that the angel could overhear them; they made all the usual remarks. They knew where Molly lived, and in their estimation—which was not unrepresentative of the world's—that automatically made her a career whore whose current hundred-percent dependency on the social only signified that she was too ugly to get the kerb-crawlers to stop. That was what they called out, anyhow, although an alky would have to have very few memory cells left to be oblivious to the fact that kerb-crawlers would stop for anything in a skirt and heels, provided that she had a hole at the right height.

Molly never rose to the bait, as Francine and some of the other residents of the B&B were wont to do, but on this particular occasion she couldn't suppress a blush. It was not on her own behalf that she suffered embarrassment but on behalf of the angel. It wasn't much of an advertisement for humankind that the Sally Ann had had to close its Temple, or that all the street scum in the neighborhood gathered there to take what advantage they could of their friendly neighborhood smuggler, or that the very same street scum were prepared to pretend that the only thing stopping her from pulling down her knickers for them was that they had better things to do with their money.

Given that the real Millennium was only ten months away Molly would have thought that even the down-and-outs would have wanted to put on a *bit* of a front while the eyes of Heaven were upon them, but no. The alkies had long since given up on propriety—and, she supposed, everything else.

The third time Molly saw the angel he was sitting at a two-seater table crammed into an alcove in the public library. He was reading the *Independent*. Of his wings there was now not the slightest trace, and his raincoat, although it couldn't have been cheap—if, in fact, he'd purchased it instead of miraculously spinning it out of some mysterious utility fog—was stained, as if he'd been sleeping rough. His hair was mousy brown, just beginning to thin at the back. In spite of all this, there was no hesitation in her recognition. She'd seen him twice already, and she hadn't forgotten the finely-sculpted lines of his face. Three days' worth of stubble couldn't hide the fact that he was the most beautiful man presently in the world. Elvis would have wept in envy, even before the immortal worms got to work on his insides.

Molly looked away as soon as she saw him, but she'd already taken note of the fact that the only empty seat left on the entire ground floor was the one opposite the angel, and she knew before she went up the stairs to REFERENCE that there wouldn't be any room up there because of all the kids from the college filling in their free periods. When she got to REFERENCE she went over to the encyclopedias. She hesitated over the *Britannica* and the *Catholic Encyclopedia*, but in the end she took the *Encyclopedia of Fantasy* off the shelf. It seemed, on the whole, to be the most sensible place to look up ANGELS.

She read through the article, committed a handful of names to memory, and then went back down to the card catalogue to check whether the books were in the lending stock. She always used the card catalogue instead of the computer because it felt nicer. She'd hoped the library might at least have *The Revolt of the Angels* or *The Wonderful Visit*, but they didn't. Out of print, out of mind. What they did have back in REFERENCE, however, was a two-volume edition of Old Testament Apocrypha and Pseudoepigraphia, so she went upstairs again and hauled out the unwieldy volume containing the *Book of Enoch*. Then she took it downstairs, planted it on the table at which the angel was sitting, and plonked herself with almost-equal emphasis in the vacant chair.

It didn't occur to Molly to wonder whether the angel might be reading the *Independent* as a matter of choice. She'd spent enough time taking advantage of the free central heating to know that no one came into the library because they were keen to find out what was happening in the world. The ones who were so desperate to get in that they would be queuing up at opening time always grabbed the *Sun*, the *Mirror* and the *Mail* first, then the *Express* and the *Guardian*. Then the ones who were pretending hardest that they were really earning their Jobseeker's Allowance would grab the *Times*, the *Telegraph* and the local rag. The *Independent* was always the last to go, left for the attention of the poor sucker who had no choices left.

She had opened her own book and read the first four pages of *Enoch*, including the footnotes, before the angel finally condescended to lower the *Independent* sufficiently to let his eyes peep over. She waited a full three seconds before raising her own head so that she could meet his curious but mildly suspicious gaze. The angel's eyes were the bluest she had ever seen. They were bluer than the bluest sky on the brightest summer day there had ever been. They were the only thing left that would have immediately informed the most casual observer, seeing him for the first time, that their owner was, in fact, an angel.

To show off her erudition, Molly had already prepared an apposite quote. She wasn't entirely sure which James Bond book it came from, but thought it was probably *Goldfinger*. "Once is happenstance," she said. "Twice is coincidence. Three times is . . . are you looking for me, by any chance?"

"No," said the angel, too bluntly to allow her to savor the music of his voice.

"Oh," said Molly, wondering whether she ought to be relieved or hurt. " Well, if you'd care to tell me who you *are* looking for, maybe I can help. You don't seem to be having much success on your own."

"I'm not looking for anyone," the angel said. He didn't seem particularly well-spoken.

"No message to deliver?" Molly queried. "No mission to carry out?"

"No," said the angel.

"You're just not playing the game, are you?" Molly said. "What's the matter—don't you have TV in Heaven?"

The angel lowered the *Independent* and displayed the entirety of his incredibly beautiful but unshaven face. He seemed to be trying to formulate a question. Molly guessed that she was the first human being he'd talked to, and figured that she ought to help him out.

"Well," she said, "if you haven't come to deliver a message, and you aren't here to befriend and redirect some poor unfortunate who's on the brink of making a morally disastrous decision, what *are* you doing way down on *terra firma*?"

The angel didn't even blink. "I fell," he said.

It wasn't what he said that bowled Molly over but the way he said it. She'd spoken lightly, as if the whole thing were a joke, not because she thought it was but because that was the only way she knew of dealing with a situation she'd never encountered before. He could have said exactly the same words in that sort of way and it would have been funny. It *could* have been pure stand-up, the kind of thing that got Eddie Izzard a big laugh—but it wasn't. It was deadly serious. Even though Molly was sitting there with the *Book of Enoch* open on the desk, its pages well-nigh tabloid size, it didn't even occur to her to connect "I fell" with the war in Heaven or *Paradise Lost* or the angels that had begat the Nephilim on the lucky daughters of men. She had heard "I fell" spoken in exactly that manner, in exactly that tone, by neighbors in the bedsit, by companions in group and by fellow shelf-stackers on the very few occasions when the temp agency managed to get her work in spite of her record, her history, her lack of a proper address and her general Oxfam-dressed appearance.

Oddly enough, she couldn't quite remember whether she'd ever said it herself. She'd certainly sported the bruises more than once in the hectic days when she'd copped for the kids, so she knew it wasn't a lie. It never was a lie, although everyone always thought it was. Even when you got a push in the back, or a fist in your face, it wasn't a lie. The fact that an angel could say it certainly proved that, even if it proved nothing else.

A few more minutes passed before Molly recovered herself sufficiently to say: "When you say *fell*, you do mean from Heaven, I suppose—not from the Land of Dreams, or any cop-out along those lines."

"From Heaven," the angel confirmed. Nobody with eyes like those could be capable of copping out, any more than he could be capable of copping for a couple of kids.

Molly took the angel round the corner to The Greasy Spoon, whose proprietor hadn't quite got to grips with the concept of irony when he'd changed its name from The Bistro. She offered to buy the angel something to eat, but he told her that he didn't need food *as such*. She ordered the all-day breakfast and a pot of tea for two.

"I shouldn't really have to do this," she explained to him, figuring that he had to be pretty innocent in the ways of the world if he'd had to make do with the *Independent* since his arrival. "Being in a B&B, I ought to get breakfast *included*. That's what the second B stands for, after all—but standards have slipped down here. On the other hand, it's better than a lot of places. The girls on the game are very good about only doing it in alleyways and cars, for the sake of the kids, and we've all got our own sinks and electric kettles, and the loos aren't that bad, considering, and the TV in the sitting room is always replaced the day after it gets nicked, and we've got cable. I'm in the smallest room, of course, but you could say that I'm in the lap of luxury compared to most, because my kids are still out to foster. Unfortunately, just about the last way you can score any points when you get that close to the bottom is to get your kids back, so I'm actually reckoned to be not yet off the mark, even though I've kicked everything but the Prozac and the over-the-counter tranks disguised as antihistamines. Some would say that my brain chemistry is fried anyhow, but I don't think so— and at least I've got guts, to say that to an angel. I have the breakfast at lunchtime because it's cheaper than anything actually called *lunch* and if you only have one real meal a day it's better to have it in the middle. Can't cook in the rooms, you see, except for cup-a-soup and other just-add-boiling-water crap, and who can stomach that? What's Heaven like, exactly?"

"It's not *like* anything," the angel said, unhelpfully.

"Nice gardens? Pleasant weather? Bright light?" Molly prompted, figuring that any hint at all would be better than nothing, and that she really ought to try to bring the angel out of himself a little. If he hadn't been sent to deliver a message, the fact that he had accepted the lunch invitation, even though he didn't need food *as such*, suggested that maybe he had been sent as some kind of *test*.

"None of that," he said.

"*None* of it! What about singing? Surely you were in the choir. Doesn't it get boring, just bathing in the presence of God, century after century?"

"No," he said. "There's no time in Heaven."

"No *time*?" Molly hadn't been expecting that. "What keeps everything from happening at once then?"

"Nothing," he informed her, calmly. "Everything does happen at once." He sipped his tea but it was still too hot, and probably too sharp for his celestially-softened palate.

"You'd better put some sugar in it," Molly said, passing him the thing that looked like a giant salt cellar with a chimney. "That's a bit rotten, don't you think? The preachers promise eternity. Don't you think the dead might be a little disappointed when they get there and find that their stay is considerably shorter than a split nanosecond? If Saatchi and Saatchi tried that the Advertising Standards Authority would be down on them like a ton of bricks."

"It's not *shorter* than anything," the angel said. "You have to set aside that whole way of thinking. Paradise isn't a *place* at all. The human imagination is too narrowly attuned to mere existence to encompass its essence."

Molly couldn't help but wonder whether she'd first caught sight of him just too late to see the clipboard and blue pencil disappear.

"So what did you do?" she said.

"We don't *do* anything," he began—but she immediately saw that he'd got hold of the wrong end of the stick.

"I said what *did* you do," she reminded him. "I've given up fishing for descriptions. I mean, what did *you* do to qualify for the drop. With Lucifer it was pride, with the fathers of the Nephilim it was presumably lust. That still leaves five deadly sins untapped by angelkind. *Please* don't tell me it was sloth."

The angel made a face. He'd obviously put too much sugar in the tea. "I fell," he repeated, in the same stubbornly heart-melting fashion. It wasn't a lie. Whatever he was covering up, whoever he was protecting, it wasn't a lie.

Molly sighed, but she didn't have the heart to be sarcastic. "So what are the other fallen angels doing these days?" she asked. She was genuinely interested. "According to Enoch, they taught mankind the fundamentals of technology and civilization, but the skills they passed on must have become obsolete ages ago. Unless, of course, they got more out of government retraining schemes than I ever did."

"I don't know," he said.

"But you're hoping to make contact, right? Or maybe not. I mean, if the fallen angels are all in Hell, you'd probably rather stay here. Always assuming, of course, that this isn't Hell and that I *am* out of it. That's Mephistopheles, you know." She felt slightly ashamed of showing off, especially as she'd only seen the *Dr. Faustus* movie with Richard Burton, way back in the days when she'd had the falling habit herself. At least she'd always had her own TV in those days; the only way to keep a TV was to have a bloke around who could nick someone else's when your own got burgled. Sometimes, she wondered whether there were any real victims anymore, or whether there was just a vast population of knocked-off TVs that were kept constantly in circulation by the beating heart of larcenous intent. The ones that kept reappearing in the sitting room certainly hadn't come from Comet.

"I don't know anything about Hell," the angel said, stuffily, "but I know this isn't it."

Molly could see that it was going to be hard work getting any more out of him. She was half-inclined to drop it and go back to ignoring him, just like everybody else. Hadn't she already told herself that it was the sensible thing to do? But she couldn't rid herself of the nagging suspicion that even if Elvis hadn't been what she needed to get year zero off to a flying start, the angel might be.

"If you're not going to drink that tea," she said, in the end, "you might as well give it here and sod off."

There was a long pause while the angel considered his options. In the end, he decided not to give her the tea. He forced himself to drink. After two or three further sips he seemed to get used to the sweetness. The color of his eyes was like a sky looking down on someplace as far away as Molly could imagine—and she was not an unimaginative person.

"Well," Molly said, even though she knew it would make her sound like a social worker, "if it's nectar you want, you'll have to get up again, won't you? It's the only way to get over the falling habit—believe me, I know. Stick around here, and it isn't just the tea that will go from bad to worse. It won't be just a matter of losing the wings and your raincoat turning into something a flasher would be ashamed to open up. I saw what happened to Elvis when the serum got to work, and it wasn't a pretty sight." She figured that it was safe to mention Elvis to the angel. If you couldn't trust an angel not to shop you to the moral guardians of society, who could you trust?

The angel still didn't reply. He was now so deeply absorbed in the tea that he was at risk of becoming obsessed, and Molly began to wonder whether it had really been a kindness to tell him to sweeten it. Fortunately, she was spared the temptation to offer him a sausage or a bit of fried bread. She'd been hungry. Conversation always gave her an appetite—*real* conversation, that is, not the kind of chatting that the women in the B&B went in for.

"Of course," she said, figuring that if she were going to come on like a social worker she might as well go the whole hog, "you have to *want* to get up again. Nobody can help you if you won't be helped. Maybe you'd be happier down here on Earth. There's not much to recommend it, I suppose, but we do have *time*—all the time in the world. Places, too, though rumor has it they're not as various as they used to be. Look, you're not exactly making this easy for me, are you? I mean, I'm trying to do you a *good turn* here. Who knows—this may be my last chance to qualify for Heaven? You could at least pretend that you're interested. Think of it as an episode of *Touched by a Human*. I can only do so much—at the end of the day, it's up to you."

"Yes," he said, betraying a hint of positivity for the first time. "I can see that. But it's hard for me, too."

The tone of his voice melted her heart all over again. The words *I fell* echoed in her mind, and echoed and echoed.

"It's okay," she said. "If you guys really did teach us the fundamentals of technology and civilization, we owe you one. Like they say in America, if you can't pay back, pay forward. Between the two of us, we'll get it figured out. You lucked out—hardly anyone around here spends more time in the library than me, and I don't just *pretend* to read. You can come back to the B&B with me if you like, but you can't stay the night. It's the rules, and I can't afford to get chucked out, for the kids' sake." She was telling the truth about not pretending to read.

She loved the Penguin *Dictionary of Quotations*, where Oscar Wilde had observed that it was better to be beautiful than good, but better to be good than ugly. If the beautiful angel wasn't going to cuddle her, she could at least pretend that it was her decision, her choice, her ruling.

"I understand," he said, although it wasn't at all clear what he understood—or was prepared to pretend that he understood, given that he probably didn't know anything at all about anything outside of a Heaven that wasn't a place and didn't even have time.

"Okay," she said. "Let's go."

The alkies didn't say a word when Molly and the angel walked past the old Salvation Army Temple, but that was probably because the cider had taken the edge off their wit. There was no sign of Saint Luke or his boozemobile but the down-and-outs had obviously experienced a visitation. They weren't as blissful as crackheads blessed by Saint John, but they weren't as mean as they were when they had hangovers.

There were five pre-schoolers playing on the stairs at the B&B, and a couple of the mums popped their heads out to make sure that the visitor wasn't an obvious child molester, but neither passed any comment on the unlikelihood of Molly keeping company with an angel. They just stared, with eyes the color of dirty dishwater—eyes incapable of reflecting anything but the dullest winter sky.

The angel was appropriately impressed by the tidiness of Molly's room, although it represented a very modest victory over the forces of chaos. She'd moved the wardrobe to cover up the corner where the mold kept growing on the wall, and she'd put the rug she'd salvaged from a skip over the shiny grease patch on the carpet. The bed was made and there wasn't a single item of clothing draped over the back of the chair. Only the curtains were seriously disgusting, and she couldn't be expected to take *them* to the launderette. The angel didn't even glance at the curtains; a true representative of the Good, he let his eyes wander over the piles of books stacked—*almost* neatly—under the window, at the foot of the bed and all around the sink.

"Burglars never pinch books," she told him. "No point. And before you ask, I haven't read them all. I picked most of them up going through the boxes people leave at the side when the recycling bin gets too full, and I always figure it's better to take the ones that you might never get around to reading than leave anything you might regret not having picked up when you run out of ones you're actually keen on. Anyway, big thick paperbacks make bloody good draught-excluders."

The angel turned to look at her, more appraisingly than before. Molly was alarmed to note that the summer sky had already begun to fade from his eyes. At what point, she wondered, would he pass the point of no return? And what would happen to him then? Would he have to fight just to hang on to human status? *Could* he hang on to human status, if that became his fallback position, or would he just keep on sliding, all the way to Lucifer and Hell?

When the angel sat down on the bed, slumping like Annie after a bad abduction experience or Francine after an extra-generous hit, Molly knew that she had her work cut out, but it was too late to complain. She'd already accepted the responsibility.

Maybe, she thought, this was the best way to make a new start—not by grabbing something new for yourself but by doing something new for someone else. Maybe, in the great cosmic scheme of things, you were supposed to build up a little moral credit before you could get the go-ahead to turn your own life around. If so, this was going to take even more imagination and ingenuity than letting Elvis down gently.

"I suppose you've tried praying?" Molly said, dispiritedly.

"I've *tried*," the angel said, "but I seem to have lost the knack." He looked up at her with his wonderful blue eyes, as if he were expecting a sympathetic pat on the head. Molly had to resist the temptation to join him. Now that he'd taken his raincoat off, his relatively unspoiled suit made him look way too good for this kind of environment, and she couldn't bear the prospect of seeing him flinch and move away if her cellulite should accidentally come into contact with his thigh.

"I think I tried it myself once," she said. "Way back when. It didn't do any good, even though I was still a virgin and didn't understand the chorus of 'Ebenezer Good.' Maybe I couldn't take it seriously enough— but lack of faith is one problem *you* shouldn't have. I suppose there's no point in asking what God's like. He's not *like* anything, is he? He just *is*."

"That's right," said the angel.

"Thought so. You haven't a fucking clue, have you? Down here, you're completely out of your depth."

Because she was looking him right in the eye she saw the color weaken when she pronounced the obscenity, and was stricken by the terrible thought that if this *was* a test, she must be more than halfway to failing by now whether she stooped to further obscenity or not. She was suddenly struck by a sense of awkward urgency. This was Earth, after all, and time was of the essence here. The angel probably couldn't stand much more exposure to the forces of change and decay—and as soon as she'd condescended to notice his presence in the world she'd become time's accomplice, aiding and abetting its patient assault on his divinity. If she wasn't part of the solution, she was part of the problem. She couldn't just wash her hands of this one.

As that revelation roughly took hold of her, Molly felt that she would have given anything in the world for the answer to the angel's problem to be easy. Love would have been *so* easy, but she already knew that it wasn't even worth a try. She knew beyond the shadow of a doubt that if she could only get the angel to take the least little bit of pleasure in her, she could do it with love and not just with lust, but she also knew far better than he did—with luck, far better than he ever would—where the limitations of reality lay.

It had been easier by far with Elvis. Elvis, immortality serum or no immortality serum, had already been finished. The angel, God bless him, hadn't even started. No matter what his timeless experience in Heaven had been like, and no matter what it was that had caused God to knock him down, the angel hadn't even *begun*. Molly supposed that you had to get used to being in time before you could get to grips with beginning, and that the angel simply hadn't had long enough, or help enough, even to think about what it would *mean* to pull himself back together.

"Well," she said, slightly startled by the desperation in her voice, "there are a few more things that aren't even worth trying. I think we can take it for granted that Prozac isn't the answer in this particular case, and Freudian analysis wouldn't get us anywhere even if we had the time. We need a fix that's quick, but one that isn't chemical." She nearly added *and doesn't involve fucking* but she caught herself in time. She didn't want to labor the point, or deepen the blue of his eyes any further than it was already deepened. Hastily, she added: "It might help if you could bring yourself to tell me exactly why you stand in need of absolution." No sooner had she said it, however, than she jumped to the conclusion that it probably wouldn't.

"I fell," said the angel, yet again.

There was nothing in the least infuriating about the repetition, because the pathos wrapped up in the remark was still undergoing a stage-by-stage metamorphosis that had not yet reached its heart-rending end.

That had to be the key, Molly thought. That had to be the vital clue, the vital cue, the vital Q to which she was required to find the A.

"I'm stupid, aren't I?" Molly whispered. "You keep telling me what the matter is, and I just keep missing it. I keep getting hung up on the questions that don't have any answers, like where you fell from and what made you fall, but the real point is that you're *still falling*, faster and faster, into time and into place and into the vortex of creation. Of course you don't know *why*, because there is no *why* in Heaven. All the worldly whys are in Hell, aren't they? Every last one."

"I don't know," said the angel, proving her point.

Molly realized that when she had first seen the angel he had been over six feet tall. Even in the library he'd topped five-seven, but now he was no taller than she was. In a matter of hours, he'd be no bigger than a child, but he'd still be too old to grow wings and fly, even in his imagination—and her presence was making it worse. Her nearness was accelerating the process. She was a carrier of time and place, and she was furthering the angel's infection with every breath she took, but she knew that it wouldn't do any good at all to send him back out on to the street. There were five billion people in the great wide world, and they had thousands of years of history in them, and the people closest to hand were as riddled and raddled with contagion as all the rest.

In spite of her resolution, Molly sat down on the bed, next to the angel. He didn't reach out to her, but at least he didn't move away. He wasn't afraid.

She closed her eyes, as if she were a little girl confronted with a birthday cake or some other everyday prodigy, who had to close her eyes to make a wish if she were to stand any chance at all of making it come true.

"I'll tell you a funny thing about the human brain, Mr. Angel," she said, speaking out of the darkness. "There are any number of ways to jolt it out of everyday misery, and all of them work for a while, but you can never get more than the merest delusory glimpse of Heaven. If you do something like heroin the brain just stops producing happy chemicals of its own, so when you try to give it up you just go crazy. It's different with Es and acid, but not so very different. Whatever the stuff gives you, you stop giving yourself, and when you stop doing the stuff because the effect's worn thin, you've lost it. People think it's just drugs, but it isn't. It's the same with everything you do that allows you to grasp the merest atom of delight. Fucking, dreaming, reading, kids . . . everything. Whatever gets you an inch nearer to Heaven only tantalizes once or twice, and then it starts to become as ordinary as anything else, and leaves you without the ability to do it for yourself if you don't get the fix—and if you can't handle that, you just go crazy.

"I don't have the slightest idea what Heaven is really like, Mr. Angel, and I can't tell you anything about Hell, but I can tell you this: if you intend to stay here, you have to be able to handle it without going crazy. You have to realize that everything you try, everything you do and everything you think of will only seem to work once or twice, and that the best you can hope for afterwards is that things will stay *ordinary*. If you can't help going crazy, everything you think and feel and do thereafter will be a matter of trying to get back to the beginning, of trying to hold on without shrinking any further and losing any more—because time leads nowhere except death, and you just have to learn to handle that, and get what you can out of a world without a Heaven. If you came here thinking that time heals, forget it, because time *wastes*. If you came here looking for a place to be, you shouldn't have bothered, because there's no place like home—and I don't mean that there's no place *like* home, I mean that there's *no place* even remotely like what you'd really like to think of as *home*, but you have to get used to that and make do with what there is, one way or another. You just have to *get used* to it, and *make do with what there is*, or else you get crazier and crazier and crazier until there's nothing left at all. Down here, you have to accept things as they are if you want to make a new start, because there's no other way to *begin*. Even in year zero, you have to see things as they are. There's no other way, except to oblivion.

"So if I were you, Mr. Angel, I'd stop fucking around down here where you don't belong and go back where you came from, where you don't have any time to waste or any place to call anything. It doesn't matter how or why you fell—what you have to do is get up again, while you still can. If you don't, you'll become just as human as the rest of us, and the only way to get up will be the hard way. That's the choice: either you get back up, *right now*, or you stay here and rot. Just *do it*. I know it's the most difficult thing in the world, but that's all there is to it, and all there can be to it. It's what all of us have to do, one way or another. I'm going to open my eyes now, *and I want to see you gone*."

Molly knew, even before she opened her eyes, that the angel would be gone, and so he was—because he was still an angel, even if his wings had gone into hiding. She had pronounced far too many obscenities to sustain the sky in his eyes. She had shown him darkness, and she had scared him as shitless as only an entity that didn't need food *as such* could be.

She wished that someone had done as much for her, way back when, although she knew perfectly well that she wouldn't have been able to take it in. Whatever else she'd been, she was no angel—but whatever she'd been, this was year zero and she was now the kind of person who could touch an angel and do him a good turn. She had to be. There wasn't any other option left.

She also knew, though, even before she got down to the serious business of planning the rest of her day, that she would probably never know *for sure* whether she had passed the test, if it actually had been a test, or whether the angel really had decided to go back to the place from which he had fallen instead of all the way to Hell. In her experience, people mostly did go back to the place from which they had fallen, if they only could—and she now had no good reason to suppose that angels were any different—although sometimes, like little anorectic Annie, they simply couldn't.

That was why, when people like her said "I fell," it was hardly ever a lie—but that was why people like her who still had it in them to get up again did get up, even though they had no way to do it but the hard way.

S.D. WATKINS, PAINTER OF PORTRAITS

Steve Rasnic Tem

STEVE RASNIC TEM's latest book is a collection of all his collaborations with wife Melanie Tem: *In Concert*, published by Centipede Press. He has recent and forthcoming stories in *Crimewave*, *Null Immortalis*, *The Black Book of Horror*, *Asimov's* and the anthology *Werewolves and Shape Shifters*, edited by John Skipp.

"In the early stages of thinking about a story I find that stray, rather disparate ideas may wander into the net," reveals the author. "I'm often not sure how they're going to fit, or if they're nothing more than some random distraction.

"In this case I gave the protagonist my own suspicion of complex metaphor (believing it usually hides something we're not meant to know). And I've often wondered about the painters of classical religious art, or anyone devoting their lives to what some would call 'imaginary beings.'

"I suppose we could consider fantasy and horror writers as part of that category (the devotees, not the imaginary beings)."

THE OLD PRIEST WAS DRUNK, but Watkins did not think he would pass out soon. The priest was pouring himself his sixth, or seventh glass of wine. The portrait painter had been so engrossed in his sketches of too many lines, too many choices, that he had lost count. But he had carefully watered the wine down beforehand so that the priest would get drunk, yet still remain conscious through this, the first portrait sitting.

Watkins himself did not drink at all, but after hours of intense drawing he would not have called himself sober. He watched as his wounded hand made lines that leapt away from the body, rose from the shoulders as if the old priest's arthritic joints and twisted bones were reforming themselves into something that might launch the failing body toward Heaven. Here and there his blood spotted the page.

"So many lines, why do you make so many lines? Did they teach you that in art school?" The priest's boozy breath against the side of his face made him feel ill.

Watkins twisted in his chair. "I told you this is all preparation. I begin the painting tomorrow. This is nothing for you to see. You should be in your chair—this is a portrait *sitting*, remember? You should be sitting, posing."

The priest staggered back to his chair in front of the fire, his voluminous black cassock casting broad shadows over Watkin's front room, alternating with the warm, sudden flushes of firelight. It brought an otherworldly illumination to the paintings covering every inch of the walls: all of them of angels in various poses, all of them gorgeous, and none of them by Watkins himself. They had all been painted by his father Martin, who had been a genius.

The priest had his hand affectionately around the wine bottle, gazing at this patchwork hallucination of angelic obsession. "When I came here looking for a painter, I thought it would be your father."

"The fact that no one at St. Anthony's knew my father has been dead more than ten years speaks volumes."

The priest nodded sadly, tipping dangerously forward. "He painted most of the murals in the church, and the fine details in the transepts. Admirers come from thousands of miles."

"And for which he was seriously underpaid." Watkins raised his hand against the possible response. "I did not say the church cheated him. St. Anthony's gave him what he asked for. But it was far too little pay for an artist of his genius, as his children and widow would be happy to tell you. I am not my father. Myself, I can only paint what I can see. I have come to be satisfied with that. I'm certainly good enough to paint a portrait for the church hall, which I will do for a modest fee, but one appropriate to my level of talent."

"Is this why you do not attend Mass, my son?"

Watkins bridled at the term, but said nothing immediately. Instead he focused on the lines framing the priest's nose, his ill-proportioned ears, the deceptively simple crack of a mouth. He made ten lines where only one was required. His father used to admonish him, *It betrays a lack of faith, Son. Make the single line with confidence, then go on to the next. In time they will be the right lines, if you persist.*

"I enjoy the searching for a final image," he said now, to the priest. "That is why I make so many lines."

"And yet you say you draw only what you can see."

"I do. But in the face there is every person you used to be, and every person you will become. The lines, the planes, are all there. I draw what I see, but sometimes I think I see too much."

"And this was your father's method as well?"

Watkins kept his face calm, composed, even as the evolving shape on his sketch pad erupted, lines spinning off cheekbones, lines twirling off that nasty, no-lipped mouth that spat out the priest's portion of their conversation, hair lines and skin lines and ley lines transversing the page, transmuting, leaving mysterious pockets where eyes might take seed and grow. "My father needed no framework—he was like God's camera. His lines, his proportions, all perfection. Michelangelo, Da Vinci, they might have learned a thing or two from my father. He painted angels with flesh the texture of air, captured their flight on the end of his brush and suffused his colors with their yearning spirits.

"Pardon me, Father, but if there is a God you will find him walking through my father's work." He gestured to the painting high on the wall behind him. "Look at that one with the clouds, the angel's form just slipping out of the mist. You see such clouds and the fact that an angel hides among them shouldn't surprise you. No one since Turner has painted skies more magnificent than my father's, and that is simply one particular sample of his powers."

Gazing at the painting the priest drunkenly attempted to cross himself, and failed. "And that is why you no longer attend Mass, my son? Because our sacraments pale before your father's great talent?"

"I understand that Father Gavin administers the sacrament, and has for years. He is the one who counsels the ill and the downtrodden. Your duties are strictly administrative, are they not? And yet you are the one whose portrait will be hung in the church hall."

"Admittedly, I have no talent for people. I never have. Frankly I find the general populace annoying—all their petty concerns, when there are things of such spiritual beauty to contemplate, such as your father's fine paintings. But I am the older priest—it is our bishop's wish that I have my painting done first. I would not claim that I am deserving of the honor."

"And yet you have not turned it down."

"I have not turned it down." The elderly priest looked into his empty glass, then filled it slowly, shakily, struggling to spill as little of the precious wine as possible. "You admire your father's work so much, and you belittle your own. Is it possible you resent your father's talent, and that is why you no longer attend Mass at St. Anthony's, because you would be forced to encounter his finest work there—the 'Three Angels and the One,' 'The Thousand Eyes of the Seraphim' or his magnificent 'Sancte Deus'? Or perhaps you fancy yourself some condemned child, fallen from grace after disappointing his father? Or a rebel, is that the way you think of yourself, Mr. S.D. Watkins, Painter of Portraits?"

"But, old man, who could be more of a rebel than the priest who hates his parishioners?"

The priest paused, then gulped down most of his glass. The wine seemed to have hoarsened his voice. "Your initials, S.D.? I do not believe I have ever encountered your first name. Surely he did not name you after his greatest painting?"

"My father was an intense, at times obsessive, artist. But he was not insane. My first name is Samuel, middle name Daniel," the younger Watkins lied.

The priest shone his munificent smile and unfocused gaze on the portrait painter. "I believe your wound is bleeding again, a bit more copiously, I fear."

Watkins held up his right hand, gazing at it as if he'd never seen it before. The bandage wrapping his palm was soiled and fraying, and so thin it appeared painted on, the texture reminding him, in fact, of a shroud his father had once painted over a contorted Jesus. The heart of the bandage was stained with a starburst black and maroon. "This is no problem. I hold the brush at the tips of my fingers, using my whole arm to move it across the canvas. As my father always told me, 'When you hold it too tightly, you disconnect yourself from the thing you've embraced.'"

"But you're ruining the page, my son."

"I've changed my mind—we will dispense with further sketching. I will go attend to this, fetch a fresh bottle of wine, and when I return we will begin the painting proper. And I will tell you why I no longer attend Mass."

Watkins went down into the cellar, grabbed a bottle of wine he had not watered down, and turned to the ramshackle cabinet mounted at a slant to the dirty cement wall. He peeled the bandage off his hand and dropped it. He pulled out fresh gauze from the cabinet, aware of all his paintings staring at his back, but he did not turn around. He groped about the table beneath the cabinet, found a dirty paintbrush, and jammed it into the open wound. He ground the brush into the raw tissues, tried to keep his eyes clear to watch, but they involuntarily clamped shut. He wrapped the clean gauze around his hand with his eyes closed. Overhead he could hear the priest singing to himself.

He painted the background in tones taken from the priest's flesh illuminated by the flicker of firelight, then gradually darkened the lines so that the edge of a bookcase appeared, then a hot patch of fireplace. The priest stared with eyes wide open, wine glass tilted almost to the point of a nasty spill. Watkins thought he might actually be napping. He began to carve the form out of the bruised tones swimming behind the nodding priest. He looked carefully at the air surrounding the withered head atop the shivering shoulders, and painted what he saw there, the colors vibrating until the features became indistinct. But there was something there, if he could only see well enough to capture it.

"Is it the church's recent troubles with—indiscretion. Is that what keeps you away, my son? Perhaps some unfortunate incident when you were a boy?"

Watkins was somewhat startled by the priest's coherence, when he'd been thinking the aging cleric on the verge of unconsciousness. "I would hardly call those troubles recent. And no, I was not fondled by some randy member of the clergy. Not that any of that improves the possibility of my attendance."

The priest nodded in agreement or perhaps simply in response to some inner, alcohol-induced rhythm. "It is a sad state of affairs. In the priesthood we yearn for the beautiful, for a spiritual life which will raise us above the concerns of the everyday. But we find we must wait so very long. Some find that beautiful spirit in children, and they lose their perspective. They simply lose their way."

"And you, are you saying you lost your way?"

"Don't be ridiculous. I, for one, have never found any special beauty in children. They are simply loud, and unformed. But have you bought into the news propaganda—do you see all of us as monsters?"

"Many priests came into our home while my father was alive. Some seemed rather ordinary. And others, although I did not 'buy in' to their beliefs necessarily, are still among the most admirable, unselfish human beings I have ever met."

The priest sighed, laughed. "I could not say so, from my experience."

Watkins concentrated on getting the eyes right. If the eyes were not correct no other part of the portrait could compensate. "So are you saying your faith is not so strong?"

"There is nothing wrong with my faith in God, Child. It is human beings I have trouble with."

"So you believe there is evil in the world."

"Are you saying there is not?"

"No, but I would ask why. Your god, my father's god, is he not omnipotent? If so, how can he allow evil?"

The priest laughed. "Perhaps your doubts of your own originality are justified, S.D. Watkins. The question of evil? Why do the wicked prosper while the righteous suffer? If I could answer that perhaps they would make me a bishop! It goes back to the fallen angels, I suppose. But such philosophical questions are not for the likes of us. You must simply have faith, my son."

"The fallen angels. The ones who rebelled?"

"Lucifer sought to overthrow God. He had to be dealt with."

"It sounds like an adventure story. An action movie."

"Oh, I believe it may be the greatest adventure story of all time."

"I suppose I don't believe the spiritual underpinnings of our existence should sound like an adventure story."

The priest leaned forward. "Son, are you in pain?"

Watkins became aware then that he had been supporting his wounded hand with the stronger one. His inflamed fingers barely kept their grip on the brush. Together they moved around the canvas making marks and elaborating on the hunched form of the priest in the middle of the composition. In the painting the priest's face was still not focused. The angles of the shoulders were all wrong, or perhaps they were, at last, correct. "It is always painful to see clearly, Father."

The priest snorted. "It is always painful to imagine more than you can be."

"Are you referring to yourself? I only paint what I am able to see. My father the great Martin Watkins, painter of angels, he was the one with imagination."

Watkins calmed himself, forcing his brush hand to move at a more leisurely pace around the canvas, making corrections and adjustments, redefining lines, picking up details, using his pain as a kind of compass, or diviner, to guide him.

"Perhaps we should stop. I believe I may have drunk too much wine."

"Just stay with me a while longer, Father—I'm not yet ready to take a break. I don't want to lose the thread that will lead me into your true portrait. Tell me some stories. Tell me about the giants."

"You mean Fe Fi Fo Fum, that sort of thing?"

"Don't be coy. Speak to me of the giants in the Bible. They were the offspring of the angels and human women, were they not?"

"Oh, that's simply part of the *Jewish* writings. The Book of Enoch, the Dead Sea Scrolls, that sort of thing. Nothing to take very seriously. Please do not tell me you stay away from the church because of giants!"

"Why, Father, the way you said *Jewish*—are you a bigot?"

The priest said nothing for a time. The only sound was the vigorous scratching Watkins made against the canvas, with too much force and too little paint. Finally the priest replied, "Yes, I am, but I would like to imagine that someday I will be a better man."

"Sorry. I don't possess that kind of imagination. Remember, I paint what I see."

Watkins continued to paint vigorously. Paint and blood splattered his face, dripped down his arm to pool on the canvas.

"The angels had their way with human women, thereby corrupting humankind. It is a distasteful story."

"But they not only corrupted them sexually—they corrupted them in other ways, did they not?"

"Things we were not intended to know."

"Perhaps they taught us how to create art."

"Their offspring were easily recognized. Even after the giants disguised themselves as normal they could be identified by their double rows of teeth, their distortions."

"Congenital malformations."

"Oh, I would never say that."

"Of course you wouldn't say that." Watkins' brush traveled over the sharp shoulders of the priest's image. The shoulders began to transform, the flesh rising off the body. "But this story of giants, it sounds like the kind of lie you would tell yourself, like I'm a good priest, or I'm not a bigot, or I am this great, undiscovered artistic talent. A lie that makes you feel better about yourself."

"I don't believe I understand."

"Humanity didn't want to believe they were descended from this mating with angels, so they invented giants as carriers of the tainted blood."

"Watkins, that is insanity. I will pray for you, my son."

"Thank you. Your portrait is complete, by the way. I will send my bill directly to the bishop, if you don't mind."

"Perhaps that would be best."

"Come look at it, tell me if it's an accurate likeness, in your opinion."

"Why, I have had so much wine. I really don't believe I can reclaim my feet."

"Take your time, Father. I will leave it on the easel. If you'll excuse me I'd best go take care of my hand again."

Watkins took a last glance at his painting. The image of the priest was still somewhat hunched, but it was rising to its feet, dragged heavenward by the translucent distortions in the shoulders and back and the warped transmutations in the flesh of the chest area, just opening up and catching the air.

"I really don't believe I can stand," the priest muttered.

"Have faith. Your faith may comfort you. When I was small I would watch my father paint the angels. Here, and in St. Anthony's. I know now he painted other things during that period, a number of landscapes, some studies of workers down at the docks, but those canvases were lost among these countless images of angels, floating, sitting, standing casually or at attention, singing, dancing, doing for the most part what human beings do, except that they were larger than life, possessed of a kind of inner illumination."

The priest stirred enough to say, "Lovely."

"I suppose. But you know what bothered me? He'd modeled them after relatives, after neighbors, and some of the local priests. Not only their faces, but something about their postures, the general attitudes they expressed. I did not want to see it, but I could not deny my eyes. After that I could not look at any of those people the way I had before."

Down in the cellar Watkins flipped on the light and gazed sadly at his heavenly host of creations staring out from their less-than-perfect, overworked canvases: their warped backs, their distorting faces, their double, sometimes triple rows of teeth. Their clouds of eyes. Their six wings. Their wings pulled from ruined flesh as if by a giant hand, leaving but a broken stalk of ethereal flesh, and still their mouths forced open, praising all that is holy, Sancte Deus, Amen.

Upstairs he could hear the old priest falling, dragging himself to his portrait, weeping.

BEING RIGHT
Michael Marshall Smith

MICHAEL MARSHALL SMITH is a novelist and screenwriter who lives in North London with his wife, son and two cats.

Under that name he has published around seventy short stories and three novels—*Only Forward*, *Spares* and *One of Us*—winning the Philip K. Dick, International Horror Guild, August Derleth and British Fantasy awards, as well as France's Prix Morane.

Writing as "Michael Marshall," he has published five internationally best-selling thrillers, including *The Straw Men*, *The Intruders* and *Bad Things*, with *The Breakers* forthcoming. *The Servants*, a ghostly short novel set at the British seaside, recently appeared under the byline "M.M. Smith."

"There's nothing I enjoy more than heading out to a pub with my wife and spending the night setting the world to rights," admits the author. "Sometimes, however, it can seem that I can do rather more listening than speaking.

"Then one night I discovered, to my bewilderment, that she felt exactly the same. She could not be more wrong, of course, and so from here came the idea of some kind of objective measurement—over not just one evening, but a lifetime . . ."

IT WAS MONDAY, the fourth day of their vacation, and the fourth solid day of rain. This didn't bother Dan unduly—you didn't come to London, London in February, moreover, if you were looking to work on your tan—and they'd packed accordingly. The city was moreover full of museums, galleries, stores: it had history up the wazzoo, a lot of good restaurants and nearly as many Starbucks as at home. If you could bear to get a little damp in between stops, there was a good time to be had whatever the precipitation situation. The forecast—which Dan knew all about, having been woken by it at 5:30 that morning—said the weather was going to get better as the week went on. Which was hopeful, but either way, it was something you couldn't do anything about. The weather was simply there. You had to just accept it, adjust your plans accordingly, move on. There was no point complaining. No point going on and on and *on*.

What you *could* affect, on the other hand, was jetlag.

If you were flying to Europe—which they had done many, many times since the kids left home—there was a simple procedure to follow. You were going to land in the early morning, so it made sense to catch some sleep on the plane (however fractured and tossy-turny, even a little helps). Then from the minute you arrived on foreign shores you locked yourself mentally to the new slot, and you stayed awake until the time you would normally at home. That way your body quickly got itself into some new kind of understanding, and you were so bushed by the time it came to turn in that you'd sleep regardless. Might be a couple of days where you felt draggy late afternoon, but otherwise you'd be okay.

This is what Dan had done. This is what he always did.

Marcia, she did it different.

Despite the fact they'd discussed it, she stayed awake the whole flight. Said she'd found it impossible to sleep, though Dan had managed to catch an hour or two—not much, but enough to make a difference, to con the body into believing it had been through some kind of night. Then, when they'd gotten to the hotel just before lunch, she'd started yawning, muttering about a nap. Dan told her to keep going—but mid-afternoon still found her spark out on the bed. Dan left her there and went for a stroll around the surrounding blocks. Sure, he felt a little spacey and weird, but he kind of enjoyed the feeling, and the walk. It served as a first recon of the neighborhood, informing him where the cafés where, the nearest bookstore, all of that. It reminded you, too, that you'd done a pretty strange thing, traveled a long way, and that you weren't at home anymore. For Dan, this walk was the opening ceremony of the vacation. It said: Here I Am.

When he got back to the hotel, Marcia was in the shower. They went out, had another little walk, and then dinner in the nearest restaurant. By ten o'clock Dan was utterly beat, and ready for bed. Marcia was speeding by then, however, and wanted to talk up the issues around Proposition 7, the *cause de jour* back home in Oregon. Dan hadn't much cared about P7 when on his own turf (it was going to be defeated, which was a shame, but that's what people are like), and sure as hell didn't care about it now. What was the point of coming to another country if you were going to mire yourself in the same old crap?

When he eventually said this, yawning massively, Marcia led the discussion into a playful analysis of why he was apparently unable to enter into any kind of intellectual dialogue that wasn't about books, before deftly turning back to Proposition 7.

This lasted a further twenty-five minutes. When Dan finally said he was just going to have to go to bed, she shook her head and stood up. First evening of the holiday ruined, her body language said: thank you once again, my brutish husband. Thanks a lot.

Dan slept like a baby that night.

Marcia, not so well.

They spent the next couple of days getting some tourism done, seeing the iconic sights, ticking the big ones off the list. Dan was happy to do this, knowing they'd relax by the weekend, find their vacation feet, be able to kick back and do their own thing. By Saturday he was locked on GMT, the lingering late-afternoon slump nothing that an extra-shot latté couldn't shake off. Marcia meanwhile was getting further and further out of sync, however. She was waking at six, five, four in the morning: sitting up in bed reading (and reading a novel set in America, naturally, or else one of the magazines she'd brought from home); alternatively, as on the Monday morning, turning the television on—quietly, of course, but you could still hear the tube crackle—and obsessing about the rain.

The real problem wasn't the jetlag, annoying though it was (when it could've been so easily avoided). Dan could sympathize with jetlag. Not sleeping, it's no fun. You lie there on your back staring up at an unfamiliar ceiling and your brain goes round and round and round. He had sympathy with sleeplessness. What drove him quietly nuts was the *mentioning* of it, the endless fricking . . . talk.

It was the same when Marcia had a cold. Dan got a cold, he took some tablets, waited for it to go away. He'd snuffle and wheeze a little, but you couldn't do anything about that. With Dan, a cold lasted four days, tops, soup to nuts, first sneeze to oh-it's-gone. With Marcia a cold was a two-week miniseries, an HBO Big Season Event. The first signs would be noted, discussed, held up for scrutiny. The danger of an approaching malaise would be flagged, and the particular inconvenience of its timing loudly mourned. Nine times out of ten this phase would last a single evening—and then the symptoms would disappear, having never been anything more than two sneezes, or a mild headache. Sometimes the cold would arrive for real, however— and she would wander down the next morning wrapped in a blanket, face crumpled, nose red, hair all crazy.

And then, for at least a week, the *mentioning of it*.

The constant updates—as if, twenty times a day, he'd said to her, "Now, darling, tell me *exactly* how every single little bit of your body feels, and don't stint on the detail. Really. I *have* to know." The sinus report. The lower back state-of-play. The throat film-at-eleven—but first here's a message from our sponsor, Runny Noses R Us.

The cold would go away, eventually. Two days of noting its passing, and she'd be fine—would return, in fact, to the woman who said she never got colds, not ever. That's when Dan knew he was in trouble. Ten days of reduced conversation would mean she was full to the brim with observations of pith and moment, stuff that simply *had* to get out of her head before it popped. Any chat, no matter how relaxed, could get suddenly derailed into a discussion of the major or minor issues of the day/year/century, with Marcia being firm but fair, subtle but strident, as if performing to a sizable radio audience. His participation was allowed once in a while, as a foil, a sentence thrown in as by an interviewer. Other than that, she'd just roll. Any suggestion that the length and depth of discussion was inappropriate to a dinner out at a local restaurant, to Sunday breakfast, or to when he was trying to have a quiet bath, would be met with the masterfully oblique suggestion that he just hadn't thought about the issues enough, and that anyway he'd had his say and it was her turn now.

Followed by more discussion.

It was on one of these occasions, a romantic supper that had turned into a two-hour debate on their town's zoning regulations, that Dan had first fantasized about the notion of some kind of independent adjudication: the idea that there might be some agency to which he could appeal, not with ill will, but just so he could be proved right— just so that it could be established, once and for all, that she did hog discussions, cheated in arguments (by shifting the topic whenever she realized she was on shaky grounds), and got mini-colds once a month.

He loved his wife and wouldn't want her any different. But just once in a while he wished there was some way of proving that *he was right*.

No one was more surprised than he to find out that actually, there was.

• • • • •

The bookstore was in a side street halfway down Charing Cross Road. When they'd last been to London, back in the mid-1990s, the area had been wall-to-wall books. Like everywhere else in the world, it was now feeling the dual pinch of the megastores and online auction sites. The specialty shops were still in place, but the second-hand and antiquarian had closed or gone to seed, and there was a big hole left by the demise of a former Borders.

Having left Marcia back at the hotel in the health spa for the morning, Dan was mildly ticked to find he'd done the street with an hour and a half to spare. He didn't want to go back early, kick his heels in the hotel. Marcia had been her most jetlagged yet that morning, and very down about the weather. He'd been unsympathetic on two subjects over which he considered himself powerless, and sharp words had been spoken.

On a whim, he started poking around the uncharted streets just behind the main road, and it was here that he found Pandora's Books. A little wooden shop front, the name appropriately picked out in faded gold paint. The window was littered with a random selection of ancient-looking volumes, none of which he'd heard of. Perfect. Especially as it was beginning to drizzle. Again.

The smell made him smile as soon as he was inside. Old, forgotten paper, books foxed and creased and bumped. The scent of old shelves and venerable dust added their own welcome notes. It was the way these places *should* smell, the smell of peace and quiet and your own thoughts, the odor of not being in a hurry. The room wasn't too big— probably only twenty feet by fifteen—but the high shelves packed into it, along with the dim light, made it seem larger. In the back there were wooden staircases leading both up and down, neither marked "Private," promising more of the same (and second-hand bookstores are all about promise). There was a little desk over on the right, piled high with books waiting categorization, but nobody behind it, or in sight. Dan dithered, then propped his bag against the desk. Usually bookstores preferred it that way, to discourage shoplifters, and it would leave both hands free.

He worked his way down from the top. They had a whole lot of books, that was for damned sure. Most of the stuff on the upper level was modern and of no interest, though he did find a pulp paperback worth keeping in his hand. He thought he heard someone coming up the stairs while he turned this book over, debating the couple of pounds it would cost, but when he looked up no one was there. By the time he got back to street level they'd evidently headed down to the basement.

He took his time around the shelves on the ground floor, as many were dedicated to local history. In the end he found one thing he thought was a definite, plus a couple of maybes. Depended on whether they shipped. The book he wanted was heavy—a vast Victorian facsimile of an older history of London—and he went over to prop it up against his bag. As he did so he thought he heard someone coming into the room from the back, but when he turned, a small loving-your-store smile on his face, there was no one there. Evidently just a noise from upstairs. Booksellers creep in mysterious ways, their alphabetizing to perform.

It was in the basement that he found the book.

At first he thought there was nothing for him down there: the room was only half the size of the higher floors, and had none of their sense of order. Tomes of all ages and conditions were piled onto cases in danger of imminent collapse. There was a strong smell of damp down there, too, doubtless caused or at least enhanced by the grim-looking patches on the walls. The plaster had come away in many places, revealing seeping brickwork behind.

Dan poked around for a while nonetheless, shoving aside piles of bashed-up book-length ephemera (do your own accounts, learn Spanish in twenty seconds, find your inner you and dream your inner dream), finding and quickly rejecting a few older tomes. It's a shame when the floor you do last has the least of interest in it, but sometimes that's just the way it is. He was about to give up and go pay for what he'd already put aside, when a bookcase half-hidden right at the end caught his eye. He decided to check it out. He was in no hurry, after all.

He'd thought from a distance these books were much older than the rest, but he soon saw they were not. Most were Everyman Editions, leather-bound and quite attractive, but commonplace and not worth the carrying. He had already turned away when something made him turn back and look again. He stood square onto the case and ran his eyes back and forth in a grid pattern. He'd evidently glimpsed something without really seeing it. He wasn't expecting much, but it would be mildly interesting to see what had caught his eye. Eventually he found it, a book whose spine was much more scuffed up than the rest.

He gently eased it out. It was called *Hopes of a Lesser Demon, Part II*, which was kind of odd, for a start. It was a small, chunky thing with battered boards and old leather covers; about an inch thick, six inches high, and four deep. The title on the spine seemed to have been handwritten in ink. When Dan turned to the front the frontispiece claimed the book had been published in Rome in 1641, but that couldn't be right. For a start, that meant it should have been in Latin, or Italian at the very least. It wasn't. It was in English, for the most part.

As he leafed through the book it also seemed clear that it could never actually have been published in this form at all. Chunks of it did look very old, the paper spotted and towelly, the text in languages he didn't understand and typefaces that were hard to read. Others had been printed far more recently; the paper fresh and glossy, the subjects contemporary. Though there were sections in French and German and something Eastern European, plus something he guessed was Korean from its similarity to the signs on a food market he walked by back home.

It was also far from clear what the book was *about*.

There was a sermon on chastity, a few pages on deciduous trees. Part seemed to be a travel guide to Bavaria, with spotty black-and-white plates that must have been taken before the First World War. A polemic on some obscure Middle Eastern sect was followed by a stretch of love poetry, which had mathematical equations in the footnotes, and proceeded by two handwritten pages of what looked like the accounts of a sugar plantation in the West Indies in the eighteenth century. There was no sense to it whatsoever, and yet at the bottom of each page was a folio—a page number—and the ordering of these numerals was consistent from front to back, regardless of subject change or whether they were printed in decaying hand-plated Gothic type or super-crisp computer-generated Gill Sans.

Dan flipped back to the front, and saw a price written there in pencil. Five pounds. Eight–nine bucks. Hmm. He already wanted the book, without really knowing why.

He glanced through the pages a little further, looking for an excuse to turn his impulse into a no-brainer, and finding merely further pockets of unrelated non-information. A handful of reproductions of watercolors, none by artists he recognized, and few of them any good. A list of popular meadows in Armenia. A section on advanced electronic engineering, complete with circuit diagrams, then a Da Vinci-like ink sketch of a man holding an axe, followed by a long portion of what seemed to be an illustrated children's book, about a happy dog.

And then there were the "Invocations."

The paper of this section was very, very old, and the writing had been entered by hand. Portions had faded back almost to nothing, and even those that were strong weren't very easy to read. The first page seemed to be a kind of index. Item One read: "The Vision of Love's Arc invocation—for to glimpse what man or woman (or both) shall come into your life, hopefully." Item Eleven: "The Sadness of Cattle Invocation—the purpose being to make less gloomy your livestock in the night." Item Twenty-Two: "The Regeneration of Heat invocation—a most useful gesture for the revitalization of a time-cooled hot beverage."

What? A spell to warm up a cup of coffee?

That was silly. The whole index was dumb, in fact, the most stupid section of what was evidently a very stupid book. Dan had more-or-less changed his mind about buying it—five pounds was five pounds, after all, and the book was surprisingly heavy for its size—when he caught sight of the last entry in the index:

Item Thirty-Eight: "The Listening Angel—an invocation for to prove whether you are right."

Frowning, Dan flicked to the indicated page and read just enough to establish that yes, this meant exactly what he thought it did.

He seemed suddenly to hear a rushing noise, quite loud, like the tread of a hundred feet, or the beat of thousands of tiny wings. He closed the book and hurried up the stairs.

There was still no one at the desk, though he saw the explanation for the sound he'd heard. It was raining properly outside now, raining hard. The store's dim lamps struggled against the lowering darkness.

Dan waited for a few moments, moving impatiently from foot to foot, and then ventured to call out. There was no response. He waited a little longer, then strode to the back of the store and hiked up the stairs. There was no one up there. No one in the basement, either, when he went back down to look. He found himself back at street level, standing again in front of a desk which was still deserted.

Dan dug in his wallet and took out a five pound note. He put it on the desk and picked up his bag. He left the big Victorian book behind. It no longer seemed very interesting.

When he got back to the hotel he was soaked, and surprised to discover he was also late. Somehow it had become three o'clock. He was half-expecting to find Marcia waiting huffily in the lobby, but she wasn't there. He took the elevator up to the room. It was empty. Baffled, he called the spa—and was relieved to find that a woman of his wife's description was currently fast asleep on one of the loungers around the pool. Relieved and, of course, irritated.

He left the book on the bed and wandered around the hotel room, drying his hair with a towel. He *could* go down and wake Marcia, remind her they were supposed to be . . . but what was the point? By the time she was dressed it would be too late to get to the Tate. And he would also, he realized, have to account for the fact he'd returned well after he'd said he would. It was not the first time, and "looking at books" never seemed to be a good-enough explanation.

He set up the room's coffee machine and waited for it to do its thing. Meanwhile he sat in the chair at the desk, and watched the book on the bed. It wasn't moving, naturally, and there was no danger that it would. And yet . . . it didn't feel as if he was merely looking at it. Of course you couldn't actually "watch" something if it wasn't doing anything, though, right? And yet. And yet.

When coffee was made, he went and picked the book up. At first he couldn't find the Index of Invocations. After dipping into the book at random, he started at the beginning and rigorously leafed through from front to back. He saw a lot of odd things, but not the index. His heart, which had been beating rather faster that usual, gradually returned to normal. He flicked through the book again, more slowly, obscurely relieved. He had imagined it, that was all. Perhaps it had just been a kind of delayed jetlag fever: annoyance at the crossed words that morning, a fantasy born of the dust and damp of the shop . . .

Then he found them. The Invocations, sandwiched between two sections he *knew* he'd seen on the front-to-back pass. Whatever.

He scanned a few of the other entries:

"Item Twenty-Four: The Strengthening of Bark—a whisper for aiding the defenses of a tree or bush (of considerable size) that is under attack."

"Item Ninety: The Hail of Destiny—a snap to force unto yourself the attentions of any passing taxi cab."

"Item Six: The Flattening Stroke—for to redress a planet that has become mistakenly round. Use only once."

But they were just diversions. Very quickly he made it down to Item Thirty-Eight, then flicked through the pages until he again found the one that entry referred to.

As he opened the page he heard the sound again, the beating of wings.

A glimpse out of the window confirmed that this was, for a second time, merely an increase in the volume of rain outside. Odd how it kept happening, though. And how dark it had become.

The instructions on the page were short, and the ingredients it called for were not unduly hard to come by.

Marcia still hadn't returned.

Dan didn't see how he had much choice but to give it a try.

Half an hour later he was standing on the roof of the hotel. This hadn't been easy to bring about, but the recipe stipulated that the invoker must be both outside (in the sense of "not within a structure") and at the highest place available within one hundred horizontal feet of his or her position when the book had been most recently opened. Once he'd worked out what this meant, Dan took the elevator to the highest floor of the hotel—the twelfth—but knew somehow this wouldn't be enough. Plus, if something was going to happen, he didn't want to be interrupted by another guest heading back to their room. A certain amount of poking around led him to a door around a corner, which was marked STORES. There were indeed stores inside, and Dan helped himself to a bath towel, but at the back was another door. Opening this led to a dark interior staircase which led upwards.

At the top was a metal door. It was locked. Of course. Dan kicked at it, impotently. He could hear the sound of rain beyond it. He was so close. He kicked again, the lock clicked, and the door swung open a foot.

The sound of rain was suddenly far louder, and Dan saw it was now pelting down outside. Putting aside the question of why the door was now unlocked, he wrapped the towel around his head, left the book on the floor where it wouldn't get wet, and stepped outside.

A very large, flat area lay in front of him, the roof of the hotel. Various protuberances stuck up here and there, some disgorging steam or smoke, many with fans which lazily cycled round. Piles of forgotten wood and other detritus lay against the low wall which went right around the edges. The grey surface of the roof was hidden in places by sizable pools of water, which reflected a blackening sky which seemed to be getting lower and lower.

Dan walked right out to the center of the roof and stopped. London was spread around him, albeit obscured by sheets of rain and gathering gloom. The towel was soon soaked, and he took it off. Evidently you just had to take this experience as it came. He had memorized the invocation. It wasn't hard. It was so straightforward, in fact, that it was ludicrous to believe it would achieve anything.

Nonetheless, he unwrapped the hand towel he'd brought up from the room. Inside were three things. A small sample of his saliva, in one of the room's water glasses: a "secretion" had been called for, and saliva was as far as he was prepared to go. A few strands of Marcia's hair, easily gleaned from her brush, wrapped in a piece of toilet tissue, and also put into the glass. Rather more trickily, a postcard to Marcia's sister. The recipe called for "a sample of both their words," and didn't explain it any more clearly than that. This defeated Dan until he noticed the postcard, written the previous evening in the bar and now lying on the desk awaiting a stamp. Most of it was in Marcia's hand, but he'd added a cheery sentence at the bottom. Would it do? Dan supposed he was about to find out. He rolled the postcard and put it into the glass, too.

He straightened, and quickly threw his hand up into the air. He was a fool, he knew, and braced himself for the immediate return of the glass, possibly onto his head.

It didn't come back down.

After a second he looked up, and saw that the glass had disappeared.

The rain had started falling harder, too, and now it really did sound like wings.

Parts of the sky slowly seemed to detach themselves from the rest, patches of darkness gathering as if a cloud were settling over the hotel, wisps of it catching on the buildings across the street, like the ghosts of future fires.

The sound of traffic seemed to get both louder and further away. Dan listened to it, and to the rain as it fell, until the two noises became one and entered his head, and disappeared, leaving it empty and still.

"Seventy-eight percent," said a voice.

Dan turned. Behind him, something was sitting on the low wall at the edge of the roof.

It was about twelve feet tall, the white of old, tarnished marble, and difficult to see. It seemed to sit hunched on the wall, huge wings hanging off its shoulders. It appeared a little uncomfortable, as if finding itself in the wrong place, somewhere either too hot or too cold.

"Are you the angel?" Dan said.

"Over the length of the marriage, you have spoken twenty-two percent of the time," the figure said. Its face was turned away from him, hidden behind long wet hair. Its voice was cold, dry, and seemed to come to Dan both via his ears and up through his legs. "If you limit the enquiry to periods of discussion that could be considered of academic or of purely hypothetical interest, then her contribution rises to eighty-six percent. This peaks, under the influence of alcohol, at ninety-four percent."

"Then I am right," Dan said. "I knew it."

The angel gave no indication it had heard. "If considered in terms of total words uttered, rather than time spent speaking, the breakdown is about the same. The shortness and lack of fluidity of your sentences is somewhat counterbalanced by the speed of your attempts to pack them in the short intervals available."

"Now hold on," Dan said. He started to walk forward, but a loud, heavy movement of the angel's wings warned him to stay where he was. Somewhere, far away, there was the rumble of thunder. "What do you mean, 'lack of fluidity'?"

"Caused merely by the lack of opportunity for you to get into your stride," the angel said. "Of course."

Dan nodded, mollified. "Thank you," he said. "Now. How do I . . .?"

"Sometimes she even talks when you're not there," the angel said. "Quite often, in fact."

"And you listen?"

"Of course. It's what I do."

Dan frowned. "What kind of things does she say?"

"She hopes your kids are safe."

"Well, so do I."

"Yes, but she says it out loud. And her words are heard."

"Okay," Dan said. He was cold. Unbelievably, it was starting to rain harder, the sky pressing closer down. His hair was plastered to his skull, water running down his face. "What . . . else does she say?"

It seemed like the angel was turning to look at him, but when the movement was finished it was still looking another way. "She says it makes her sad when the children call, and you hand the phone straight to her, after merely grunting hello. She tries not to resent the fact you make no effort with her friends, and that—and these are my figures, not hers—you are on average responsible for less than four percent of the conversation when they're around. She has issues with the fact that you seem to believe her having a massage once in a while is a big indulgence, when you spend three times as much every month on books which you'll mostly never read, and often don't even open again. She feels hurt when you look at her as if wondering what she is harping on about, and why. She wishes that once in a while you would handle her in the way you do an interesting book—and says you used to, once."

Dan smiled tightly.

"Well, that's all very interesting. Thanks for your time. And your unbiased opinion."

The angel rolled its shoulders, as if preparing to leave. "She cares about things. Who do you think we're in favor of: those who care about things, or those who don't?"

Dan said nothing.

"And the colds," the angel added. "Who do you think they're worse for, her or you?"

"I've got to go," Dan said. "I assume you will let yourself out."

He headed back toward the metal door, sloshing straight through the puddles. He didn't want this anymore. Sometimes the person you love is a pain in the ass. He wished he could have left it that. The rain drummed on the roof like the turning of a million dusty pages. He felt suddenly tired, fifty years of coffee gone sour. With each step it became harder to remember what had just happened, or to believe it, or to remember why he'd wanted to know.

He was reaching for the handle on the door when the angel spoke again. It sounded different. Quieter, further away, as if only a memory of itself.

"When she cannot sleep she lies awake and hopes you still love her."

Dan stopped dead in his tracks, and turned. "Of course I do," he said, stricken. "She must know that, surely."

The angel was fading now, the steady flap of its wings turning back to rain, the grey of its skin becoming cloud once more. As it stood, it turned into rising mist in front of his eyes, its words coming to him as cold wind, blown his way by the beating of those wings.

It said: "For her, the sound of the two of you talking together is like the smell of books. Do you think she doesn't notice, when you believe you're being good about being bored? Sometimes that's why she keeps talking, because she panics when she fears you might not find her interesting anymore."

It said: "This 'peace and quiet' you believe you want so much: what is it for? What thoughts do you harbor, so valuable they are worth wishing quietness upon someone who loves you so much? Meanwhile she fears for all the ways that things can go wrong in the world, and become still, and lose strength and fall apart."

It said: "If she dies before you do, which she might, will you then still wish you'd spent more time in silence? When you live in that endless quiet after, in those years of deadening cloud and solitude, what might you be prepared to promise, to give, to hear just one word more from her?"

Then the wind dropped and it was gone.

Dan stood on the roof a full five minutes longer. When he stepped back through the metal door into the hotel, he found the book was gone. He hurried down the stairs, through the store cupboard, and ran to the elevator.

When he let himself back into the hotel room, he heard the sound of Marcia in the bath.

"Dan?" she said quickly, "Is that you?"

"Yes," he said.

"Where have you *been*?"

"Got caught out in the rain," he said, carefully, not yet wanting to go in, not yet ready to see her face. "I'm sorry. Had to hunker down and wait inside somewhere while it passed over. I called the room. You weren't here."

"Fell asleep," she said, sheepishly. There was silence for a moment. Then she said: "I missed, you."

"I missed you, too." He took his jacket off and hung it up in the wardrobe to dry. "You okay?"

"You know, I think I'm coming down with a cold."

Dan rolled his eyes, but called room service to bring up tea, lemon and honey, before going to help wash her hair. She told him about the spa in the hotel. He told her about his walk, leaving out Pandora's Books. The two of them sat companionably with their words in the warm bathroom, the world cold and wet outside. They decided to order food to their room. They watched TV, read a little, went to bed.

In the small hours of the night, while Marcia fitfully dozed, the listening angel came into the room and touched her brow, whispering to her to worry no more, for a while.

When Dan woke in the morning, Marcia was asleep next to him. It rained a little as they ate breakfast together, but after that the day was fine.

NOVUS ORDO ANGELORUM

Jay Lake

Desire

THE ANGEL OF DESIRE bares her breasts, nipples hard in the dreaming wind of night. Her hair flows from her head like smoke in the autumn sky. It is every shade of black and grey—desire is the province of each age of life, not just callow youth nor addled dotage nor even obsessed middle years.

Desire's wings stretch wide as any angel's, but their plumage is rare. They look to have been patched together from a very congeries of birds; the mountain teratornis and the lammergeyer, the great golden eagles of the Arabian desert and the condor in his snowbound fastness. Every child dreams of flight, waking to be mocked by the birds. Her wings bear the burden of those dreams, which unfold in later life to the wretched obsessions that drive men mad.

But it is in her eyes, the gaze of Desire, where this angel's true power lies. They are rimmed with kohl, draped with lashes like a dark spray of rust. Their brown depths are drowning pools of lust. To catch her glance is to feel your heart stop, to feel blood cold in your arms and hot in your groin. No one, no age or gender, is safe from her eyes, so Desire wears a mask of silk and leather with a coiled snake worked upon it in tiny rubies formed from the blood of those she has loved.

In her hooded beauty she reminds us that Love is the greatest and most terrible of God's gifts.

Despair

Desire's fraternal twin Despair is a young man with hollow eyes and a sunken chest. His hair is the eerie pallor of the starving, the icy white frizz grown by a corpse in its coffin. His skin is so pale as to be almost blue. Despair looks like every student pulled from a morgue freezer, caught on the wrong side of that balancing point between potential and disaster.

His wings are different from his sister's, composed of what might be called the ghosts of feathers, only brittle shafts and lacy ribs, without soft plumage to fill them out. Despair wears them wound close and tight to his body, just over the leather greatcoat that flaps around his calves. He dresses in torn black denim and an array of ropy scars. Everyone who ever cut themselves in his name has inflicted their own wound upon him.

Despair's power is in his body. Even in shadow, the angle of his repose can cause a man to slump, a woman to turn away with tear-burned eyes. To meet Despair full on, his every muscle broadcasting the hopeless music of the world, is to lay down meek in the street and end your struggle.

He is both God's invitation and warning to stray from faith.

Chance

There is another angel, distant cousin to those already named, the angel of Chance. Chance is an elegant young man. His blond hair flips back in a wave. He favors pastel polo shirts and stylish white slacks. His wings are discreet, a clever accessory to be admired by the matrons of River Oaks or Telegraph Hill, while granddaughters at the country club blush behind their Shirley Temples and whisper youthful scandal of Chance's single silver earring.

Chance is not concerned with wagering, or the lottery, but rather the common happenstances of life. A missed flight, that relieves the annoyed traveler of death by burning jet fuel hours later in an Iowa cornfield. The flat tire that keeps the family Camry from a patch of black ice, leaving slick, spinning death for someone less favored. Hands bumping together over a book on sale at Powell's, leading to coffee, then pizza, then a wild night of passion followed by a lifetime of contentment.

You could pass Chance on the street and never really know him except by the twenty-dollar bill you later find stuck to your shoe. Chance is God's reminder to us that order is not one of the forces of the world.

Flora

Flora is the angel of plants and flowers. Her work is found among the world's oldest and quietest citizens. She wears flowing silks borrowed from her friends among the mulberry leaves, and crowns of whatever blooms that hour and season, be it the moss rose or the orchid. Her wings are spiders' webs, pale traceries glimmering by moonlight. It is the sight of Flora moving through the gardens of night that gave rise to legends of fairies.

Flora's hair is all the colors of the natural world, a rainbow turned to river. Her eyes are the brown of soil one moment, the blue of water the next. Her smile is tiny, pursed, a soon-to-open rose. Her heart is just as thorny.

Do not mistake Flora for a benign power. Trees with their roots rend the mightiest works of man. The least lichen is the death of rocks. Your bones will someday be her province, once the worms have cast you out. More patient than Time, she carries worlds in her hands and love of all that grows in her heart.

No one knows what God thought when He set her into the world, but remember that it was sweet Flora who set the order of the plantings in the Garden. It was she that tended the orchards. It was she that placed the fig leaves where a shamed man might find them, and it was she that grew the apple tree where a woman of intellect might climb on advice of a snake.

Word

Word is the oldest angel of all. He is sometimes called "God's grandfather." He carries his age well. It shows only in the webbing of lines around his pale, blind eyes, and the stiffness in his step. He has a shock of red hair that lifts in a mutable fire from his head, so that Word is always as tall as he needs to be. His skin is dark as well-baked bread. His face is the face of Everyman.

Blind as he is, Word needs no cane, for his wings serve him well. They arch high as a house, more like the wings of a moth than a bird. Their sensitive fibers build for him a picture of the world. He wears no clothes for textiles would block his wings and pain his senses. Even in his nakedness Word is wrapped in glory.

For you see, in the beginning Word made the world upon the waters when God spat Word from His mouth. Later, Word made flesh. Without their tongues, men would be no more than animals. Without Word, men's tongues would be no more than meat.

Word is the beacon of our minds and the light of our days, withered proxy for an absent God.

SARIELA; OR, SPIRITUAL DYSFUNCTION & COUNTERANGELIC LONGINGS: A CASE STUDY IN ONE ACT

Michael Bishop

MICHAEL BISHOP's novels include the Nebula Award–winning *No Enemy but Time*, the Mythopoeic Fantasy Award–winning *Unicorn Mountain* and the Locus Award–winning *Brittle Innings*.

His short fiction has appeared in seven collections, but recent uncollected stories include "The Door Gunner" and "Bears Discover Smut," both recipients of the Southeastern Science Fiction Association Award for short fiction, and "The Pile," recipient of the 2009 Shirley Jackson Award for short story.

He has also edited a number of books, including, most recently, *A Cross of Centuries: Twenty-Five Imaginative Tales About the Christ* and, with Steven Utley, *Passing for Human*.

"I originally wrote the one-act play 'Sariela' for the angel-themed anthology *Heaven Sent*, edited by Peter Crowther," explains Bishop, "and mostly recall great glee at turning my studies of angelic hierarchies and an interest in 'counterangelic longings' into remunerative fictive drama.

"I also take some pride in turning the male angel 'Sariel' into the female 'Sariela' and in referencing Milton's *Paradise Lost* on the provocative question of angelic sex."

NIGHT. *The interior of the Cat's Eye Bar, Grill, & Pinball Parlor on the outskirts of Ackley, Georgia, U.S.A. To the right (from the audience's point of view), a pair of high-finned, cut-down 1957 Chevy convertibles (one hot pink, one turquoise) set together bumper to bumper on blocks: the bar.*

Nine stools in front of it. upended airplane turbines with revolving leather seats. A mirror behind the bar reflects liquor bottles and glasses; it wears a swag of fishing net and is plastered with beer ads, travel stickers, and soiled pieces of U.S. and Latin American highway maps.

Left of the double-car bar, and up a half step, extends a sawdust-sprinkled drinking area, jukebox room, and dance floor. Rickety tables and cane-back chairs make a ragged archipelago across this expanse. A bank of lit-up Li'l Abner, Snuffy Smith, and Grandpa Clampett pinball machines share rear-wall space with a jukebox, a Roller Derby video game, and an art-deco thermoplastic Drew Barrymore umbrella and fly-reel stand.

A few shadowy HUMAN FIGURES slump at the back tables, nursing their booze and/or piecing together jigsaw puzzles of the Little Grand Canyon, loglike alligators in the Okefeenokee Swamp, or the Waving Girl statue on Savannah's River Street. A downstage table to the far left sits vacant, with a battered dessert cart behind it and an overgrown bonsai apple tree in a glazed Ming pot to one side in front of it . . . as a pretentious mythological symbol.

It is a chilly, damp Friday, the seventh of January, ano Domini 1994 (as ostensibly civilized western Earthlings reckon, subdivide, and pigeonhole time), but in the Cat's Eye—except for the video game and the Lucite umbrella stand—it could be 1963 (before John F. Kennedy's assassination), 1972 (shortly after the breakup of the Beatles), 1985 (near the premiere of A Lie of the Mind *at the Promenade Theater), or 1991 (the evening the Minneapolis Twins took the World Series from the Atlanta Braves in a domed stadium draped, it appeared to many Braves fans watching on television, with Hefty trash bags).*

The BARTENDER, a handsome twenty six-year-old farm-boy type with a long jaw and mismatched ears, sets a rosy cherub (raspberry ginger ale and Albigensian bitters) before his four-year-old son, AUBREY, and squints ceilingward. AUBREY floats a worm-eaten pecan in his rosy cherub and repeatedly kicks the rear door of the turquoise Chevy with his Payless penny loafers. The other five PATRONS at the car bar ignore the boy's toe drumming.

BARTENDER: Raphael? (*Squints, cocks his head, listens.*) Hey, Raffy, your table's ready.

RAPHAEL materializes at the table by the dessert cart and the symbolic bonsai. His head nearly touches the ceiling. He wears tight black leather pants, a beaded Choctaw vest over his otherwise unclad torso, and a white terrycloth headband on which the Magic Marker motto BEGOTTEN TO RAZE HELL is fuzzily emblazoned. He has huge wings, a single pair only.

He sits, props one wing, the left, on the dessert cart, and holds the other aloft so that it casts an oxymoronically luminous shadow over the entire dance floor, even to the near edge of the double-Chevy bar. He glances at his naked wrist, shakes his head disgustedly, and looks about the Cat's Eye as if for a waitress or a tardy drinking chum.

RAPHAEL: Hashmal, we have an appointment. Appear at your earliest convenience. Please.

HASHMAL manifests at the bar, between AUBREY and a hungover PATRON who doesn't even notice the chief of the angelic order known as dominions. HASHMAL—like RAPHAEL, a daunting seven feet tall—wears a brocaded jerkin, plum-colored tights with a sewn-in codpiece, and calf-high, slipper-soled, suede boots.

He pays for a draft Michelob Dark and turns to carry it up the half-step and across the floor to RAPHAEL's table. His pivot causes havoc: HASHMAL's wings trail him like a pair of feathery drag chutes, sweeping a Coors Silver Bullet, a highball glass of Wild Turkey, the ignition key to a Dodge Dakota pickup, and a woman's tortoise-shell compact onto the butt- and sawdust-strewn floor.

AUBREY looks after HASHMAL wide-eyed, but no one else at the bar reacts, either to mumble, "Watch it, buddy," or to snatch a wisp of down from one of his pillaging wings.

HASHMAL sits across from RAPHAEL, toasts him, and grimaces when the jukebox starts to shake the joint with the raucous Garth Brooks anthem, "Friends in Low Places."

RAPHAEL: You're inappropriately dressed.

HASHMAL: Beelzebub calling Moloch vile.

RAPHAEL: I mean for the era.

HASHMAL. I manifested. Never mind my attire. Just tell what urgency requires my presence *here*.

RAPHAEL: Sariela, of whom I have charge as captain of all guardian spirits. You, as captain of the order regulating angelic duties, need to hear how Sariela has proved negligent, just as I need your advice and counsel about what to do to help this unhappy spirit.

HASHMAL: *Sariela?* The name has a slippery sort of familiarity.

RAPHAEL: May I tell you the story?

HASHMAL: You do outrank me. Always have. Always will.

RAPHAEL (*refolding his wings, leaning forward*): We posted Sariela, a guardian of deliberately feminine aspect, to protect a newlywed couple from this very town, Ackley, Georgia, U.S.A.; Earth; Sol Planetary System; Milky Way Galaxy; Local Cluster Number—

HASHMAL: I know where we are.

RAPHAEL (*sotto voce*): If not when. (*Aloud:*) The couple to whom we posted Sariela go by the names Philip and Angel Marie Hembree. We sent her—

HASHMAL: Angel Marie? The woman's name is Angel Marie? How odd. Such ironic synchronicity.

RAPHAEL: A simple coincidence. It's only a name. In any event, we posted Sariela to the Hembrees on their wedding day, August 15, *anno Domini* 1993, the thirty-second anniversary of Philip's birth. Angel Marie had insisted that they marry on this day as a precaution against Philip ever forgetting their wedding anniversary. This same stratagem had also worked for her previous husband, Bobby Dean Gilbert, who died in 1989 in a collision between a trailer truck carrying a load of Christmas trees—Frasier firs, primarily—and the Gilberts' rattletrap 1978 Toyota Corolla.

HASHMAL: Both husbands were born on the same day?

RAPHAEL: No. *No!* Listen! This accident occurred on a fog-blanketed switchback of a North Georgia mountain, and Bobby Dean died instantly, impaled boccally by the trunk of a Frasier fir and thoracically by the Corolla's steering column.

HASHMAL (*shuddering*): Praise God our basic incorporeality frees us from any fear of impalement. (*Arches one eyebrow.*) Or we'd play hell dancing on the heads of pins, wouldn't we?

RAPHAEL (*impatiently*): Angel Marie, on the other hand, survived the accident, but with crippling injuries from which she still quietly struggles to recover. Her survival owes much to the professionalism of the Georgia Highway Patrol and a pair of Emergency Medical Service personnel who drove her to the county hospital.

A few weeks later, as a physical-therapy patient in the Cobalt Springs Rehabilitation Center here in Ackley, she met Philip Hembree, driving instructor for the resident disabled and also the teenage progeny of the Center's senior medical and administrative personnel. Blessedly, Angel Marie fell in the first category. Philip found her a much less demanding, and exasperating, student than the overweight male quadruple amputee, Carrol Bricknell, who could negotiate Ackley's back roads only with the aid of an experimental voice-activated computerized guidance unit and a strap-on chin pointer that its manufacturer refers to whimsically as either a "directional diviner" or a "unicorn wand." So, as you can imagine, Philip was predisposed to welcome Angel Marie into his customized, state-provided instructional vehicle as a student. In fact, he—

HASHMAL: Forgive, but these proliferating details overwhelm me. Of what sin of omission or commission is Sariela guilty? Has she somehow sabotaged the well-being or happiness of the Hembrees?

RAPHAEL: Oh, no. Far from it.

HASHMAL: What, then?

RAPHAEL: The trouble lies in Sariela's untoward response to a very specific, and somewhat delicate, manifestation of the Hembrees' admittedly exemplary mutual regard. I dilate on the human beings under her novice protection to give you a clearer insight into her anomalous attitudes and behavior. Must I cut to the vulgar chase? Or may I give you all the facts necessary to reach an informed and sagacious judgment?

HASHMAL: Pardon my impatience. Enlighten me fully.

RAPHAEL: Technically, Sariela served as Angel Marie's guardian. She replaced the quasi-disgraced Cristiana, who only by her pinion tips contrived to save her ward's life in that wreck with the Christmas-tree truck. Cristiana, I regret to report, has since lapsed into a vegetative spiritual funk—but that's another story. Sariela, despite her posting as Angel Marie's protector, had a sidelong responsibility to Philip, a professed agnostic, and this extra duty made her the *de facto* guardian of the Hembrees as a couple.

HASHMAL: Yes, yes. I understand.

RAPHAEL: Philip's agnosticism denies him a separate angel, of course, but his "goodness"—a state without heavenly imprimatur, albeit one that usually elicits unofficial seraphic approval of a conditional sort—did in fact put him in line for collateral protection. We hope to win him through Angel Marie, for, in the Apostle Paul's take on such matters, "Even if some do not obey the word, they, without a word, may be won by the conduct of their wives . . ." At which point, of course, we would delightedly grant the redeemed man a guardian exclusively his own.

HASHMAL: I have another appointment two decades into the next millennium. Could we speed this up a bit?

RAPHAEL: Sure. (*Aside:*) But visit a haberdasher before you go to keep that appointment. (*To Hashmal*): At the Cobalt Springs Rehabilitation Center, Philip chastely courted Angel Marie through the latter two years of her convalescence, physical therapy, and fight for psychosomatic wholeness. He entered the relationship a long-term bachelor and, in his own self-mocking phrase, a "recidivist virgin," whatever degree of celibacy *that* implies. The result was—once Angel Marie had placed her late spouse at a psychological remove, and Philip and she had fallen in love and married—their union had the recurrent, uh, libidinous enthusiasm one would expect in the conjugal relations of much younger adult lovers. You see, from the vantage of a woman once satisfactorily yoked to an athletic hedonist—namely, Bobby Dean—Angel Marie had much to teach Philip, even while recovering from her severely crippling injuries. Philip, in turn, had much to offer Angel Marie from the hand-on perspective—metaphorically extended to the act of erotic intercourse—of a driving instructor for the "physically challenged."

HASHMAL: You're blushing.

RAPHAEL: That's impossible.

HASHMAL: Perhaps you're right. Go on.

RAPHAEL: The early weeks of the Hembrees' marriage—the past four months, in fact—exposed Sariela to such a repeated commotion of eroticism, whether obstreperous or tender, quick or protracted, that it at first unhinged and eventually totally transfigured her. Sariela, rather than formulating strategies to protect the couple from accidents, evil-doers or harmful individual or joint decisions, began to obsess on the apparent joy of, well, *carnality*—especially in the divinely sanctioned context of marriage. For these reasons, I guess, Sariela gave herself over to a most unangelic pornographic voyeurism.

HASHMAL: My God! Didn't you reprimand her?

RAPHAEL: Despite her preoccupation, she held the Hembrees entire, as individuals and as a couple.

HASHMAL: Of course she did. Barring unwanted pregnancies, communicable diseases, and mattress fires, bed is a haven from danger. But surely you took steps, however feeble, to reclaim Sariela from her obsession?

RAPHAEL: What would you have done?

HASHMAL (*after thinking this over*): Summoned counselors, persons of good judgment and experience, to expostulate with her, to expatiate upon the pitfalls of—

RAPHAEL: And so I did. (*He snaps his fingers, and a bewigged and somewhat bemused MALE FIGURE, in the garb of an eighteenth-century British gentleman, appears on the dance floor. No one else in the Cat's Eye pays the newcomer any heed.*) Look there. (*Tendering introductions*): Hashmal, Philip Dormer Stanhope, Fourth Earl of Chesterfield. Lord Chesterfield, Hashmal the Dominion. Sorry to yank you so unceremoniously out of the afterlife again, but my colleague here has questioned the course I pursued in attempting to treat Sariela's unseemly variety of spiritual dysfunction.

CHESTERFIELD: Ah, yes, Sariela. A charming sprite. (*He approaches the table.*) Altogether charming.

RAPHAEL: I summoned you to counsel her, sir, because in your earthly incarnation you once made a rather witty, not to say astute, observation about the manifold disadvantages of human reproductive liaisons.

CHESTERFIELD: Sex?

RAPHAEL (*grimacing*): As you prefer.

CHESTERFIELD (*quoting himself*): "The cost is exorbitant, the pleasure is momentary, and the position is ridiculous."

RAPHAEL: That's it.

CHESTERFIELD: And, just as you wished, Your Seraphacy, I took that very epigram to Sariela.

HASHMAL (*fascinated*): And how did she respond?

RAPHAEL *snaps his fingers again, and CHESTERFIELD vanishes, demanifesting without so much as a hollow pop. RAPHAEL snaps them again, and Sariela materializes in the center of the grungy dance floor. The jukebox plays "God Didn't Make Honky-Tonk Angels."*

SARIELA stands nearly six feet tall, her svelte body draped in a flowing, snow-white robe. She has a noble, startlingly beautiful face—that of either a somewhat feminine man or a rather masculine woman—and her wings sprout from her shoulder blades like impotent, if shapely, nubs.

SARIELA: "The best is free of either payment or guilt, one may protract or re-experience the pleasure, and imaginative partakers may vary the position."

RAPHAEL: God have mercy.

HASHMAL (*caught off guard*): How clever! (*Recovering*): But how crass. Never do I pity the Almighty's fallen creatures more than when I hear tell of them in the reason-annihilating throes of recreational passion. And you, Sariela my dear, have fallen prey to the meretricious allure of the activity that even Lord Chesterton, as a frail mortal, had the wisdom to adjudge specious and demeaning?

SARIELA (*unabashed*): I confess it. Also that it profoundly irks me that I can't indulge.

RAPHAEL (*to HASHMAL*): She's bright. Her counter to Lord Chesterfield's *bon mot* was virtually instantaneous.

HASHMAL (*to SARIELA*): I congratulate on your quick thinking, if not on your tact.

SARIELA: Each parry of my tripartite reply sprang from the Chesterfieldian clause that it contradicts. He smoked me out.

HASHMAL: I take it you don't like the man.

SARIELA: Despite Samuel Johnson's ill-tempered diatribes against him, Lord Chesterfield was—and remains, even in God's unimpeachable Heaven—the perfect gentleman. But that doesn't negate my view that as a living human being he scantly deserved the functional genitals vouchsafed him.

RAPHAEL: Child, come over here. Sit down with Hashmal and me. Have a glass of wine.

SARIELA: I'd prefer ouzo, for all the feeble kick it affords intelligences without digestive tracts.

RAPHAEL: Come on. Don't quibble over drinks.

He pats the table. SARIELA stalks over to it, scrapes a chair away from it, twirls the chair around, and straddles the chair like a lean chip-on-the-shoulder cowpoke.

SARIELA: I'm not really quibbling over booze. I'm grousing about our asensual incorporeality.

HASHMAL: Oh. I see. Of course.

RAPHAEL (*shouting*): Bartender, another Michelob Dark, a glass of Zinfandel, and an "ouzo" for the lady!

BARTENDER (*shouting back*): You got it, Raffy!

HASHMAL: "Raffy"?

As the ANGELS talk, the BARTENDER prepares their drinks, sets them on a cork-bottomed tray, and eventually dispatches little AUBREY across the room to them with the tray.

RAPHAEL: I've made dozens of trips to Ackley over the past few months. What's so heinous about some friendly banter with the local tavern keeper?

HASHMAL: Nothing. Not a thing.

SARIELA: I'd like to taste what I eat and drink. I'd like to process my food and liquids internally. I'd like to excrete them, once processed. Not to put too fastidious a label on it, I'd also like to screw.

HASHMAL (*off-guard again*): Who?

SARIELA: "Whom," I think you mean. Anyone. Well, *almost* anyone. Almost anyone with the requisite anatomical equipment, the tactile sensitivity to enjoy the performance, and the courtesy to impart gratification in turn—if, that is, I were so constituted as to experience such pleasures.

AUBREY arrives with the drinks, distributes them, gives a mannerly, if awkward, bow, and retreats.

SARIELA (*nodding at the boy*): Even that living prepubescent facsimile of a Renaissance putto has more erogenous impulses and tissues than we do. It's outrageous.

RAPHAEL (*to HASHMAL*): You see. She has a virulent case of spiritual dysfunction, with counterangelic longings of such insistent strength that—were she to publish her discontent in Heaven—she could wreak havoc among all nine orders.

SARIELA: Hogwash.

RAPHAEL: Do you *deny* that you suffer an uncommon—for angels—spiritual dysfunction?

SARIELA: Do you deny that we have "genitals," albeit ones that generate neither offspring nor waste, so that we would do better to call them "naturalia," "privates" or even "doodads"?

HASHMAL (*his interest wholly engaged*): Why, I never think about them at all.

SARIELA: And why should you? They don't *do* anything. We can neither squirt nor swyve. Yours may swing some, guys, but mine merely—I don't know, *reside*. It's a joke: a sick, sad, unfunny joke.

RAPHAEL: Sariela, they exist at all only when we incarnate as emissaries to humanity. Why rail against their absence of functionality when, ordinarily, we have our essence as bodiless spirits about the Holy Throne.

SARIELA: Because the Occupant of the Throne should not have made us, even in our roles as emissaries, as sexless as kewpie dolls. Instead, He made me in my guise as a guardian with what I now recognize as a nearly perfect simulacrum of the quiff of an adult human female. (*She starts to hike up the hem of her robe.*) Look.

RAPHAEL (*catching her wrist*): There's no need. We believe you.

HASHMAL: "Quiff?"

SARIELA: You guys could show me yours. I wouldn't mind. All I've had to go by—the Hembrees being my first assignment and my access to photographic representations virtually nil—is Philip's endearing set: so soft in repose, so salient in arousal.

RAPHAEL: Sariela!

SARIELA: Phooey. Why this avoidance? This shame? This Puritanical squeamishness?

HASHMAL: I don't think that's wholly fair. After all, *I'm* wearing a codpiece.

SARIELA: All right, then. Unbutton it. Snap it out.

HASHMAL (*flustered*): No, thank you. I couldn't.

RAPHAEL: Such prurient curiosity ill serves you, Sariela. But

I'd argue that our "shame"—a decent, angelic shame—stems from sympathy for our fallen wards.

HASHMAL: Or maybe from the realization that our equipment has only a place-holding, or representational, function. Wow, that is a downer.

SARIELA: Crap. (*She knocks back the shot glass of ouzo, or whatever, that AUBREY has brought her and runs her tongue around her lips sensually.*) Double crap.

RAPHAEL: Why these mad physical desires? Why such sighing and panting? Sariela, you have in you the distilled essence of pure spirit, whatever your current status as a guardian.

SARIELA: And yet I want . . . I want to get it on. The Hembrees have corrupted me past recall or liberated me to joys I'm helpless to know—except, that is, in the witnessing, the hearing, and the heat of my fancy, where such joys, worse luck, seem only to carbonize and drift away.

The jukebox plays Hank Williams's "I'm So Lonesome I Could Cry." A MAN and a WOMAN at the back of the room get up, clasp each other, and shuffle about the dance floor, more like shadows than apprehendable human beings. SARIELA stands.

SARIELA (*enraged*): How can you dance to that song? (*The COUPLE ignores her.*) Two people dancing together are "lonesome" only on sufferance! Stop it! (*A beat or two, then:*) I said, *Stop it!*

The COUPLE goes on dancing. The three ANGELS watch in a mood of perplexity (RAPHAEL, HASHMAL) or of raw disgruntlement (SARIELA). The song ends, the MAN and the WOMAN sit back down, the jukebox lever-locks an old Eddie Arnold 45 r.p.m. disk into play position: "Welcome to My World."

SARIELA paces beside the table, methodically rather than feverishly— in the same studied way that she wrings her hands and clenches her jaw. RAPHAEL and HASHMAL regard her with abashed wonder. At one point, they exchange a helpless shrug. Finally, SARIELA slams herself back into her chair and stares glassily out over the bar's clientele.

SARIELA: You guys are firing me, right?

RAPHAEL: Unless you can quell this morbid infatuation with the concupiscent, we'll surely post you back to Guardian Dispatch Central for, well, retraining.

SARIELA: Mothballing, you mean.

RAPHAEL: Nonsense. You can't—

SARIELA: Endless spiritual storage. Eternity will closet, then disassemble, and then wholly absorb me.

HASHMAL: Never. Never. We *love* you, Sariela.

SARIELA: Not as Philip Hembree loves his Angel Marie. Or vice versa.

RAPHAEL: Vice—animal frailty—has more to do with it than you seem willing to admit.

SARIELA (*acidly quoting*): "Love not the Heavenly Spirits, and how their love / Express they, by looks only, or do they mix / Irradiance, virtual or immediate touch?"

RAPHAEL: I beg your pardon.

HASHMAL (*enthusiastically*): Adam's appeal to Raphael—to you, Your Radiant Seraphacy—toward the end of the eighth book of Milton's *Paradise Lost*.

SARIELA (*to RAPHAEL*): It made you blush, for your smile "glowed / Celestial rosy-red, Love's proper hue," and you said to Adam, "Let it suffice that—"

RAPHAEL: You suppose me, after all these countless eons, a halo-bearing illiterate? I know what I said. (*Rises and strides about in peeved majesty.*) Through Mr. Milton's cheeky ventriloquism, I replied

". . . Let it suffice thee that thou know'st
Us happy, and without Love no happiness.
Whatever pure thou may in the body enjoy'st
(And pure thou were created) we enjoy
In eminence, and obstacle find none
Of membrane, joint or limb, exclusive bars;

Easier than air with air, if Spirits embrace,
Total they mix, union of pure with pure
Desiring, nor restrained conveyance need
As flesh to mix with flesh, or soul with soul."

HASHMAL (*clapping mildly, once*): Bravo.

RAPHAEL: Stifle it. (*To SARIELA:*) A bit earlier, my namesake cautioned Adam to remember—as I caution you, Sariela—that

". . . Love refines
The thoughts, and heart enlarges, hath his seat
In Reason, and is judicious, is the scale
By which to heavenly love thou may'st ascend,
Not sunk in carnal pleasure, for which cause
Among the beasts no mate for thee was found."

SARIELA: Then the beasts among whom no mate was found for *me*, a guardian spirit, are those same dear, lascivious monkeys whom you posted me to defend. Is that it?

RAPHAEL: Exactly, my pretty picket.

SARIELA: Fine. But the ache persists. The hunger, too. In recesses I fear inaccessible.

RAPHAEL (*to HASHMAL*): You've got an appointment elsewhere, I believe.

HASHMAL: I do?

RAPHAEL: So you said. Feel free to depart for it.

HASHMAL (*somewhat bemusedly*): Thank you. (*He demanifests, promptly and entirely.*)

Meanwhile, RAPHAEL swings around SARIELA's chair, stalks to the bonsai apple tree, pulls from it a small crimson fruit, and extends the fruit to SARIELA.

RAPHAEL: Here. For your ache. For your hunger.

SARIELA (*examining it*): I wouldn't have supposed apples in season. And the hunger of which I spoke doesn't submit to this sort of feeding.

RAPHAEL: Taste it. Take a bite.

SARIELA: A bite will engulf it.

RAPHAEL: Please. For me.

SARIELA takes a bite. The bite does encompass the tiny apple. She marvels at her empty hand and savors the fruit's peculiar taste. Then she swallows and smiles.

SARIELA: Yes. I see.

RAPHAEL:

"Whatever pure they in the body enjoy'st
(And pure thou wert created) *we* enjoy
In eminence, and obstacle find none
Of membrane, joint, or limb . . ."

SARIELA (*radiant*): I understand. But show me. No one has ever showed me.

RAPHAEL: An anomalous—indeed, an unforgivable—hole in your education.

SARIELA: Fill it. Please.

RAPHAEL: Immediately. But not here. (*Takes SARIELA's hand, guides her to her feet. Then, as they tower in the center of the dance floor, he clicks his heels together three times.*) Presto, Sariela: The Rapture!

RAPHAEL and SARIELA vanish, hand in hand, from the Cat's Eye. Over the dying strains of "Midnight Train from Georgia," a riff of laughter from the departing SARIELA. Then the dance floor stands empty, and the only audible sound is that of AUBREY's toes kicking the turquoise Chevy.

A door to the right of the car bar opens, and a MAN in his mid-thirties wrestles a wheelchair containing a smiling young WOMAN over the Cat's Eye's threshold. Every PATRON at the bar looks toward the newcomers, including AUBREY, who stops kicking the bar's body metal.

BARTENDER (*affectionately*): Hey, Phil! Hey, Angel Marie!

ANGEL MARIE: Hey, Troy.

PHILIP: How goes it, Troy?

BARTENDER: Can't complain. The usual?

ANGEL MARIE: Sure. And rack up some songs by the King.

BARTENDER: You got it.

PHILIP wheels ANGEL MARIE past the bar, tilts her chair so that it rolls onto the dance floor, and pushes her to the table where the three ANGELS sat. Here he parks his wife and sits in RAPHAEL's former spot. AUBREY carries the HEMBREES a couple of amber longnecks, while the BARTENDER leaves the bar to feed the jukebox a handful of coins.

BARTENDER *(over his shoulder)*: Y'all trust me to do this?

PHILIP *(nuzzling ANGEL MARIE and prompting a series of giggles)*: Why shouldn't we?

BARTENDER: It's out of my era. I'm a Travis Tritt kind of guy. *(To ANGEL MARIE:)* Hey, darlin', need a bodyguard?

ANGEL MARIE: Got one. Got one real close.

BARTENDER: I'd say. Well, Aubrey and me're real proud to have you all here.

ANGEL MARIE *(glancing at him)*: You are? Why?

BARTENDER: The head-in-the-clouds riffraff leaves and the bona fide class comes in.

ANGEL MARIE: What?

AUBREY pulls a fruit off the bonsai apple tree and hands it to ANGEL MARIE, who gives him an appreciative buss and takes a dainty bite of the apple. THE BARENDER comes over, picks up AUBREY, and totes him back down to the bar. From the jukebox, "Love Me Tender." A MAN and a WOMAN get up from a shadowy rear table, embrace, and box-step slowly about the floor. ANGEL MARIE takes what's left of her apple and feeds it to PHILIP.

PHILIP: Mmmmmm. Delicious.

ANGEL MARIE: Even half-bitten?

PHILIP *(nuzzling her)*: Even half-bitten.

The lights fade. Soon, about all the audience can discern is ANGEL MARIE outlined in her wheelchair and PHILIP's silhouette leaning into hers. The King continues to croon and the rapt COUPLE to step about rhythmically in swirls of shoe-displaced sawdust. . . .

WITH THE ANGELS

Ramsey Campbell

RAMSEY CAMPBELL was born in Liverpool, where he still lives with his wife Jenny. His first book, a collection of stories entitled *The Inhabitant of the Lake and Less Welcome Tenants*, was published by August Derleth's legendary Arkham House imprint in 1964. Since then his novels have included *The Doll Who Ate His Mother*, *The Face That Must Die*, *The Nameless*, *Incarnate*, *The Hungry Moon*, *Ancient Images*, *The Count of Eleven*, *The Long Lost*, *Pact of the Fathers*, *The Darkest Part of the Woods*, *The Grin of the Dark*, *Thieving Fear* and *Creatures of the Pool*.

His short fiction has been collected in such volumes as *Demons by Daylight*, *The Height of the Scream*, *Dark Companions*, *Scared Stiff*, *Waking Nightmares*, *Cold Print*, *Alone with the Horrors*, *Ghosts and Grisly Things*, *Told by the Dead* and *Just Behind You*. He has also edited a number of anthologies, including *New Terrors*, *New Tales of the Cthulhu Mythos*, *Fine Frights: Stories That Scared Me*, *Uncanny Banquet*, *Meddling with Ghosts* and *Gathering the Bones: Original Stories from the World's Masters of Horror* (with Dennis Etchison and Jack Dann).

The author's latest novel is *Solomon Kane* (based on the recent film and various drafts of the screenplay, it attempts both to capture the film and include deleted elements that director Michael Bassett would have liked to include). Forthcoming is another novel, *The Seven Days of Cain*, while *Ghosts Know* is in progress.

Ramsey Campbell has won multiple World Fantasy Awards, British Fantasy Awards and Bram Stoker Awards, and is a recipient of the World Horror Convention Grand Master Award, the Horror Writers Association Lifetime Achievement Award, the Howie Award of the H.P. Lovecraft Film Festival for Lifetime Achievement, and the International Horror Guild's Living Legend Award. A film reviewer for BBC Radio Merseyside since 1969, he is also president of both the British Fantasy Society and the Society of Fantastic Films.

"My fellow clansman Paul Campbell will remember the birth of this tale," he reveals. "At the Dead Dog party after the 2010 World Horror Convention in Brighton, someone was throwing a delighted toddler into the air. I was ambushed by an idea and had to apologize to Paul for rushing away to my room to scribble notes. The result is here."

AS CYNTHIA DROVE BETWEEN the massive mossy posts where the gates used to be, Karen said "Were you little when you lived here, Auntie Jackie?"

"Not as little as I was," Cynthia said.

"That's right," Jacqueline said while the poplars alongside the high walls darkened the car, "I'm even older than your grandmother."

Karen and Valerie giggled and then looked for other amusement. "What's this house called, Brian?" Valerie enquired.

"The Populars," the four-year-old declared and set about punching his sisters almost before they began to laugh.

"Now, you three," Cynthia intervened. "You said you'd show Jackie how good you can be."

No doubt she meant her sister to feel more included. "Can't we play?" said Brian as if Jacqueline were a disapproving bystander.

"I expect you may," Jacqueline said, having glanced at Cynthia. "Just don't get yourselves dirty or do any damage or go anywhere you shouldn't or that's dangerous."

Brian and the eight-year-old twins barely waited for Cynthia to haul two-handed at the brake before they piled out of the Volvo and chased across the forecourt into the weedy garden. "Do try and let them be children," Cynthia murmured.

"I wasn't aware I could change them." Jacqueline managed not to groan while she unbent her stiff limbs and clambered out of the car. "I shouldn't think they would take much notice of me," she said, supporting herself on the hot roof as she turned to the house.

Despite the August sunlight, it seemed darker than its neighbours, not just because of the shadows of the trees, which still put her in mind of a graveyard. More than a century's worth of winds across the moors outside the Yorkshire town had plastered the large house with grime. The windows on the topmost floor were half the size of those on the other two storeys, one reason why she'd striven in her childhood not to think they resembled the eyes of a spider, any more than the porch between the downstairs rooms looked like a voracious vertical mouth. She was far from a child now, and she strode or at any rate limped to the porch, only to have to wait for her sister to bring the keys. As Cynthia thrust one into the first rusty lock the twins scampered over, pursued by their brother. "Throw me up again," he cried.

"Where did he get that from?"

"From being a child, I should think," Cynthia said. "Don't you remember what it was like?"

Jacqueline did, not least because of Brian's demand. She found some breath as she watched the girls take their brother by the arms and swing him into the air. "Again," he cried.

"We're tired now," Karen told him. "We want to see in the house."

"Maybe grandma and auntie will give you a throw if you're good," Valerie said.

"Not just now," Jacqueline said at once.

Cynthia raised her eyebrows high enough to turn her eyes blank as she twisted the second key. The door lumbered inwards a few inches and then baulked. She was trying to nudge the obstruction aside with the door when Brian made for the gap. "Don't," Jacqueline blurted, catching him by the shoulder.

"Good heavens, Jackie, what's the matter now?"

"We don't want the children in there until we know what state it's in, do we?"

"Just see if you can squeeze past and shift whatever's there, Brian."

Jacqueline felt unworthy of consideration. She could only watch the boy wriggle around the edge of the door and vanish into the gloom. She heard fumbling and rustling, but of course this didn't mean some desiccated presence was at large in the vestibule. Why didn't Brian speak? She was about to prompt him until he called "It's just some old letters and papers."

When he reappeared with several free newspapers that looked as dusty as their news, Cynthia eased the door past him. A handful of brown envelopes contained electricity bills that grew redder as they came up to date, which made Jacqueline wonder "Won't the lights work?"

"I expect so if we really need them." Cynthia advanced into the wide hall beyond the vestibule and poked at the nearest switch. Grit ground inside the mechanism, but the bulbs in the hall chandelier stayed as dull as the mass of crystal teardrops. "Never mind," Cynthia said, having tested every switch in the column on the wall without result. "As I say, we won't need them."

The grimy skylight above the stairwell illuminated the hall enough to show that the dark wallpaper was even hairier than Jacqueline remembered. It had always made her think of the fur of a great spider, and now it was blotchy with damp. The children were already running up the left-hand staircase and across the first-floor landing, under which the chandelier dangled like a spider on a thread. "Don't go out of sight," Cynthia told them, "until we see what's what."

"Chase me." Brian ran down the other stairs, one of which rattled like a lid beneath the heavy carpet. "Chase," he cried and dashed across the hall to race upstairs again.

"Don't keep running up and down unless you want to make me ill," Jacqueline's grandmother would have said. The incessant rumble of footsteps might have presaged a storm on the way to turning the hall even gloomier, so that Jacqueline strode as steadily as she could towards the nearest room. She had to pass one of the hall mirrors, which appeared to show a dark blotch hovering in wait for the children. The shapeless sagging darkness at the top of the grimy oval was a stain, and she needn't have waited to see the children run downstairs out of its reach. "Do you want the mirror?" Cynthia said. "I expect it would clean up."

"I don't know what I want from this house," Jacqueline said.

She mustn't say she would prefer the children not to be in it. She couldn't even suggest sending them outside in case the garden concealed dangers—broken glass, rusty metal, holes in the ground. The children were staying with Cynthia while her son and his partner holidayed in Morocco, but couldn't she have chosen a better time to go through the house before it was put up for sale? She frowned at Jacqueline and then followed her into the dining-room.

Although the heavy curtains were tied back from the large windows, the room wasn't much brighter than the hall. It was steeped in the shadows of the poplars, and the tall panes were spotted with earth. A spider's nest of a chandelier loomed above the long table set for an elaborate dinner for six. That had been Cynthia's idea when they'd moved their parents to the rest home; she'd meant to convince any thieves that the house was still occupied, but to Jacqueline it felt like preserving a past that she'd hoped to outgrow. She remembered being made to sit up stiffly at the table, to hold her utensils just so, to cover her lap nicely with her napkin, not to speak or to make the slightest noise with any of her food. Too much of this upbringing had lodged inside her, but was that why she felt uneasy with the children in the house? "Are you taking anything out of here?" Cynthia said.

"There's nothing here for me, Cynthia. You have whatever you want and don't worry about me."

Cynthia gazed at her as they headed for the breakfast room. The chandelier stirred as the children ran above it once again, but Jacqueline told herself that was nothing like her nightmares—at least, not very like. She was unnerved to hear Cynthia exclaim "There it is."

The breakfast room was borrowing light from the large back garden, but not much, since the overgrown expanse lay in the shadow of the house. The weighty table had spread its wings and was attended by six straight-backed ponderous chairs, but Cynthia was holding out her hands to the high chair in the darkest corner of the room. "Do you remember sitting in that?" she apparently hoped. "I think I do."

"I wouldn't," Jacqueline said.

She hadn't needed it to make her feel restricted at the table, where breakfast with her grandparents had been as formal as dinner. "Nothing here either," she declared and limped into the hall.

The mirror on the far side was discoloured too. She glimpsed the children's blurred shapes streaming up into a pendulous darkness and heard the agitated jangle of the chandelier as she made for the lounge. The leather suite looked immovable with age, and only the television went some way towards bringing the room up to date, though the screen was as blank as an uninscribed stone. She remembered having to sit silent for hours while her parents and grandparents listened to the radio for news about the war—her grandmother hadn't liked children out of her sight in the house. The dresser was still full of china she'd been forbidden to venture near, which was grey with dust and the dimness. Cynthia had been allowed to crawl around the room— indulged for being younger or because their grandmother liked babies in the house. "I'll leave you to it," she said as Cynthia followed her in.

She was hoping to find more light in the kitchen, but it didn't show her much that she wanted to see. While the refrigerator was relatively modern, not to mention tall enough for somebody to stand in, it felt out of place. The black iron range still occupied most of one wall, and the old stained marble sink projected from another. Massive cabinets and heavy chests of drawers helped box in the hulking table scored by knives. It used to remind her of an operating table, even though she hadn't thought she would grow up to be a nurse. She was distracted by the children as they ran into the kitchen. "Can we have a drink?" Karen said for all of them.

"May we?" Valerie amended.

"Please." Once she'd been echoed Jacqueline said "I'll find you some glasses. Let the tap run."

When she opened a cupboard she thought for a moment that the stack of plates was covered by a greyish doily. Several objects as long as a baby's fingers but thinner even than their bones flinched out of sight, and she saw the plates were draped with a mass of cobwebs. She slammed the door as Karen used both hands to twist the cold tap. It uttered a dry gurgle rather too reminiscent of sounds she used to hear while working in the geriatric ward, and she wondered if the supply had been turned off. Then a gout of dark liquid spattered the sink, and a gush of rusty water darkened the marble. As Karen struggled to shut it off Valerie enquired "Did you have to drink that, auntie?"

"I had to put up with a lot you wouldn't be expected to."

"We won't, then. Aren't there any other drinks?"

"And things to eat," Brian said at once.

"I'm sure there's nothing." When the children gazed at her with various degrees of patience Jacqueline opened the refrigerator, trying not to think that the compartments could harbour bodies smaller than Brian's. All she found were a bottle of mouldering milk and half a loaf as hard as a rusk. "I'm afraid you'll have to do without," she said.

How often had her grandmother said that? Supposedly she'd been just as parsimonious before the war. Jacqueline didn't want to sound like her, but when Brian took hold of the handle of a drawer that was level with his head she couldn't help blurting "Stay away from there."

At least she didn't add "We've lost enough children." As the boy stepped back Cynthia hurried into the kitchen. "What are you doing now?"

"We don't want them playing with knives, do we?" Jacqueline said.

"I know you're too sensible, Brian."

Was that aimed just at him? As Cynthia opened the cupboards the children resumed chasing up the stairs. Presumably the creature

Jacqueline had glimpsed was staying out of sight, and so were any more like it. When Cynthia made for the hall Jacqueline said "I'll be up in a minute."

Although she didn't linger in the kitchen, she couldn't leave her memories behind. How many children had her grandmother lost that she'd been so afraid of losing any more? By pestering her mother Jacqueline had learned they'd been stillborn, which had reminded her how often her grandmother told her to keep still. More than once today Jacqueline had refrained from saying that to the twins and to Brian in particular. Their clamour seemed to fill the hall and resonate all the way up the house, so that she could have thought the reverberations were shaking the mirrors, disturbing the suspended mass of darkness like a web in which a spider had come to life. "Can we go up to the top now?" Brian said.

"Please don't," Jacqueline called.

It took Cynthia's stare to establish that the boy hadn't been asking Jacqueline. "Why can't we?" Karen protested, and Valerie contributed "We only want to see."

"I'm sure you can," Cynthia said. "Just wait till we're all up there."

Before tramping into the nearest bedroom she gave her sister one more look, and Jacqueline felt as blameworthy as their grandmother used to make her feel. Why couldn't she watch over the children from the hall? She tilted her head back on her shaky neck to gaze up the stairwell. Sometimes her grandfather would raise his eyes ceilingwards as his wife found yet another reason to rebuke Jacqueline, only for the woman to say "If you look like that you'll see where you're going." Presumably she'd meant heaven, and perhaps she was there now, if there was such a place. Jacqueline imagined her sailing upwards like a husk on a wind; she'd already seemed withered all those years ago, and not just physically either. Was that why Jacqueline had thought the stillbirths must be shrivelled too? They would have ended up like that, but she needn't think about it now, if ever. She glanced towards the children and saw movement above them.

She must have seen the shadows of the treetops—thin shapes that appeared to start out of the corners under the roof before darting back into the gloom. As she tried to grasp how those shadows could reach so far beyond the confines of the skylight, Cynthia peered out of the nearest bedroom. "Jackie, aren't you coming to look?"

Jacqueline couldn't think for all the noise. "If you three will give us some peace for a while," she said louder than she liked. "And stay with us. We don't want you going anywhere that isn't safe."

"You heard your aunt," Cynthia said, sounding unnecessarily like a resentful child.

As Brian trudged after the twins to follow Cynthia into her grandmother's bedroom Jacqueline remembered never being let in there. Later her parents had made it their room—had tried, at any rate. While they'd doubled the size of the bed, the rest of the furniture was still her grandmother's, and she could have fancied that all the swarthy wood was helping the room glower at the intrusion. She couldn't imagine her parents sharing a bed there, let alone performing any activity in it, but she didn't want to think about such things at all. "Not for me," she said and made for the next room.

Not much had changed since it had been her grandfather's, which meant it still seemed to belong to his wife. It felt like her disapproval rendered solid by not just the narrow single bed but the rest of the dark furniture that duplicated hers, having been her choice. She'd disapproved of almost anything related to Jacqueline, not least her husband playing with their granddaughter. Jacqueline avoided glancing up at any restlessness under the roof while she crossed the landing to the other front bedroom. As she gazed at the two single beds that remained since the cot had been disposed of, the children ran to cluster around her in the doorway. "This was your room, wasn't it?" Valerie said.

"Yours and our grandma's," Karen amended.

"No," Jacqueline said, "it was hers and our mother's and father's."

In fact she hadn't been sent to the top floor until Cynthia was born. Their grandfather had told her she was going to stay with the angels, though his wife frowned at the idea. Jacqueline would have found it more appealing if she hadn't already been led to believe that all the stillbirths were living with the angels. She hardly knew why she was continuing to explore the house. Though the cast-iron bath had been replaced by a fibreglass tub as blue as the toilet and sink, she still remembered flinching from the chilly metal. After Cynthia's birth their grandmother had taken over bathing Jacqueline, scrubbing her with such relentless harshness that it had felt like a penance. When it was over at last, her grandfather would do his best to raise her spirits. "Now you're clean enough for the angels," he would say and throw her up in the air.

"If you're good the angels will catch you"—but of course he did, which had always made her wonder what would happen to her if she wasn't good enough. She'd seemed to glimpse that thought in her grandmother's eyes, or had it been a wish? What would have caught her if she'd failed to live up to requirements? As she tried to forget the conclusion she'd reached Brian said "Where did they put you, then?"

"They kept me right up at the top."

"Can we see?"

"Yes, let's," said Valerie, and Karen ran after him as well.

Jacqueline was opening her mouth to delay them when Cynthia said "You'll be going up there now, won't you? You can keep an eye on them."

It was a rebuke for not helping enough with the children, or for interfering too much, or perhaps for Jacqueline's growing nervousness. Anger at her childish fancies sent her stumping halfway up the topmost flight of stairs before she faltered. Clouds had gathered like a lifetime's worth of dust above the skylight, and perhaps that was why the top floor seemed to darken as she climbed towards it, so that all the corners were even harder to distinguish—she could almost have thought the mass of dimness was solidifying. "Where were you, auntie?" Karen said.

"In there," said Jacqueline and hurried to join them outside the nearest room.

It wasn't as vast as she remembered, though certainly large enough to daunt a small child. The ceiling stooped to the front wall, squashing the window, from which the shadows of the poplars seemed to creep up the gloomy incline to acquire more substance under the roof at the back of the room. The grimy window smudged the premature twilight, which had very little to illuminate, since the room was bare of furniture and even of a carpet. "Did you have to sleep on the floor?" Valerie said. "Were you very bad?"

"Of course not," Jacqueline declared. It felt as if her memories had been thrown out—as if she hadn't experienced them—but she knew better. She'd lain on the cramped bed hemmed in by dour furniture and cut off from everyone else in the house by the dark that occupied the stairs. She would have prayed if that mightn't have roused what she dreaded. If the babies were with the angels, mustn't that imply they weren't angels themselves? Being stillbirths needn't mean they would keep still—Jacqueline never could when she was told. Suppose they were what caught you if you weren't good? She'd felt as if she had been sent away from her family for bad behaviour. All too soon she'd heard noises that suggested tiny withered limbs were stirring, and glimpsed movements in the highest corners of the room.

She must have been hearing the poplars and seeing their shadows. As she turned away from the emptied bedroom she caught sight of the room opposite, which was full of items covered with dustsheets. Had she ever known what the sheets concealed? She'd imagined they hid some secret that children weren't supposed to learn, but they'd also reminded her of enormous masses of cobweb. She could have thought the denizens of the webs were liable to crawl out of the dimness, and she was absurdly relieved to see Cynthia coming upstairs. "I'll leave you to it," Jacqueline said. "I'll be waiting down below."

It wasn't only the top floor she wanted to leave behind. She'd remembered what she'd once done to her sister. The war had been over at last, and she'd been trusted to look after Cynthia while the adults planned the future. The sisters had only been allowed to play with their toys in the hall, where Jacqueline had done her best to distract the toddler from straying into any of the rooms they weren't supposed to enter by themselves—in fact, every room. At last she'd grown impatient with her sister's mischief, and in a wicked moment she'd wondered what would catch Cynthia if she tossed her high. As she'd thrown her sister into the air with all her strength she'd realised that she didn't want to know, certainly not at Cynthia's expense—as she'd seen dwarfish shrivelled figures darting out of every corner in the dark above the stairwell and scuttling down to seize their prize. They'd come head first, so that she'd seen their bald scalps wrinkled like walnuts before she glimpsed their hungry withered faces. Then Cynthia had fallen back into her arms, though Jacqueline had barely managed to keep hold of her. Squeezing her eyes shut, she'd hugged her sister until she'd felt able to risk seeing they were alone in the vault of the hall.

There was no use telling herself that she'd taken back her unforgivable wish. She might have injured the toddler even by catching her—she might have broken her frail neck. She ought to have known that, and perhaps she had. Being expected to behave badly had made her act that way, but she felt as if all the nightmares that were stored in the house had festered and gained strength over the years. When she reached the foot of the stairs at last she carried on out of the house.

The poplars stooped to greet her with a wordless murmur. A wind was rising under the sunless sky. It was gentle on her face—it seemed to promise tenderness she couldn't recall having experienced, certainly not once Cynthia was born. Perhaps it could soothe away her memories, and she was raising her face to it when Brian appeared in the porch. "What are you doing, auntie?"

"Just being by myself."

She thought that was pointed enough until he skipped out of the house. "Is it time now?"

Why couldn't Cynthia have kept him with her? No doubt she thought it was Jacqueline's turn. "Time for what?" Jacqueline couldn't avoid asking.

"You said you'd give me a throw."

She'd said she wouldn't then, not that she would sometime. Just the same, perhaps she could. It might be a way of leaving the house behind and all it represented to her. It would prove she deserved to be trusted with him, as she ought not to have been trusted with little Cynthia. "Come on then," she said.

As soon as she held out her arms he ran and leapt into them. "Careful," she gasped, laughing as she recovered her balance. "Are you ready?" she said and threw the small body into the air.

She was surprised how light he was, or how much strength she had at her disposal. He came down giggling, and she caught him. "Again," he cried.

"Just once more," Jacqueline said. She threw him higher this time, and he giggled louder. Cynthia often said that children kept you young, and Jacqueline thought it was true after all. Brian fell into her arms and she hugged him. "Again," he could hardly beg for giggling.

"Now what did I just say?" Nevertheless she threw him so high that her arms trembled with the effort, and the poplars nodded as if they were approving her accomplishment. She clutched at Brian as he came down with an impact that made her shoulders ache. "Higher," he pleaded almost incoherently. "Higher."

"This really is the last time, Brian." She crouched as if the stooping poplars had pushed her down. Tensing her whole body, she reared up to fling him into the pendulous gloom with all her strength.

For a moment she thought only the wind was reaching for him as it bowed the trees and dislodged objects from the foliage—leaves that rustled, twigs that scraped and rattled. But the thin shapes weren't falling, they were scurrying head first down the tree-trunks at a speed that seemed to leave time behind. Some of them had no shape they could have lived with, and some might never have had any skin. She saw their shrivelled eyes glimmer eagerly and their toothless mouths gape with an identical infantile hunger. Their combined weight bowed the lowest branches while they extended arms like withered sticks to snatch the child.

In that helpless instant Jacqueline was overwhelmed by a feeling she would never have admitted—a rush of childish glee, of utter irresponsibility. For a moment she was no longer a nurse, not even a retired one as old as some of her patients had been. She shouldn't have put Brian at risk, but now he was beyond saving. Then he fell out of the dark beneath the poplars, in which there was no longer any sign of life, and she made a grab at him. The strength had left her arms, and he struck the hard earth with a thud that put her in mind of the fall of a lid.

"Brian?" she said and bent groaning to him. "Brian," she repeated, apparently loud enough to be audible all the way up the house. She heard her old window rumble open, and Cynthia's cry: "What have you done now?" She heard footsteps thunder down the stairs, and turned away from the small still body beneath the uninhabited trees as her sister dashed out of the porch. Jacqueline had just one thought, but surely it must make a difference. "Nothing caught him," she said.

THINGS I DIDN'T KNOW MY FATHER KNEW

Peter Crowther

PETER CROWTHER is the recipient of numerous awards for his writing, his editing and, as publisher, for the hugely successful PS Publishing imprint.

As well as being widely translated, his short stories have been adapted for TV on both sides of the Atlantic and collected in *The Longest Single Note*, *Lonesome Roads*, *Songs of Leaving*, *Cold Comforts*, *The Spaces Between the Lines*, *The Land at the End of the Working Day* and the upcoming *Things I Didn't Know My Father Knew*.

He is the co-author (with James Lovegrove) of the novel *Escardy Gap* and author of the Forever Twilight science-fiction/horror cycle (*Darkness, Darkness* and *Windows to the Soul* are already available, with *Darkness Rising* forthcoming). His short Halloween novel, *By Wizard Oak and Fairy Stream*, is published by Earthling.

Crowther lives and works with his wife and business partner, Nicky, on Britain's scenic Yorkshire coast.

"I confess I've never understood when genre writers say they don't believe in the stuff they're writing," reveals the author. "Me, I believe it all—vampires, werewolves, ghosts, goblins, aliens, Santa, monsters frozen in the ice, fairies, the perfect pint of Guinness . . . the whole schtick. And I'm particularly strong on the belief that, one day, I'll see my parents again.

"So, impatient as ever about waiting to find out first-hand, I indulge myself every once in a while and I write something that'll enable me to spend some time with them . . . at least on paper.

"'Things I Didn't Know My Father Knew' is the product of one of these selfish little jaunts, written at a time when I desperately wanted to see my dad again and give him a big hug. Needless to say, it's dedicated to him and to all fathers taken prematurely from their kids. Plus it's for the kids who, although maybe grown up a little, still miss 'em like crazy.

"Love ya, Dad!"

If there is an afterlife, let it be a small town
gentle as this spot at just this instant.
— "In Cheever Country" by Dana Gioia

SOMETHING WAS DIFFERENT.

Bennett Differing opened his eyes and listened, and tried to pinpoint what was wrong. Then he realized. He couldn't hear his wife's breathing.

He shuffled over, pulling the bedclothes with him, and stared at the empty space beside him on the bed. Shelley wasn't there. He looked across at the clock and frowned. It was too early for her to get up. She always stayed in bed until he was out of the shower. Why would she be getting up at this time?

Then he remembered. She was meeting her sister, going to the mall for their annual shop-till-you-drop spree.

As if on cue, Shelley's voice rang out. "Honey?"

"Yeah, I'm up," Bennett shouted to the ceiling.

"Well, I'm on my way. Lisa gets in at 8:15."

Bennett nodded to the empty room. Around a yawn, he said, "Have fun."

"Will do," she shouted.

"Take care."

He could hear her feet on the polished wooden floor of the hallway downstairs, going first one way and then another—Shelley suddenly remembering things, like car keys, house keys, purse.

"Will do," she shouted. "It's a lovely morning."

Bennett flopped back onto the bed. "Good." The word came out as a mutter wrapped up in another yawn.

"What?"

"I said, *good*. I'm thrilled for you."

The feet downstairs clumped back into the kitchen. "I'll be home around eight. Lisa's getting her bus at seven."

"Okay."

The sound of feet stopped and then he heard them coming quickly up the stairs. "Can't go without giving you a kiss," Shelley said as she ran into the bedroom. Now that the door had been opened he could hear the radio downstairs.

She leaned across him and kissed him on the forehead, making a smacking sound. He knew she had made a lipstick mark, could see the mischievous glint in her eyes as she surveyed her work with a satisfied smile.

She ruffled his hair lovingly. "What are you going to be doing today?"

Bennett shrugged, yawned and turned his face away from her. He could taste the staleness of sleep still in his mouth.

"Oh, this and that."

"Words!" Shelley snapped at him, jabbing a finger in his stomach. "Make sure you do your words before you deal with e-mails." She smiled and rubbed his stomach—another sign of affection. "Will you be okay?" The question came complete with inflection and frown.

"Sure," Bennett said. "I'll be fine. I'll get lots done."

"Promise?"

"Promise." He raised his clenched fist to his head and tapped two fingers against his temple. "Scouts' honor, ma'am. I'll do my words."

She stood up and picked up her watch from the table by her side of the bed. Strapping it onto her wrist, she said, "Well, have a good day. There's a sandwich in the refrigerator."

"Great."

She stopped at the bedroom door and scrunched herself up excitedly. "You know . . . ," she said, rubbing her hands together, " . . . you can smell it."

Bennett shuffled up and rested his head on his hand. "Smell what?"

Shelley frowned. "Christmas, of course." She straightened her sweater where she had rucked it out of her skirt. "You can smell it everywhere: the cold . . . and the presents, eggnog, warm biscuits. The skies are clear and the air is crisp . . ." Bennett half-imagined he could hear sleigh bells and his wife nodded as though in response to his thoughts. "And I think we're going to have some snow," she added with a devilish smile—she knew Bennett hated snow.

Bennett groaned. "Oh goody."

She waved a hand at him. "You know, you're turning into Scrooge."

He flopped his head onto the pillow. "Bah, humbug!"

Shelley smiled. "Okay, I'm on my way. See you tonight."

"Yeah, see you," he said to the slowly closing door.

It seemed like no time at all before the front door slammed and he heard the Buick's engine fire into life. Then three soft pips on the horn as Shelley pulled out of the driveway.

Suddenly the house was quiet, the only sound the sound of the car moving off along the street. Then, around the silence, drifting through it like a boat across a still lake, the sound of the radio gave a sense of life, albeit muffled.

Bennett could hear a funky jingle and the weatherman distantly telling anyone in Forest Plains who was bothering to listen at this time in the morning just what the weather was doing. Rain coming in from the west, heat coming in from the east . . . all elemental life was there: winds, twisters, cold fronts circling, warm fronts sneaking up for the kill, maybe even a tremor or two.

"Maybe even snow!" he said to the pillow.

But there *was* something else, too. Even *he* could smell it. Smell it in the air. *Was* it Christmas? Did Christmas *have* a smell . . . a smell all of its own, not just the associated things that society had tacked onto it?

Bennett sat up in bed and looked at the clock. It was a little before seven, two minutes to his alarm ringing, the clock dancing side to side like on the cartoon shows, demanding attention like a family pet, craving a human touch to let it know its job was done for another night. He leaned over and hit the switch.

The clock seemed to settle on its curlicued haunches and Bennett half-imagined it pouting because he had robbed it of its daily chore.

He yawned, scratched places that itched, and threw back the sheets. It was cool. Cool but not cold.

Bennett slid his legs out of bed and rested his feet on the floor. It was part of the getting-up process, a kind of airlock sandwiched between sleep and wakefulness. The first ritual of the day.

He sniffed a bear-sized sniff and drew in everything and anything.

Somewhere in that sniff, alongside the fresh coffee and toasted bread smells that Shelley had left behind in the kitchen and which were now threading their way through the house, were the smells of his bedroom and his clothes, the wood grains and varnish of the furniture, the oily odors imbued by the machines that had stitched the mosaic linen of the curtains and stamped the twists and whorls on the bedside lampshades; old smells, new smells. Unknown smells. Smells from near and faraway . . . smells of other people, other places, other times.

And small-town smells. Plenty of those . . . so different to the smells of the city, New York City, where Bennett had worked as an insurance adjuster for twenty years before turning to writing full-time and hiding himself and Shelley away in Forest Plains . . . a town as close to all the picket-fenced and town-squared small towns as could possibly exist outside the pages of an old well-thumbed *Post*, particularly in these dog days of the second millennium.

He sniffed again and glanced at the window.

Outside, over the street, gulls were circling. On the wires running across the posts that stood sentry-like alongside the grassy lawns, the neighborhood regulars—sparrows, chaffinches and thrushes—were perched . . . like hick locals lazing on a front porch watching an invasion of bike riders crazy-wheeling and whooping around the square.

Bennett frowned and got to his feet, finding new places to scratch as he staggered to the window. Now he could see what was happening.

"Huh!" was all he could think of to say. Someone had taken the world while he had been dragging himself from his bed. Someone had stolen everything that was familiar and had covered it with gauze. But this was a moving gauze, a diaphanous graveyard mist that, even as he watched, was drifting along Sycamore Street, swirling around the tree trunks, twisting itself like ribbons through the leafless branches, washing up the sidewalks to the polished lawns and onwards, stealthily, reaching, conquering and owning, pausing every now and again to check out a crumpled brown leaf before moving on.

He leaned on the sill and yawned again.

It was the mist he could smell. He wondered why Shelley hadn't mentioned it. He'd have told her to take special care. In fact, if he had known it was this bad—because it *was* getting bad . . . thickening by the second, it seemed—he'd have driven her over to the train station at Walton Flats. And anyway, hadn't she said that the skies were clear? He looked both ways along the street. Maybe it *had* been clear when she looked out, but that must have been some time ago.

Bennett frowned. Well, whatever it *had* been . . . it was foggy now.

Now the mist was pooling all around, settling itself onto the trees and the pavement, resting on the sidewalks and the dew-covered lawns, investigating the promise of warmth offered by his partly open window.

The mist had a clean, sharp smell, snaking across the sill and around him into the room, sliding beneath the bed and inside the louvered wardrobe doors, checking out the threads, evaluating the labels. Evaluating *him*.

Bennett watched it.

Soon it would make its way out of the bedroom door and onto the landing. It would find the spare bedroom—*nothing here, boys . . . let's move on*—and then the stairs leading down to the kitchen and the tinny radio sounds.

Bennett stretched and threw the window wide.

A boy appeared out of the mist, dodging the tendrils that grasped for but never quite caught hold of his bicycle wheels. The boy was standing on the pedals, pumping like mad, a cowlick pasted down on his forehead, a brown leather sack crossed across his chest and filled with news and stories, comments, cartoons and quotes. The boy reached into his sack, pulled out a rolled-up paper and made to throw, his arm pulled back like a Major League pitcher. As the paper left his hand, spinning through the milky air, he caught sight of Bennett and smiled.

"Hey, Mist' Diff'ring!" the boy yelled, a *Just Dennis* kind of boy, his voice sounding echoey and artificial in the silent, mist-shrouded street.

Forest Plains was full of boys just like this one, all tow-heads, patched denims and checked shirts. But many of them didn't have names, at least not names that Bennett knew. They were just boys, boys who whispered giggling and mysterious behind your back when you bought something—*anything*—in the drugstore; boys who viewed any structure as merely something else to climb; boys who propped up the summertime street corners, drinking in the life and the sounds and the energy; boys with secret names . . . names like "Ace" and "Skugs."

He'd heard two of them talking in the drugstore just the day before yesterday, the one of them calling over to the other—*Hey Skugs, get a load of that, will ya!*—holding up a comic book, his eyes glaring proudly as though he were responsible for the book and the story and the artwork. And the second boy had dutifully sidled up the aisle to his friend, and equally dutifully exclaimed *Wow!* as he was shown a couple of interior pages. *Wow! Neato!*

Bennett had wanted to interrupt, stop the boys in the middle of their comic book explorations, and ask, *What kind of a name do you have to wind up with Skugs?* But he knew it wouldn't make sense. It would be Charles or James—which would only explain "Chuck" or "Jim"—and the surname would probably be Daniels or Henderson, both equally unhelpful. And that would have meant him having to ask, *So why "Skugs"?* and then the boys would have looked at each other, shrugged, dumped the comic book back on the rack and run out of the store giggling.

Bennett suddenly felt that *he* wanted to be standing out in an early-morning street, alone with an invading mist, hair-plastered onto his forehead, Schwinn between his legs and his old leather *Grit* sack around his shoulder, drinking in the sights and smells and sounds of a life still new . . . still filled with so many possibilities. Suddenly he wanted a secret name of his own . . . one that made no sense at all and that would make adults frown and shake their heads as he ran off laughing into the life that lay ahead.

He wondered what the secret name was for the boy in the street and, for a second, considered asking him. But then he thought better of it. At least he knew this kid's *real* name: it was Will Cerf.

Bennett waved. "Hey Will. Looks a little misty out there," he shouted as the paper hit the screen door below him, its *thud* sounding like a pistol crack.

"Fog," the boy retorted, his face serious, brow furrowed.

Fog. Such an evocative word when spoken by a voice and a mind still alive to things not so easily explained by the meteorological charts on the morning news programs.

The boy stopped the bike and straddled it, one foot on the curb, and waved an arm back in the direction he'd just ridden. "Coming in thick and fast," he said, sounding for all the world like a tow-headed Paul Revere thumbing back over his shoulder at the advancing British troops. For a second or so, Bennett glanced in the direction indicated and felt a small gnawing mixture of apprehension and wonder.

"Down by the scrapyard," Will Cerf added. "Cold, too," he almost concluded. "And damp." The boy rubbed his arms to confirm his report.

Bennett nodded absently and looked back along the street.

Already the first fingers of fog had consolidated, holding tight onto picket fence and garage handle, wrapping themselves across fender and grill, posting sentries beside tree trunks and fall-pipes, settling down alongside discarded or forgotten toys lying dew-covered on the leaf-stained lawns.

"Gotta go," Will Cerf said, a hint of sagacious regret in his voice.

"Me, too," Bennett said. "You take care now."

The boy already had his head down, was already reaching into that voluminous bag of news and views, his feet pumping down on those pedals, the tires *shhhh*ing along the pavement. "Will do," came the reply as another airborne newspaper flew through the mist, gossamer fingers prodding and poking it as it passed by. "You, too," he added over his shoulder.

And then, as if by magic, Will Cerf disappeared into the whiteness banked across the street in front of Jack and Jenny Coppertone's house. The whiteness accepted him—*greedily*, Bennett thought . . . immediately wishing he hadn't used that word—and stretched over to Audrey Chermola's Dodge, checking out the JESUS SAVES sticker on the back fender before swirling around the rain barrel out in front of her garage, climbing up the pipe and over the flat roof to the back yard beyond.

Bennett pulled the window closed.

Outside visibility was worsening.

Now the power lines and their silent bird population had gone. Even the posts were indistinct, like they were only possible *ideas* for posts . . . hastily sketched suggestions for where they might be placed. The Hells Angels gulls had gone, too. He leaned forward and looked up into the air to see if he could see any shapes negotiating the milky currents, but the sky appeared to be deserted.

Deserted and white.

As he watched, a milky swirl of that whiteness rushed at the glass of the window, making him pull back with a start . . . it was as though the mist had momentarily sensed him watching it, like a shark suddenly becoming aware of the presence of the caged underwater cameraman and his deep-sixed recording lens. Then the cushion of mist moved off, lumbering, up and over the house . . . out of sight. Bennett craned forward and tried to look up after it . . . to see what it was doing now.

Just for a second, he considered running to the spare bedroom, where Shelley always kept a window wide to air the room . . .

But then his bladder reminded him it needed emptying. He turned away from the window and padded out to the bathroom.

Taking a pee, Bennett was suddenly pleased that Shelley wasn't downstairs. Pleased that she hadn't heard the newspaper hit the screen door because then she would open it, bring the paper inside into the warmth.

And that would mean she would let the fog inside.

He *hmph*ed and shook his head, flushed the toilet.

Downstairs, on the radio, The Mamas and Papas were complaining that all the leaves were brown. Bennett knew how they felt: roll on summer!

He closed the bathroom door and stepped into the warmth of the shower, feeling it revitalize his skin.

Through the steamed-up glass of the shower stall, Bennett could see the whiteness pressing against the bathroom window. Like it was watching him. Lathering his hair, he tried to recall whether he had heard the radio anchorman mention the fog.

After the shower, Bennett shaved.

The man staring back at him looked familiar but older. The intense light above the mirror seemed to accentuate the pores and creases, picked out the wattled fold of skin beneath his chin . . . a fold that, no matter how hard he tried and how hard he stretched back his head, stoically refused to flatten out. That same light also highlighted the shine of head through what used to be thick hair, the final few stalks now looking like a platoon of soldiers abandoned by their comrades. If he were still able to have a secret name now, it would be "Baldy" or "Tubby" or maybe even "Turkeyneck." As he shaved, he tried to think of what names he *did* have as a boy: he was sure he used to have one, and that it had annoyed him for a time, but he could only think of Ben.

He pulled on the same things he'd been wearing last night. Despite the fact he had two closets literally brimming with shirts and sweaters, jogging pants and old denims that were too threadbare to wear outside the confines of the house, Bennett considered the wearing of yesterday's clothing as something of a treat . . . and something naughty, something he could get away with the way he used to get away with it as a kid.

There were so few things an adult could get away with.

Feeling better, more refreshed, he opened the bathroom door and stepped out onto the landing. As he neared the staircase he could hear thick static growling downstairs and, just for a second, he almost shouted out his wife's name as a question, even though he knew she was long gone to the mall.

He padded downstairs slower than usual, checking the layout over the rim of the handrail as the next floor came into view.

In the kitchen everything was neat and Shelley had left out the cutting board, a jar of marmalade and a new loaf out of the freezer. The coffee smelled good. But first things first: he had to attend to the radio. Bennett leaned on the counter and pushed a couple of the pre-set buttons to zone in on another station . . . anything to relieve that static. But each time he hit a button, it was the same . . . didn't even falter, just kept on crackling and hissing and . . .

whispering

something else. He leaned closer, put his ear against the speaker and listened. Was there a station there? Could he hear someone talking, talking quietly . . . *very* quietly indeed? Maybe that was it: maybe it was the volume. He twizzled the dial on the side but the static just got louder.

Bennett stepped back and looked at the radio, frowning. He had been sure he could hear something behind the static but now it was gone. He switched it off and on again, got the same, and then switched it off. He'd watch TV.

After flicking the set forward and backward through all the available channels, Bennett gave up. Static, static everywhere. Static and voices, soft faraway whispering voices . . . saying things—he was sure they were there and they were saying things, but he just couldn't get them to register. He tossed the remote onto the sofa and sat for a few minutes in the silence.

Coffee. That was what he needed. That would make things right.

He strolled back into the kitchen, poured a cup and walked across the hall into his office.

The cumulative smell of books and words met him as it always did, welcomed him back for another day.

He powered up the old Aptiva, heard it click once—the single bell-tone it always made—and then watched the screen go fuzzy.

"Huh? What the hell's going on here?" he asked the room.

The millions of words and sentences tucked up in the double-stacked shelves of books and magazines shuffled amongst themselves but, clearly unable to come up with a good response, remained silent.

Bennett placed his coffee on his mouse mat and shuffled the mouse. Nothing. The computer wouldn't even boot up. He pressed the volume button on the CD-ROM speakers and heard the static invade his office.

Along with the faraway whispering voices.

He flipped the Rolodex until he got the number for the maintenance people and pressed the hands-free key on the fax/telephone at the side of his desk. This time he knew there were voices in that white haze of crackle coming from the fax machine . . . and the voices sounded like they were chuckling.

Forgetting the coffee, he went out into the lounge and picked up the handset of the house line.

It was the sound of the sea and the wind, the hiss of the tallest trees bending to the elements, the hum of the Earth spinning. All this and nothing more. Nothing more except for the unmistakable sound of someone—some*thing*—calling his name . . . calling it as though in a dream.

Now the panic really set in. It had already been lit and its flames fanned without him even seeing the first sparks, but when Bennett walked quickly to the front door, opened it and stepped out onto the stoop, the fire became a conflagration in his stomach.

The fog was everywhere, thick and solid, unmoving and ungiving, leaving no single discernible landmark of the street he and Shelley had lived in for more than twenty years. It was an alien landscape—no, not so much a landscape as a canvas . . . a blank canvas sitting on an old easel in a musty loft somewhere in the Twilight Zone, and Bennett was the only dab of color to be found on it.

And he felt even he was fading fast.

He stared towards the drive at the side of the house and was pleased to see that he could make out the fence running between his property and Jerry and Amy Sondheim's. He didn't know whether to be relieved or dismayed by the fact that Shelley had the car. Then he decided he was relieved: if the car *had* been there, he would have gone to it, slid into his familiar position behind the wheel and driven off.

Driven off where? a soft voice asked quietly in the back of his head.

Bennett nodded. He couldn't have driven anywhere in this. Nobody could drive anywhere in this. Christ, what the hell *was* it?

He stared into the whiteness trying to see if there was just the tiniest hint of movement. There was none. The fog looked like a painted surface, as though the entire planet was sinking into a sea of mist, submerging itself forever, removing all traces of recognizability. No radio or TV, no telephones . . . not even any Internet! Was this the way it was all going to end? The whole planet being cut off from itself as though nothing existed? As though nothing had *ever* existed?

It was right then—as Bennett was looking first to the left along

Sycamore Street to where it intersected with Masham Lane, trying to imagine the old bench Charley Sputterenk erected in memory of his wife, Hazel, and then to the right, down towards Main Street, trying to see if he could hear the distant sound of moving traffic—that he heard something moving in the fog.

He snapped his head back to face front and stared, stared hard. But he couldn't see anything . . . except now the mist seemed to be swirling a little, right in front of his face . . . as though something was pushing it towards him. Something coming towards him and displacing it . . .

"Hello?" His voice sounded weak and querulous and he hated himself for it. Hated himself but was unable to do anything about it. The mist continued to swirl and Bennett's eyes started to ache with the effort.

"Somebody out there? Need any help?"

This time he had tried to make his tone initially mock-serious—*Jesus Christ, is this some weather or what?*—and then helpful . . . a fog-bound Samaritan calling to a lost and weary traveler.

The sound came again—a hesitant shuffle of shoes on sidewalk, perhaps?—and was accompanied by what sounded to be a cough or a low, throaty rumble.

Bennett took a step back, reaching his hand behind until it touched the reassuring surface of the doorjamb, and felt something under his foot. Quickly glancing down he saw the folded newspaper. There was something sticking out of it, a gaudily-colored handbill protruding from the printed pages.

He bent down and scooped up the paper and its contents and then backed fully into the house, allowing the screen door to slam and pushing the house door closed without turning around, and securing the deadbolts top and bottom before turning the key.

There had been no sound out there, no sound at all. And there should have been. Even if the fog had shrouded the entire county—though it was far more likely that it had merely entrapped Forest Plains, and possibly only a couple of the town's many streets—he should have been able to stand on his own doorstep and hear something . . . a siren, a voice, a car engine, someone's dog howling at the sudden claustrophobic curtain that had dropped down.

But it was silent out there.

More silent than he could ever have imagined.

And he should have been able to see *something* . . . anything at all: a glimpse of windowpane across the street, the muted and silhouetted outlines of roof gable or drainpipe, the indistinct shape of a parked car whose owner was either unable or unwilling to brave the murk.

But there was nothing to see at all through the whiteness.

The thought came to him

. . . somehow I don't think we're in Kansas any more, Toto

that it wasn't Sycamore Street at all. And it wasn't Forest Plains. And the mall where Shelley was shopping-till-she-dropped with her sister Lisa was a world away.

He went to the window at the side of the door and looked out into the street. It was the same as before. He could see his own drive and his own lawn run down to the sidewalk, and he could see the vague outline of the road . . . but nothing more.

The handbill slipped out of the newspaper and fluttered to the floor at his feet just as he thought for a moment that he could see a shape forming out in the whiteness, but nothing appeared . . . though the mist now seemed to be swirling thickly in the middle of the street.

Bennett lifted the handbill and stared at it.

It was just a regular-sized insert, like any of the ones that dropped out of Bennett's *Men's Journal* or Shelley's *Vanity Fair* . . . ablaze with color and just three lines of curlicued fonts, seraphed letters and ubiquitous exclamation marks, all of the text bold, some of it italicized.

It read:

CONGRATULATIONS TO <u>BENNETT DIFFERING</u>!

in huge letters in the very center of the sheet, with Bennett's name appearing to have been typed into place on a line. Below that, the handbill announced

YOU HAVE WON A VISIT FROM <u>YOUR FATHER</u>!

with the words appearing in slightly smaller lettering, employing the best sideshow-barker's spiel, and in a typesetting nightmare of a mixture of small caps, dropped first letters and the typed-in words YOUR FATHER. And then:

HAVE A GOOD TIME!

And that was that.

Bennett turned the sheet over to see if there was anything on the back, but there was only a pattern of swirling lines, like the ones printed for security on foreign currency.

Won? How could he have won anything when he didn't recall even entering any competitions? And his father? John Differing had been dead some twenty-seven years. Maybe it was some kind of gag. Maybe everyone on the street—maybe even everyone in Forest Plains—was receiving a similar handbill in their newspaper. Bennett wished he could ask young Will Cerf to look in the other papers he was delivering to check out that particular theory.

Outside, a *haurrrnk!* Sounded . . . like a ship's horn.

Bennett looked up at the window and saw a shape forming out of the thick swirls of mist in the middle of the street. Someone was walking towards the house . . . walking slowly, even awkwardly. Someone had been hurt.

With the handbill still clutched in his hand, Bennett rushed to the door and started to release the deadbolts. But then he stopped.

Who was this person? Maybe it was some kind of weirdo, some transient brought in with the fog . . . like the guys that howl at a full moon. And here was Bennett busily opening the door to let him inside.

He pushed the top bolt home again and moved back to the window.

The shape was now fully emerged from the mist: it was a man, a man in a dark suit, no topcoat—*no topcoat!* and in this weather!—and wearing a hat. Bennett immediately assumed an age for the man—he had to be older than seventy, maybe even eighty, to be wearing a hat. Hardly anyone he knew wore hats these days, at least around Forest Plains.

The figure stopped for a moment and moved its head from side to side like he was checking out the houses. The man had to have 20/20 vision no matter how old he was: when Bennett was last outside he wasn't able to see across the street let alone distinguish one house from another.

When the man started moving again, Bennett thought there was something familiar about him. Maybe he'd come out of Jack Coppertone's house across the street . . . it wasn't Jack himself—too old, though Bennett still couldn't see the man's face—but it could be Jenny's father. Bennett rubbed the glass and remembered that the mist was outside the window, not inside. But, no, it couldn't be Jenny's father—he was a short man, and fat. Whereas the man walking across the street was tall and slim, a soldier's gait, straight-backed and confident . . . despite the fact that he had just had to stop and check which house he was heading for. Whatever, and whoever the man was, Bennett didn't think he posed a problem . . . and he *could* be in difficulty. Lost at the very least. And it would be good to speak with somebody.

He moved back to the door, released the last bolt and pulled it open.

The man's shoes on the black surface of the street made a *click-clack* sound. The mist swirling around his arms and legs looked like an oriental dancer's veils, clinging one second and voluminous the next . . . and brought with it now the unmistakable sound of distant voices muttering and whispering. Then his face appeared, frowning and unsure, one eye narrowed in an effort to make some sense of the house and the man standing before him, the shadow of the hat brim moving up and down on his forehead as he strode forward.

He looked wary, this fog-brought stranger from afar. And well he might do.

The house, Bennett knew, he had never seen before.

And when he had last seen the man standing before him in this alien street, the man had been little more than a boy.

The whispering voices echoed the word "boy" in Bennett's head like circling gulls warning of bad weather out on the coast.

He successfully fought off the urge to cut and run back into the house—to throw the deadbolts across—how appropriate that word suddenly seemed: dead-bolts—to bar the stranger's way . . . to erase the errant foolishness of what he was thinking, of the silly *déjà vu* sense he had ever seen the man before. But he was just a man, this stranger to Forest Plains . . . a man lost and alone, maybe with a broken-down Olds or Chevy a couple of blocks parked up somewhere down near the intersection with Main Street, a trusted and faithful vehicular retainer that he cleaned and polished every Sunday but which now languished with a flooded carburetor or a busted muffler trailing down on the road.

The man stopped and looked at Bennett, just twenty or thirty feet between them, the man out on the sidewalk and Bennett standing in the open doorway of his home, screen door leaning against him, the fresh and welcoming lights spilling out onto the mist which held their shine on its back and shifted it around like St. Elmo's Fire.

"Hey," Bennett said softly.

The man shifted his head to one side, looked to the left and then to the right. Then nodded.

Bennett crumpled the handbill into a ball and thrust it into his pants pocket. "Quite a morning."

"Quite a morning," came the response.

It was as though someone had pumped air or water or some kind of helium gas into Bennett's head. There were things in there—sleeping things, memory things that lay dormant and dust-covered like old furniture in a forgotten home that you suddenly and unexpectedly went back to one magical day . . . things awoken by three simple and unexciting words delivered in a familiar voice and a familiar drawl the accuracy of which he thought he had misplaced—or, more realistically, had filed away and ignored.

These things grew to full height and shape and revealed themselves as remembered incidents . . . and the incidents brought remembered voices and remembered words: these were real memories . . . not the cloying waves of rose-colored-eyepiece nostalgia that he got watching a re-run of favorite childhood TV show or hearing a snatch of a one-time favorite song. He saw this man—many versions of him, each older or younger than the one before—playing ball, laughing, talking . . . saw him asleep.

"You lost?"

The man looked around for a few seconds and then looked back at Bennett. "I guess so. Where am I?"

"This is Forest Plains."

"Where's that?"

Bennett shrugged and tried to stop his knees shaking. "It's just a town. Where are you heading?"

"I'm going—" The man paused and closed his eyes. When he opened them, he smiled at Bennett. "Home," he said. "I'm going home."

Bennett nodded. "You want to come in for a while? Have a cup of coffee?" He had never heard of a ghost that came in for coffee but, what the hell . . . all of this was crazy so anything was possible. He glanced along the street and saw that the mist seemed to be thinning out, the first vague shapes and outlines of the houses opposite taking hesitant form.

The man followed Bennett's stare and when he turned back there was a wistful smile on his mouth. "Can't stay too long," he said.

"No," Bennett agreed. He nodded to the fog. "Bad day."

The man turned around but didn't comment. Then he said, "You ever think it's like some kind of vehicle? Like a massive ocean liner?"

"What? The fog?"

The man nodded, gave a little flick of his shoulders, and stared back into the mist. "Like some huge machine," he said, "drifting along soundlessly and then—" he snapped his fingers "—suddenly pulling into a port or a station, somewhere we've not seen for a long time . . . sometimes for so long it's like . . . like we've never seen it at all. And it reveals something that you weren't expecting . . . weren't expecting simply because you don't know how far you've traveled." He turned back. "How far not just in distance but in time."

"In time?" Bennett said, glancing out at the swirling mist. "Like a time machine," he said.

The man smiled, the intensity suddenly falling away. "Yeah, like a time machine. Or something like that."

Bennett stepped aside and ushered the man into the house.

The man who looked for all the world like John Differing removed his hat and held it by the brim with both hands at his waist. Looking around the kitchen, he said, "Nice place."

Bennett closed the door and stood alongside the man, noting with an inexplicable sadness that he seemed to be around four or five inches shorter than he remembered. He followed the man's stare and drank in the microwave oven, the polished electric hobs, the chest freezer over by the back door, the small TV set on the breakfast counter. What would these things look like to someone who had not been around since 1972?

"*We* like it," Bennett responded simply. "So, coffee?"

The man shrugged as Bennett walked across the kitchen to the sink. "Whatever you're making."

"Coffee's fresh. Shelley—my wife—she made it. It might have gotten a little strong, sitting. I'll just boil some water."

"Uh huh. She here?"

"Shelley? No, she's out. Shopping. Christmas shopping. With her sister. Does it every year." Placing the kettle on its electric base, Bennett pulled a chair from the table. "You want to sit down?"

The man shook his head. "No, I don't think I can stay that long. Don't want to get too settled."

"Right."

The man placed his hat on the table and straightened his shoulders. "Mind if I look around?"

"No, no . . . go right ahead. Coffee'll be ready in a couple of minutes."

He watched the old man walk off along the hallway and tried to think of all the things he wanted to ask him. Things like, what was it like . . . where he was now? Things like, did he know who he was . . . and that he was dead? Did he even know that Bennett was—

"This your office?" The voice drifted along the hallway and broke Bennett's train of thought.

"Yes." The kettle clicked off and Bennett poured water into the electric coffee jug.

"You work from home?" The voice had moved back into the hallway.

"Yeah. I gave up my day job about five years ago. I write full-time now." He went to the refrigerator and got a carton of milk.

Pouring steaming coffee into a couple of mugs, Bennett wondered what the hell he was doing. The fog and the fact that it had cut him off from civilization had messed up his head. A stupid handbill—he felt in his pocket to make sure it was still there . . . make sure he hadn't imagined it—some half-baked ramblings about the fog maybe being a time machine that the dead used to travel back and forth, and the appearance of a man who looked a little like his father had freaked him out. Looked like his father! What the hell was that? He hadn't even *seen* his father for twenty-seven years.

He shook his head and added milk to the mugs. The fact was he had invited some guy into the house, for crissakes. Shelley would go ape-shit when she found out. *If* he told her, of course. Putting the milk back in the refrigerator, he suddenly thought that maybe Shelley *would* find out . . . when she got home and found her husband lying in the kitchen with a knife in his—

"What kind of stuff do you write?" the man asked, standing right behind him in the kitchen.

"Shit!" He spun around and banged into the refrigerator door.

"Pardon me?"

"You startled me."

"Sorry."

"That's okay. I'm sorry for—"

"Didn't mean to do that."

"Really, it's okay." He closed the refrigerator door and took a deep breath. "Guess I must be a little nervous." He waved a hand at the window. "The fog."

The man walked across to the counter by the sink and nodded to the window. "Looks like it's clearing up." He reached a hand out towards the two mugs and said, "Either?"

Nodding, Bennett said, "Yeah, neither of them have sugar, though. There's a bowl over to your—"

"I don't take it." He picked up one of the mugs and, closing his eyes, took a sip. "Mmm, now that's good. You don't know how good coffee tastes until you haven't had it for a while."

The man continued to sip at his coffee, eyes downcast, as though studying the swirling brown liquid.

Bennett considered just coming right out with it there and then, confronting this familiar man with the belief that he was Bennett's very own father. But the more he watched him, the more Bennett wondered whether he was just imagining things . . . even worse, whether he was in some way trying to bring his father back. After all, who ever heard of a handbill that advertised returning dead relatives. He may just be putting two and two together and getting five.

On the other hand, maybe it *was* his father. It could well be that there were forces or powers at large in the universe that made such things possible. Maybe Rod Serling had had it right after all. Maybe the dead did use mist as a means of getting around—so many movies had already figured that one out . . . and maybe they did travel in time.

Bennett took a sip of his own coffee and thought of something he had often pondered over: if a chair falls over in an empty house miles from anywhere, does it make a sound? Natural laws dictate that it must do, but there were plenty of instances of natural law seemingly not figuring out. The thing was—the thing with the chair in the deserted house—there was no way of proving or disproving it . . . because the only way to prove it was to have someone present at the falling over, which destroyed one of the criteria for the experiment. So maybe whatever one *wanted* to believe could hold true.

The same applied to the man in Bennett's kitchen. So long as Bennett didn't actually come right out and ask him and risk the wrong response.

John Differing? No, name's Bill Patterson, live over to Dawson Corner, got a flooded Packard couple blocks down the street, and a wife in it—Ellie's her name—busting to get home soon as this fog's cleared up

it was safe to assume the man was Bennett's father. And the plain fact was there were so many things that supported such a belief. Thinks like . . .

"My father drank his coffee that way, sipping," Bennett said, pushing the encroaching silence back into the corners of the room where it didn't pose a threat.

The man looked up at Bennett and smiled. "Yeah?"

Bennett nodded. "Looked a lot like you do, too."

"That right?"

Bennett took a deep breath. "He died more than twenty-seven years ago. He was fifty-eight." He took another sip and said, "How old are *you*? If you don't mind my—"

"Don't mind at all. I'm fifty-eight myself."

"Huh," Bennett said, shaking his head. "Quite a coincidence."

"Looks like it's a day for them," the man said as he lowered his cup down in front of his waist. "My boy—my *son*—he always wanted to be a writer."

"Yeah?"

"Yeah. I must say, I never had much faith in that. Seemed like a waste of time to me." He lifted the cup again. "But a man can be wrong.

Could be he made a go of it." His mouth broke into a soft smile. "Could even be he'll get real successful a little ways down the track."

Bennett wanted to ask if the man ever *saw* his son these days, but that would have been breaking the rules of the game . . . just as it would have been courting disaster. The response could be *Sure, saw Jack just last week and he's doing fine*. And Bennett didn't want that response. But the more they talked, the more sure he became.

They talked of the man's past and of the friends he used to have.

They talked of places he had lived and things he had done.

And in amongst all the talk, all the people and all the places and all the things, there were people and places and things that rang large bells in Bennett's mind—so many coincidences—but there were also several people and places and things that didn't mean anything at all. Things Bennett had never known about his father. But he still refrained from asking anything that might place the man in some kind of cosmic glitch . . . or that might provoke an answer that would break the spell.

In turn, Bennett told the man things about his father . . . things that not only was he sure his father had never known but also that he himself hadn't known. Not *really* known . . . not known in that surface area of day-to-day consciousness that we can access whenever we want.

And each time Bennett said something, the man nodded slowly, a soft smile playing on his lips, and he would say, "Is that right?" or "You don't say" or, more than once, "You make him sound like quite a man."

"He was. Quite a man."

For a second, the man looked like he was about to say something, the edge of his tongue peeking between those gently smiling lips

thank you

but he seemed to think better of it and whatever it had been was consigned to silence.

Bennett placed his mug on the counter and pulled the handbill from his pocket. "You believe in ghosts?" he asked.

"Ghosts?"

"Mm hmm." He moved across to the man and showed him the handbill. "Got this today, in the newspaper. Ever hear of anything like that?"

The man shook his head. "Can't say that I have, no."

"You think such a thing is possible?"

The man shrugged. "They do say anything's possible. Maybe ghosts see everything in one hit . . . the then, the now and the to come. Maybe time doesn't mean anything at all to them. Could be they just hop right on board of their fog time machine and go wherever or whenever they've a mind."

Bennett looked again at the handbill, his eyes tracing those curly letters. "But why would they want to come back . . . ghosts, I mean?"

"Maybe because they forget what things were like? Forget the folks they left behind? They say the living forget the dead after a while: well, maybe it works both ways." He shrugged again, looked down into his coffee. "Who knows."

Was the man nervous? Bennett frowned. Maybe he was breaking some kind of celestial rules by moving the conversation to a point where the man would have no choice but to corroborate Bennett's belief . . . and maybe that would mean—

He thrust the handbill back into his pocket and the man looked immediately relieved, if still a little apprehensive.

"Yeah, well," Bennett said in a dismissive tone, "what are ghosts but memories?"

The man nodded. "Right. Memories. I like that. And what is Heaven but a small town . . . a small town like this one. A small town that's just a little ways up or down the track."

Now it was Bennett's turn to nod. "You know," Bennett went on, "we used to play a game, back when I was a kid, where we used to say which sense we would keep if we were forced to give up all but one of the senses, and why.

"Kids would say, 'hearing' and they'd say 'because I couldn't listen my records,' or they'd say 'sight,' 'because I couldn't read my comic books or watch TV or go to the movies.'"

"And what did you say?"

Bennett smiled. This was a story he'd told his father on more than one occasion. "I used to say I wouldn't give up my memory, because without my memory nothing that had ever happened to me would mean anything. Everything I am—forget the skin and flesh and bone, forget the muscles and the sinews and the arteries—*every*thing I am is memories."

The man smiled. "You ever stop to think that maybe you're a ghost?"

Bennett laughed. "Did *you*?"

And the man joined in on the laughter. "An angel, maybe."

"An angel?"

The man shrugged. "A messenger. That's what angels are . . . messengers."

"Yeah? And what's your message?"

The man laughed. "Oh, that would be telling now. Wouldn't it."

Bennett suddenly realized he could now see the house across the street quite clearly. Could see the front door opening . . . could see the unmistakable outline of Jenny Coppertone stepping out onto the front step, staring up into the sky. Then she turned around and went back into the house.

Bennett heard the muted sound of a door slamming.

The fog's hold on the world was weakening.

He looked across at the man standing in front of the sink, saw him frowning at the mug of coffee, shuffling his arms around like he was having difficulty with it. Maybe it was too hot for him . . . but, hadn't he been drinking it all this time?

Outside, a car went by slowly, its lights playing on the mist.

Then the *haurrrnk!* blasted again, the same sound he'd heard before . . . but different in tone now. This time it sounded more like a warning.

The man dropped the mug and Bennett watched it bounce once, coffee spraying across the floor and the table legs and the chairs.

Bennett watched it roll to a stop—amazingly unbroken—before he looked up. The man was looking across at him, his face looking a little pale . . . and a little sad.

"I couldn't . . . I couldn't keep a hold of it," he said.

"You have to go," Bennett said. He knew it deep in his heart . . . deep in that place where he knew everything there *was* to know.

"Yes, I have to go."

"I'll see you off—"

The man held up his hand. "No," he snapped. And then, "No, I'm sure you've got things to do . . . things to be getting on with."

"Memories to build," Bennett added.

"Right, memories to build." He moved forward from the counter, unsteadily at first, watching his feet move one in front of the other as though he were walking a tightrope. Bennett made to give him a hand but the man pulled away. "Can't do that," he said.

They stood looking at each other for what seemed like a long time, Bennett desperately wanting to take that one step forward—that one step that would carry him twenty-seven years—and wrap his arms around his father, bury his face in his father's neck and smell his old familiar smells, smells whose aroma he couldn't recall . . . how desperately he wanted to give new life to old memories. But he knew he could not.

As he reached the door, the man stopped for a second and turned around. "You know, my son, when he was a kid, he had a nickname."

Bennett smiled. "Yeah? What was it?"

"Bubber."

"Bubber?" *Oh my god . . . Bubber . . . it was Bubber because I—*

"He had a stutter—nothing too bad, but it was there—and his name was . . . his name began with a B."

Bennett could feel his eyes misting up.

"Kids can be cruel, can't they?"

It was all he could do to nod.

The door closed, the screen door slammed a ricochet *rat-a-tat* and Bennett was alone again . . . more alone than he had ever felt in his life. "Take care," he said to the empty kitchen.

And you, a voice said somewhere inside his head.

He waited a full minute before he went to the door and opened it, stepped out into the fresh December air and walked to the street. "And what was the message, old timer?" he said.

The fog had gone and the watery winter sun was struggling through the overhead early-morning haze.

Cars were moving up and down, people were walking on the sidewalks, but there was no sign of the man.

"Hey, Bennett!"

Bennett gave a wave to Jack Coppertone as he pulled the handbill from his pants pocket. It was now a flyer for The Science Fiction Book Club; maybe that was what it had always been. As he folded it carefully, thinking back to that final sight of his visitor pulling open the door, he suddenly turned and ran back to the house.

On the table, right where the man had placed it, was a hat.

The message!

Bennett walked carefully across the kitchen, heart beating so hard he thought it was going to burst through his chest and his shirt, and reached for it, closing his eyes, expecting to connect with just more empty air.

But his fingers touched material.

And he lifted it, not daring to open his eyes . . . he was breaking rules here, of that he was sure . . . but maybe, just maybe, if only one or maybe two senses were working, he could pull it off. He lifted the hat up and buried his face inside the brim.

What are ghosts but memories? he heard himself saying from just a few minutes earlier. And there they were . . . memories. The only question was, were they from the past or the future?

Almost as soon as he had breathed in, the fragrance dissipated until there was only the smell of soap and the feel of Bennett's empty hands cradling his face. But deep inside his head, the memories were still there, smelling fresh as blue bonnets in spring air.

Haurrrnnnnnnnnk!

Bennett looked at the window and saw that it had started to snow.

THE FOLD

Conrad Williams

CONRAD WILLIAMS is the author of the novels *Head Injuries*, *London Revenant*, *The Unblemished*, *One*, *Decay Inevitable*, *Blonde on a Stick* and *Loss of Separation*. He has also written four novellas: "Nearly People," "Game," "The Scalding Rooms" and "Rain."

Williams is a past recipient of the British Fantasy Award, the Littlewood Arc Prize and the International Horror Guild Award. He is the author of more than eighty short stories, some of which appear in his first collection, *Use Once Then Destroy*. A new collection, *Open Heart Surgery*, is forthcoming from PS Publishing, as is the anthology *Gutshot*, which marks his debut as an editor.

The author lives in Manchester, England, with his wife, three sons and a big Maine coon cat.

"The idea for this story came during a visit to my favorite Manchester bookshop, Sharston Books, which is based in a warehouse on an industrial estate," Williams explains. "There are thousands of books there, and it would take you years of browsing to assess them all. There are two levels and, sometimes, when it's quiet, it is possible to hear the people on the upper level moving from stack to stack.

"There are the usual creaks and groans that you find in an old building, but there's something odd about it, too, something about people flicking through ancient pages, picking up books that might not exist anywhere other than this place in which one is standing.

"There are books here that are so buried that it's feasible they've never been opened since the shop began trading, twelve years ago. It seemed a great place to locate a story involving creatures that are beyond history."

During his research, Williams stumbled upon a list of names attributed to fallen angels and their origins: "I liked the name 'Malpas,'" he says, "and when I saw that this was an angel who appeared as a crow, I felt that it was too good an opportunity not to put in some references to this most horror-friendly of birds."

MALPAS HALTED AT THE FOOT of the stone steps outside his tower block and, as always, glanced behind him to check that nobody had followed him home. Black snow edged the pavements. The moon was the merest swipe of light, like an afterthought in a painting of the night. Malpas' breath came in white flutes.

It was taking longer to cross town. He could feel death in his bones, worming, trying to break him down, but he was a tough old bird. It would be some time yet.

"If at all," he muttered, and began to climb.

The lifts were working, thank Christ, and he ascended to the twelfth floor and pulled out from his pocket a bunch of old, discolored keys. As he reached for the lock, his eye caught the scar in the pad of fat at the base of his left thumb. It was like a star; its twin lay on the back of his hand. *Where the angels kissed you*, his mother had once told him.

Inside, he threw off his coat and scarf and sat in the armchair by the window. The dark seemed fastened to the planet; on some nights, especially in winter, he could believe that it would never go away, that it was adhered for good to everything. Whenever he looked in the mirror—or, as now, caught his reflection in the muddied glass of the window—it might be the case that he had spent eons in the dark, and had evolved to cope better with it.

His eyes were like two faded smears of ash on a pale grey cloth. His hair, once so black it seemed to contain streaks of blue, was white. He had never liked his mouth, a ruddy, wide crevice: his large, hooked nose seemed to be permanently trying to obscure the horror of it. He kept that mouth closed for much of the time. He watched the street for a while. A taxi. A bus. A man in a wheelchair being pushed across the road. A man—a blind man—with a white stick, tapping at the pavement, head ranging around as if he could see what surrounded him. What looked like wings were attached to his back, but then Malpas saw that it was a pale grey rucksack. *Getting old, going blind myself*, he thought.

After he had rested and his breath and color had returned some, he moved to the back room, where his bed and his workbench lay, each covered in books and photograph albums, craft tools and ancient maps of the world. He never slept in here; his armchair was for dreams. This was his store room and sanctuary. He worked hard in here. So it was now.

He switched on the radio and twiddled the tuner until he found a station playing classical music. He rolled up his shirtsleeves and leaned over the dead carrion crow. Rigor mortis had drawn its wings in towards the body. Malpas stretched them out and parted the feathers on the chest until he could feel the crest of its breastbone. He nicked the skin with his scalpel and gently peeled the membrane away from the bone. He kept peeling and teasing with the scalpel, sprinkling borax on to the meat to keep it dry, until the body of the bird had been separated from its chamber of skin.

He snipped away the joints at the extremities and turned his attention to the neck. He pulled the skin gently away from the skull, like a hood that has been drawn too tightly. He dug out the eyes with tweezers, packing the sockets with borax and fiberglass wool. The thing looked like some ghastly, famished creature emerging from a covering of snow.

Malpas was unfazed by the grisly aspects of this work. It calmed him. To see the anatomy of a once-living creature was like being admitted to view a sacred secret.

He scoured the skull of its contents and packed it. He threaded fake eyes through the padding in the sockets and carefully introduced the skull back to its skin hood. He had been working solidly for three hours now. The tower block was still and quiet. He could believe there was nothing else in the world but for him and Messiaen and this broken pound or so of *Corvus corone*.

He had no idea how he possessed the taxidermist's skill. Presumably, at some point, he had taken a course; he couldn't remember. But then, the same could be said about any aspect of his life. He had stumbled blindly through his sixty-odd years, groping for sense and stability, trying to understand other people and keep a lid on the fear he had of space and time.

He wished he had known his parents, his father particularly. He had a thing about dads, and wished he could have been one. He felt, sometimes, that he was a forsaken speck, a fluke, a freak, something never meant to have known the beat of a heartbeat, or the spark of a thought. The fragility of life assaulted him every morning when he turned a newspaper page or switched channels on the television.

The heart was a gnarly old muscle but it was shockingly small. And everything it was connected to was frail. Veins that you could pop open with your fingers like a peapod. The slapdash muddle of organs in the chest cavity. The brain wobbling precariously on top of a spine: it was like some joke, some plate-spinning trick, doomed to failure. There were so many ways to die, so many different insults and assaults the body could suffer, that it was astonishing so many people made it into old age, but then it wasn't really old age at all. The puff of the world's oldest person was an unheard gasp in the roaring, nine-billion-year life-span of the sun. Being surrounded by a family, knowing the warmth of a child's soft skin, would help him sit easier with all of that.

He broke off from his work at a little before 1:00 a.m. He poured himself a small whisky and sat in his chair, watching the other tower blocks in his estate, the lights switching off, and the bodies moving within each TV screen window. He tried to remember a time before he was old, but it was difficult. There was a suggestion of youth, at some point, but, as in the aging eye, there was a misty cataract preventing him from seeing anything in detail.

He finished his drink and rubbed at his face and his hands, until the stiffness had been chased from them. He returned to the crow and finished the job. The last thing he did, before sewing the cavity shut, was to carefully insert a golden hair from a tin he kept in his tool drawer. There was a lock of hair in there, belonging to a boy that had died in childhood. Something he had come across over the years. Something he felt it was important to own.

By 3:00 a.m. the bird was ready. He packaged it in bubble wrap and folded brown paper around it, securing everything with string. He went back to his chair. He thought a little about this strange flourish that he discharged at the end of each commission but could not remember the origin of it. A secret, a private signature most likely? It didn't really matter, but he couldn't stop now. He felt he owed it to the dead boy, whoever he had been. It was some skewed way of keeping him vital in this world. He went back to his chair and drank some more and watched some more and fell asleep.

In the morning he awakened to an ash-colored sky. He had been dreaming of his own father, of whom he might have resembled. Cary Grant, perhaps. Or Johnny Weissmuller. At some point that man must have picked him up, cuddled him, tickled him, made him laugh.

The taste of digesting whisky was unpleasant at the back of his mouth. It was too cold to wash, or change his clothes. He took scant pleasure from the fact that, as an old man, he could pretty well do as he pleased in matters of personal hygiene, for he had nobody to chide him about it.

He took a bus from his flat to a crossroads half a mile north, where he caught a connection that took him to the neighboring district, a matter of a ten-minute journey. Here he disembarked and walked the final quarter of a mile to the industrial estate.

He breakfasted on toast and tea at a café patronized by yellow-jacketed construction crew, long-distance lorry drivers, and staff from the various offices nearby. At 9:30 a.m., he walked to a car park around which were arranged a carpet show room, a garage and an old factory that had been converted into a second-hand bookshop. A bicycle had been padlocked to a security gate in front of the old warehouse roller door, a door that had not seen use since the factory's closure, some fifteen years before.

Now it was rusted and, in all probability, sealed shut. Access was via a side door plastered with political slogans and stickers and cuttings from local newspapers bemoaning Oxfam's impact on independent booksellers. Malpas tapped on the glass twice and opened the door.

Clive Grealish was sitting at his customary spot behind the counter, his hands—shaking violently with Parkinson's disease—attempting to fish a teabag from a mug.

"Good morning, Anders," he said, as Malpas placed the package on the counter, amid the usual detritus: receipt rolls, books that needed pricing, paper bags, pencils. As usual, Grealish did not look up to acknowledge his old friend. Malpas saw only the top of his head, the upper edges of his brown spectacle frames.

It was quiet in the factory; the thousands of books had dampened sound so that it fell dead at the moment it was made. Beyond the walls, Malpas could hear plenty: the slam of a plastic bin lid, the rattle of an extractor fan, a muted radio, traffic roaring up and down the main road.

Grealish took the bird and hurriedly concealed it within a drawer beneath the counter. Malpas fancied he saw his forehead gleam more sharply; was the man sweating?

"You never look at me, Clive," he said, "when we talk. And, come to think of it, when we don't talk, either. When we stand together in . . . companionable silence."

"What of it?" Grealish said, fiddling with his teaspoon.

Malpas gazed off down the narrow aisle that ran through the factory. Every window had been blocked out by volumes.

"Nothing," Malpas said. "I just wonder, sometimes, if I, well, if there's something about me that . . . unnerves you."

"Your line of questioning," Grealish said, and attempted a chuckle that sounded like something ill living just inside his mouth. "That unnerves me."

"Why?" He was struggling now to remember when or how they had become friends, and whether, after all, "friends" was an inaccurate way of describing their relationship.

"It doesn't matter," Grealish said. He opened his wallet and dug out a fifty-pound note. "No more birds, please."

Malpas was shocked. "But this is my livelihood. You've always told me that you have no problem selling them on. And I've never asked you for more. I know you must make quite a bit of profit on these—"

"No more birds." And now he did look at Malpas, and although light glinted off the lenses of his spectacles, obscuring his eyes, Malpas could sense the fear in them. "There's nothing more I can do for you."

"What do you mean? I never saw myself as a charity case."

Footsteps shifted across the floor above. The unmistakable sound of a book being slid from a shelf. Grealish recoiled, as if struck. "I didn't hear anybody come in," he said.

"Relax, Clive," Malpas said. "This is a shop. The door is unlocked. People come here to buy things, don't they?"

"I've been sitting here since I opened up. Nobody came in." Again he was averting his gaze, as if a small sun had suddenly exploded within Malpas' face, too bright to behold. He seemed eager to keep talking though, now. It seemed he was fishing for some sort of explanation from Malpas, but he couldn't give it. Not one that satisfied, at least.

He said: "Maybe you locked him in when you closed yesterday." It was meant light-heartedly, but Grealish did not take it that way. He stood up, then sat back down, wiped his face with a creased blue handkerchief snatched from his pocket. Malpas was irritated that the focus of their discussion had shifted. He tried to steer Grealish back to the matter of stuffed crows and regular payments, but Grealish was transfixed by the upper floor. His gaze followed an imagined route taken by this phantom customer.

"Clive, it could just be a trapped bird—"

Grealish shot him a hot look then, as if he had said something accidentally profound, but did not answer.

"—or a collapsed bookshelf. You overstock them, you know."

Grealish agreed, or at least allowed himself to be ameliorated by the suggestion. He said, with a graveness that Malpas found odd: "There are words in this old bookshop that might never be unearthed."

"We have to talk," Malpas said. "You can't just release me like this."

"Release you," Grealish said, weakly, his voice barely containing enough air for the words to carry upon it. He said more, but the sense was lost upon the older man. Was it something like *If only it were so simple?*

"I can't, I won't talk now," Grealish said. He was staring at the puckered, long-sealed wound on Malpas' hand with grim fascination. "Maybe later. Yes, later. Come back when I close, at seven tonight. We'll go for a drink."

He reached out and shook Malpas' hand in an action that was almost savage; later, Malpas would notice that Grealish had left scratch marks in his skin. There was nothing for it; Grealish had become a closed door, his eyes fast on his accounts ledger, his hands moving ceaselessly, like a cellist applying vibrato to a note. Outside in the weak sunshine, Malpas turned and stared back at the bookshop's upper floor windows, hoping to catch sight of a warped shelf, or a pigeon fluttering at the glass, trying to escape.

He thought there was a shadow for a second, but noticed that a cloud racing across the sun might have caused a similar effect.

He fingered the crisp banknote in his pocket as he walked back to the bus stop. Where would the money he needed to survive come from now? He shook his head; he simply must force Grealish to U-turn on his decision. He thought of nothing else on the way home and, as he approached the concourse beneath his block of flats, felt a jolt of shock. There, lying by the entrance, was a dead crow. It was as if the ferocity of his concentration had summoned it.

He laughed, a papery little thing. He rubbed his lips and bent over the carcass. The scar on his hand throbbed, as it did whenever he was in the vicinity of these dead birds: some psychosomatic trigger, some sympathetic twinge.

The body was intact, there was no spoiling, no deformation. The bird was almost inviting him to resurrect it, to rediscover its menace and might. Quickly, Malpas scooped it up and placed it in the pocket of his raincoat. He would put his all into this job. He would show Grealish that skills such as his were rare in the extreme. His customers would not find artistry again so easily. He would give them this chance to reconsider.

In the lift up to his floor he paused, felt a moment's panic. Something Grealish had said, something in the mess of nonsense he had spouted. *No more birds.* Was that some kind of disguised invitation to carry on, but to bring . . . *differently*? Malpas' fingers twitched with the key in the lock as he dwelt upon the possible significance of what had been said. Might desperation have muddied his interpretation? Given it a weight that he hadn't grasped at the time? Was Grealish leaving the door open to him to deliver more . . . exotic fauna?

He shook away the thought and strode to the door. Inside, he felt instantly comforted by its old smells of coffee grounds and whisky and soap. He placed the bird on his work surface and shrugged off his jacket. He was tired. It was edging into late afternoon already. He couldn't work out where the day had gone. He fixed himself a plate of sandwiches and a strong whisky and soda and ate the food standing by the window, looking out at the encroaching dusk.

Movement, something other than the usual winding-down machinations of the buildings and roads that surrounded him. Something that didn't sit happily with him. He scanned the windows and streets, looking for the awkward, or the ill-fitting, or the plain wrong.

A woman shook a rug out of her fifteenth-story window. Two men with gelled hair laughed on their way to the main road, shoes buffed, shirts open to the throat in defiance of the chill. A man in a suit cycled past. He imagined it to be a father hurrying home to play with his son. Sometimes, Malpas dreamed he could feel the warm magic of a boy's scalp beneath his fingers, but he would always wake alone, cheated of such fancy, and would feel diminished for it.

Movement again. This time he latched on to it. In the concrete mandala that formed a centerpiece to the three towers, he saw the blind man from the previous day, mooching around near a bench. His movements were jerky, as if Malpas were watching a poorly rendered sequence from a stop-motion film. He seemed to be staggering. Malpas wondered if he was all right.

He raised his fingers to his tired eyes and rubbed, gently. He heard the gentle susurration of his eyebrows as his knuckles brushed against them. When he opened his eyes again, the blind man was staring directly at him. Malpas stepped back, involuntarily, as if the heat from the man's gaze had been palpable.

He reached out a hand and switched off the lamp. Presently, he felt brave enough to return to the window. The blind man was gone. But gone where? And why should it bother him so? He had seen him twice in two days. That was hardly grounds for suspicion.

Perhaps he was not so blind. Dark glasses and a white stick didn't mean that he didn't have some vision. Blindness never really meant total blindness, did it?

He looked down at his hands to find them shaking, an awful parody of Grealish's disease. He could not work like this. He fixed himself another, weaker drink, and turned on the taps in the bathtub. He fetched the radio and tuned it to a channel broadcasting political debate. He needed other voices; it didn't matter what they were talking about.

When the water was just this side of uncomfortably hot, Malpas undressed and immersed himself, by gasping degrees. The heat and the background babble and the whisky helped to loosen the tension in his shoulders and back. He was aghast at the extent of his unraveling. Every day he must be drawn tight as an over-wound watch. It was no way for a man approaching retirement age to live his life. He must do more for himself. Find time to relax. Make time in which to treat himself like this.

He laid his head against the back of the tub and allowed the water to come up around his ears. He closed his eyes and placed a hot, sodden flannel over his face. *Blind now, like you. What do you see? What do you think of? What extra do you hear?*

The lift doors opening on his floor. The scuff of shoes along the corridor. The push of air as the swing doors are opened. *That's what you hear.*

He sat up, abruptly, in the bath, his buttocks squeaking on the acrylic. He pulled away the flannel and cold air assaulted his skin. He felt his flesh pimple, despite the hot water. Malpas thought he could hear the door being tested. The hinges creaked, the letterbox inched open and closed. He imagined hands pressed against the wood, feeling for weak spots, measuring resistance. Or it could just be the remnants of this stressful day, jangling around in his dark places.

He got out of the bath and wrapped a towel around his torso. He gazed at the line of light beneath his front door: unbroken. There was nobody out there. To confirm this, he strode over to the door and yanked it open. The corridor was empty. Malpas stared for a while at the area in front of his door, where a faded sisal mat haltingly bade WELCOME, as if he could see the footprints of another, a heat signature, shimmers in the air to suggest a recent presence.

He was about to close the door when a jinking shadow on the wall at the end of the corridor caught his attention: its author was descending the stairs. Malpas' courage was such that he almost called out a hello to halt the intruder and invite him back. Have it out. Bring about a resolution. But even as he thought this, the shadow grew still, as if it had caught the flavor of his intent.

It spooked Malpas. It was as if, although it could only be coincidence, he was being read, *anticipated*.

Malpas closed the door, and, as an afterthought, trying to shut his mind to the ludicrousness of the situation, shunted all thought of who this person was, or might be, from his mind.

If you cast him out, he can't . . . *smell* you.

And that was the nub of it, the thing that bothered Malpas most. He felt as if he were being subtly hunted. And that his exposure was down to him. His own behavior had allowed this proximity. Someone was tracking him down.

He dressed quickly and approached his work area. Routine and familiarity flooded him with calm, with confidence. Work would drive out the fear from his body, at least for a little while. As before, he positioned the bird, stretched out its wings against the jealous clench of rigor mortis, and reached for his scalpel. In the second his eyes were averted from the carcass, there came a voice, cracked, tiny, filled with loathing:

Don't you touch me. Don't you cut me.

Malpas did not look again at the crow. He put down his tools and stood up straight. He wiped away a tear and went to the door where he shrugged on his raincoat. He stood there, in the dark, for a few seconds, but there was only quiet now.

It almost might not have happened, but the voice was like soil under the fingernails, difficult to get out. He opened the door and a figure shrouded in shadow peeled back its hood, and a layer or two of what writhed within it, to show him the decaying mouth that he would spend forever being crammed into . . .

If only. Death, suddenly, felt like the sweetest release from this tiring life.

He closed the door, wondering for a mad second if he should not have opened a window so that the bird could find its way home, and shuffled off in the direction of his pursuer, down the stairs, into the street, where mist was piling in off the canal and the streetlights were splintering with all the moisture in the air.

He walked for two hours, avoiding the buses, wishing to stave off the various unpleasant possibilities for as long as he could. Finally, he reached the industrial wasteland. No cars or people around now, just acres of lonely concrete and steel and glass. Exotic weeds—that would have been ignored during the day—shivered in a cracked forecourt, becoming something alien, something out of faerie. Through the fear, or perhaps enhanced by it, grey, uninteresting things could be seen to possess beauty.

He stood for a while, freezing cold and stiffening already from his marathon walk, but rapt at the coils and flutes and spines that frothed from every acid-green nub on its slender stem. There was a pattern here, as there was in everything in nature, he thought. Fingerprints on everything. A cipher beyond the skill of any master code-breaker.

For a moment, he thought he had it. A maddening glimpse of what it meant to be alive, but then a shroud was drawn back over the answer, and perhaps that was for the best, for what mind could cope with such knowledge without going utterly mad?

Roused from this torpor, he cast about him, trying to get a sense of where he was in relation to the factory. Everything seemed different in the dark, without people and traffic to provide some kind of milling compass. But there was an angle of office block, and the zig-zag of a fire escape attached to it, that snagged on his memory. Up ahead, in a building he could not yet see the edges of, lights burned in the windows still, while all around was absolute black. His heart jumped at this, and he took it as a good sign.

The door was still unlocked. Not so good. Not so good.

"Clive?" he called out. His voice seemed to alter the balance of the factory. A dozen different creaks and groans and sighs came to him as the shop's walls realigned itself around this sudden acoustic assault. But none of them, he was sure, were organic. "Clive?"

He stared at the counter. It was an object lesson in chaos, as usual, but it seemed there was something else about it, something violent. He couldn't put his finger on it, but something about that layout told him that his friend and patron was dead.

There was no blood. No scorch marks from a sawn-off shotgun. No smell of eroded leather and wood from a beaker of flung hydrochloric acid. Just . . . something in the crazed arrangement of papers. Perhaps Grealish's hand, as it slid back across the surface, making its final adjustments, had the signature of death about it.

Whatever it was, Malpas approached the counter expecting to find the worst. Instead he looked down upon an empty seat. Grealish did not lie beneath it, his face slackened by the immense boredom of eternity. A half-finished mug of tea was cold on the countertop.

He made two tours of the factory, calling Clive's name every few seconds. There was no sign of him in any aisle. The airbrushed faces of celebrities in the biographical section grinned at him at the things they had witnessed. Paperback jackets in the crime and horror section offered every possible suggestion as to what might have happened. The dust in here had been disturbed and redistributed, added to by whatever had come to take Grealish away. For surely, he had been kidnapped. Malpas' panic would not allow any rational alternative.

He went behind the counter—the floor was covered in newspapers and invoices and dockets—and reached for the phone, intent on allowing the police to sort out the matter, when he saw himself disappear into the corner of a small, black-and-white screen.

The CCTV system. He located the tape player and saw that it was empty. He cursed. Grealish had forgotten to load a cassette. But he knew that this was unlikely. Grealish was one of the most crime-conscious, paranoid individuals he had ever met. In a cupboard next to the player he found dozens of cassettes. Every one of them had been labeled and Grealish's neat handwriting provided a date and times for each recording. There was no tape covering this morning's events, when Grealish had effectively sacked Malpas.

Malpas sighed. Something bad had happened here, he was sure of it, but the evidence did not suggest foul play. He shook his head. There was no evidence. A mug of unwanted tea. Any moment, he would hear the flush of a toilet and Grealish would return with his newspaper, wanting to know why Malpas was standing in a staff-only area.

But the lack of a cassette in the player, that was not like his friend. He would not have gone home without turning off the lights and locking up. Despite the apparent lack of a crime and a perpetrator, Malpas felt threat in the factory, close against him, smothering, despite its cavernous interior. Every second he spent here was a second closer to something awful befalling him, he was convinced of it.

He caught himself staring at the door—for minutes, it must have been—waiting for it to swing inward and something formed from the night's unedifying ingredients, the dark, the diesel exhaust, the fog, would swarm inside and slice him apart on its razorwire teeth.

He stepped back and something cracked underfoot. He shifted his balance so that his full weight would not crush what he suspected to be beneath this slew of paper: a cassette. This day's date was written on the label. A long crack ran across its surface, but the tape beneath was not disturbed. He could only hope it would still function when he fed it to the loading tray.

The unbearably long wait as the tape whined and whirred into position and was rewound. White noise. Flickers and jags. And Grealish's bookshop in smeared black, white and grey. The playback was shared between various areas of the factory. The counter area, the delivery bay at the rear of the building, and two views from the upper floor.

Malpas had arrived not long after the shop had opened, yet he refrained from messing around with the cueing buttons. If the cassette was damaged, he didn't want to risk snapping it by placing any further tension on the tape.

He saw the empty loading bay with its collection of rotting pallets and recycling bins, its surface pockmarked with craters and patches of ragwort. He saw the counter where Grealish sipped his tea and leaned over his ledger like a monk illustrating scriptures. He saw the upper floor east and then the upper floor west, where books were crammed into mazy shelves two or three levels deep.

Watching the screen refresh every ten seconds or so, Malpas' thoughts began to drift. He pictured customers that had become lost in the aisles, claimed by the dust and cobwebs, assimilated by the books themselves, so deep in the factory that they would never be found, their flesh and bones and organs turned by weird, literary alchemy into text.

The loading bay, the counter, the upper floor. The loading bay, the counter, the upper floor.

Malpas saw Grealish's head snap up. He watched as his own raincoat moved towards the counter, the crow in the parcel tucked under his arm. Shadow fussed about Malpas' head like a cloud of midges. The image stuttered and warped. Malpas smelled hot plastic and wondered if the fracture in the housing had caused the tape to catch and overheat. But the image settled and jumped upstairs.

Another shadow now, emerging from the stacks of books like a surge of spilled liquid. Cut to the loading bay. Cut to the counter. Grealish magicking away the parcel and averting his gaze. Speaking. He could just make out the words: *There are words in this old shop that must never be unearthed.* Malpas frowned.

Cut to the upper floor. A figure moving away from the camera. In the next shot, from the other end of the factory, the figure calmly approached, but began to shiver and jerk violently before any identification could be made. The loading bay and its enviable space. Grealish again, using his hands to indicate to Malpas that their partnership was over. Handing over the fifty. Both heads snapping to the side at a sound coming from above. By the time the camera had returned to the counter, Malpas had left and Grealish was still staring up at the ceiling.

The upper floor showed the figure descending. Regardless of what might happen to the tape, Malpas stabbed the pause button as the head sank into view. It jumped around in apparent disregard of the state Malpas had deigned for it. A face, of sorts. The eyes were broad black holes: sunglasses, surely, although Malpas could no longer be sure. The mouth was too thin and corrupted by movement to register on the image. As he watched, the eyes seemed to enlarge, as if they were ink stains on tissue paper.

He released the pause and the figure sank out of view. By the time the camera had returned to the counter, Grealish was sitting bolt upright in his chair, his face a ruin of fear and panic and . . . what looked like rapture. His eyes were closed, the pen in his hand moving all the while.

A shadow was sliding into the frame. It was huge, cuneiform, as if the person casting it had spread a cloak above his head, as children do with their coats in playgrounds, pretending to be vampires. Light filled the screen, so bright that Malpas had to turn away. The tape ended.

There are words in this old shop that must never be unearthed.

Must? Surely Grealish had said "might"? Perhaps he had, and Malpas' lip-reading skills were in need of a polish. Did it matter, anyway?

But then he thought it did. He was convinced Grealish had given him a lead. But if there was a message for him in this shop, it might take him centuries to unveil it, even if he were to know what it was he was looking for. The tape played on, showing its empty rooms. Eventually, the steam from Grealish's mug disappeared.

Malpas sat down on the chair and leaned across Grealish's ledger. Surely not, he thought. But he pushed back and raised the great, heavy cover. No figures in here. No debit and credit columns. In Grealish's tiny, tidy handwriting—he had managed to squeeze three lines of text into lines meant for one—was a journal stretching back decades, to when Grealish was a child.

Malpas gathered up the great book and, struggling with its weight, hurried out of the door and into the estate. He caught a taxi home, only cursing, for a moment, the extravagance of such action. His own accounts could wait if there was something in this book that might yet save his friend.

On the way he checked regularly through the back window to see if the cab was being followed, but the traffic was light and there was no obvious tail. The driver, thankfully, did not try to engage him in conversation. He tapped guitarist's fingernails against the steering wheel in time to a song that was inaudible to Malpas' ears.

He paid the driver, not waiting to receive his paltry change, and hurried through the entrance doors to the lift. Two boys of around ten years old were hunched by its side, their mouths smacking around wads of gum, trying to start a fire with pages torn from a pornographic magazine. They ignored Malpas completely. He was used to it, and grateful, too. He didn't engage with any of his neighbors, nor they with him. It was better, safer, that way, he thought now, as he ascended.

Safer for whom? A voice, raucous, raw, asked him as he approached his front door, shaking the key free of the bunch. *You . . . or them?*

He teased the door open and shifted the keys into the center of his palm, curling his hand into a fist, the blades of the keys sticking out among his knuckles. "Get out!" he shouted, but his voice wouldn't back up the intimidation he'd intended.

He stepped into the flat, but he knew, he felt, that it was empty. Nothing had been disturbed here. He closed the door and rubbed his forehead, as if this might prove to him that the voice was coming from his own head. He placed the ledger on the sofa and mixed himself a strong whisky and soda. On the way back, he picked up his magnifying glass from the workbench, hesitating only slightly when he thought that the crow's eyes had swiveled a fraction to watch him.

Nonsense. But he threw a cloth over the bird anyway, to conceal it.

He sat down and opened the ledger to the latest entry. Yesterday's date. Something had interrupted Grealish because he had not completed the last sentence in the final paragraph. The handwriting was no longer pristine, it was all over the paper:

I can only do so much to help him. But I am getting old. Getting weak. Jumping at shadows. The barriers I erected have all come crashing down. I'm the final obstacle. Some guardian I turned out to be. I could do with a guardian angel of my own. But I gave my all and I tried my best. It is of some comfort to me to know that I will not be present at the grand judgment, the fiery end. I hope, only, that it comes quickly for him, and that he is not given a glimpse of what he once was. And yes, it comes on, now it comes on, and I feel its heat, but I will not look up. I will not look into that sunken face. I will not scream for mercy, Samael, blind God, destroyer, you foul reaper, you evil shephe.

Malpas lifted his glass to take another drink only to find it already empty. His heart was beating bird-fast. Black spots burst across his vision. What was this? What was this madness? He had never marked Grealish down as the type to rant. He was calm, ordered, punctilious in the extreme. Yet maybe this ledger was where he allowed his pressure seal to vent steam. Wasn't it true that the quietest of us were the ones to keep your eye on?

He flicked back a few dozen pages. Entries from five years previously:

We lose our way, sometimes. The map is ignored because we come to know a place so intimately, or we think we do. There's always a left turn to catch us out. Always a misremembered street or a white space that we didn't recall in the A-Z. Finding your way back, geographically (or otherwise), is difficult when you've spent so long wandering lonely paths. What you believe is real is a forgotten or a binned version of the cartographer's sketchbook. You walk in missteps. You fumble at doors that ought never to have been erected. You stumble blindly down alleys fringed with things that would have you open to the spine in seconds were you to wander off the track. You lose your wings. The skin heals over. You forget how to fly. You search for love, or friendship, or warmth and all the while it's all of these things and none of these things. You seek home. You look to be back among the magnificent beasts of your upbringing. A childhood that lasted for millennia.

And back. Ten years, now.

In this way, he . . . shall we say . . . keeps the wolves from the door. Every suture, every bond, every socket sewn shut serves, in some small way, to lock his secret away for a little longer. To misdirect his predator. It masks him, this business. And there is poetry here, is there not? In these suspended lives there can be identified his own life, put on hold while he flaps around. One of his own birds. Fragile. Canny. Carrion-eater.

Towards the front of the ledger, Malpas was amazed, and shocked, to find pictures of himself in the ledger's earliest pages, drawn in a childish hand by Grealish who, judging by the dates, could have been no older than seven. Here he was, unchanged (apart from his black hair) and his hunched posture, wearing his black, shabby raincoat, strutting about like, well, he supposed, like some crow. A silver chain led from his hand up, into the sky, where it seemed to be tethered into the heart of the sun. And now, after further scrutiny, the raincoat appeared to be nothing of the sort. It was scruffy, long wings; oily feathers folded into themselves. He felt his shoulder blades twitch as if in recognition.

Where the angels kissed you.

Malpas jerked his head towards the cracked, rasping voice, so violently he felt a pain tear through the base of his skull. The cloth was shifting above the dead crow.

He could not get up. Fear had nailed him fast to the sofa. He watched as the crow shifted and began clearing its lungs with its awful, hacking call. The cloth fell away from it, and the crow was revealed as a creature half-completed, a taxidermist's project gone wrong, something sent to the production stages before the blueprint had been signed off.

This was no sacred secret. This was Nature's joke. It cried out again and the sound rattled the windows. Its organs writhed in the cavity of its chest like parasitic worms squirming in the remains of roadkill. Its beak was a soft, grey facsimile of the real thing.

Malpas watched, horrified, as it dropped off, so much necrotic tissue. The blind man was in its face, now, writhing there like a nightmare made solid. It flexed its wings and a cloud of ash and soil was flung up around the bird, obscuring the room behind it, and dimming the light.

Too late he realized who had laid this bird in his path. He had been trapped by the commitment to his own bleak hobby.

I have searched for you for so long, Malpas. I have traveled a universe of distance on this unedifying little rock, trying to catch your scent.

Malpas tried for a moment to believe that this was an illusion, that he was inventing horror to punish himself. But all too soon he saw that it was real. "What did you do to Grealish?"

He feared you, did you know that? His entire life he was scared to the marrow of you. He protected you with his all, though.

"What?" Malpas' lips had turned to shavings of wood.

There are some here, still, who would sacrifice their life to save someone lower than the low. But I'm here to tell you your exile is over. We're taking you back into the fold.

Malpas thought of the crows he had so lovingly restored for Grealish, and he grasped the significance of the hairs, used in a bid to confuse that monster's scent, to sidetrack him, delay him all this time from having Malpas within reach of his black, ancient claws. He wondered now, about the boy and who he was. He wondered, as vomit sprang to his throat, if he himself, after all, might have killed him. Grealish, too, had died for this deceit. He had known who Malpas was, and had managed to live with it, when such knowledge might dash the sense from other men's brains and turn them into idiots.

He owed Grealish one last display of solidarity. The sore points at his shoulder blades sparked to life. He understood the origin of their pain, now. Nothing so mundane as arthritis. A part of him, hidden, buried, knew what it meant to fly, understood the thrill. It might be lovely to know that experience once more. But what he had forgotten, what he didn't know, couldn't harm him.

His wings might have been torn from him by demons . . . or they might simply have turned vestigial, forgotten, withered from lack of use . . . well, it didn't matter anymore.

Despite his monumental age, he was more a man of this world than Samael's rarefied clime.

He drained his glass and threw it at the crow. The blind man ducked it, roared, enlarged. Malpas was laughing by now. He knew he was free. Even as Samael flicked his wrist and sent a hot, liquid chain of gold towards his hand, Malpas was moving, finding a speed that he had not known for centuries. The chain rammed home into the scar, but it was a restraint that had no strength for what he had planned.

Malpas flung himself at the window as Samael shrieked his objection and, in a matter of seconds, in the instant before impact, Malpas saw himself as a child, many thousands of years previously. It was an image that stayed with him for the mere moments that he remained airborne. Yet he was able to call out, at the moment of his death, the word that meant more to him than any other in his charmed existence: "*Father*."

BASILEUS
Robert Silverberg

ROBERT SILVERBERG is a multiple winner of both the Hugo and Nebula awards, and he was named a Grand Master by the Science Fiction/Fantasy Writers of America in 2004. He began submitting stories to science fiction magazines in his early teens, and his first published novel, a children's book entitled *Revolt on Alpha C*, appeared in 1955. He won his first Hugo Award the following year.

Always a prolific writer—for the first four years of his career he reputedly wrote a million words a year—his numerous books include such novels as *To Open the Sky*, *To Live Again*, *Dying Inside*, *Nightwings* and *Lord Valentine's Castle*. The latter became the basis for his popular Majipoor series, set on the eponymous alien planet. A rare new fantasy novella, "The Last Song of Orpheus," was recently published by Subterranean Press.

"'Basileus' is about a computer nerd who can call up real angels on his computer," explains the author. "It's full of convincing-sounding stuff about hardware, software, programming and such. It brims with incidental detail about the special qualities of particular angels.

" I don't believe in the existence of angels. And I had never used a computer at the time, back in October of 1982, when I wrote the story.

"You see what tricky characters professional writers of fiction are? When I sit down to write a story, I'm willing to tell you any damn thing at all, and I'm capable of making you believe it, because for the time that I'm writing the story I believe it myself.

"In the case of 'Basileus' I needed a story idea and I had, for the moment, run absolutely dry. One tactic that I've sometimes used when stuck for an idea is to grab two unrelated concepts at random, jam them together, and see if they strike any sparks. I tried it. I picked up the day's newspaper and glanced quickly at two different pages.

The most interesting words that rose to my eye were 'computers' and 'angels.'"

"All right. I had my story then and there. I had to write about angels as though I had spent my whole life conversing with them and knew them all by their first names. But I stockpile oddball reference books for just such moments, and among them was a copy of Gustav Davidson's *Dictionary of Angels*. (Due credit is given in the story.) I began to leaf through it. Very quickly I read on past 'Gabriel' and 'Michael' and 'Raphael' into the more esoteric ones like 'Israfel,' who will blow the trumpet to get the Day of Judgment under way, and 'Anaphaxeton,' who will summon the entire universe before the court. Once I had found them, I knew that I had the dramatic situation around which to build my plot. The Day of Judgment! Of course, I saw right away that I'd have to invent a few angels of my own to make things work out, but that was no problem; inventing things like angels is what I'm paid to do, and I'm probably at least as good at it as some of the people who had invented the ones who fill the pages of Gustav Davidson's immense dictionary.

"What about the computer stuff, though? Me, with my manual typewriter? So I had a few conversations with that all-knowing computer expert Jerry Pournelle, and he not only explained the whole business to me but sent me a twenty-page letter, telling me what to look for when I went computer-shopping.

"And so I wrote 'Basileus.'

"I managed the job in four or five days. In fact, it was the last work of fiction I would ever write on a typewriter. A few weeks later I was a full-fledged computer user at last, embroiled in the intricacies of my giant-lobster story, 'Homefaring,' and praying each hour that the damned machine would do what I wanted it to do.

"You know to whom I was praying, of course. Israfel. Anaphaxeton. Basileus."

IN THE SHIMMERING lemon-yellow October light Cunningham touches the keys of his terminal and summons angels. An instant to load the program, an instant to bring the file up, and there they are, ready to spout from the screen at his command: Apollyon, Anauel, Uriel and all the rest. Uriel is the angel of thunder and terror; Apollyon is the Destroyer, the angel of the bottomless pit; Anauel is the angel of bankers and commission brokers. Cunningham is fascinated by the multifarious duties and tasks, both exalted and humble, that are assigned to the angels. "Every visible thing in the world is put under the charge of an angel," said St. Augustine in *The Eight Questions*.

Cunningham has 1,114 angels in his computer now. He adds a few more each night, though he knows that he has a long way to go before he has them all. In the fourteenth century the number of angels was reckoned by the Kabbalists, with some precision, at 301,655,722. Albertus Magnus had earlier calculated that each choir of angels held 6,666 legions, and each legion 6,666 angels; even without knowing the number of choirs, one can see that that produces rather a higher total. And in the Talmud, Rabbi Jochanan proposed that new angels are born "with every utterance that goes forth from the mouth of the Holy One, blessed be He."

If Rabbi Jochanan is correct, the number of angels is infinite. Cunningham's personal computer, though it has extraordinary add-on memory capacity and is capable, if he chooses, of tapping into the huge mainframe machines of the Defense Department, has no very practical way of handling an infinity. But he is doing his best. To have 1,114 angels on-line already, after only eight months of part-time programming, is no small achievement.

One of his favorites of the moment is Harahel, the angel of archives, libraries and rare cabinets. Cunningham has designated Harahel also the angel of computers: it seems appropriate. He invokes Harahel often, to discuss the evolving niceties of data processing with him. But he has many other favorites, and his tastes run somewhat to the sinister: Azrael, the angel of death, for example, and Arioch, the angel of vengeance, and Zebuleon, one of the nine angels who will govern at the end of the world. It is Cunningham's job, from eight to four every working day, to devise programs for the interception of incoming Soviet nuclear warheads, and that, perhaps, has inclined him towards the more apocalyptic members of the angelic host.

He invokes Harahel now. He has bad news for him. The invocation that he uses is a standard one that he found in Arthur Edward Waite's *The Lemegeton, or The Lesser Key of Solomon*, and he has dedicated one of his function keys to its text, so that a single keystroke suffices to load it. "I do invocate, conjure and command thee, O thou Spirit N, to appear and to show thyself visibly unto me before this Circle in fair and comely shape," is the way it begins, and it proceeds to utilize various secret and potent names of God in the summoning of Spirit N—such names as Zabaoth and Elion and of course Adonai—and it concludes, "I do potently exorcise thee that thou appearest here to fulfil my will in all things which seem good unto me. Wherefore, come thou, visibly, peaceably and affably, now, without delay, to manifest that which I desire, speaking with a clear and perfect voice, intelligibly, and to mine understanding." All that takes but a microsecond, and another moment to enter in the name of Harahel as Spirit N, and there the angel is on the screen.

"I am here at your summons," he announces.

Cunningham works with his angels from five to seven every evening. Then he has dinner. He lives alone, in a neat little flat a few blocks west of the Bayshore Freeway, and does not spend much of his time socializing. He thinks of himself as a pleasant man, a sociable man, and he may very well be right about that; but the pattern of his life has been a solitary one. He is thirty-seven years old, five feet eleven, with red hair, pale blue eyes, and a light dusting of freckles on his cheeks. He did his undergraduate work at Cal Tech, his postgraduate studies at Stanford, and for the last nine years he has been involved in ultra-sensitive military-computer projects in Northern California. He has never married. Sometimes he works with his angels again after dinner, from eight to ten, but hardly ever any later than that. At ten he always goes to bed. He is a very methodical person.

He has given Harahel the physical form of his own first computer, a little Radio Shack TRS-80, with wings flanking the screen. He had thought originally to make the appearance of his angels more abstract—showing Harahel as a sheaf of kilobytes, for example—but like many of Cunningham's best and most austere ideas it had turned out impractical in the execution, since abstract concepts did not translate well into graphics for him. "I want to notify you," Cunningham says, "of a shift in jurisdiction." He speaks English with his angels. He has it on good, though apocryphal, authority that the primary language of the angels is Hebrew, but his computer's audio algorithms have no Hebrew capacity, nor does Cunningham. But they speak English readily enough with him: they have no choice. "From now on," Cunningham tells Harahel, "your domain is limited to hardware only."

Angry green lines rapidly cross and recross Harahel's screen. "By whose authority do you—"

"It isn't a question of authority," Cunningham replies smoothly. "It's a question of precision. I've just read Vretil into the database, and I have to code his functions. He's the recording angel, after all. So to some degree he overlaps your territory."

"Ah," says Harahel, sounding melancholy. "I was hoping you wouldn't bother about him."

"How can I overlook such an important angel? 'Scribe of the knowledge of the Most High,' according to the Book of Enoch. 'Keeper of the heavenly books and records,' 'Quicker in wisdom than the other archangels.'"

"If he's so quick," says Harahel sullenly, "give *him* the hardware. That's what governs the response time, you know."

"I understand. But he maintains the lists. That's database."

"And where does the database live? The hardware!"

"Listen, this isn't easy for me," Cunningham says. "But I have to be fair. I know you'll agree that some division of responsibilities is in order. And I'm giving him all databases and related software. You keep the rest."

"Screens. Terminals. CPUs. Big deal."

"But without you, he's nothing, Harahel. Anyway, you've always been in charge of cabinets, haven't you?"

"And archives and libraries," the angel says. "Don't forget that."

"I'm not. But what's a library? Is it the books and shelves and stacks, or the words on the pages? We have to distinguish the container from the thing contained."

"A grammarian," Harahel sighs. "A hair-splitter. A casuist."

"Look, Vretil wants the hardware, too. But he's willing to compromise. Are you?"

"You start to sound less and less like our programmer and more and more like the Almighty every day," says Harahel.

"Don't blaspheme," Cunningham tells him. "Please. Is it agreed? Hardware only?"

"You win," says the angel. "But you always do, naturally."

Naturally. Cunningham is the one with his hands on the keyboard, controlling things. The angels, though they are eloquent enough and have distinct and passionate personalities, are mere magnetic impulses deep within. In any contest with Cunningham they don't stand a chance. Cunningham, though he tries always to play the game by the rules, knows that, and so do they.

It makes him uncomfortable to think about it, but the role he plays is definitely god-like in all essential ways. He puts the angels into the computer; he gives them their tasks, their personalities and their physical appearances; he summons them or leaves them uncalled, as he wishes.

A god-like role, yes. But Cunningham resists confronting that notion. He does not believe he is trying to be God; he does not even want to think about God. His family had been on comfortable terms with God—Uncle Tim was a priest, there was an archbishop somewhere back a few generations, his parents and sisters moved cozily within the divine presence as within a warm bath—but he himself, unable to quantify the Godhead, preferred to sidestep any thought of it. There were other, more immediate matters to engage his concern. His mother had wanted him to go into the priesthood, of all things, but Cunningham had averted that by demonstrating so visible and virtuosic a skill at mathematics that even she could see he was destined for science. Then she had prayed for a Nobel Prize in physics for him; but he had preferred computer technology. "Well," she said, "a Nobel in computers. I ask the Virgin daily."

"There's no Nobel in computers, Mom," he told her. But he suspects she still offers novenas for it.

The angel project had begun as a lark, but had escalated swiftly into an obsession. He was reading Gustav Davidson's old *Dictionary of Angels*, and when he came upon the description of the angel Adramelech, who had rebelled with Satan and had been cast from Heaven, Cunningham thought it might be amusing to build his computer simulation and talk with it. Davidson said that Adramelech was sometimes shown as a winged and bearded lion, and sometimes as a mule with feathers, and sometimes as a peacock, and that one poet had described him as "the enemy of God, greater in malice, guile, ambition and mischief than Satan, a fiend more curst, a deeper hypocrite." That was appealing. Well, why not build him? The graphics were easy—Cunningham chose the winged-lion form—but getting the personality constructed involved a month of intense labor and some consultations with the artificial-intelligence people over at Kestrel Institute. But finally Adramelech was on line, suave and diabolical, talking amiably of his days as an Assyrian god and his conversations with Beelzebub, who had named him Chancellor of the Order of the Fly (Grand Cross).

Next, Cunningham did Asmodeus, another fallen angel, said to be the inventor of dancing, gambling, music, drama, French fashions and other frivolities. Cunningham made him look like a very dashing

Beverly Hills Iranian, with a pair of tiny wings at his collar. It was Asmodeus who suggested that Cunningham continue the project; so he brought Gabriel and Raphael on line to provide some balance between good and evil, and then Forcas, the angel who renders people invisible, restores lost property and teaches logic and rhetoric in Hell; and by that time Cunningham was hooked.

He surrounded himself with arcane lore: M.R. James' editions of the Apocrypha, Waite's *Book of Ceremonial Magic* and *Holy Kabbalah,* the *Mystical Theology and Celestial Hierarchies* of Dionysius the Areopagite, and dozens of related works that he called up from the Stanford database in a kind of manic fervor. As he codified his systems, he became able to put in five, eight, a dozen angels a night; one June evening, staying up well past his usual time, he managed thirty-seven. As the population grew, it took on weight and substance, for one angel cross-filed another, and they behaved now as though they held long conversations with one another even when Cunningham was occupied elsewhere.

The question of actual *belief* in angels, like that of belief in God Himself, never arose in him. His project was purely a technical challenge, not a theological exploration. Once, at lunch, he told a co-worker what he was doing, and got a chilly blank stare. "Angels? *Angels?* Flying around with big flapping wings, passing miracles? You aren't seriously telling me that you believe in angels, are you, Dan?"

To which Cunningham replied, "You don't have to believe in angels to make use of them. I'm not always sure I believe in electrons and protons. I know I've never seen any. But I make use of them."

"And what use do you make of angels?"

But Cunningham had lost interest in the discussion.

He divides his evenings between calling up his angels for conversations and programming additional ones into his pantheon. That requires continuous intensive research, for the literature of angels is extraordinarily large, and he is thorough in everything he does. The research is time-consuming, for he wants his angels to meet every scholarly test of authenticity. He pores constantly over such works as Ginzberg's seven-volume *Legends of the Jews,* Clement of Alexandria's *Prophetic Eclogues,* Blavatsky's *The Secret Doctrine.*

It is the early part of the evening. He brings up Hagith, ruler of the planet Venus and commander of 4,000 legions of spirits, and asks him details of the transmutation of metals, which is Hagith's speciality. He summons Hadraniel, who in Kabbalistic lore is a porter at the second gate of Heaven, and whose voice, when he proclaims the will of the Lord, penetrates through 200,000 universes; he questions the angel about his meeting with Moses, who uttered the Supreme Name at him and made him tremble. And then Cunningham sends for Israfel the four-winged, whose feet are under the seventh earth, and whose head reaches to the pillars of the divine throne. It will be Israfel's task to blow the trumpet that announces the arrival of the Day of Judgment. Cunningham asks him to take a few trial riffs now—"just for practice," he says, but Israfel declines, saying he cannot touch his instrument until he receives the signal, and the command sequence for that, says the angel, is nowhere to be found in the software Cunningham has thus far constructed.

When he wearies of talking with the angels, Cunningham begins the evening's programming. By now the algorithms are second nature and he can enter angels into the computer in a matter of minutes, once he has done the research. This evening he inserts nine more. Then he opens a beer, sits back, lets the day wind to its close.

He thinks he understands why he has become so intensely involved with this enterprise. It is because he must contend each day in his daily work with matters of terrifying apocalyptic import: nothing less, indeed, than the impending destruction of the world. Cunningham works routinely with megadeath simulation. For six hours a day he sets up hypothetical situations in which Country A goes into alert mode, expecting an attack from Country B, which thereupon begins to suspect a pre-emptive strike and commences a defensive response, which leads Country A to escalate its own readiness, and so on until the bombs are in the air. He is aware, as are many thoughtful people both in Country A and Country B, that the possibility of computer-generated misinformation leading to a nuclear holocaust increases each year, as the time-window for correcting a malfunction diminishes. Cunningham also knows something that very few others do, or perhaps no one else at all: that it is now possible to send a signal to the giant computers—to Theirs or Ours, it makes no difference—that will be indistinguishable from the impulses that an actual flight of airborne warhead-bearing missiles would generate. If such a signal is permitted to enter the system, a minimum of eleven minutes, at the present time, will be needed to carry out fail-safe determination of its authenticity. That, at the present time, is too long to wait to decide whether the incoming missiles are real: a much swifter response is required.

Cunningham, when he designed his missile-simulating signal, thought at once of erasing his work. But he could not bring himself to do that: the program was too elegant, too perfect. On the other hand, he was afraid to tell anyone about it, for fear that it would be taken beyond his level of classification at once, and sealed away from him. He does not want that, for he dreams of finding an antidote for it, some sort of resonating inquiry mode that will distinguish all true alarms from false. When he has it, if he ever does, he will present both modes, in a single package, to Defense. Meanwhile he bears the burden of suppressing a concept of overwhelming strategic importance. He has never done anything like that before. And he does not delude himself into thinking his mind is unique: if he could devise something like this, someone else probably could do it also, perhaps someone on the other side. True, it is a useless, suicidal program. But it would not be the first suicidal program to be devised in the interests of military security.

He knows he must take his simulator to his superiors before much more time goes by. And under the strain of that knowledge, he is beginning to show distinct signs of erosion. He mingles less and less with other people; he has unpleasant dreams and occasional periods of insomnia; he has lost his appetite and looks gaunt and haggard. The angel project is his only useful diversion, his chief distraction, his one avenue of escape.

For all his scrupulous scholarship, Cunningham has not hesitated to invent a few angels of his own. Uraniel is one of his: the angel of radioactive decay, with a face of whirling electron shells. And he has coined Dimitrion, too: the angel of Russian literature, whose wings are sleighs and whose head is a snow-covered samovar. Cunningham feels no guilt over such whimsies. It is his computer, after all, and his program. And he knows he is not the first to concoct angels. Blake engendered platoons of them in his poems: Urizen and Ore and Enitharmon and more. Milton, he suspects, populated *Paradise Lost* with dozens of sprites of his own invention. Gurdjieff and Aleister Crowley and even Pope Gregory the Great had their turns at amplifying the angelic roster: why then not also Dan Cunningham of Palo Alto, California? So from time to time he works one up on his own. His most recent is the dread high lord Basileus, to whom Cunningham has given the title of Emperor of the Angels. Basileus is still incomplete: Cunningham has not arrived at his physical appearance, nor his specific functions, other than to make him the chief administrator of the angelic horde. But there is something unsatisfactory about imagining a new archangel, when Gabriel, Raphael and Michael already constitute the high command. Basileus needs more work. Cunningham puts him aside, and begins to key in Duma, the angel of silence and of the stillness of death, thousand-eyed, armed with a fiery rod. His style in angels is getting darker and darker.

On a misty, rainy night in late October, a woman from San Francisco whom he knows in a distant, occasional way phones to invite him to a party. Her name is Joanna; she is in her mid-thirties, a biologist working for one of the little gene-splicing outfits in Berkeley; Cunningham had

had a brief and vague affair with her five or six years back, when she was at Stanford, and since then they have kept fitfully in touch, with long intervals elapsing between meetings. He has not seen her or heard from her in over a year. "It's going to be an interesting bunch," she tells him. "A futurologist from New York, Thomson the sociobiology man, a couple of video poets, and someone from the chimpanzee-language outfit, and I forget the rest, but they all sounded first-rate."

Cunningham hates parties. They bore and jangle him. No matter how first-rate the people are, he thinks, real interchange of ideas is impossible in a large random group, and the best one can hope for is some pleasant low-level chatter. He would rather be alone with his angels than waste an evening that way.

On the other hand, it has been so long since he has done anything of a social nature that he has trouble remembering what the last gathering was. As he had been telling himself all his life, he needs to get out more often. He likes Joanna and it's about time they got together, he thinks, and he fears that if he turns her down she may not call again for years. And the gentle patter of the rain, coming on this mild evening after the long dry months of summer, has left him feeling uncharacteristically relaxed, open, accessible.

"All right," he says. "I'll be glad to go."

The party is in San Mateo, on Saturday night. He takes down the address. They arrange to meet there. Perhaps she'll come home with him afterwards, he thinks; San Mateo is only fifteen minutes from his house, and she'll have a much longer drive back up to San Francisco. The thought surprises him. He had supposed he had lost all interest in her that way; he had supposed he had lost all interest in anyone that way, as a matter of fact.

Three days before the party, he decides to call Joanna and cancel. The idea of milling about in a roomful of strangers appalls him. He can't imagine, now, why he ever agreed to go. Better to stay home alone and pass a long rainy night designing angels and conversing with Uriel, Ithuriel, Raphael, Gabriel.

But as he goes towards the telephone, that renewed hunger for solitude vanishes as swiftly as it came. He *does* want to go to the party. He *does* want to see Joanna: very much, indeed. It startles him to realize that he positively yearns for some change in his rigid routine, some escape from his little apartment, its elaborate computer hook-up, even its angels.

Cunningham imagines himself at the party, in some brightly lit room in a handsome redwood-and-glass house perched in the hills above San Mateo. He stands with his back to the vast sparkling wraparound window, a drink in his hand, and he is holding forth, dominating the conversation, sharing his rich stock of angel lore with a fascinated audience.

"Yes, 300 million of them," he is saying, "and each with his fixed function. Angels don't have free will, you know. It's Church doctrine that they're created with it, but at the moment of their birth they're given the choice of opting for God or against Him, and the choice is irrevocable. Once they've made it they're unalterably fixed, for good or for evil. Oh, and angels are born circumcised, too. At least the Angels of Sanctification and the Angels of Glory are, and probably the seventy Angels of the Presence."

"Does that mean that all angels are male?" asks a slender dark-haired woman.

"Strictly speaking, they're bodiless and therefore without sex," Cunningham tells her. "But in fact the religions that believe in angels are mainly patriarchal ones, and when the angels are visualized they tend to be portrayed as men. Although some of them, apparently, can change sex at will. Milton tells us that in *Paradise Lost*: 'Spirits when they please can either sex assume, or both; so soft and uncompounded is their essence pure.' And some angels seem to be envisioned as female in the first place. There's the Shekinah, for instance, 'the bride of God,' the manifestation of His glory indwelling in human beings.

There's Sophia, the angel of wisdom. And Lilith, Adam's first wife, the demon of lust—"

"Are demons considered angels, then?" a tall professorial-looking man wants to know.

"Of course. They're the angels who opted away from God. But they're angels nevertheless, even if we mortals perceive their aspects as demonic or diabolical."

He goes on and on. They all listen as though he is God's own messenger. He speaks of the hierarchies of angels—the seraphim, cherubim, thrones, dominations, principalities, powers, virtues, archangels and angels—and he tells them of the various lists of the seven great angels, which differ so greatly once one gets beyond Michael, Gabriel and Raphael, and he speaks of the 90,000 angels of destruction and the 300 angels of light, he conjures up the seven angels with seven trumpets from the Book of Revelation, he tells them which angels rule the seven days of the week and which the hours of the day and night, he pours forth the wondrous angelic names, Zadkiel, Hashmal, Orphaniel, Jehudiel, Phaleg, Zagzagel. There is no end to it. He is in his glory. He is a fount of arcana. Then the manic mood passes. He is alone in his room; there is no eager audience. Once again he thinks he will skip the party. No. No. He will go. He wants to see Joanna.

He goes to his terminal and calls up two final angels before bedtime: Leviathan and Behemoth. Behemoth is the great hippopotamus-angel, the vast beast of darkness, the angel of chaos. Leviathan is his mate, the mighty she-whale, the splendid sea serpent. They dance for him on the screen. Behemoth's huge mouth yawns wide. Leviathan gapes even more awesomely. "We are getting hungry," they tell him. "When is feeding time?" In rabbinical lore, these two will swallow all the damned souls at the end of days. Cunningham tosses them some electronic sardines and sends them away. As he closes his eyes he invokes Poteh, the angel of oblivion, and falls into a black dreamless sleep.

• • • • •

At his desk the next morning he is at work on a standard item, a glitch-clearing program for the third-quadrant surveillance satellites, when he finds himself unaccountably trembling. That has never happened to him before. His fingernails look almost white, his wrists are rigid, his hands are quivering. He feels chilled. It is as though he has not slept for days. In the washroom he clings to the sink and stares at his pallid, sweaty face. Someone comes up behind him and says, "You all right, Dan?"

"Yeah. Just a little attack of the queasies."

"All that wild living in the middle of the week wears a man down," the other says, and moves along. The social necessities have been observed: a question, a non-committal answer, a quip, goodbye. He could have been having a stroke here and they would have played it the same way. Cunningham has no close friends at the office. He knows that they regard him as eccentric—eccentric in the wrong way, not lively and quirky but just a peculiar kind of hermit—and getting worse all the time. I could destroy the world, he thinks. I could go into the Big Room and type for fifteen seconds, and we'd be on all-out alert a minute later and the bombs would be coming down from orbit six minutes later. I could give that signal. I could really do it. I could do it right now.

Waves of nausea sweep him and he grips the edge of the sink until the last racking spasm is over. Then he cleans his face and, calmer now, returns to his desk to stare at the little green symbols on the screen.

That evening, still trying to find a function for Basileus, Cunningham discovers himself thinking of demons, and of one demon not in the classical demonology—Maxwell's Demon, the one that the physicist James Clerk Maxwell postulated to send fast-moving molecules in one direction and slow ones in another, thereby providing an ultra-efficient method for heating and refrigeration. Perhaps some sort of filtering role could be devised for Basileus. Last week a few of the loftier angels had been complaining about the proximity to them of certain fallen angels within the computer. "There's a smell of brimstone on this disk that I don't like," Gabriel had said. Cunningham wonders if he could make Basileus a kind of traffic manager within the program: let him sit in there and ship the celestial angels into one sector of a disk, the fallen ones to another.

The idea appeals to him for about thirty seconds. Then he sees how fundamentally trivial it is. He doesn't need an angel for a job like that; a little simple software could do it. Cunningham's corollary to Kant's categorical imperative: *Never use an angel as mere software.* He smiles, possibly for the first time all week. Why, he doesn't even need software. He can handle it himself, simply by assigning princes of Heaven to one file and demons to a different one. It hadn't seemed necessary to segregate his angels that way, or he would have done it from the start. But if they were complaining—

He begins to flange up a sorting program to separate the files. It should have taken him a few minutes, but he finds himself working in a rambling, muddled way, doing an untypically sloppy job. With a quick swipe he erases what he has done. Gabriel would have to put up with the reek of brimstone a little longer, he thinks.

There is a dull throbbing pain just behind his eyes. His throat is dry, his lips feel parched. Basileus would have to wait a little longer, too. Cunningham keys up another angel, allowing his fingers to choose for him, and finds himself looking at a blank-faced angel with a gleaming metal skin. One of the early ones, Cunningham realizes. "I don't remember your name," he says. "Who are you?"

"I am Anaphaxeton."

"And your function?"

"When my name is pronounced aloud, I will cause the angels to summon the entire universe before the bar of justice on Judgment Day."

"Oh, Jesus," Cunningham says. "I don't want you tonight."

He sends Anaphaxeton away and finds himself with the dark angel Apollyon, fish-scales, dragon-wings, bear-feet, breathing fire and smoke, holding the key to the Abyss. "No," Cunningham says, and brings up Michael, standing with drawn sword over Jerusalem, and sends him away only to find on the screen an angel with 70,000 feet and 4,000 wings, who is Azrael, the angel of death. "No," says Cunningham again. "Not you. Oh, Christ!" A vengeful army crowds his computer. On his screen there passes a flurrying regiment of wings and eyes and beaks. He shivers and shuts the system down for the night. Jesus, he thinks. Jesus, Jesus, Jesus. All night long suns explode in his brain.

On Friday his supervisor, Ned Harris, saunters to his desk in an unusually folksy way and asks him if he's going to be doing anything interesting this weekend. Cunningham shrugs. "A party Saturday night, that's about all. Why?"

"Thought you might be going off on a fishing trip, or something. Looks like the last nice weekend before the rainy season sets in, wouldn't you say?"

"I'm not a fisherman, Ned."

"Take some kind of trip. Drive down to Monterey, maybe. Or up into the wine country."

"What are you getting at?" Cunningham asks.

"You look like you could use a little change of pace," Harris says amiably. "A couple of days off. You've been crunching numbers so hard they're starting to crunch you, is my guess."

"It's that obvious?"

Harris nods. "You're tired, Dan. It shows. We're a little like air traffic controllers around here, you know, working so hard we start to dream about blips on the screen. That's no good. Get the hell out of town, fellow. The Defense Department can operate without you for a while. Okay? Take Monday off. Tuesday, even. I can't afford to have a fine mind like yours going goofy from fatigue, Dan."

"All right, Ned. Sure. Thanks."

His hands are shaking again. His fingernails are colorless.

"And get a good early start on the weekend, too. No need for you to hang around here today until four."

"If that's okay—"

"Go on. Shoo!"

Cunningham closes down his desk and makes his way uncertainly out of the building. The security guards wave at him. Everyone seems to know he's being sent home early. Is this what it's like to crack up on the job? He wanders about the parking lot for a little while, not sure where he has left his car. At last he finds it, and drives home at thirty miles an hour, with horns honking at him all the way as he wanders up the freeway.

He settles wearily in front of his computer and brings the system on line, calling for Harahel. Surely the angel of computers will not plague him with apocalyptic matters.

Harahel says, "Well, we've worked out your Basileus problem for you."

"You have?"

"Uriel had the basic idea, building on your Maxwell's Demon notion. Israfel and Azrael developed it some. What's needed is an angel embodying God's justice and God's mercy. A kind of evaluator, a filtering angel. He weighs deeds in the balance, and arrives at a verdict."

"What's new about that?" Cunningham asks. "Something like that's built into every mythology from Sumer and Egypt on. There's always a mechanism for evaluating the souls of the dead—this one goes to Paradise, this one goes to Hell—"

"Wait," Harahel says. "I wasn't finished. I'm not talking about the evaluation of individual souls."

"What then?"

"Worlds," the angel replies. "Basileus will be the judge of worlds. He holds an entire planet up to scrutiny and decides whether it's time to call for the last trump."

"Part of the machinery of Judgment, you mean?"

"Exactly. He's the one who presents the evidence to God and helps Him make His decision. And then he's the one who tells Israfel to blow the trumpet, and he's the one who calls out the name of Anaphaxeton to bring everyone before the bar. He's the prime apocalyptic angel, the destroyer of worlds. And we thought you might make him look like—"

"Ah," Cunningham says. "Not now. Let's talk about that some other time."

He shuts the system down, pours himself a drink, sits staring out the window at the big eucalyptus tree in the front yard. After a while it begins to rain. Not such a good weekend for a drive into the country after all, he thinks. He does not turn the computer on again that evening.

Despite everything, Cunningham goes to the party. Joanna is not there. She has phoned to cancel, late Saturday afternoon, pleading a bad cold. He detects no sound of a cold in her voice, but perhaps she is telling the truth. Or possibly she has found something better to do on Saturday night. But he is already geared for party-going, and he is so tired, so eroded, that it is more effort to change his internal program than it is to follow through on the original schedule. So about eight that evening he drives up to San Mateo, through a light drizzle.

The party turns out not to be in the glamorous hills west of town, but in a small cramped condominium close to the heart of the city, furnished with what looks like somebody's college-era chairs and couches and bookshelves. A cheap stereo is playing the pop music of a dozen years ago, and a sputtering screen provides a crude computer-generated light show. The host is some sort of marketing exec for a large video-games company in San Jose, and most of the guests look vaguely corporate, too. The futurologist from New York has sent his regrets; the famous sociobiologist has also somehow failed to arrive; the video poets are two San Francisco gays who will talk only to each other, and stray not very far from the bar; the expert on teaching chimpanzees to speak is in the red-faced-and-sweaty stage of being drunk, and is working hard at seducing a plump woman festooned with astrological jewelry. Cunningham, numb, drifts through the party as though he is made of ectoplasm. He speaks to no one, no one speaks to him. Some jugs of red wine are open on a table by the window, and he pours himself a glassful. There he stands, immobile, imprisoned by inertia. He imagines himself suddenly making a speech about angels, telling everyone how Ithuriel touched Satan with his spear in the Garden of Eden as the Fiend crouched next to Eve, and how the hierarch Ataphiel keeps Heaven aloft by balancing it on three fingers. But he says nothing. After a time he finds himself approached by a lean, leathery-looking woman with glittering eyes, who says, "And what do you do?"

"I'm a programmer," Cunningham says. "Mainly I talk to angels. But I also do national security stuff."

"Angels?" she says, and laughs in a brittle, tinkling way. "You talk to angels? I've never heard anyone say that before." She pours herself a drink and moves quickly elsewhere.

"Angels?" says the astrological woman. "Did someone say angels?"

Cunningham smiles and shrugs and looks out the window. It is raining harder. I should go home, he thinks. There is absolutely no point in being here. He fills his glass again. The chimpanzee man is still working on the astrologer, but she seems to be trying to get free of him and come over to Cunningham. To discuss angels with him? She is heavy-breasted, a little wall-eyed, sloppy-looking. He does not want to discuss angels with her. He does not want to discuss angels with anyone. He holds his place at the window until it definitely does appear that the astrologer is heading his way; then he drifts towards the door. She says, "I heard you say you were interested in angels. Angels are a special field of mine, you know. I've studied with—"

"Angles," Cunningham says. "I play the angles. That's what I said. I'm a professional gambler."

"Wait," she says, but he moves past her and out into the night. It takes him a long while to find his key and get his car unlocked, and the rain soaks him to the skin, but that does not bother him. He is home a little before midnight.

He brings Raphael on line. The great archangel radiates a beautiful golden glow.

"You will be Basileus," Raphael tells him. "We've decided it by a vote, hierarchy by hierarchy. Everyone agrees."

"I can't be an angel. I'm human," Cunningham replies.

"There's ample precedent. Enoch was carried off to Heaven and became an angel. So was Elijah. St. John the Baptist was actually an angel. You will become Basileus. We've already done the program for you. It's on the disk: just call him up and you'll see. Your own face, looking out at you."

"No," Cunningham says.

"How can you refuse?"

"Are you really Raphael? You sound like someone from the other side. A tempter. Asmodeus. Astaroth. Belphegor."

"I am Raphael. And you are Basileus."

Cunningham considers it. He is so very tired that he can barely think. An angel. Why not? A rainy Saturday night, a lousy party, a splitting headache: come home and find out you've been made an angel, and given a high place in the hierarchy. Why not? Why the hell not?

"All right," he says. "I'm Basileus."

He puts his hands on the keys and taps out a simple formulation that goes straight down the pipe into the Defense Department's big Northern California system. With an alteration of two keystrokes he sends the same message to the Soviets. Why not? Redundancy is the soul of security. The world now has about six minutes left. Cunningham has always been good with computers. He knows their secret language as few people before him have.

Then he brings Raphael on the screen again.

"You should see yourself as Basileus while there's still time," the archangel says.

"Yes. Of course. What's the access key?"

Raphael tells him. Cunningham begins to set it up.

Come now, Basileus! We are one!

Cunningham stares at the screen with growing wonder and delight, while the clock continues to tick.

BEAUTIFUL MEN

Christopher Fowler

CHRISTOPHER FOWLER was born in Greenwich, London. He is the award-winning author of ten short story collections and thirty novels, including eight volumes in the popular Bryant & May series of mysteries.

Fowler has fulfilled several schoolboy fantasies—releasing a terrible Christmas pop single, becoming a male model, posing as the villain in a Batman graphic novel, running a nightclub, appearing in *The Pan Books of Horror Stories* and standing in for James Bond.

His work divides into black comedy, horror, mystery and tales unclassifiable enough to have publishers tearing their hair out. The author's often hilarious and moving autobiography, *Paperboy*—about growing up in London in the 1950s and '60s—was published in 2009.

"This story came to me while I was sitting where Ryan sits at the start and end of the tale," Fowler reveals. "It's my favorite sunset spot in the world, and I've sat there at points of my life that have ranged from great happiness to terrible despair.

"I'm calmed by urban environments, and imagined angels in a form that would suit the city. I assumed that any messenger from the heavens would be an equally wonderful and terrible thing—there would be no joyous news without the tragic equivalent. Nice is also the city of beautiful men."

The Coast

OUT IN THE BAY, the last jet-skiers are looping past each other in the setting sun. Nearby, on Cap Ferrat, the summer parties are coming to an end. The Mistrale is rising, whipping petals and pine needles into the air, stippling the surfaces of sapphire swimming pools. This year the Russians have moved in, filling the hotels vacated by Americans. Everyone wants to know where the Americans have gone. They are fondly remembered; in past times they were generous and jovial, but now they have completely vanished. Restaurant owners blame politics, but only in the vaguest terms. The Riviera towns are safe havens, far from the threat of fundamentalist attack. Nobody here feels like the end of the world would affect them.

The hot winds are still bringing firestorms to the hills. Yellow seaplanes blast the flames with seawater, but already there are fewer people to witness the drama. Houses are being locked up for the coming winter. Entire areas are falling asleep, even though the temperature has barely dropped from the height of summer. Many slumber beneath the cliffs of the Massif Central, the great fold of rock that creates a microclimate so warm it is nicknamed "Little Africa," perfect for growing figs and clementines, perfect for hiding from the world.

The light hurts Ryan's corneas. The low sun on the sea fractures and pierces, but he will not don his glasses, for he must see everything now. Speedboats burn the last of their precious petrol cutting geometric patterns through the azure waves. A fierce golden light bathes the pink breast-shaped cone of the Negresco, and turns the slow curve of the Promenade Des Anglais into a shimmering ribbon, studded with the rubies of homegoing brake lights.

Ryan checks his Rolex and begins the countdown in his head. Already the first neon striplights are outlining the hotels of Nice. The last ferry of the evening is arriving from Corsica. The pizza restaurants in the port are preparing themselves for the extra business it will bring. The buildings have drawn in the brightness of the day and will feed it back as night energy. Everything is interlocked, as unstoppable as time, and will remain so until the very last moment.

Ryan leans against the warm stone of the seat and turns up the music in his headphones. He smiles at those who pass and waits for the vermilion dusk, patiently watching as the city goes about its business, tethered to routine, absorbing upset, heedless of harm, happy to exist at all.

And he thinks to himself, what a wonderful world.

The Girls
On June 13th exactly four months earlier, he is seated in much the same pose but further around the bay, in a pulsing basement nightclub with sweating red walls, like a chamber of the heart. He watches as three glistening girls with thick St. Petersburg accents squeeze together for their web-cam interviewer, pushing for screen space.

They are being interviewed about what they look for in a man. The interview is being projected on high-res screens all around the room, greedily repeating their behavioral tics in fierce scarlets and cyans, like coursework for anthropology students. The girls shriek that their guys need broad shoulders and firm definition and a sense of humor, but above all property, nice cars and lots of money. He studies them from the bar and thinks it odd that those who see the most beauty in the world are the least equipped to handle it. And those who see nothing at all are the best survivors, at least while their looks hold out.

Ryan examines these Russian dolls with a dispassionate eye, and tries to see what they want him to see. All he can find is what's on display; bleach-cuts and cleavages and flicking hair, posing bodies, thrusting hips, tossed heads, sparkling jewelry, forced laughter revealing weirdly whitened teeth. He makes himself listen, because all he can really hear is a sort of hysterical high-pitched squeaking in the background while their sexual postures talk over them. Men only hear bodies in nightclubs.

Unraveling their logomania, he tries to form an opinion about what they're saying, even though the effort nearly kills him. He thinks: *That's what you tell everyone you want, but I know you; you'll settle for less, much less because eventually you'll have to. Because girls like you are ten a penny here and beautiful men with lots of money might want you but only for a night, then they'll throw you out without breakfast and drive away to someone else. Why? Because they can and you can't without looking like hookers.*

That's not sexist, he thinks, *that's practical.*

The girls of the Cote D'Azur ask for a lot but have to settle for very little. They'll date a man who disappears for days at a time, who lies to them constantly, who'll never hold down a job or have any money, who's as fat and bald and ugly as a pig, who'll let them down every single time. They pretend they want perfection, but their expectations are gradually reduced to such a low level that their men can get away with anything.

Ryan blames the Single Switch, a mutant autogenesis hardwired inside girls' brains that trips one day, and suddenly a light shines behind their eyes telling them to find a man fast and have a child. This is the moment when their ideals carbonize and they behave like someone blindfolded for a party game, rushing about to grab the first shiny male who comes within range, no matter how venal, bitter and hate-filled they are. Because many men really hate women, hate them so much that they can barely prevent themselves from lashing out. But the Riviera girls have to pair off before they spend too much time alone and turn strange, devoting themselves to horoscopes, crystals and cat sanctuaries, and filling their homes with false memories.

That's not unfair, he thinks, *that's realistic.*

• • • • •

The One

Ryan knows this to be the case because he is the kind of man the desperate girls chase. He always goes after the silly, pretty ones because he ticks all their boxes. Youth? He'll say he's twenty-six when he's actually twenty-nine. Job? He's employed in broadband sales and marketing at Cap 3000, the vast shopping mall to the west of Nice. Looks? His hair is thinning, his gut stretching, but he has an olive tan and height is a big advantage. Sixty percent of all CEOs are over six feet tall, he reminds himself, and nearly all are men. Personality? He can make a girl laugh and feel that they have the measure of him. Brains? He graduated languages and new technologies, and is unusually well-read. Money? He's on a good salary, has just been promoted, gets new cars and annual bonuses. Eligibility? He's single! There are no ugly surprises and no hidden children.

Willingness to commit?

Ryan is dating an awful lot of women in this, the year before his thirtieth birthday, two or three at any one time. But in the nightclub that night, on May 13th, he meets Lainey Gray, a tall, thin-shouldered American who teaches at a language school in Villefranche. She talks to him on the cancer deck, a rubbish-strewn stairwell at the rear of the building where the patrons once took drugs instead of sneaking smokes, and catches him before his psychic armor goes on. None of Ryan's usual nonsense works on her. She studies him with detached amusement, a half-smile playing on crimson frosted lips, and he knows she can see right through him. But she sticks around, because she is waiting for him to exhaust his bag of tricks, and wants to see what's left behind.

Smart girl.

Maybe too smart. There's Ryan thinking he's laying traps to catch her, and she's already caught him. Over the next month they meet six times before she even lets him touch her. You can love a girl like that.

Their first six dates:

An unwatchable dubbed rom-com with Sarah Jessica Parker at the Nice Etoile. They reach a mutual decision to leave before the end and go for pasta in the Old Town. A Warhol exhibition at the Museum of Modern Art, followed by a brasserie meal in Place Messena. She goes to his flat but only stays for coffee. His best friend Sean's birthday party at the K Club. Ryan drops a couple of pills but doesn't tell her. He genuinely believes she hasn't noticed, until she stares hard at him and suddenly goes home on her scooter without saying a word. A crowded lunch in the Cours Salaya where they have to shout and mime across the table to each other. The afternoon is spent pushing through crowds of tourists on the Promenade Des Anglais. He goes to her flat in Mont Boron, but she coolly kicks him out after an hour, explaining that she has to get up early next morning. *Mesrine* parts 1 and 2 followed by icy steel platters of *fruits de mer* at the Café De Turin. He eats a bad oyster. A party for one of her work colleagues, Marisia, at the Chinatown dim sum restaurant. Ryan leaves her there with the intention of calling another girl, but something prevents him.

Then, a few days after that, the walls come down between them.

From date seven onwards they're at each other like dogs on a hot Spanish street. Lainey can't keep her hands off Ryan. Ryan doesn't have time to look at anyone else, and isn't interested anyway. A couple of his former girlfriends leave sulky messages but he puts them off, then deletes them from his mobile.

Over the next three months, Ryan and Lainey continue to grow closer. They have their first argument, then fuck like lunatics. Devastated by the thought of someone else's happiness, many of their single friends stop bothering to call. Ryan meets Lainey's parents on their first overseas visit. They're sweet and totally confused by Europe. Ryan realizes that he has been caught, but enjoys this strange sensation without understanding why. One day the pair find themselves in Habitat and Ryan thinks: *Oh shit, we're choosing furniture together. She must be The One.*

• • • • •

The Chasm

Ryan knows what's coming next, but finds the idea of a mapped and stable future depressing beyond all endurance. He has always assumed there would be more to life than just finding a mate and slowly turning into his father, but the odds are against him. He becomes depressed, and has no idea what it will take to excite and revitalize him, so he simply allows events to take their natural course. Like the girls being interviewed in the club, he sees little real point to life, which makes him well equipped to survive it. But surviving isn't living.

Lainey does not share his pessimism, but senses an emerging pattern of hairline fractures between them. The gaps quickly expand until they join to form a chasm. Ryan knows that his girlfriend has a passionate, wayward spirit, but fears for the emptiness in himself. He has nothing to offer her. He never bares his soul because he is not sure he has one.

And Nice has a raffish charm that takes away any sense of urgency, a sense of elegant disgrace that encourages bad behavior. The town gave the world a healthy salad and the word "tourism," but not much else. The rest of its pleasures have to be patiently uncovered. The English built its extraordinary coast road, where hookers in Barbarella outfits now cruise beside grannies, rollerbladers and *petanque* players.

Whether he ends up staying with Lainey or not, Ryan thinks he'll stay on. He feels more settled here than in England. This is the city he dreams of most—slightly disturbing, slightly surreal, filled with the sensual luxuries of wasted time. Watching the sunset liners returning from the south, he is so filled with the desire for tropical deceptions that it's possible to not to see the new poor: the McDonald's outlets, the lost Algerian children, the tramps asleep in doorways. Like California, this part of Europe has become the place to head when you're too rich, too recognizable, too stupid, too burned out to live anywhere else. It's expensive and selfish, and no one here cares whether you clean pools or once opened for Oasis.

Ryan marks time and watches the world, his compass spinning.

For all he knows, he might love Lainey. But he doesn't love her enough.

The Beautiful Men

Then, something inexplicable happens that ends his former life.

Lainey has a loud friend called Lex, an easyJet steward based at Gatwick who flirts and theatrically emphasizes his words, punctuating his conversations with expansive hand gestures, and Ryan wants to argue with him every time they meet, so he finds excuses not to meet up with Lainey whenever she makes arrangements for them.

But one night the trio end up having a good time, mainly because Lex stops trying so hard to be liked. Three days later Ryan meets the pair of them at a new bar in the port, and that is where he first notices them, standing right in the center of the room.

The beautiful men.

Ryan assumes they're gay; anyone would. He figures that the new acceptance of gay men gives them permission to be as ordinary as everyone else, and now most of them are. The flamboyant clothes and outrageous behavior of the past has been relegated to old photographs, the former ghettos have been decimated by rent hikes and invading coffee shops. The bars which were once the exclusive province of Riviera queens are now as blended as the wines served in them. But, just as one would occasionally spot a small flock of stunning, unattainable girls, as attenuated and exotic as African flamingos, Ryan starts to notice the beautiful men, half-a-dozen of them, each so ridiculously perfect that he can't imagine what they ever looked like as children. He wonders if they have been conjured into existence by a coalescence of pure atoms, or perhaps they are man-made and spend their nights floating in amniotic fluids being recharged.

Each night they drift into Lex's favorite bar, Le Six, and order cocktails, standing apart from everyone else, not even looking around, just quietly talking to each other, so unreal that you want to pinch their flesh for reassurance.

Lainey notices them and Lex definitely notices them, and everyone assumes they're models because their expensive clothes are casually immaculate and their hair and skin looks retouched. They are all in their early twenties, tall, dark, thick-armed and slender-waisted, with an other-worldly presence that rises above traditional notions of beauty. *Nicois* men are naturally dark and beautiful, so it takes a lot to stand out.

It is strange that Ryan should even notice them at all, but the simple truth is that they disturb him. They are the wind in the tops of the pines, the tremble of the seismometer needle before a quake. They ruffle still waters and scatter seagulls, they part crowds and make cats cower. They appear shallow to the point of absurdity yet are somehow the opposite, as if they are magnetically connected to life, as if they are the essence of life itself.

The Seventh

As soon as Ryan sees them, he starts seeing them everywhere he goes, throughout the bars and restaurants and art galleries of Nice, on empty night streets and at busy midday intersections, the same six beautiful men, all in dark glasses, all standing a little apart from one another, never touching anyone else, moving aside so that they don't come into contact with mere mortals, as though something cataclysmic would happen if they did.

And then one day, they are joined by a seventh, the most perfect one of all.

Ryan cannot describe him without sounding infatuated. The object of his obsession is well over two meters tall, with tousled black hair and clear dark skin, a wide jaw and the strangest blue eyes Ryan has ever seen on a real human being. He never wears shades. He is muscled and long in the thighs, wears a steel and leather bracelet on his right arm, skinny jeans and shiny black boots, a jet shirt open at the neck. And when he has occasion to smile, something astonishing happens. He draws down the stars. The air fills with errant electricity, and seems in danger of igniting.

"They started turning up about six weeks ago," says Lex one night when the three of them are at the bar. He eyes them with a combination of lust and fury. "They always hang around together. Never talk to anyone else. Probably nobody's good enough for them."

"And you're staring at the tall one," Lainey tells Ryan.

"No, I'm not," he lies indignantly.

"Yes, you are. You may not realize it but you can't take your eyes off him."

"He's wearing a great shirt. And you've got to admit he's hot, for a guy. I'm comfortable with my sexuality. It doesn't make me gay to say that."

"No, I guess not," Lainey sighs. "You're not being judgmental, which is a good thing."

"Do you know how much effort it takes to look that hot?" asks Lex. "I bet he gets up at five in the morning to start his workout and conduct some kind of intense moisturizing program. They all have eight-packs now, it's the new musculature. He's probably a model or a professional whore, which amounts to the same thing."

Here's the odd thing, thinks Ryan. *When you experience extreme beauty, you tend to think of it as other-worldly, but I see the opposite in this man. I'm drawn because he's completely at ease in his world, entirely connected with it. He is no angel; he smokes and drinks and has a dirty laugh, but there's something so unknowable and expansive about him that you can't help but be fascinated.*

The Pursuit

Something very strange is happening to Ryan, and he knows it. It feels like love but can't be, surely. He fights against the word "obsessed," but the more he sees, the more he wants to see, and when the beautiful men aren't there he feels a little more lost, and little less alive.

"Charisma" means "bearing the gift of divine grace," and that is what they have, the beautiful men, a coalescence that begins to escalate when they enter a room, perhaps not a physical heat but something Ryan perceives to be uncomfortably hot. He begins finding excuses to hang out in their neighborhood—the bars and restaurants to the east of Avenue Jean Medecin. He starts lying to Lainey about where he is going, but Lex sees him around and clearly decides to keep his counsel.

Ryan continues to change each time he sees them. He feels a disgust at the way he's behaved with girls in the past, as if just being in proximity to these demigods somehow has the potential to make him a better person.

But it is a drug. Each time he sees their leader he wants something more. In the crowded bars of dying summer he can stand quite close, but it still isn't enough. He tries to hear what the beautiful men are saying to each other, but can never catch the words. Then one night when Lainey has a cold and is staying home, the two men find themselves pressed close together in a scruffy pub behind the flower market. It is the first time Ryan sees him without his friends. He raises his eyes to find his searching gaze returned.

The effect is one of electrocution.

Ryan went to a Catholic school and emerged with a tangle of doubts and suspicions he has never bothered to work through, but this man presses against his heart and catches his breath between parted lips, inhaling and returning it to the universe in an act so perversely religious that he almost faints. He shakes his head as if to clear the clouds from it, but the sensation only grows. The man is still staring at him. It's as if he does not entirely occupy the space in which he stands. The weight of him is slightly blurred, shimmering with dark matter.

Holding his stare, the man steps back towards the door, and Ryan can only follow.

Outside a light rain sparkles in yellow squares of light. They walk in silence through the streaming alleyways of the Old Town. Ryan follows, knowing that he would pass through fire to remain this close. He sees how others move out of their way, as if the sight disturbs them in some fundamental manner. They reach the square of Sainte Reparate and slip inside the church. Within the cool grey space, Ryan instantly loses the sights and sounds of the city. Beneath the church's old wooden roof the man he is following stops in the deserted nave and slowly turns. He watches as Ryan draws closer, and closer still.

The Admission

Ryan is suddenly filled with terror. He cannot comprehend what he is doing here. It makes no sense at all, and feels as dangerous as tapping Death on the shoulder. The man he has followed is watching him with a mystifying, silent blankness. Their faces are lit by the guttering penance candles that line the pews.

Ryan takes a step closer, so that they are but a forearm's length apart.

"My name is Phosphoros," says the man in clear but oddly weighted English. "You must not touch me. But you can answer this for me."

Ryan stops and waits while Phosphoros, the light-bearer, the morning star, taps out a battered cigarette and lights it, the flame streaking his wet face with gold. "Why are you here?"

"I don't know."

"Think about your answer very carefully. I must ask again. Why are you here?"

"Because I love you." Ryan cannot believe he has said this, and tries to bite back the words.

"You don't know me."

"I don't have to. I just know what I feel."

"It is very dangerous for you."

"I don't care."

"You understand what I am."

"I think so."

"And you are not afraid."

"No."

It might be Ryan's imagination, but the beautiful man's mouth appears to be moving out of synch with his voice, like a poorly dubbed film. The words of Phosphoros resound in Ryan's head, disorienting him.

"Why are *you* here?" Ryan throws the question back.

Phosphoros sighs. "We are the rebels. We believe that people should be told. We will probably be punished when we return."

"What should we be told?"

"That you cannot be saved."

Ryan touches his forefinger to his chest and looks around. "You think that's what I want? To be saved?"

"I do not mean you. I mean the world. You will dissipate to atoms very soon now. All humans will. Do you think it will help to know what is going to happen?"

Ryan cannot think of an answer. He had not been expecting to trigger some kind of metaphysical debate in a French church. It briefly crosses his mind that the man with whom he has become obsessed is mad or drugged, just another beautiful burnout who's had too many late nights. But Ryan needs to believe. He wants answers. It is human nature to seek solutions.

"You're saying the world is going to end? No, it wouldn't help me to know how. But it would change me."

"And you want to change."

"Yes."

"Why?"

"Because I don't like myself. I'm lost. I think most of us are."

"Then come to me." Phosphoros holds out his arms in welcome.

The Vision

The pose bothers Ryan, reminding him of a hyper-real life-sized statue of Jesus in the chapel at his old school. Yet he steps into his angel's embrace without hesitation, and feels his warm arms close like wings about his shoulders.

Phosphoros flicks aside his cigarette, exhales and kisses Ryan fully and deeply. It should feel like a sacrilegious act, but is the reverse.

There is a sensation of molten rain in Ryan's mouth that floods down his throat and into his chest, setting his soul aflame.

The grey walls of the church fall away and he sees. Truly, he sees.

It will begin exactly six weeks after this night. The future unfolds in flashes of brilliance that damage his eyes.

A huge bomb detonates in a Siberian oilfield.

The Russians blast the most important Sunni temple in the Middle East.

Saudi Arabia collapses into a state of civil war.

The oil pipelines are cut. The troops are unable to hold back the crowds.

The loss of oil stops electricity, and the loss of electricity stops water. America attempts to form alliances, but is rebuffed. China no longer needs its help. Elderly men shout across vast tables. The crowds mill like panicked animals. The buildings fall. The West is left unprotected, and like a card house it collapses.

The end comes with indecent speed, but the suffering lingers on for years. After-images of cataclysm roll past in a blur of pixels, endlessly looped on the world's dying television screens. The future screams, then starves, then whimpers, then fades to a nagging soundless pain that reduces everyone to animals, then insects, then microbes.

The Decision

Ryan breaks free, severing the circuit. The walls of the church close back in. He blinks and tries to focus. "This is why you're here," he says, forming the words with difficulty, as if drunk. "You know what's about to happen. You're testing us, to see if we should know as well."

"We're here to help. You need to tell me. The decision is yours."

"How many others have you asked?"

"We have only asked the ones who have seen us for what we are. The ones who are drawn to us against their natures. We need to know how you wish to survive, with or without this terrible knowledge."

"If everything will be gone in just a few passes of the sun," Ryan replies, "I want to be awake, not asleep. If I can't survive, I want to live. Please, don't take the memory away. Leave it inside me."

"As you wish." The angel Phosphoros seizes him by the hair and kisses him with a vicious force, and this time it feels as if some part of his soul is being restored, forcing the fire of life into him, so that even though he is shivering and frozen in the darkened church, every nerve in his body is alive with energy.

Phosphoros releases him and studies his face to remember it. "I should tell you that all the humans we approached reached this consensus," he says. "You are the last one to be asked. The seven of us were right to come here, right to question. Upon our return we will throw ourselves upon the mercy of our elders, and present the evidence of your strength. If we are successful in our entreaties, we will end the world a few seconds before you yourselves can destroy it, in a vast and sudden conflagration, so loud that it is silent, so bright that it is blackness, and there will be no anguish, no suffering, nothing left at all. I hope this is of consolation to you."

"I don't need to be consoled," Ryan tells the angel. "I feel—" He struggles to find the right word. "—completed."

Phosphorus releases him and steps back, to be joined by his six friends, who slowly emerge from the shadows. Ryan follows them outside and watches as they rise up in the rain and become streams of luminescence that burst and glow within the night clouds over the sea, before finally vanishing from sight.

Ryan finds that he is quite alone. His sense of loss is like a bruise upon his heart. He thinks of Phosphoros soaring away, of the risk he took to prove the strength of man, but the sensation of love is quickly replaced by confusion. He cannot understand what he is doing here. His chest is sore. He feels as if he is recovering from a great sickness. Digging his mobile from his jacket pocket, he is about to call Lainey but changes his mind. All he knows now is that he needs to be by himself.

The knowledge he has been given carries an enormous weight, and he must rediscover of his spirit.

In the time that's left his journey takes him back to his family in London, and then to the shoreline of Nice once more, where he feels most at rest. By the time he returns, America has recalled its citizens and Lainey has gone. Nobody knows where she is. Ryan knows he will never see her again.

The End

And now, with just minutes to go before the end of the world, he leans back against the warm stone of the seat, and turns up the music in his headphones. He smiles at the passing pedestrians and looks down at the bay, waiting for the angelic interception, the soundless flare of vermilion light that will tell him they succeeded. He watches as the city goes about its business, tethered to routine, heedless of harm, happy to exist at all.

Once he was lost and miserable. But now the precise details of the world's conclusion are burned into his cortex. He understands the fall of angels, the hopes of men, the nature of love. Ryan smiles to himself, truly content for the first and only time in his life.

He knows that there are others out there who were touched, who are now watching and waiting for the final hour to arrive. He thanks the beautiful men. He knows that joy has the breadth of an atom, and is quickly gone. But while it is here it must be treasured, for there is nothing else that we can do.

Here it comes.

GOING BAD

Jay Lake

"INNOCENCE ALWAYS WAS A RECIPE for disaster." Sesalem kept one hand on the issue thirty-eight that protruded from the holster at his back like a warm, black egg stuck halfway out of the hen.

A nervous habit.

Corpses made him nervous.

Fork-Foot, his Infernal Liaison, walked around the body, kicking it with needled claws. Sesalem winced at this contamination of evidence. Eight feet tall, jeweled with glittering scales, and armored with Infernal Immunity, there was little the detective could do to influence the demon.

"Not innocent." Fork-Foot growled like machine screws in a blender. "Stupid."

The alley was narrow, three stories of age-blackened brick on each side lined with greasy dumpsters. Portland had been a nice town, back before the Rapture. Now they were lucky just to keep the murder rate down.

It was no comfort that a good number of the victims got up off their tables at the morgue and walked out. Or sometimes clawed their way from the earth, much later.

"She came down here," Sesalem said. He framed his thoughts into a narrative as he always did when working a case. "For . . . something. To find help, to offer help. Not to score, I don't think. Though someone scored *off* of her."

The victim was perhaps sixteen, African-American with short wiry hair. She'd been carrying a canvas bag from the Albina Church of God in Christ All-Saved and wearing a white sundress. At least, they assumed it had been a sundress. Covering her head, the bag had been tugged off by a forensics tech who now waited for the detective to finish his meditative contemplation.

Sesalem couldn't imagine any local nut-cutter carrying that bag. It had to belong to her. Logo aside, it was too clean for downtown.

"Stupid," rumbled Fork-Foot. "I tell you, you listen. People never listen." His voice faded to a ritualistic grumble.

"Was the perp one of yours?" If so, case closed, and move on. Make a call to her parents, if she had any they could find.

"No. Aura's no good."

Demons killed for sport, about like people ate and slept—automatic as breathing, hard to get through the day without. Most victims were in free-kill zones, where there was no call for investigation. Even when not, the crime was usually so obvious as to merit only the most cursory review.

People killed for sport, too, some of them far too emboldened by the demon-haunted world of the Rapture. That was still illegal. In theory.

"What about one of the Damned?"

"No." Fork-Foot offered no further explanation, but his word was literally law.

Sesalem sighed. "One of ours, then." He nodded at the forensics tech. "Okay, Jackie. Do your stuff, tag and bag her then ship her to county. Somebody text me if we get a positive ID from this mess. And . . . be kind." Sometimes it took a soul a while to realize it was finished with life.

He walked back to his parked car, ignoring the stabbing pain in his kidneys. Those who hadn't rammed broken-necked through the roofs of their houses and cars to go to Jesus during the Rapture were mostly Afflicted since. Kidney stones sucked, but it beat having snake hair or tear ducts that dripped shit.

Fork-Foot leaned on the fender of Sesalem's car, a short wheelbase Toyota Land Cruiser painted to resemble a zebra—if zebras had balloon tires and bull bars. The metal groaned, eliciting a sympathetic wince from Sesalem.

"Not one of yours, either." Fork-Foot's tongue shot out of his muzzle to lick one eyeball.

"Not one of ours?" Sesalem asked. "That doesn't leave a lot of options."

"Them." Fork-Foot pointed at the sky. He locked his thumbs to make butterfly wings. "Bird brains."

Not butterfly wings, Sesalem realized. Angel wings. "I don't believe it."

Fork-Foot shrugged, then jumped straight up to the top of the building they had been standing in front of. Sesalem watched the demon leap across the stunted skyline of the Pearl District. It was headed downtown, presumably for the local demon's nest in Pioneer Courthouse.

"Angels." Sesalem shook his head. "No way."

The instant message came through on his cell phone's tiny screen about two hours later. Sesalem was eating a pork burrito in front of a little trailer on Southwest Fifth.

Alley vict Sheshondra Rouse 17 yrs Albina resident cause of death heart failure. Mutilation post-mort.

Post-mortem mutilation? Not demon work, then. Pre-mortem was their style. They definitely preferred to prolong the suffering.

The pay phone a few yards to his left began ringing. Sesalem glanced at it, then at the *vieja* running the trailer. She shrugged. Cell phones had continued to work pretty well since the arrival of the Legions of

Hell, but the landlines had really suffered. They mostly worked by Demonic—or sometimes Divine—intervention.

Rational people didn't answer ringing phones.

Rational people didn't work Homicide in a demon-haunted world, either. Sesalem walked over and picked up the receiver. "Hello?" he said cautiously.

"Detective Sesalem." It was a distant, tinny voice, the line crackling with static and cross-talk in some guttural tongue. "This is Control."

Control. What the few agents of the Divine still on Earth called their semi-mythical upstream management. Parallel to the demons' New Jersey headquarters, in a sense. Either this was some joker with brass balls the size of coconuts or Heaven was calling.

Under the circumstances, Sesalem went along with it. "Sure. Go ahead, Control."

"Back off the Rouse case. Let it go, and return to doing good works."

"Good works my ass," Sesalem snapped, his own self-discipline slipping. "Too damned late for that." He slammed the handset down onto the hook. He truly hated being told what to do.

Then he sat down to finish his burrito and think about why a birdbrain would commit murder. The pay phone rang again, but he ignored the noise.

It had to be murder. Otherwise Control wouldn't have bothered to call him. And it wasn't a demon. Notoriously dishonest as they were, he couldn't figure why Fork-Foot would bother to lie.

But Fork-Foot had hinted at something.

Sesalem needed the demon again, needed to know what Fork-Foot knew. He walked far enough away from the still-ringing pay phone to dial Fork-Foot's pager from his cell phone.

Fork-Foot dropped to the bricks of Southwest Fifth like a runaway freight elevator. Sesalem flinched from the cloud of chips and dust accompanied by a stench like an electrical short. Brimstone would have been an improvement.

"Nothing to liaise here," said Fork-Foot in his metal-shredding voice as he looked around. "You got something personal to discuss?"

Cut to the chase, thought Sesalem. Don't extemporize, don't apologize. Just look him in the eye pits and talk. The detective took a deep breath. "Why would an angel have murdered Sheshondra Rouse?"

Fork-Foot shrugged. It was like watching an earthquake ripple through a wall. "Why not?"

"They're forces of good."

Fork-Foot laughed. At least Sesalem thought it might be a laugh. "Read the Bible, little man. Angels are no different from demons. Just prettier wardrobe, better public relations."

"This isn't Gomorrah. It's Portland. She was a good kid from the Albina neighborhood. There's no *reason*."

"Even angels got to play."

"Sport? That's all you think it was? A sport killing, like one of your hunts through Old Town?"

"You better off believing that."

What the hell did that mean? "Better off than what? Some dead black kid?"

"Better off than some dead black detective," said Fork-Foot.

"Tell me," hissed Sesalem, his voice dropping like it did when he was sweating a perp.

"Already did," said Fork-Foot. "Don't need to page me no more."

Then the demon was gone in a swirl of brick dust. All around Sesalem, phones were ringing, from office windows, from passing cars, his own cell.

Back at the crime scene, Sesalem left his cruiser blocking the mouth of the alley. There was nothing left but draggled police tape and some empty film canisters. Forensics still hadn't gone all digital.

He stood where Sheshondra Rouse had screamed her last. Black paint had been hastily slopped over whatever stains had resisted the quicklime and hot water the clean-up crew normally employed. It was still sticky, already crisscrossed with boot prints, clawed demon feet and a motorcycle.

"Why'd you die here, baby?" he asked the brick walls. Somehow this didn't seem like angel play.

"Angels are no different from demons," Fork-Foot had said.

Did they ever change sides?

As if summoned by the thought, a rush of warm, moist air blew in, Leviathan itself breathing upon the alley, followed by a flutter of wings. The angel landed next to Sesalem in a straight drop eerily reminiscent of Fork-Foot's most recent appearance.

It was almost seven feet tall, cadaverously thin, with junkie arms—all slack, stringy muscles and blue tendons. It wore leather pants with buckled motorcycle boots. The angel's bare chest was covered with an ornate tattoo of Michelangelo's *La Pieta*. Great grey wings swept behind the angel, matching greasy grey dreadlocks and sea-grey eyes. The angel had silver rings on each finger and he smelled like an overheated motorcycle.

"Just because we're good," the angel said, as if picking up a prior conversation, "doesn't mean we're nice."

"The good don't kill the innocent." Sesalem palmed his thirty-eight. Even loaded with silver bullets dipped in holy water and myrrh, the gun wouldn't do much for him now. It still made him feel better.

"The good do what they can in these late days." The angel glanced at the sticky paint on the pavement. "She would have met someone. He would have been the wrong person, led her places she shouldn't go. She had power in her, detective. Power that could have blossomed into something terrible."

"People get crucified on traffic lights in this town," said Sesalem. "I got a new definition of 'terrible.' So why not just turn her around and point her home? Or better yet, kill that wrong person. He might have deserved it."

The angel shook its head. "There were no good exits from this alley for Sheshondra Rouse."

"You needed him," breathed Sesalem in a burst of insight, "him but not her. He's a source or a contact or something. She was someone who had some spiritual power, loose in the world. Disposable."

"My war never ends, Detective. Does yours?"

Was it a man Rouse had come to see? An angel? Or a demon?

There didn't seem to be a difference.

"One of your people went bad," Sesalem said. "She died for it."

"Almost correct," said the angel. "One of theirs went good. But he needed a soul to carry him upward."

Then the angel vanished, leaving a swirling grey feather perhaps a yard long. Sesalem holstered the gun, snatched the feather from the air, and trudged back toward his Land Cruiser.

All four tires were flat, slashed by needled claws. Sesalem looked back down the alley in time to catch a beam of light, a young black girl standing in it, talking to a tall, bejeweled demon—Fork-Foot?

Then they were gone.

It was a long walk home. He threw his cell phone in the river to stop it ringing, following it with his badge, but kept the feather. "How good is good?" he asked it.

There was no answer.

ABOUT THE EDITOR

STEPHEN JONES lives in London, England. He is the winner of three World Fantasy Awards, four Horror Writers Association Bram Stoker Awards and three International Horror Guild Awards, as well as being a twenty-one-times recipient of the British Fantasy Award and a Hugo Award nominee. A former television producer/director and genre movie publicist and consultant (the first three *Hellraiser* movies, *Night Life*, *Nightbreed*, *Split Second*, *Mind Ripper*, *Last Gasp*, etc.), he is the co-editor of *Horror: 100 Best Books*, *Horror: Another 100 Best Books*, *The Best Horror from Fantasy Tales*, *Gaslight & Ghosts*, *Now We Are Sick*, *H.P. Lovecraft's Book of Horror*, *The Anthology of Fantasy & the Supernatural*, *Secret City: Strange Tales of London*, *Great Ghost Stories*, *Tales to Freeze the Blood: More Great Ghost Stories* and the *Dark Terrors*, *Dark Voices* and *Fantasy Tales* series. He has written *Coraline: A Visual Companion*, *Stardust: The Visual Companion*, *Creepshows: The Illustrated Stephen King Movie Guide*, *The Essential Monster Movie Guide*, *The Illustrated Vampire Movie Guide*, *The Illustrated Dinosaur Movie Guide*, *The Illustrated Frankenstein Movie Guide* and *The Illustrated Werewolf Movie Guide*, and compiled The Mammoth Book of Best New Horror series, *The Mammoth Book of Terror*, *The Mammoth Book of Vampires*, *The Mammoth Book of Zombies*, *The Mammoth Book of Werewolves*, *The Mammoth Book of Frankenstein*, *The Mammoth Book of Dracula*, *The Mammoth Book of Vampire Stories by Women*, *The Mammoth Book of New Terror*, *The Mammoth Book of Monsters*, *Shadows over Innsmouth*, *Weird Shadows over Innsmouth*, *Dark Detectives*, *Dancing with the Dark*, *Dark of the Night*, *White of the Moon*, *Keep Out the Night*, *By Moonlight Only*, *Don't Turn Out the Light*, *H.P. Lovecraft's Book of the Supernatural*, *Travellers in Darkness*, *Summer Chills*, *Brighton Shock!*, *Exorcisms and Ecstasies* by Karl Edward Wagner, *The Vampire Stories of R. Chetwynd-Hayes*, *Phantoms and Fiends* and *Frights and Fancies* by R. Chetwynd-Hayes, *James Herbert: By Horror Haunted*, *Basil Copper: A Life in Books*, *Necronomicon: The Best Weird Tales of H.P. Lovecraft*, *The Complete Chronicles of Conan* and *Conan's Brethren* by Robert E. Howard, *The Emperor of Dreams: The Lost Worlds of Clark Ashton Smith*, *Sea-Kings of Mars and Otherworldly Stories* by Leigh Brackett, *The Mark of the Beast and Other Fantastical Tales* by Rudyard Kipling, *Darkness Mist & Shadow: The Collected Macabre Tales of Basil Copper*, *Pelican Cay & Other Disquieting Tales* by David Case, *Clive Barker's A-Z of Horror*, *Clive Barker's Shadows in Eden*, *Clive Barker's The Nightbreed Chronicles*, *The Hellraiser Chronicles* and volumes of poetry by H.P. Lovecraft, Robert E. Howard and Clark Ashton Smith. A Guest of Honor at the 2002 World Fantasy Convention in Minneapolis, Minnesota, and the 2004 World Horror Convention in Phoenix, Arizona, he has been a guest lecturer at UCLA in California and London's Kingston University and St. Mary's University College. You can visit his website at *www.stephenjoneseditor.com*.